Overlord

The prequel to The Unraveling series

El McInerney

Book Cover by 100 Covers

Map by Stardust Book Services

Icelands
Crendar
Endless Sea
Western Sea
Great Maelstrom
Chelak Islands
N
Vycenia
Northland
Neopoli
Deepwood
Wren
River Arin
Glade
Arindel
Snowhorn Mtns.
Sorin
Ferin
Yaro
Tarsis
Middle Passage
Straits of Ruin
Kharas
Greatport
The Federation
Tine
Skywarden Mtns.
Riftlands
The Blade
Nazare
Nazarene River
The Federation

Contents

Chapter 1

"Must it take you half the day to get ready?" Gidion's father, Conal, exclaimed from the doorway of their peddler's caravan.

Gidion ignored him and continued to fill his sack with the magical glowglobes and heatstones he planned to sell at market.

"If you'd done that last night like I said—"

"I'm ready now, alright?" Gidion snapped. He pulled the drawstrings on his sack, then got to his feet and slung it over his shoulder.

Conal opened his mouth again, and Gidion braced himself for another stinging comment. But instead, his father shook his head and went down the steps that took him outside. Gidion took two long strides to the doorway and leaped straight onto the ground, the impact satisfying against his feet.

Conal shut and locked the door behind him, not with a key but a weave-lock that only another weaver mage would be able to undo. Which meant it was virtually impregnable, as weavers didn't commonly come around these parts.

I shouldn't be here, either, Gidion thought bitterly. *I should be studying at the Spire to learn warcraft magic so I can finally confront* her. *But no, I'm supposed to hide instead like a frightened mouse and live like a common peddler.* His eyes took in the wagon. Its freshly varnished wood gleamed in the early morning light, and bright red lettering proclaimed its purpose: "Goods, cloths, and knick-knacks." Gidion's lip curled. How he hated the thing.

He turned back to find his father creating a defensive weave around their two horses to stop anyone from stealing them. They were comfortably grazing the yellow grass, unbothered by the use of magic so close to them. "I still don't understand why we aren't driving the wagon all the way into town."

Conal tied off the weave. "Tine will be packed on a day like today. It will be hard to get stabling."

"Not impossible, though, given how *early* it still is." Gidion looked meaningfully at the washed-out blue of the sky.

"Don't try my patience." Conal slung his own sack over his shoulders and started marching toward the road, hidden behind a line of leafy trees.

Don't try mine, Gidion thought. But he followed, the contents of his sack jarring painfully against his back. They soon reached the road and turned toward the sun, which wreathed the stone walls of Tine, their destination, in gold. While wide enough for two wagons to pass, the road was no more than a dirt track, and dust puffed and gathered around their sandaled feet as they walked. It had been hard baked by the sun for many weeks and was riven with fine, long cracks. Gidion had been glad of the dry spring at first. There was nothing worse than pushing the caravan through the churn of bad Kharasian roads after heavy rainfall. But now, looking at the rolling meadowlands with their shriveled grass and drooping flower heads, he wished the rain would come again. He wished it were cooler too, because it was impossible to sleep indoors, and no amount of washing could remove the pungent smell of the salve he used to keep the insects from biting.

When they reached the gate into Tine, they found it heavily guarded by Federation soldiers in their blood red tunics. The two men who stopped them had dark eyes beneath their egg-shaped steel helms. Their skin was even darker, too dark for natives of Kharas, and they sported trim chin beards. Zenians, for sure.

"Papers," said the taller of the two. He spoke Zenian with a native accent, confirming Gidion's suspicions.

It also happened to be the Common Tongue of the Federation, so Gidion spoke it well. A peddler needed to. He reached inside his belt pouch for his identity documents and handed them over, his father doing the same.

The guard squinted at them, then jerked his head toward their packs. "What's in those?

"Goods for market, sir," Conal said.

Gidion hated his father's tone, the way he pandered to the soldiers. They were weaver mages—they should be above this kind of thing.

"Show here," the guard demanded, ignoring Conal to focus on Gidion.

"With pleasure. I love an eager customer," Gidion said, barely hiding his sarcasm. The man's expression hardened, but Gidion took his pack off and opened it up.

"Take everything out."

Gidion forced out a smile. "My goods look much better when they're not covered in dust. Why don't you take this and have a root around?" Gidion thrust his pack toward the guard.

"You want to spend the afternoon in the stocks?" he snapped.

"Apologies for my boy," Conal said, already removing items from his sack. "I've yet to knock some sense into him."

You knock me about plenty. Nonetheless, Gidion copied his father and began to remove the items from his pack, setting them out carefully, one by one. But the second guard, from impatience or malice, grabbed Gidion's pack and upended it so that everything emptied out into a little pile on the ground. He used a hand to spread the goods out, scanning them, then opening pouches and spilling their contents into the dust. Gidion clenched his teeth, barely restraining himself from making a biting comment. He would need to clean everything.

The first guard picked up a red drawstring pouch and removed a round, milky stone that fit neatly into his palm. "What's this? A glowglobe?"

"Of the finest quality," Gidion replied.

"Where'd you get it?"

"We get our weaver's supplies from Kharas," Conal interjected.

The guard's eyes narrowed, and the other man stopped searching his father's goods to leer at Gidion threateningly.

Gidion cranked out another smile. "The guarantee is in the bag."

The guard snorted but looked again and drew out a small piece of paper. It bore the signature and address of a weaver named Jerald Kiltour. Jerald was an old friend of Conal's from their Spire days and provided the guarantee and repair services for the glowglobes Gidion made. The guard ran his eyes over Gidion and Conal, taking in their breeches and shirts, both made of good cotton and well cut. With a snort, he placed the glowglobe and guarantee back into the pouch. But he wasn't done yet. "Empty your pockets."

"I'm afraid there's nothing for sale in my pockets," Gidion said, spreading his hands in a gesture of helplessness.

In answer, the guard grabbed him and yanked his arms behind his back, keeping a painful grip on him. The other began to pat him down, finding his purse and pulling it out of his pocket. He opened it up, then plucked out a silver coin and held it to the light.

"I didn't realize you were tasked with checking the purity of our metal," Gidion said, although he knew with a sinking heart what was coming. "But you'll find it's all good coin."

The guard removed more silver from his purse before tossing the purse onto the ground next to his things.

"I hope you're not planning to keep those coins," Gidion said. "We've got materials to buy and a stall to rent."

Conal rushed to intervene. "I'm sorry, pay my son no mind. We'll just—"

"Seems like you make a lot more money than any ordinary peddlers should," the guard interrupted. "Some might call you thieves."

"My dear sirs, the thief here is not me," Gidion said, unable to stop his anger from creeping into his voice.

"You want the whip, do you?" the guard holding him said, right into his ear, making him jump.

Gidion struggled, but the guard only held on tighter, his breath hot against Gidion's neck. "You can't just take our money!" he exclaimed.

"Fine for resisting search," the other guard snapped. "Now move on, or it's the stocks *and* the whip you'll get."

Gidion glared at him, breathing heavily, his vision spinning. The guard smirked, enjoying his power. *Ilk take them.* He let the Tapestry become visible before his eyes. Hundreds of thousands of tiny shimmering threads woven together to form the fabric of the world—he only had to pluck a few, make the guards feel his own power.

"Please, sirs. He's only a silly boy. I'll get him in hand," Conal said, shooting Gidion a furious look. There was fear in his eyes, too, and Gidion reluctantly released the threads.

The guard shoved Gidion away from him, making him stumble. "Gather your things and get out of my sight."

They hunkered down to sweep their things into their pack, along with a good portion of dust.

"Idiot!" Conal said as they passed into the town. "How many times have I told you to keep your mouth shut!"

Gidion kicked at the ground. "How many times must we let these pricks humiliate us?"

"Like it or not, we need them."

"Seems to me the Feds are worse thieves than the Riftlanders. At least, the Riftlanders are open about it."

"Trust me, we're better off under Federation rule than at the mercy of those brutes," Conal said.

Gidion couldn't disagree with him. They'd fought off Riftlanders often enough on the roads. If he had any complaint, it was that the Federation didn't have enough soldiers to keep the peace. All merchants had to travel with their own guard around these parts. The only reason Conal and Gidion didn't was that his father was a full weaver mage and had trained at the Spire. *Where I should be training too.* The thought made his fingers curl tightly in on themselves. He was fed up of running. Fed up of fawning to idiot guards. And all because of his father's paranoia over *her*.

They'd marched almost to the center before he began to calm down. But, at last, the sights and smells of the town began to work on him, undoing the hard knot in his throat and belly. Breathing deeply, he took in the aroma of cookpots and the scent of wood smoke, the stink of packed bodies and the stench of animal dung—the smells of ordinary life and ordinary people. Then, just as deliberately, he focused his attention on the buildings on either side of him. Much like the rest of the province, they rose up to one or two stories of thick, red-plastered stone, with small, round windows to keep out the heat of summer and the cold of winter, and flat roofs for washing and open-grill cooking.

As they came to the end of the street, a shrieking boy raced across his path, almost tripping him. Four others followed, mouths stretched open with grinning intent. Gidion watched the boy veer into an alleyway and wondered what it would have been like to grow up with other children and have a house and a mother.

The market square opened ahead of them. It was large, spreading out as far as the eye could see on every side. The area nearest him had been sectioned off for livestock pens and was already crowded with horses, pigs, sheep, and cows. Sun-browned men—and a few women too—walked among the pens, opening mouths and lifting hooves, haggling with farmers and holding up coins to the light.

In the center stood a huge, white canvas awning on sturdy poles. Beneath it, sellers were setting up their stalls in lines or serving early customers. Strings of brightly colored flags ran along the sides of the awning, and more crossed the open parts of the square. No doubt the flags had been hung to add brightness to the festive day, but they seemed limp and sad in the still air.

Then, his eyes fell on the stocks to his right. Three ochre-skinned men locked by the ankles, heads hanging, faces blistering from the sun. Their heads shaved, their scalps covered in half-healed cuts. Riftlanders. Must have been there for a couple of days at least.

But it wasn't they that caught his attention. It was an ear. An ear with a large nail driven through it, pinning it, and the Riftlander who owned it, to the near post of the stocks. The post was only shoulder-height, forcing the prisoner into an uncomfortable half crouch. His legs were trembling, and every time he shifted his weight, he winced in pain. Fresh blood dribbled down from the ear and down his bare chest. Gidion clamped an instinctive hand to his own ear. He was about to turn away, but an impulse sent him over to the prisoners instead. Uncorking his waterskin, he stretched it out to the nailed man.

Before the prisoner could take it, a guard appeared and slapped Gidion's arm down, spraying water all over him. "No succor for Rift Rats. Get yourself off!"

Gidion bit back a retort, his eyes meeting those of the nailed man. An anger there to match his own.

"Are you determined to stir up trouble wherever we go?" Conal cried. "Those are Riftlanders, and be glad they're safely locked up."

"I know what they are," Gidion said. "And at least they aren't hypocrites like the Fed—"

"Shut your fool mouth!"

They were still dangerously close to the Federation guards, Gidion realized. He hated his father for being right, but self-preservation won out, and he clamped his teeth together.

They headed across the other end of the vast square to the Market Inn. It rose a full four stories, its buildings and outhouses taking up a third of the square. Long tables and benches had been set outside under a green awning, occupied by men, women, and children breakfasting, or in the case of the first, drinking a morning ale. The windowsills on the ground floor held baskets of tired flowers, and there was a sign above the door with a painting of a bunch of grapes and a bed, the universal Kharasian symbol for an inn.

"I'll go in and get us a stall. Wait here, and don't stir up trouble," Conal said.

As he went inside, Gidion thought about the Spire again. His father could only control him until he hit eighteen years of age. After that, Gidion was considered a full man. He could leave, then, go and learn warcraft magic under the great warweaver Arianna Velden. And once he was ready, he'd stop this running and hiding, and go after the Ilk mage who'd murdered his mother. *I'll go. I have to.* He was still lost in these thoughts when his father returned, bearing a wooden chit.

"Over there." Conal jerked his chin to the right.

Their stall was at the end of a row on the busy side. Conal always paid a premium to ensure they were well seen. As Gidion took each object from his pack, he wiped the dust off it with the polishing cloth he always carried. First out went the glowglobes and heatstones, sitting on top of their red pouches so customers could see their size, color, and shape. The heatstones were rectangular slabs of veined black soaprock, two inches thick, just able to fit into his pack. Designed to heat a small room rather than to cook on, they were unlikely to sell today. But some people planned in advance, and they might not often see heatstones at the market, especially at the price they'd offer. He'd made them during the winter, cutting and shaping the rock, and then impregnating it with a weave that could be triggered by rubbing an activation stone against the surface. But the glowglobes were Gidion's specialty and particular talent. Only the wealthiest of the townspeople could afford them, for his were of the best quality. They had other lighting devices for poorer folk—oil lamps, tallow candles, and flint fire kits purchased from a merchant in another town. It was Conal who laid these out at the very front left of the stall, with the glowglobes and heatstones sitting proudly behind.

On the right hand side, Conal set out wooden carvings of people and animals he'd made and painted himself—figurines for children's games, including Federation soldiers, Riftlanders, weavers, wagoneers, and serving girls. Last of all, Conal put out their small weighing scales and touchstone, for checking any silver or gold they were given. These were mostly for show because their weaver's gift enabled them to reliably determine the alloys in coins. Gidion was even better at it than his father. No cheat ever got past him, though many had tried.

Their first customer came soon after, a young mother clutching a squalling baby. "Morning, sirs, I'm looking for something special for my Berit. He's five today." She jigged her baby up and down, peering around its head to look at the items on their stall.

"Does he like soldiers' games?" Conal asked.

She smiled fondly, her gaze momentarily distant. "Yellows and Reds are his favorite."

"Plenty of both here." Conal indicated yellow-painted Rift-lander men with curved blades, along with a handful of isaurs, the two-legged, lizard-like creatures that Riftlanders used instead of horses. Then he swept his hand toward the Federation replica soldiers, who all carried spears and were painted red.

"They're well made," the woman commented, lifting a soldier to look it over.

"Thank you, I made them myself. It's two for a raven. Five for two ravens," Conal replied.

The woman winced. "Times are hard, food prices have near doubled. Six of your spearmen for two?"

Conal wasn't fooled, and neither was Gidion. The quality of her dress told them she could pay the price. "I have to buy food, too," Conal said. "And this stall wasn't cheap to rent."

"Are you sure that's the best you can do?" She smiled coyly and fluttered her lashes at him.

"I'm afraid that's it."

The baby was crying even louder, making Gidion's head hurt. She jigged it up and down again, rubbing her hand against the back of its head and mumbling some soothing words. Gidion wished she would hurry up and leave with the wretched thing.

At last, having failed to silence her child, she said, "I'll pay your price, just give me two of the soldiers, two of the Riftlanders and one of the isaurs." She put a hand inside her skirts and withdrew two copper pieces.

"You can pass them to my son," Conal said as he began to wrap the figurines in hemp.

Gidion took the coins and held them up to the light—Rastian issued, with a raven on one side and last year's date on the other, 201 AR. They looked good, and he told the woman to choose the figurines she wanted. She wasn't done yet, though, her eyes going to the candles and oil lamps. "I need some scented candles," she said. "For the Procession tonight."

Hearing that made Gidion's stomach twist. He'd tried to convince his father to let him stay for the Procession of Light and the celebrations that surrounded it. But, as always, his father had forbidden it, saying it wasn't for the likes of them.

"Those are beeswax. Six ravens a pound," Conal said to the woman.

This time she didn't try to bargain with him but fished for more coins while Conal weighed out the candles.

The morning passed swiftly after that, with one customer after another keeping them busy. Eventually, Conal went to get something to eat, leaving Gidion in charge of the stall. He'd been gone just a few minutes when the red-haired foreigner appeared. He was like nobody Gidion had ever seen, looming a full four hands above him, with skin so pale it seemed to glow. A bristling beard a shade lighter than his hair covered his face and neck, and his biceps were as thick as Gidion's thighs. Bulging scars crisscrossed his forearms, one of them still angry and red. From his belt hung a short sword with a plain hilt. It looked too small for him, and Gidion reckoned he usually used another, larger weapon.

"Good afternoon. Is that a magic lamp?" He spoke Zenian with a heavy accent, and Gidion had to strain to understand him.

"It's a glowglobe if that's what you mean."

The foreigner grinned, showing a cracked front tooth. "Well, that's lucky because I lost mine, and they're not easy to replace. How much?"

"A gold falcon."

The warrior widened his eyes. "Ruination, that's a lot!" He'd switched to Vycenian, which must be his native language.

"It's a good price," Gidion replied, also in Vycenian. "And that glowglobe is better than many you'll find. Try it out yourself."

The warrior picked up the glowglobe Gidion had pointed to. It was designed to be handheld but looked tiny in his huge hand. He rolled it around between his palms for a few seconds, then uncovered it to show an intense white light. "Not bad," he said. "But worth no more than seventeen stags."

There was something he liked about the warrior. He had an open, frank manner about him and a smile that made you want to smile with him. It almost made him give in. "I'll easily get more for it than that," he said with a regretful shake of his head.

"Eighteen?"

"Nineteen."

"It *is* a pretty decent lamp, not far off Wyven quality," the warrior conceded. "Nineteen it is." He took out a purse and started to count out the silver.

Gidion set the coins onto his weighing scales, at the same time allowing the threads of the Tapestry to appear before his eyes. The threads he sought couldn't be seen, though. To test the coins' alloy, he needed to listen for a certain resonance. Very difficult to do because the differences were minuscule. But as with all such skills, Gidion had caught on quickly, and he soon determined that all the coins were good save one. However, he first made a show of testing the alloy with the touchstone and magnet. "You won't get this past me," he said, holding the bad coin out to the warrior. "There's barely any silver in it at all."

The redhead took it back and made a show of checking it. "Now that's an embarrassment," he said. "Because there's nothing I hate more than a cheat and I'm careful with my coins. You sure?"

"It's a good counterfeit," Gidion said. "But worth little more than a couple of ravens."

"Stones, I knew that fella was shifty," he muttered. He went back to his purse. "I've got a Vycenian half-consul, but they're worth a lot more than your stags."

"I'll take it with ten stags."

"Here you go then." He handed over the money.

The half-consul was a large, thick silver coin, stamped with the head of the First Consul of Vycenia in 294 AR, a curly-haired woman with a beaky nose. Seeing it made Gidion think again of how he should be there, in the Spire of Arindel, learning to be a full weaver, not here in this stinking town where soldiers stole your money and laughed about it afterward.

"Name's Ruadh Sturmson, by the way," the warrior said as he was checking the coin. "You?"

"Pep." He reached out a hand and Ruadh gave it a firm shake. His grip was painfully strong, the large fingers completely enveloping Gidion's. "I'm guessing you're not from around here?"

The warrior laughed. "Ha! No! I come from Northland, right up the freezing arse end of Vycenia."

"You've traveled far, then." Gidion finished checking the coin and put it into his purse along with the rest.

"Aye, and I'm finally traveling home. Can't wait to see northern skies again. I've had nothing but trouble since I came down here, and the Zenians seem fond of making life miserable for everyone. So tomorrow it's off to Shitass to get a ship."

Gidion frowned in confusion. "Shitass?"

"Kharas is what's written on the maps. But it stinks worse than a drunkard's arse."

"I've never been." Not entirely true, because he and his father had passed through a couple of times. Once when they were fleeing *her* and their home in Vycenia, another time to visit Conal's weaver friend Jerald. But Gidion had been too young to remember much of it.

"Well, you haven't missed much. I'm looking forward to a bit of fun tonight, I'll tell ye. The lasses here are sweet enough. I wouldn't mind warming my bed with one of them." He made a lewd face. "You got a lass?"

Gidion flushed and shook his head. He'd kissed a girl once, and she'd even let him touch her breasts. Analie was her name. But then her dad had found them and beat him with his belt. The memory of that humiliation still had a hot, sharp edge. But the things he'd done with her in his dreams!

"Stick with me tonight. I'll make sure you get to dip your wick," the warrior said, reaching across the stall to clap him hard on the shoulder. "You *are* staying tonight?"

"Too right," Gidion replied, trying to inject some of Ruadh's boisterousness into his tone. He knew his father would forbid him again if he asked. But suddenly, he was determined not to let that stop him. *I'm almost eighteen. Almost counted a full man. He can't control me forever.*

Ruadh grinned. "Tell you what, I'll leave you to your selling. I have some things to take care of. Meet you in the Market Inn after you're done, and we'll quench our thirst together, find ourselves a pair of lasses?"

Gidion returned Ruadh's grin. "I'll be there."

"Can I help you?" It was Conal, returned with wrapped food. He took in Ruadh's bulk with a frown.

"I was just leaving," Ruadh replied. "See you later, lad."

Gidion quailed, thinking his father would demand an explanation for Ruadh's parting comment.

But Conal didn't seem to have paid attention to it. "That Northlander is far from home," he commented, looking after Ruadh as he disappeared into the crowd.

Some of Gidion's tension released. "He said he's been working merchant caravans."

"Hope you kept an eye out on our goods. Sellswords are rarely honest," Conal said with a sniff.

Gidion thought about Ruadh's bad coin. Deliberate or an honest mistake? All the same, he couldn't help but feel positively toward the man. He took a deep breath, intending to tell his father he planned to stay on for the Procession. But his courage failed him, and when his father gave him a questioning look, he just said, "He bought a glowglobe."

"Did he pay full price?"

"Nineteen stags, like we agreed." It annoyed Gidion that his father seemed to consider him completely incapable of anything. But Gidion was the far better haggler than Conal was. And the only one of them who could even make glowglobes.

"Here, I got you a meat pastie." Conal handed him one of the wrapped packages.

Gidion ate silently while his father served the next few customers. But he could barely taste the food, his mind churning over ways to tell his father he planned to stay. There was no denying the fact that Conal would rage at him, probably cuff him in the ear, shout at him that he was no Lumia-worshipping heretic.

But for Gidion, the Procession of Light wasn't really about Lumia. It was about celebrating midsummer. Time and again he'd heard stories of the revelry that went on, long into the night after the Procession was over. Nonetheless, dread of his father's anger kept him quiet until it was time to put their stall away.

It was only as they were about to leave town that Gidion worked up the courage to say his piece. "I'm staying for the Procession, tonight."

Conal froze. "What did you say?"

Gidion braced himself. "I'm staying. I'm going to the Procession, I'm going to celebrate midsummer."

"Did I give you permission?" Conal said in a tight voice. The voice he used when he was about to strike Gidion.

But it only made Gidion angry in turn, chasing away his nerves. "I'm not asking for your permission. I'm going to stay."

Conal took a step toward Gidion, his right hand raised and balled into a fist.

Gidion held his ground, met his father's grey eyes unblinkingly. But his chest was heaving, his heart slamming against his ribcage.

To Gidion's surprise, Conal lowered his hand, and his voice dropped with it. "It isn't for the likes of us."

The words only stoked Gidion's fury. "You always say that!" he cried. "What's wrong with having a bit of fun? Why can't we just go and be friendly with other people for a change?"

"You know why."

"No, I don't. Are you punishing me, or is it because you're weak and old and frightened?"

Conal slapped Gidion so hard on the cheek that his ears rang. He let out a wordless snarl and threw himself at his father, fists lashing out wildly. Conal side-stepped and grabbed his wrist, his grip still strong despite his sixty-two years. Even so, Gidion easily twisted loose and away.

"Your mother—"

Gidion planted his feet and glared at him. "Go on, then, say it!"

Conal's weathered cheeks flushed a darker shade of red. He drew in a breath. "You—"

"I killed her, that's what you want to say. Go on! Go *on*!" Gidion hurled the words out with all his force, and Conal flinched as each one struck.

"That's not—' he began, hands windmilling denial.

"Say it!" Gidion cried again, his voice rising shrilly, choking on his rage. "Say it!"

But Conal stepped back, shaking his head, looking utterly lost and lonely. Gidion felt a twinge of guilt, then Conal seemed to recover and said with strength, "Fine, stay if you must stay. But for pits' sake don't do or say anything stupid. And come straight back after the Procession."

The note of command trampled down Gidion's guilt. "I'll do whatever I damn well please."

"Everything has been for you, Gidion. Everything," Conal said, his voice softening.

It was a surprise, but Gidion ignored the words, just slung his pack over his shoulder and strode toward the inn to find Ruadh.

Chapter 2

It seemed that half the town had congregated in the inn. The large windows of the common room had been thrown open, showing a mass of closely pressed bodies. Many others had taken their drinks outside to the benches in the shade. Mostly men, but a few women too, and Gidion caught the eye of one as he walked past. She was perched on the end of a bench, looking out toward the market, one bare elbow resting on the table next to a pewter cup. Raven hair tumbled in waves about her shoulders, framing a fine-boned face with a slender nose. When she saw him, she cocked her head and smiled, showing a pair of dimples and an unexpected boldness. There was something familiar about her, but he couldn't quite place it.

"She's a beaut," a voice said from behind him.

Gidion jumped. Ruadh, the red-haired warrior he'd come to meet. His face had been flamed by the sun to the same color as his hair and was shiny with sweat.

Ruadh poked him in the back. "She obviously likes you. Go ask her if she'd like a drink."

"No, I..." Gidion shook his head. Maybe if he'd been a weaver instead of a peddler.

"You need to move quickly, lad. Don't think. Just go. Worst they can do is say no."

But this wasn't true. Analie's father had taught him that with his belt, and there were fathers everywhere here. Drinking, shouting, laughing with their friends, but keeping a close eye on their daughters, nonetheless.

"Go on, you've got a good pair of shoulders on you. Girls like that." Ruadh pushed him harder in her direction.

"You go to her if you like her," Gidion said, unable to keep the sulkiness out of his voice. There was no way he was going to succeed.

"She's not my type, to be honest," Ruadh said. "I like them plumper, something to hang on to. But come on, let's go in and get a drink, warm the blood a bit and it will all be easier."

Gidion was already moving toward the inn, hating himself for his cowardice while hopeful he might get another chance to talk to her. A wave of heat and noise assaulted him when he entered the common room. His head spun, as much from the sensation as from the knowledge that he was breaking an old taboo. His father rarely allowed him to enter the taverns in the towns they visited. He strongly disapproved of drunkenness or anything that might allow Gidion to have fun, such as spending an evening drinking with a stranger. But he was a man now. He was his own man.

The room was so full that most of the patrons were standing, and being shorter than the Kharasian average, Gidion couldn't see much beyond the heads and backs of those nearest him. Ruadh, though, stood taller and broader than anyone else, and people parted automatically for him. As he squeezed through, Gidion caught glimpses of crowded tables, many covered in amber pools. His nose wrinkled reflexively at the stink of stale sweat and unwashed bodies, but then quivered at a whiff of roasting meat. He was starving.

When they reached the bar, Ruadh leaned over the counter and bellowed down at the nearest bartender, who was pouring beers from a barrel. "How's about some food and summer wine for two hard-working men here!"

The man dipped his head to show he'd heard them but served three others before finally bringing them wine in pewter cups. They ordered their food, and then Ruadh reached for his cup, taking a few large gulps before putting it down with a satisfied *thunk*. Gidion took a small sip from his. It was sweetish and slid easily across his tongue and into his throat. He drank more.

"Not too bad, eh?" Ruadh said, lifting his cup again.

"I could have a few," Gidion said with a grin.

"Aye, and we will." Ruadh finished his wine and motioned for Gidion to do the same. While Gidion was drinking, the mercenary roared down the bar for more. Then he turned back to him. "So, where are you from? You don't have the look of the folk here, yet you speak Vycenian like a native."

Gidion resorted to the usual lie. "My father hails from Vycenia and my mother from Java, but pretty much all my life I've traveled around the northern states. I spoke Vycenian from birth."

Ruadh rubbed his beard. "Java, where's that?"

"Right down on the southeast coast." Conal had picked Java for their lie because it was as far away from Kharas as could be, so people were less likely to know what a true Javan looked like.

"And you travel around on your own?"

"My father and I have a wagon."

"He didn't want to hang around?"

Thinking of his father sparked Gidion's anger. "He never does. He's old."

"Aye, there's some men seem to shrivel up as they age. You won't find me skulking in an armchair when my hair turns grey, that's for sure. But tell me, where have you traveled? Me, I've seen enough of these parts. Seems everyone around here is a bloody cheat." Then, clearly remembering the earlier business with the counterfeit, Ruadh quickly added, "I really didn't mean to give you a bad coin. That one slipped past me, makes me bloody mad when it happens."

"Plenty of people get fooled. Some of the fakes are very good."

But it was obviously a sore point with Ruadh, because he leaned in, green eyes narrowed. "Look, the world is full of selfish bastards. That's fine. Just be a selfish bastard yourself, and you're all good. But there's that and there's plain meanness. I've been run out of Ilk knows how many villages because I called someone out on their game. They don't pay up on their wagers, they're going to get it. Know what I mean? The town guard should respect a man's right to get his wagers paid. But they run me out instead—me, the one who's been stung." Ruadh banged his fist against the bar. "And the cheats. There's a lot of bloody cheats. As if it was a point of national pride. Had two merchants try to trick me out of my pay, one of them tried to rob me in the night—that one, he came in with two eyes, left with one." Ruadh laughed with relish at the memory.

To cover his discomfort, Gidion drained the rest of his wine.

The bartender came to fill their cups again, and Ruadh took a long drink. "I'd say *you* don't need to hire guards."

Gidion's fingers tightened around his cup. "What makes you say that?"

"You didn't get those shoulders riding a cart."

"Well, you're not wrong. My father and I can take care of ourselves. In fact, we were ambushed by a dozen Riftlanders once and held them off alone." He grinned proudly.

Ruadh froze in the act of raising his wine to his lips. "You fended off twelve, just the two of you! You're having me on, lad."

Gidion puffed his chest. "Just the two of us."

Ruadh set his cup back onto the table, undrunk. "No, you're having me on. I mean, I could take on three fellas at the same time, easy, as long as none of them has a bow."

There was an edge to Ruadh's tone, and Gidion worried the warrior was getting angry. Lowering his voice, he said, "I can do weaving too."

Ruadh reared back, eyes widening. "You're a bloody weaver?"

Gidion was already regretting what he'd said. Conal would be furious if he learned of it. And Ruadh didn't look too pleased. He thought quickly. "I'm not a real weaver. I can just do some bits of weaving."

Ruadh was shaking his head. "I don't like stoning weavers. Give me the skin creeps. Too many of my brothers I've seen fall to magic. It's unnatural. Not a fair fight."

Gidion's heart was plummeting, but he tried again to salvage the situation. "Weavers can't use much magic to kill people, you know. The Tapestry doesn't let us. If we try to disturb things too much, it rebounds on us and kills us instead."

Ruadh's thick, red eyebrows drew together. "I've seen weavers kill plenty of people, opening pits beneath their feet that swallowed them right up, burying armies with rocks broken from the mountain."

"Well, I suppose indirectly the magic can be used to kill more people than if you were attacking them directly with lightbolts. But there's still a limit. And weaving can be used for a lot of good too, you know. Most don't become warweavers and don't want to kill. They're builders and healers, scholars, and advisers."

"Look, I've got nothing against people fighting for a living. That's what I do. I sell the strength of my arm for silver and gold, and proud of it," Ruadh said. "But weaving's just not fair." He bashed the counter again, causing a few patrons to turn around with curious looks.

Gidion tried another gambit. "But don't you use tricks to defeat your opponents? Don't you ambush sometimes? Or set traps?"

Ruadh paused, then cocked his head to the right in concession. "Aye, I suppose I can see your point there. Still not fair, though." He shook his head, then drank more of his wine. A moment later, he smiled. "I like you anyway, lad. I'll look it over for tonight. We'll have some fun, eh?" He raised his cup toward Gidion for a toast.

Relieved, Gidion clinked his cup against Ruadh's. Their food arrived, then, steaming bowls of stew and bread, and they fell into conversation about the villages and towns they'd both visited. The warrior was a lively and funny drinking companion, who grew louder and louder the more wine he consumed. Gidion often found himself choked with laughter and once came close to falling off his stool, when the wine had worked its full mischief in his head.

"I'm going to take a piss," Ruadh said. "When I get back, we'll go out. I see they've lit a fire in the square."

Gidion watched with a smile as the warrior disappeared into the thick press of people. Then he realized just how much information he'd revealed to Ruadh, and his smile died. Still, the man was hardly an Ilk friend, if Ilk even existed still. More likely the kind of man who would slay Ilk without a second thought and look for more to kill when he was done. So Gidion pushed his worries aside and tapped his foot to the beat of the minstrel's song. It was one he knew well and that he often sang to himself on the road.

Oh, the merry wives of
Hightop
How do they like to roam
Up the hill and down the
vale
That's how they like to go –
oh!

They love to drink
They love to dance
They'll steal your heart
If they get the chance
And you'll never be right
again
Oh, the merry wives of
Hightop
How do they like to roam
Up the hill and down the
vale
That's how they like to go –
oh!

The raucous words soon had men and women stomping and singing along, and Gidion found himself raising his voice to join them, a little creakily at first, then with loud gusto as a man next to him clapped him on the shoulder and raised his cup in cheerful salute.

"You haven't got a bad singing voice for a peddler."

Gidion flushed at the insult, then realized who was speaking to him—the young woman who'd smiled at him as he went into the inn. From up close, he could see that her eyes were the color of spring violets, a color more vivid than he'd ever seen.

She was smiling again now, dimples showing. "No need to be touchy," she said. "I'm just playing with you."

He fumbled for something to say. "How do you know I'm a peddler?"

Her smile broadened. "I saw you selling glowglobes at the market."

So that was why she'd seemed familiar. "What's your name?"

"Nessa, and yours?"

"I'm Pep." He paused, then decided to take a risk. "Would you like a drink?"

"Are you only able to speak in questions?" she returned.

His cheeks burned.

But she laughed—a rich, pleasing sound. "I'd love a cup of that summer wine."

He turned back toward the barman and, imitating Ruadh's manner earlier, called for two drinks. There followed an awkward wait during which he kept his eyes fixed on the barman while being acutely aware of her presence behind him. At last, the drinks were delivered, and he handed one to her. He raised his cup to hers, daring to meet her eyes. "Happy Day of Long Light."

"May Lumia forever shine over us." Nessa's tone was laced with irony, as if she didn't really worship Lumia. But then, neither did he, and maybe she'd guessed that about him too.

"Are you from here?" He asked even though she didn't look quite like the other townsfolk. There was a strange yet familiar slant to her eyes that made her stand out.

"I grew up on a farmstead not too far away."

This caused Gidion to reappraise her. The farmsteaders around this area were strong, hard people who enclosed their homes with wooden palisades to protect against constant Riftlander raids. His eyes fell on her arms, exposed by the sleeveless green dress she wore. They were muscular and crisscrossed with scars, some puckered and red, others pale white.

"I used to be a legionnaire," Nessa said, raising her left arm as if to inspect it. "Although I picked up a few of these before I joined the legions."

The scars didn't detract at all from the inviting softness of her skin. With an effort, Gidion pulled his eyes away from it and fixed them on her face. "Did you see they had some Riftlanders in the stocks?"

"Too good for them," Nessa said viciously.

Gidion was taken aback by the strength of feeling in her tone.

"Sorry, I've had too many run-ins with them," she said. "Gets me a bit worked up." She laughed, then her expression turned flirtatious once more. "Forget them. Tell me about you." She sipped from her cup, keeping her gaze trained on him.

Gidion fumbled for something to say. "Uh, I'm just a ... I mean, I'm ..."

Evidently realizing he was incapable of a sensible answer, she followed with another question. "Was that your father with you earlier?"

The mention of his father made him stiffen reflexively. "Yes."

"He's hardly the one who makes the glowglobes, is he? We don't see them often around here."

"No, it's me who makes them."

Her eyes widened. "You're a weaver?"

He hesitated, thinking what his father would say, then of Ruadh's earlier reaction. But she seemed impressed, was leaning into him, so close he could smell her perfume, a mixture of orange blossom and vanilla. "Yes, I am," he said with a touch of pride.

But she frowned in suspicion. "You don't look much like a weaver."

It was hard to think with her so close to him. "I can show you."

"Go on then," she said with a curve of her lips to soften the challenge.

Gidion made the Tapestry visible and plucked a few threads, creating a breeze that lifted the ends of her black hair and made them dance in the air.

She laughed delightedly, clapping her hands together. "Is that you?"

He nodded, releasing the threads before anyone could notice what he was doing.

The strands of hair fell around her face, and she gave him a coy look. "Are you going to leave me blind?"

"Sorry." He took hold of the threads again.

"Not with magic," she said, her voice and eyes lowering suggestively.

He blushed. "Oh, right." Reaching out with his fingers, he gently brushed the tendrils of hair aside.

Her hand went to his, trapping it against her cheek. His eyes fixed on hers, which seemed moist, inviting. Would she let him kiss her, or was it too soon? They'd barely started talking. But the way she was looking at him, the pressure of her hand on his...

"Well, seems like *I'm* not wanted anymore." Ruadh. Gidion sprung away from Nessa, cursing the warrior silently.

"And you're...?" Nessa said, looking at Ruadh through her eyelashes.

"Ruadh Sturmson, mercenary guard, at your service," Ruadh replied with a bow and a wink.

Gidion felt a strong desire to hit the man.

"Nessa Ni'Teele." She raised her cup toward him. "Are you two with each other, then?"

"Aye, well just for the night's fun," Ruadh replied. "You staying for the Procession?"

Nessa smiled broadly. "That's why I'm here."

Gidion rushed to speak before Ruadh could get another word in. "Did you come on your own, or ..."

"I was here with some friends, but I seem to have lost them," Nessa replied with a shrug.

Gidion rushed to be helpful. "Oh, would you like us to—"

But Ruadh cut in, angering him further. "Why don't you join us, then?"

"I'd love to," Nessa replied, smiling at the mercenary.

Gidion's blood boiled. Ruadh was definitely moving in on her, the bastard.

"Let's go outside?" Ruadh said. "I hear music, which means the dancing will be starting."

"Yes, I love dancing!" Nessa said, already making her way to the door.

Gidion made to follow her, but Ruadh slapped a meaty hand on his shoulder, stalling him. "Lad, you look like you're ready to skewer me. I'm only helping."

"You basically just asked her to dance," Gidion said, his voice hard and flat.

"No, I've put it in her mind that we could go dancing. And you're going to ask her when we get out there."

Gidion's anger drained away, replaced by the familiar leaden despair. "But I don't know how." *To the pits with you, father, for not teaching me anything normal people know.*

"Reckon she can, though. So, come on, let's go out and enjoy ourselves." Ruadh pushed him forward.

Out in the square, the streaks of red and orange in the sky were losing the battle to the dark hues of night, but there was still plenty of light from other sources. The market stalls had been dismantled, along with the canvas awning, and huge, flaming torches had been wedged into the ground around the perimeter of the square. Shadows danced on the walls of the nearby buildings, like demonic creatures rising above the roiling crowd. A large bonfire provided more light at the square's east side, and people were sitting and standing around it in clumps. At the opposite end, a stage had been erected, lit on all four corners by more torches. Three musicians were performing on it—a singer who also played the lute, a drummer, and a fiddler. The space in front of the stage had been taken over by a dozen or so couples who waltzed back and forth to the music.

As Gidion watched, a heavy man wearing a purple robe and a heavy golden chain clambered up onto the platform, accompanied by another dressed in an ordinary shirt and breeches. When the band finished the tune, the purple-robed man stepped to the fore and the second man blew loudly on a horn. First low, then rising high, it rang out across the square, bringing instant quiet as all eyes turned toward them.

The man in purple spoke in a booming voice that easily carried over the crowd. "As mayor of Tine, I welcome you all to our Festival of Light. I wish you all a happy night and a season of joy and bountiful plenty." A loud cheer. "And now, to begin the feast, the band, led by the great minstrel, Galvin Goldsinger, will play the 'Dance of Lumia!'"

"I'll get us some beers," Ruadh said. He departed with a meaningful look at Gidion.

Gidion tried to pluck up the courage to ask Nessa, but she beat him to it. "Come on." She grabbed his hand. Her fingers were rough, callused, but to him felt softer than silk.

"I've never learned to dance," he said, blushing.

"What? That's a tragedy! I'll have to teach you." She pulled him toward the other dancers. When they were among them, she instructed him to put one hand around her waist and hold the other in the air.

The feeling of her lithe muscles sent spikes of desire shooting through him. She was so close to him that their bodies touched, her breasts pressing lightly against him. It made his groin swell, and he worried that she could feel it and would be offended.

But if she noticed, she didn't show it. Instead, lips curved into a smile, she instructed him to take a step back. He did as she asked, and she stepped toward him at the same time. "Now forward," she said. He obeyed, and again she followed his movement.

Back and forth they went in time to the music. But when he'd mastered this basic rhythm, she gave more complex instructions, and he began to fall apart. He'd move forward when he should move back, to one side when he should move to the other. He didn't mind when it led to their bodies colliding but squirmed every time he trod on her feet. She didn't seem to mind, though, laughing each time.

"You might make a passable dancer with a little practice," she told him after the third dance.

"It's not so different to fighting," Gidion replied, trying to make light.

"You're also a fighter?" But then she traced the line of his shoulder with her fingertips, making him shiver. "But of course you are."

Maybe now he could kiss her? Should he just do it or was it better to ask? But the words stuck in his throat. So instead, he said, "I've had my own share of run-ins with the Riftlanders."

"They're brutes, every one of them," she said.

Gidion regretted bringing them up. It had broken the warmth between them. She was clearly agitated, her violet eyes darkening with some memory, her muscles rigid, making her pull away from him. But then she seemed to get a grip on herself. "Let's not talk about them, tonight." She softened again, but he sensed residual tension in her.

"Do you enjoy the Procession of Light?" he asked to change the subject.

"More so the celebrations around it," Nessa said. "And the opportunity to dance with handsome young men." The side of her mouth quirked up while she looked at him meaningfully.

Gidion's cheeks heated. She thought him handsome?

But then she became more matter of fact. "I'm surprised *you're* here. I thought weavers hated Lumia."

"Not hate," Gidion said. "We just don't believe she exists, that worship of her is a heresy."

"In my experience, people who don't follow a religion tend to hate those who do."

It gave Gidion pause. Conal had spoken often enough of how he despised the Lumin priesthood. Gidion instinctively felt the same. "The priests, maybe," he said. "But not the people."

Three long horn blasts rang out across the square. The crowd stilled, and all eyes turned to the stage, now occupied by a single horn blower.

"Procession's starting." Ruadh's voice.

Gidion turned to find him holding three foaming beers, which he handed to Gidion and Nessa.

The hornblower exited the stage, but moments later a procession of robed figures filed on from the left. They came in male-female pairs, the first three couples dressed in robes like those of weavers from the Spire. But while his father had told him that weavers wore their robes in many colors, the robes of these people were all red, with the symbol of the Spire Weavers woven in black on their chests—a thread that spiraled around a slender, needle-like tower. The next three couples wore strange masks that lengthened their faces and gave them feline eyes Their robes were flaming orange, marked with what initially looked like the heads of two sheep in profile. But when he looked longer, the face of a sexless person stared straight out from the middle.

An optical illusion—to symbolize the illusionist mages of Eleusia, he guessed.

The twelve robed people halted on the left-hand side of the stage and fanned out into a semi-circle, alternating in red and orange. A giant figure emerged from the right, looming twice as high as the tallest of the mages. It was clothed in billowing black, the face covered with the skeleton of some wild animal, a wolf perhaps. A horn blow, low and eerie, then three deep booms from a hidden drum.

When the final drumbeat had faded, one of the male weavers stepped forward and cried out, "Father of darkness, spawner of Ilk, I am Lorias Teryanal, First of the weavers of Vycenia, and I say to you that we have come to destroy you and end your curse upon the world!"

The hooded one, who had to be the Ilk Lord, loosed a cackling laugh. "You cannot defeat me! Your power is nothing compared to mine!"

"That may once have been true, but no longer," said the man playing Lorias. "We have mastered an even stronger magic than yours."

"Couldn't they have found better actors?" Ruadh snorted.

But Gidion was rapt and made no response.

"I know what you'll try to do," the Ilk Lord said. "But if you do it, you'll destroy the world. Stop, fools, and accept me as your master. Help me rule, and you'll live forever."

Loris plucked out a large, glowing stone from his robes. It was a glowglobe, no doubt intended to represent the giant focus stone the Final Hundred had used to unleash the power that would destroy both the Ilk Lord and half the world. "We, the weaver mages of Vycenia and the illusionists of Eleusia, join our power together to send you to the void! There will be no afterlife for you, you will be unmade!" he cried, holding the stone out before him.

A bright flash of light and a deafening explosion. The Ilk Lord screamed and appeared to ignite, white smoke swirling around him. Whoops and cries of amazement from the crowd. But then it was the mages who cried out as more explosions crossed the stage, and they fell to the ground.

BOOM, BOOM, BOOM.

The drumbeats sounded all around the square, the very earth quaking under Gidion's feet. A voice cried out from somewhere on the stage. "Alas, the world is destroyed!"

A man ran out with a piece of wood painted and shaped like a gigantic wave. Others followed with thunderclouds and lightning bolts, and then giant tongues of flame and spiraling winds.

"In Arindel, they have real flames and real winds," Ruadh said. "You should see the act they put on in the Consul."

"I have to say this one is better than many I've seen," Nessa said. "But that wouldn't be hard."

There was a ripple of movement at the front of the crowd. Gidion saw a glowing figure moving through the massed bodies. The person stepped onto the stage, carrying a torch that cast a flickering light on her fine features.

Coming to a halt at the center of the stage, the young woman cried out in a ringing tone, "Be at peace, world! I am Lumia, sent by my father, Solaris, the Master of Order, and my mother, Lunari, Protectress of the Land, to return light and life to the world they made. You were punished for your sins against nature, your foolish use of magic, and your obedience to those who would unnaturally try to reshape the world. But now you know the consequences of your actions. Follow me and obey my father and mother, stop abusing the world with spinnings and weavings, and you will know light and peace."

"This isn't what really happened," Gidion said. "She's no goddess. It's a lie. It's a total lie."

"It's just a story," Ruadh said.

"It's a lie."

"Shut up!" hissed a man in front of them.

The storm bearers ran off, leaving only Lumia, Lady of Light and Banisher of the Gloom on the stage. The crowd oohed and aahed but Gidion shook his head, feeling that he was betraying himself by being there. His father, for once, had been right. It was no place for weavers.

Lumia began to speak again but was drowned out by a rising din from the darkness beyond the square.

"What's that?" Gidion said.

"Ruin and bloody Ruination!" Ruadh cried.

"What?" Gidion craned his neck to see above the crowd. The sky in the distance was orange. At first, he didn't know what he was looking at, but then it hit him. Fire. Rising up all around.

"Riftlanders!" Nessa exclaimed. "I know their calls anywhere."

Indeed, Gidion could now hear a ululant howling along with the thump of heavy feet and the clash of metal. The first of the raiders burst onto the stage, a sword piercing "Lumia" through the chest. She collapsed, a red stain spreading on her white robe.

The crowd began to panic, people trampling over themselves to get away. Nessa almost fell to the ground, Gidion put a protective arm around her, staggering as he too was shoved by the people in front of them.

"We have to get out of here!" Ruadh said. "Follow me." The big warrior began to elbow people out of the way.

Wishing he had his focus stone and staff, Gidion followed, Nessa falling in behind.

Chapter 3

But before they'd cleared the square, they came face to face with a band of Riftlanders. Big, hardened men, with long, braided black hair and arms tattooed with black stripes to show how many men they'd killed. All around them lay dead and dying townspeople—men, women, and children—cut down without regard.

But Gidion had no time to take in the horrors. The nearest attacker had reached him and was swinging a curved blade. Gidion side-stepped and spun on the ball of his foot to smash his heel into the man's midsection. He doubled over, wheezing.

Another Riftlander rushed Gidion, arm outstretched as if to grab him. But Gidion saw the flash of the knife coming low from the other side. He brought his left arm down sharply against the wrist of the man's knife hand, keeping the inside of his own wrist turned away from the blade. But the man was bigger and had the advantage of momentum, and the knife pierced the top of Gidion's leg. Hot, stinging pain, but Gidion ignored it.

As the man drew the knife back, he stepped in, grabbed hold of the attacking arm, and pulled the man toward him. The Riftlander stumbled as his weight came forward, and Gidion kneed him in the face. But he barely seemed to feel it, letting out only a low grunt before trying to wrench out of Gidion's grasp. Gidion moved with him, keeping the arm controlled, but as he tried to dislodge the knife from his fingers, the warrior managed to break free.

"I gut you like pig," he snarled in the Common Tongue. "And I cut your balls off and fill them in your throat."

The blood pulsed harder in Gidion's head, but he didn't rise to the bait, instead flicking his eyes about to check for other attackers. Ruadh was to his left, fending off two assailants with a sword he must have stolen from one. Nessa, though, had disappeared.

He'd no time to wonder what had happened to her, for the knife-wielding Riftlander lunged in again, one hand extended to try and grab Gidion, knife sweeping toward his gut. This time, Gidion was ready, and he pivoted around as the man came in, chopping down on his arms. Then he grabbed the man's wrist and the elbow of his knife hand, twisted to pull him off balance, and forced the knife from his grasp. It fell to the ground with a *thunk*, but the other was coming at him again. Gidion snapped a kick cleanly between his legs. The man howled in pain, clutching his injured parts.

Hearing movement behind him, Gidion spun around, raising his right arm in a fast swing. His knuckles smashed into the man's temple, and he instantly collapsed.

Two more Riftlanders ran toward him. Then something hard struck the middle of his back. The pain disoriented him, and he barely dodged a sword strike.

All of a sudden, a heavy force hurled him to the ground from behind. He squirmed and tried to scrabble back to his feet, but another kick sent him back down. A flashing blade, aimed at his chest.

Panicking, he opened that part of him that was always firmly blocked off. The part that held his other magic—the magic that had led to his mother's death and a lifetime of hiding. The magic he wasn't supposed to use. He gathered all his power and sent out a roaring *NO* through the threads of the Tapestry.

It happened exactly like before. Those closest staggered backward, several keeling over, including Ruadh, who fell on top of him. Gidion landed heavily, head smashing against the ground, leaving him stunned. When he'd recovered, he squirmed out from underneath the unconscious mercenary and stood up, taking a quick look around. Everyone in a six-foot radius was in a stupor, some still standing, others crouching or lying flat. No sign of Nessa.

He stood on his tiptoes and squinted into the flame-soaked night to look for her. Riftlanders everywhere, hacking down anyone in their path. Federation soldiers also in action, but seemingly outclassed by the Riftlanders, who fought with deadly grace. Some were dragging screaming women off into the dark. Frantically, he tried to tell if any of them was Nessa, but they were too far away, the fires blinding him.

He returned his gaze to the fallen men around him. They were stirring. He should run, but Ruadh was still out cold, and he didn't want to abandon the mercenary. Which left only one other option. He plucked up a fallen knife and raised it above the throat of the nearest man. But finishing the deed was easier said than done. Gidion had fought Riftlanders before, alongside his father. But what he hadn't told Ruadh was that they usually scared raiders off with a display of weaving. A few lightbolts were generally all that was needed to take out the legs of a couple before the rest went running. This was different, and the man was unconscious. Unconscious but moaning. He'd kill Gidion when he woke. Any of them would.

Gidion gritted his teeth and stabbed the knife into the man's throat. It was both easier and harder than he'd expected. The knife tip slid in easily enough, but it required brute force to slice through the tendons of the neck and cut open the main artery. The man's eyes opened as he was doing his murderous work, and Gidion read panic in them as the blood pumped out of the Riftlander's ruined neck, taking his life with it.

Gidion went to the next man. This time, he avoided looking at the other's eyes while he carved his throat open. The Riftlander gurgled and wheezed as he died, legs jerking. But Gidion just went to the next man, falling into a blurry detachment as he killed one after the other.

"Gidion!"

To his amazement, Gidion saw his father, riding on one of their horses toward him, leading the other. He was also carrying both their battlestaffs. "I saw the raiders come in on the road and followed," Conal said. "Let's go."

"What the pits just happened?" Ruadh, who was slowly getting to his feet, eyes screwed up in pain.

Conal regarded the warrior. "Are you injured?"

"Just a bump on my head." Blood trickled down his temple and into his beard.

"They're waking up," Gidion said numbly. "We need to kill them."

"What we need to do is get the pits out of here while we can," Ruadh said. "I know poor odds when I see them." The man nearest him stirred, and Ruadh stamped on his face, bursting his nose. He fell back into unconsciousness.

Gidion looked away, sickened, then realized his own hands were drenched in blood and tried to wipe them off his tunic.

"Follow me," Conal said. "Gidion, take your staff and get on Maisie."

"Nessa," Gidion said, remembering they'd lost her.

"No idea what happened to her. Hopefully, she escaped those bastards," Ruadh replied. "I'll follow you, weaver."

"She has to be somewhere." He began searching for her again.

"Come on, Gidion," Conal said. "We don't have time."

"He's right, lad. Come on."

But Gidion ignored them both. She had to be out there somewhere.

"Take your damn staff and come on!" Conal snapped, shoving the staff in Gidion's face.

Cursing, Gidion took the battlestaff from his father, then got onto Maisie's back. Together, they made for an empty side street. But they hadn't gone far when another band of Riftlanders rounded the corner ahead of them. Two of them rode on the backs of isaurs, huge, two-legged creatures with the tough, scaly hide of a lizard and jaws powerful enough to crush a man in half. It was rare to see them outside the Riftlands, and Gidion's mouth dropped at their size. But then an arrow was flying at him from the isaur's rider. He activated a shield just in time to stop it from hitting him, then began to weave a lightbolt.

Conal sent one first, but the attack just dissipated around the man. Nicoleum armor, the one thing that stopped magic from working. Gidion realized the isaur was also wearing a nicoleum chest plate. Shit.

"We have to run!" Conal cried, wheeling his horse to go down another street.

"I'm with you!" Ruadh said.

But before Gidion had the presence of mind to move, it hit him—a wave of gut-wrenching, mind-breaking terror so strong it caused his knees to buckle. Shouts and gasps echoed around him. Then he saw them, rearing up behind the Riftlanders and advancing with a creaking, rattling gait. He knew immediately what they were, for he had seen them once before.

Ilk.

Creatures made of old bones and moldering remains, vomited from the bowels of the earth. Hideous parodies of living creatures, they walked on two legs, their eyes glowing red. A fetid stench came before them, containing a poisonous dread and a promise of the grave. This, the Gloom, was their most potent weapon. But these Ilk had more mundane ones too—swords and spears clutched in bony fingers, or long talons that could disembowel their victims in a single slash.

Some of the Riftlanders screamed warnings, but too late. Arrows punched uselessly into scaly flesh and bone, not even slowing the monsters' advance.

"Anyone know what in Ruination these things are?" Ruadh cried.

Gidion had frozen. This was all his fault. He'd used his shout power, he'd brought them back. Just like what had happened with his mother.

"They're Ilk," Conal said grimly.

"Are you having me on?" Ruadh said. "There's been no Ilk for two hundred years."

"He's right," Gidion said. "They're Ilk."

"That's it, I'm out of here," Ruadh said, casting about for an avenue of escape.

"Hello, Gidion."

He'd been expecting it, waiting for it, but the sound of her voice caused him to jump nevertheless, sending his pounding heart into an even more violent rhythm. He whirled around to find her standing right behind him, shorter than he remembered, but still striking and seemingly unaged, her coppery skin glowing with health. Malai, she'd called herself when they met ten years ago, when she'd murdered his mother.

"I'll kill you," he snarled, holding his battlestaff with its long, curved blade out before him. Inside, he quaked.

"I won't hurt you," she said. "I just want to talk to you."

Indeed, Gidion saw no malice in her silvery eyes, and sensed none either. It made him no less afraid. She was an Ilk mage. "Leave, or I'll kill you!" He tried to inject power and confidence into the words, but his voice sounded thin and reedy.

"I admire your passion, Gidion, but you know you can't harm me." Malai smiled, showing a row of perfect, white teeth.

He sprinted forward, intending to run her through with his staff, but she winked out of sight and reappeared a few paces away. He remembered her doing this before, all those years ago. What magic was it? It was nothing a weaver could do.

"My creatures will dispatch those men, and then we can talk more calmly," she said.

"I've no wish to talk to you, Ilk spawner." He took hold of the threads and passed them through his focus stone to weave a lightbolt. Malai was trying to say something else, but the crackling energy of the bolt drowned out her voice as it shot toward her. Again, she disappeared, and the bolt blasted into the building behind her, sending pieces of stone shooting out. She reappeared a few paces closer to him, out of the way of the tumbling debris.

"Don't move, Gidion!" cried Conal from behind him.

He froze and a lightbolt fizzed to his left, leaving an acrid smell in its wake. Malai dodged it as she had Gidion's, and the lightbolt struck stone again. The resulting explosion left his ears ringing.

He risked a glance over his shoulder to see his father standing behind him, eyes set with determination. The Ilk were still tearing at the Riftlanders, or more precisely, the isaur, which was panicking and trying to stampede its way free.

Malai laughed. "Hello, Conal. Have you told him yet?"

Told me what?

But Conal didn't answer her. Instead, he wove, and moments later the ground around her exploded, sending her sprawling. A shower of stones fell on her, leaving her half-buried beneath them.

"Go as fast as you can to Jerald in Greatport," Conal said to Gidion. "Tell him what's happened, and he'll help. I'll follow you and find you there."

"I'm not leaving you."

"Don't be stupid. Your mother didn't sacrifice herself so that you could die here." Conal got off his horse and turned to Ruadh. "Warrior, take my mount and get my son out of here. Have this for your trouble." He threw a purse as he spoke, and Ruadh caught it easily.

"Only too happy to oblige," Ruadh said, getting onto Conal's horse.

"I'm not going," Gidion said. Malai was down. They could take her. He started weaving the threads again.

Seeing what he was doing, Conal knocked the staff out of his hands. "If you don't go, your mother's death was for nothing. Now run."

"He's right. Let's get out of here," Ruadh said.

Gidion ignored them both and bent to pick up his staff. Malai was getting to her feet again, and Conal attacked her with a lightbolt.

Again, she evaded it easily, but this time, she reappeared further away. "Don't attack the Ilk," she called. "And they'll leave you alone."

Gidion didn't answer. Tried instead to think of a new angle of attack. Eventually, she had to make a mistake, move too slowly.

Conal wove again, and again the ground erupted beneath her, throwing her back. He looked at Gidion. "Go! I can manage this."

Ruadh grabbed the horse's reins, his face grim and purposeful. "Those monsters have nearly finished with the Riftlanders. We'll be next."

Gidion wrenched the reins out of his grip, managing to half turn his horse away. Then a heavy blow landed on the back of his head, and his vision blurred and narrowed before winking out completely.

Chapter 4

Gidion's eyes opened to a low ceiling of dark wood. Faint light shone through a small window above his head. Thunderous snores rolled out from his left. Ruadh. No sign of his father. Or of Nessa. What had happened? He remembered Ilk, four of them—and *her*. He'd been hit. His hands crawled over his skull and found a large, painful lump high up at the back. *Who did that?* He flung off the sheet and swung his legs over the side of the bed. Sharp pain stabbed through his ribs, forcing a groan out of him. When the pain had died, he realized he was in his underpants. Where were his clothes? Where was *he*?

"Reckon you've got a sore head," Ruadh said, his voice still thick with sleep. "Sorry about that, but you weren't seeing sense."

Gidion swung his gaze around to Ruadh, still lying in his bed, his eyes red and half shut. "What happened? Where are we?"

"We're in Kharas." Ruadh shifted himself upright, displaying a chest covered in a carpet of red hair.

"Kharas! How many days have I been out for?"

"Three."

Gidion frowned. How was it he'd been unconscious for that long?

Ruadh obviously guessed what he was thinking. "I had a bottle of sleepfast on me."

Gidion's mouth fell open. "You *drugged* me?"

"It was for your own good."

"You didn't have the right!" Gidion said furiously. "I could have helped. We could have taken them."

"Are you bloody joking!" Ruadh exclaimed, swinging his legs around to sit on the edge of the bed. "You never told me there were Ilk after you! And a stoning Ilk mage! I didn't sign up for that!"

"Well, you can leave now. You've done your bit."

"Not quite done," Ruadh said. "I said I'd bring you to this Jerald fellow. Then we're done." He squinted at a waterskin lying on the ground next to his bed, then picked it up.

"Kharas is close enough," Gidion said sullenly.

"I'm a man of my word, and your pa paid me well." Ruadh unscrewed the lid of the waterskin and took a long drink. "And I know this city. You'll find Jerald a lot quicker with me around."

Gidion glared at him, then realized he didn't want to lose his only ally. "Fine, we go to Jerald and then we're done."

"Good." Ruadh took another swig from the skin. "I do feel you owe me a story, though. Why the pits are Ilk after you? And how is it even possible there are still any alive?"

Gidion sighed. There seemed no reason not to tell the mercenary everything at this stage. "It all started when I was seven years old."

Ruadh whistled. "That's a while ago."

Almost eleven years since it had all begun, but Gidion had long nursed the memory, could recall the scene with clarity. But he'd never had to say it aloud before, and at first, the words stuck in his throat. "It was my birthday," he said at last, staring down at his hands. "I was ... I was playing with a new puzzle I'd been given. My mother called me for dinner, but I wanted to keep playing. I was so close to the end." He forced the next words out. "She kept insisting and I got angry. I shouted at her. But it wasn't just my voice I used." He glanced up at Ruadh, who was listening intently. "It was some kind of magical power that knocked her unconscious—as if I'd hit her on the head or something. I didn't mean to, I'd no idea what I was doing." He shook his head, remembering his terror as she'd dropped to the floor, thinking he'd killed her.

"Like whatever it was you did to me and those Riftlanders in Tine?"

"Sorry about that. I panicked."

"It helped us out of a tricky spot," Ruadh said. "But please don't use it on me again. I'd a headache for a day afterward." He took another swig from the skin. "I've never seen magic like that, not in all my years warring in Tarsis."

"It's not weaver magic," Gidion said. "I'm not sure where it comes from, really."

Ruadh thumbed his beard. "Is there other kinds of magic?"

Gidion shrugged. "It's said the Eleusians could do things weavers can't, like spin illusions."

"So, what, you're Eleusian? Aren't they all dead in the Ruin?"

"No, I'm not Eleusian," Gidion said, suddenly impatient. "Do you want the story or not?"

"Aye, go on."

"A few days after my birthday, a strange woman who called herself Malai came to our village. She's the Ilk mage who appeared in Tine. She became my friend, I suppose, though I don't remember much about her. I do remember that one day she said she'd show me something incredible. She took me to the woods near our house and said we would have to pass through a gateway to see it."

"What kind of a gateway?"

Gidion shrugged. "I don't really remember. I only know it was magical, like a square had been cut out of the world, and all you could see was this sort of greyness behind it. It made me frightened. I didn't want to go with her, but she was insisting. Then my mother came and told her to let me go. She refused and my mother attacked her. Another man—another *mage*—came out of the gateway and joined the fight. My mother was a powerful weaver, and she struck him down. Malai got very angry, and that was when the Ilk came out of the gateway." He wrung his hands, rubbing one thumb over the other.

"My father arrived, and next I remember we were on a horse—my father and I, that is. We lived in Vycenia back then, in the northwest somewhere, but we went to the Federation to hide, became peddlers, changed our names. We never saw my mother again." Saying it caused his voice to crack. And saying it all out loud made it even worse. He'd abandoned his father just like he'd abandoned his mother.

"I'm sorry, lad, that's tough, losing your ma so young."

Gidion gritted his teeth. "I'll avenge her one day—I'll avenge both of them."

"Do you know what the Ilk mage wants with you?" Ruadh asked.

"No. And I don't know how she found me, although I can guess."

"This shout magic of yours?"

Gidion nodded, ashamed.

"Can you stop yourself from using it again?"

"It only happens unconsciously," Gidion said. "But I can try. I just need to stay calm, not panic."

Ruadh handed him the skin he'd been drinking from. "Have a drink, it will help."

Gidion was fiercely thirsty and took it from him. But the liquid inside burned his throat, all the way down to his belly, making him cough and setting off the pain in his ribs. "That wasn't water," he said weakly.

"No," Ruadh agreed. "But it's a fierce tonic. Now let's go down, get some food, and find this friend of your pa's."

Half an hour later, they were finally ready to leave the inn, having gone to the kitchen first to eat a quick breakfast of honeyed porridge. The innkeeper's wife told them their destination was in the western part of the city and could be reached by going through the central market square.

"I know how to get to the market," Ruadh said. "It's not too far."

When they got outside, Gidion saw that the sun had already dropped behind the high stone buildings, leaving the narrow street in shadow. They followed it onto a much wider thoroughfare, which Ruadh said would take them to the market. As they walked, Gidion looked around, trying to stir memories from his trip here as a child, but very little came other than an impression of vast buildings and frightening numbers of people. So instead, he found himself ogling the many foreigners, who seemed to have come from every corner of the world. There were men and women as pale-skinned as Ruadh, with the blond hair and blue eyes that were common in the northern parts of Vycenia and Tarsis. Others had the olive-colored skin of the southern provinces of the Federation, with dark eyes and hair to match. These were mostly men wearing long robes of white, grey, or pale green linen.

The wealthier ones adorned their hands, arms, and ears with brightly colored gems and precious metals. And whether they were local or foreign, they avoided sullying themselves in the stinking streets, traveling instead on horseback or inside carriages. More than once, he saw the footmen standing at the front of the carriages jump down with an L-shaped broom to sweep aside clumps of dirt. To stop the carriage wheels from getting stuck, he supposed. The footmen were free with any who got in their way, whacking ankles and sometimes heads with impatient curses.

Gidion found himself staring at one particular carriage, heavily ornamented with gold leaf. It was open to the air, and inside it sat an enormously fat man with nut brown skin and eyes. He wore robes of maroon silk, intricately embroidered with gold, and a forest green wrapping around his head. Next to him was a young woman with similar coloring, her white silks clinging to the curves of her slender body. Her near-black hair was tied up in a loose mass and seeded with shimmering pearls. She was leaning toward the fat man, cooling his puffed, sweating face with a white fan. Behind the carriage came three large, heavily laden wagons, pulled by teams of six horses.

"Tunian merchant," Ruadh said, catching Gidion's gaze. "Meanest bastards around. I worked as a guard on one of their trains once, thinking that with their wealth they'd pay a handsome sum. He tried his damnedest to cheat us out of our fair due, even after we fought off a good dozen bandits."

"Did you get your money in the end?" Gidion asked.

"He had a daughter used to travel with him. When we took her and threatened to share her round for a night, he paid up pretty quickly," Ruadh said, chortling.

"Would ... would you have done it? If he hadn't paid?" Gidion felt himself redden.

"To be honest, it's not my thing," Ruadh said. "I'd rather hear a woman shrieking in pleasure than in pain. Some of the men were hoping he'd say no, though. She was quite the beauty, but more valuable to him a virgin."

"Why do you say that?" Gidion asked.

"Tunians treat everything like something to be bought and sold, even their own children. Beautiful daughters fetch a good price on their wedding day. And they'll happily pawn a child to pay off a debt."

"What happens to the child?"

"Goes to live in the creditor's household to work until the debt's paid off. Pawns are as good as slaves for the time they're there. That woman you saw in the carriage, she was one."

"She didn't look like one."

"There was a collar around her neck. A very fine collar, made of silver, but still a slave's collar. Doubtful she'll ever find herself a husband now, at least not a wealthy one. If she's lucky, she'll end up a courtesan to one of their nobles."

"I thought slavery was illegal in the Federation," Gidion said.

"It is," Ruadh said. "So technically, they're not slaves, so the Feds turn a blind eye. They need Tunian nobles on side."

They were now entering Kharas market. It was even larger than the one in Tine, and people crowded its length and breadth. Not all were buying and selling, though, and the tables in front of the taverns, coffee shops, and eating houses that ringed the square were full of groups of men and women. The lively atmosphere woke an ache in Gidion, reminding him that his father was gone, quite possibly dead.

They exited the square on the western side, as instructed by the innkeeper's wife. This street was relatively wide, for it led to the West Gate, but they soon turned off into a much narrower street and then into yet another whose pavings were broken and uneven. The buildings took on a neglected appearance, their facades dirty, their wooden shutters splintered or even missing slats. The people they passed were thin and worn-looking, dressed in rough-spun clothing that showed much evidence of patching and darning. Twice, ragged young creatures came begging for coin or food, but Ruadh sent them away with a growl.

Gidion expected to see an improvement when they reached Piece Street, but it was as dilapidated as the others. Jerald's house was halfway down the street, in front of a dry fountain mottled with yellow and white lichen.

"Why's a weaver living in a place like this? Weavers have money, right?" Ruadh said, rubbing at his beard.

To Gidion, it did at least seem to be in better repair than its neighbors, although the walls clearly needed cleaning. "My father told me Jerald has always preferred to stay among the class he came from," he said. "He was raised in the slums and wanted to help the poor. He does a lot of his work for free."

"Well, let's see if he's in, eh?" Ruadh said, stepping toward the door. He raised his hand and rapped his knuckles loudly against it. There was no response. He tried again, this time more loudly. Still no answer.

"Maybe he's gone out," Gidion said. "The shutters are all closed." But a darker thought was already coming to him, and he took hold of the threads.

"I can get it open," Ruadh said. He raised a heavy-booted foot to suggest a kick.

Gidion hesitated. Jerald might be out, and if so, he wouldn't appreciate his door being kicked in. "Let's knock one more time."

Ruadh balled his right hand into a fist and hammered it against the door with such force that it shook in its frame. They waited. Still nothing.

Disappointment, fear, and impatience made Gidion want to tell Ruadh to break down the door. He forced himself to be reasonable, though. "I suppose we should come back later."

"We can go back to Market Square and get something to eat," Ruadh said. "That gruel the innkeeper's wife gave us was hardly worth the name. I need something real to fill my belly."

But as they were about to go, a faint voice pierced through the closed door. "Who is it? What do you want?"

Ruadh motioned Gidion forward and indicated he should speak.

"Weaver Jerald Kiltour. Is that you?" he said to the door, pressing his ear against it for a reply.

A pause. "Who asks?"

"Gidion, Conal's son."

Another pause. "Gidion? Truly? Wait, wait." A grating and grinding behind the door until it finally swung open, revealing a stooped old man with tufted white hair and a face like crumpled parchment. He seemed different than Gidion remembered. Diminished somehow. But that would make sense. They'd last met eleven years ago, and Gidion had only been a little boy. It was Jerald who now peered up at Gidion, his pale blue eyes watery and weak. "What brings you here? Where's your father?" He looked behind Gidion, frowning when he caught sight of Ruadh.

"I was hoping he might be with you. It's a long story."

"Ah." He looked confused for a moment, then seemed to gather himself. "I suppose you'd best come in." Jerald stepped aside to allow them into a gloomy hallway, then led them into a living room whose single small window looked out over the street. The window didn't let in much light through the chinks in the shutters, but the room brightened as Jerald triggered a glowglobe attached to the wall by the door. A large, red rug in the middle of the room gave it some warmth, but the wooden walls were bare.

"Have a seat." Jerald indicated plain wooden chairs around a rectangular table near the window. He lowered himself slowly onto one of the chairs, and Gidion imagined he could hear his knees creak.

Gidion took a seat opposite him with a growing sense of unease. Ruadh remained standing in the center of the room, towering over them in his heavy armor.

"Tell me, then, what's happened?" the weaver asked.

Gidion recounted the full story as Jerald listened quietly.

When Gidion had finished, he spoke again, "This is a terrible tale. Conal, lost to an Ilk mage." Jerald shook his head. "But you can't stay here. It's dangerous. You should go to the Spire immediately. You'll be safer there."

Despite his misery over his father's loss, Gidion perked up at Jerald's words. "That's what I thought, but pa always said I should stay away."

"Conal was always cautious. And he never liked the Spire, neither of us did." Jerald's eyes glazed over, as if he was temporarily elsewhere.

"Why did he hate it so much?"

Jerald shook himself, his gaze sharpening again. "You'll find out when you get there. But it's the safest place for you right now. And you need to finish your training."

"And what about my father? What if he's not dead and shows up?"

Jerald hesitated. "If he comes here, I'll send him to the Spire."

Gidion nodded. Again, Jerald's eyes unfocused for several heartbeats. Where was his attention going?

Gidion was about to prod him when Jerald came back to the room and spoke. "Wait a moment and I'll pen a letter of introduction."

"I want to apprentice with Arianna Velden," Gidion said eagerly.

"Let's not get ahead of ourselves," Jerald said with a weak smile. "You need to get yourself admitted as a Seeker first. And then you'll need to pass the Selection Trial."

Seeker was the name given to weaver trainees of all levels, Gidion knew, and hearing the word couldn't help but send a thrill through him.

Jerald slowly got up and shuffled over to a writing desk at the back of the room. "Danial Thane is the Head of Seekers, last I knew. I'll write you a letter for him."

"I also need new identity papers," Gidion said. "The Feds are looking for Pep on account of ... because I killed those ..."

Jerald paused, then said, "I can provide a testimony of identity. Probably best if we say you're from Vycenia." Lifting the lid of the desk, he withdrew pen, ink, and paper. He set them carefully on top of the desk, then dipped the pen into the ink. But he'd no sooner done this than the pen fell out of his hands, rolling down the desk and clattering to the floor in a spray of black ink. His head jerked backward, eyes rolling up so far that only the whites showed. Then a spasm wracked his body, and the legs of the chair rapped against the wooden floorboards.

Gidion leaped to his feet, while Ruadh drew his axe and dropped into a defensive stance. Gidion reached out to sense whether there was any weaving but felt nothing. However, his intuitive sense told him there was another presence around Jerald. He strained to understand but got nothing more.

Jerald head snapped from side to side, so sharply that Gidion thought his neck would break. He stepped toward the weaver, thinking to try and pin him down. But before he got there, the fit stopped.

Jerald's pale blue eyes found Gidion. They were startlingly lucid, unlike the haze that had clouded them before. "Get out of here!" he cried. "Don't—" His words were choked off by a return of the terrible spasms. The front legs of the chair came off the ground and it tipped over sideways, spilling the elderly weaver onto the ground.

There, his body continued to twist and contort, legs and arms flailing as if fighting off an invisible attacker.

Gidion didn't know what to do. He turned to Ruadh, who was still standing there, holding his ax.

"Don't look at me, I don't know what in Ruination's going on," the warrior said, nostrils flaring. He glanced toward the door. "But maybe we should do as he says."

"We can't just leave him," Gidion said. He moved forward, not really knowing what to do but thinking he had to try something. Hunkering down next to the weaver, he put a hand onto his forehead, pushing out with his intuition, trying to sense what was going on. The old man's eyes fixed on Gidion again. "Trust no one," he hissed. Then a long scream erupted from his throat. "No, leave me be!" he cried. He clutched his head with his hands, pulling at it as if trying to tear it off his shoulders.

Again, the piercing scream, and Gidion reared back, hand coming free of Jerald's forehead. A glow of power leaped up around the old weaver. Too late, Gidion realized what he was doing. Blinding blue light blazed all around him, completely consuming his body. As the light died, a strong smell of cooking meat reached Gidion's nose.

"Ilk take me," Ruadh said softly. "Is he after burning himself alive?"

Gidion stared at the weaver's body, the smoking black rags that covered his bony frame. He seemed to have burned from the inside out, perhaps holding so much of the Tapestry that the power of it overwhelmed him. But that couldn't be right.

"Why the pits did he do that?" Ruadh said.

"It's like he was fighting someone," Gidion said. "Like someone invisible was attacking him." He looked around, half-expecting to see an Ilk mage jumping out from behind a piece of furniture. But that was crazy. Gidion would have seen the weaves, sensed the magic if someone had struck Jerald.

"That's it, I'm out of here," Ruadh said. "Whoever it is he was fighting is probably going to come after us next, and I'm not fighting any more bloody weavers." He started marching to the door and, after a final glance around the room, Gidion followed him.

He half expected a horde of Ilk in the street outside, but everything was completely ordinary. He realized he was shaking and swallowed hard, trying to calm himself.

"Right, I'm off to find me a ship," Ruadh said.

"Where to?" Gidion said, still in a daze. *He didn't kill himself deliberately, he didn't. Someone attacked him. He was talking to someone. Malai?* He looked up and down the street again, then up at the rooftops, but nothing.

"I'm going to Arindel."

"Let me come with you," Gidion said.

"Nah, lad, I'm not up to this. I hate weavers—no offense."

Gidion resorted to begging. "Please. I have to go there anyway. Can't we travel together?"

"You need some money? Here." Ruadh fished out some silvers from the purse that Conal had given him.

"It's not that. I've no idea how to even get a ship, or ..." Gidion found tears springing to his eyes and turned his face away in shame.

Ruadh regarded him silently, then sighed. "Fine, I suppose your pa gave me enough coin. We'll need to find a captain who's able to avoid customs and checks so we can get you out without questions."

Gidion roughly rubbed his eyes with the back of his arm. "Where do we do that?"

"There's a couple of taverns down by the docks where the captains drink. We'll find one there."

Gidion thought of Jerald, lying dead in the house. Maybe he should seal it off. If there was some kind of dark magic in there, he didn't want someone just stumbling onto it. "Just a moment." He put his hands against the door and created a locking weave that would hold it shut against ordinary passersby. "Alright, I'm ready."

Chapter 5

The winds were against them, so they didn't reach Arindel until the sun had broken the horizon the day after they set sail. Gidion tried his best to sleep in the hammock he'd been assigned under mildewed blankets provided by the captain, but only Ruadh seemed able to ignore the chill enough to actually get any sleep. Gidion reckoned it was because the mercenary had shared in the crew's liquor the evening before. He'd managed to befriend half the men on board by the time they were out of the harbor, his voice and laugh booming across the main deck for much of the day. Gidion had joined them in the drinking for a while, but he was feeling every one of his injuries and soon decided he was better off resting in the hammock.

Now, they were near the prow of the ship, gazing at the rapidly approaching port. There seemed to be hundreds of vessels, some moving slowly, others resting at the wharves that jutted into the River Arin at regular intervals. Smaller, cargo-laden boats crowded among them, manned by teams of men who shouted in unison as they heaved on the oars. The white stone walls of the city were visible beyond, stretching from east to west on either side of the river.

But it was the Spire that pulled and caught his attention. Even though his father had told him it wasn't a single spire, but a central one surrounded by six others, the sight of them startled him. They gleamed softly in the morning sunshine, so tall that their needle-like tips seemed to graze the pale blue sky. His answers were waiting there. If only he could transport himself instantly—it seemed suddenly as if he couldn't wait another breath, another heartbeat, to finally pass beyond its walls.

"There's your needle," Ruadh said, standing next to him.

"Have you ever been inside?"

"Are you joking?" Ruadh snorted.

"We're docking soon! Get your things together," called the second mate.

Gidion didn't need to be told twice. He was eager to get off the ship, to finally penetrate a city that had long had the status of legend in his mind. Although he'd barely slept, he felt fully alert and brimming with energy. His meeting with fate was close. The only dent in his mood was his missing father, but there was still a chance Conal would follow, or so he tried to tell himself.

The sailors scurried up and down the ship like spiders, shortening and furling sails so that the ship's movement slowed. Soon after, it began to veer left toward an empty dock not far from the city walls. When they were close, some of the men leaped over the side of the ship and onto the wharf, carrying thick ropes over their shoulders. They used the ropes to guide the ship in the rest of the way and then moor it firmly by wrapping the ropes around heavy iron rings attached to the wharf.

"Right, let's get off this tub," Ruadh said. "I want my breakfast on dry land."

They were off the ship almost as soon as the crew had laid down the gangplank, making their way along a paved road they'd been told would bring them to Rivergate. The road passed between rows of large stone warehouses that ran parallel to the river. Sun-browned dock workers hauled sacks, rolled barrels, and wheeled carts from the waterside to the warehouses, some of them singing, others silent except to bellow curses at those who got in their way. The stink of fish guts came to Gidion on the brisk breeze, and his nose wrinkled reflexively.

Ahead of them loomed the city wall. As they got closer, Gidion saw it was entirely smooth, as if the white stone had been melted and molded—probably by magic. It was ringed on the outside by a wide, water-filled moat that drew from the River Arin. The river itself flowed into the city under a set of three archways, and boats laden with goods were being rowed in and out.

They crossed the moat not too far from the river using a wooden drawbridge. The water was green and sluggish but not the filthy sludge Gidion had seen in Kharas. Four guards stood outside the massive black iron gates, but they didn't seem too bothered with checking who was going in.

They stepped onto a wide boulevard paved in white stone. Of the stinking gutters that had lined the streets of Kharas there was no trace, and even the animal dirt seemed to be at a minimum. The silvery lengths of the Spire were clearly visible beyond the buildings. There, at last, Gidion would meet his destiny. A thrum of excitement ran through him.

"This is Merchant's Walk," Ruadh said. "It's all shops and merchant's storehouses in this quarter. This part is for ordinary folks. Part closest to Eagle Bridge is for the rich."

The buildings did indeed all seem to be offering things for sale. There were chandlers, tailors, cloth merchants, and milliners, among others. Most shops were still closed, but their wares were visible behind large glass windows. The glass was the clearest he'd ever seen. Weaver work, no doubt. Some part of him, the peddling part, wanted to get a closer look, see what could be bought here for a good price and sold for a better one elsewhere. But that life was gone, along with his father. His throat tightened, and he swallowed.

When they reached the third crossroad, Ruadh came to a stop. "This is as far as I go," he said. "There's a passable inn down this way." He pointed down a street to the left. "The Silver Sword. I'm going to hole up there while I look for a job."

"So you don't want to come to the Spire?" Gidion said, knowing the answer but wishing it were otherwise. He'd grown fond of Ruadh, and the man was the closest thing he had to a friend.

"I like you, Gid, but I've had my fill of weavers." Ruadh sounded genuinely regretful, but the words pierced Gidion's gut like knives, leaving him with a hollowed-out feeling. "To get to the Spire, keep on this road for ten or so blocks," Ruadh continued. "Then take a right turn down West Street. The street names are all carved into the stone on the left-hand corners so keep your eye out for it." He pointed up to the corner of the street he was about to turn into, and Gidion saw the words "Targin Street" etched into the wall. "West Street will bring you straight to Eagle Bridge and then onto the Passage of the Spire."

"Will I see you again?" Gidion managed. He felt nauseous at the thought of continuing alone, without the comfort of even one human being beside him.

But if Ruadh noticed his unhappiness, he showed no sign of it. "You know where to find me if you want me." He clapped Gidion on the shoulder and then walked off, leading his horse by the reins.

Gidion watched him go, fighting a sudden urge to cry. The warrior had invited Gidion to find him again, but it had sounded like a throwaway comment. Gidion was alone now, more than ever. He watched until Ruadh disappeared into the mob crowding the street, then turned his attention to the Spire. He girded himself. There, his greatest hopes lay. There, at last, he might find a place where he belonged.

Hiking his pack on his shoulders, he followed Ruadh's directions to reach the famed Eagle Bridge. It was easy to see why it was so named, flanked as it was by a pair of marble eagles with half-spread wings, their golden beaks bright against the black of their heads.

The Passage of the Spire was as wide as Merchant's Walk. But it was clearly home to much wealthier people, with large buildings fronted by flower-filled gardens whose perfume filled the air. The few people in the street were servants hurrying about on errands, while the owners of the houses clattered past in elegant carriages.

The Spire lay right ahead of Gidion. It stood on a high, terraced plateau, each terrace brimming with summer flowers, while thick green vines spilled down the sides. Gidion had expected to feel a strong hum of weaving as he approached, but there was only the faintest shiver. It made sense, though. His father had told him that the Spire was enveloped in a powerful concealing weave, which dampened the sound of magic use.

There were two ways to get to the top of the plateau, Gidion knew. One was to take the one thousand steps that ran from street level to the main gates. The other was via a rising platform called a levitator. If he recalled rightly, it was accessed through a short tunnel to the right of the steps, which he soon spotted. A young woman wearing pale-blue livery stood outside it. Up close, he saw her tunic was embroidered with a single spire surrounded by a spiraling thread. The official Spire symbol.

"Can I go up?" Gidion asked uncertainly.

"Of course." She put a hand to the door and Gidion felt a brief hum of weaving before the door slid open to the side. Beyond it was a small, circular chamber. "In you go."

Gidion stepped through and the door slid closed behind him. A pressure under his feet told him that the levitator was rising. He could tell it was powered by a complex weave but couldn't fully make sense of it. The Eleusians were the true experts at this kind of thing. And many things that weavers had once been able to do, they could do no longer, the art lost in the Ruin.

The levitator soon stopped, and the door slid open again. He stepped out onto a grassy plaza. To his left, the city spread out below him in pearly magnificence, while to his right rose the high, crystalline wall that surrounded the Spire. He stopped for a moment to take in the view of the city, then turned his attention to the Spire and its gates of gold. They were open but flanked by four guards—two men and two women. The women had battlestaffs, marking them as weavers, while the men carried normal spears. All four blocked his way as he approached.

"State your business," said one of the women, her voice as sharp as her nose and the cut of her short hair.

"I'm here to start training as a weaver." He raised his staff to draw her attention to it.

She seemed unimpressed. "New Seeker intake takes place on the Day of the Spinners. Come back then."

That was still over two months away. He wasn't that long to get in! "I need to see Magister Thane. I've got important information to share with him."

The guard laughed. Then stopped suddenly. "Wait, you're serious?"

"It's urgent," he said. *The Ilk are after me. She's going to come for me. Jerald's dead.* "I've got information about a dead weaver."

"Who?" said the other weaver guard, who seemed younger than the first, her eyes softer and rounder.

Heartened, he said, "Jerald Kiltour."

The weavers exchanged glances, shaking their heads. "Never heard the name," said the first.

Gidion ground his teeth in frustration. What more could he say?

"Go on, scoot away from here," she continued, shooing him away like he was a dog.

Gidion quelled his anger with difficulty. He clearly needed to raise the stakes, convince these fools he was serious. "I'm pretty sure Jerald was murdered by an Ilk mage."

"And I suppose you had a load of Ilk after you," said the second weaver with a roll of her eyes.

Gidion plunged on desperately. "Yes, four of them. And I can see you don't believe me. But I'm telling you the truth, I swear it."

Now all four started laughing. "Alright, boy, you've had your joke, now piss off," said one of the men.

Gidion tried to pour every ounce of sincerity into his tone. "Please, this isn't a joke. I'm being chased by the Ilk mage, and if I stay in the city, she might find me. I really, really need to speak to Magister Thane."

"Our patience will only last so long," said the first woman, all traces of laughter gone.

He needed another tactic. The other weaver didn't seem as determined to keep him out. Maybe she could be worked on. So he kept his gaze on her as he asked his next question. "Can I at least write him a note? If I turn out to be telling the truth and he finds out, he probably won't thank you for turning me away."

That finally swayed the second weaver, who rolled her eyes and sighed. "Okay, fine. Come here with me and you can write him something."

"I don't ..." said the first, but then shrugged, as if she couldn't be bothered arguing further.

The other took Gidion into the guardhouse and slid pen and paper toward him.

Gidion scrawled his name and his father's and his information about Jerald and the Ilk. "Will you deliver it to him now?"

"I'm not your messenger," she sniffed. "It will get picked up later."

Gidion sighed in frustration but couldn't think of anything else. "Fine, I'll wait outside the gates until I get a response."

"You could be waiting a long time. Come back tomorrow."

"I'd rather be here."

She frowned at that, and he sensed that she might even be starting to believe him. But she said nothing, just folded the piece of paper and waved him out.

He took up position on one of the benches directly outside the gates. Let Malai come for him here, within view of the weavers. At least they'd have to believe him.

Several hours passed with no shade to protect him from the heat of the sun. His ribs ached abominably, but he resisted the temptation to lie on the bench. He had to avoid any sign of weakness.

As he waited, many weavers walked in and out of the Spire, and even more non-weavers. For all he knew, one of them was Thane, a matter that frustrated him greatly. He asked the guards periodically if the note had been delivered yet, until finally, they snapped that if he approached them one more time, they'd remove him from the plaza.

But his determination finally seemed to convince them that he was serious, and at midday, one of the spear wielders came to tell him the note had been sent to Thane. He also offered Gidion a drink of water from his waterskin. But the sun was low in the sky when Gidion finally heard his name being called.

Famished and parched, he limped up to the gate. Standing next to the guards was a man dressed in high-collared robes of midnight blue with the sign of the Spire embroidered in gold over the left breast. His features were striking—long-lashed eyes, cheekbones as keen as a blade, pale blond hair that curled artfully around his ears. "Hello, Gidion. I'm Magister Thane," he said in a rich tenor. "I hear you have a story to tell me." He smiled then, his cheeks dimpling into crescents. It was a surprisingly warm and welcoming smile, and a layer of tension slid off Gidion. To the guards, Thane said, "I'll take it from here. And please don't mention it to anyone else. We don't want to stir up a panic."

"Of course, Magister," they said in a chorus, bowing.

Thane was silent as he led Gidion into the Spire grounds, only speaking when out of earshot of the guards. "I sincerely hope you aren't wasting my time."

"I promise I'm telling the truth," Gidion said. "I was in Kharas and—"

But Thane cut him off. "Don't speak of it now where others can hear. We'll go to my rooms, and you can tell me your story there."

Chapter 6

Gidion tried to keep himself from gawping like a fool at the glittering lengths of the towers beyond the gates. They were constructed from rose-tinted crystal, but he couldn't make out individual bricks, as if the towers had risen up ready-formed from the ground. The crystal was translucent without being transparent, and slender, tube-like walkways connected each tower to the next on two levels, the first about a third of the way up and the second two-thirds. They also connected to the central tower like the spokes of a wheel. The effect was surely deliberate to remind all who gazed upon them of the Spinners, the gods the weavers still worshipped.

Thane angled left toward the south-western tower. He moved in an unhurried manner, although Gidion sensed an urgency in the man. But Gidion was grateful for it, as his leg had started to hurt again, worsening his limp. And he was so hungry and thirsty he felt dizzy. If Thane noticed his state, though, he said nothing.

At last, they reached the entrance to the tower. Its vast, silver doors were open, so they went through and into a short passageway that opened into a large internal courtyard. Before Gidion was a pool surrounded by leafy plants, and in the center of the pool rose a long hollow shaft that went all the way up to the top of the tower.

Thane allowed him no time to take it all in, though, going straight to a narrow bridge that spanned the pool and gave access to the shaft. Gidion peered down at the pool as they crossed, finding it tiled with a blue-green mosaic of the Spire symbol. Small, fat fish in red and gold moved lazily about in the water.

Inside the shaft, as Gidion had suspected, was a levitator. Thane activated it with a press of his finger and the levitator rose, coming to a smooth stop at the top level. Thane led him around to the right and took the second bridge they came to. Even though it had waist-high rails, Gidion had the dizzying sensation of stepping out into a chasm. He kept his gaze firmly on Thane's back and tried not to think of what would happen if he were to slip and fall.

The bridge brought them to a colonnaded passageway that circled the tower's perimeter. But Thane only took him a few paces along before stopping at a door made of rich wood and carved with the symbol of an open book. Thane pressed his palm against the center of the door, and it swung smoothly open.

The room they entered had an exterior crystal wall that acted like a giant window, causing Gidion to frown in puzzlement. Was it weaving that made the walls opaque only when looking from the outside in? Or was it something to do with the crystal itself? And despite the evening sunlight spilling into the room, it was pleasantly cool, as if the crystal deflected some of the heat. Would that make it cold in the winter, then? He had a feeling not, but the weaves in the crystal were so densely knotted he couldn't say for sure.

The floor was tiled in white but covered in rugs of soft greens and blues. A suite of chairs carved from dark wood surrounded a matching table on the interior side of the room. The legs of the table and chairs were curved like bows, very unlike any style of furniture Gidion had ever seen. The window side, which overlooked a garden of roses, was crowded with leafy plants, some almost as tall as trees. Amidst the plants were two white couches facing each other across a low, finely carved wooden table.

"A common Eleusian affectation," Thane said, noting the direction of his gaze. "While the Eleusians were great workers of stone, they also prized gardens, and brought flowers and plants indoors as much as they could."

"It's beautiful," Gidion said.

A smile flickered across Thane's face. "Beauty is important in a world so often filled with ugliness." He motioned Gidion toward the couches. "Sit. Are you thirsty?"

"Yes, Magister." He was hungry too but decided it was politer not to mention it.

Gidion perched awkwardly on the edge of one of the couches while Thane went to a porcelain pitcher sitting on a side table and poured water into a silver cup. He handed it to Gidion before seating himself on the couch opposite, his legs crossed, his hands clasped over his lap. He waited until Gidion had drunk his fill before speaking. "Perhaps you can start by telling me where you got that weaver's staff from. It's dangerous in the hands of an untrained novice." Thane smiled to take the edge off his words.

"I'm not a novice," Gidion said, heating. "My father has trained me, and he gave me this staff."

Thane's right eyebrow arched in surprise. "He trained you himself? Why didn't he send you here? He surely knows the rules."

"We lived in the Federation. The rules are different there."

"So they are," Thane said, his expression growing thoughtful before sharpening again. "But you said in your note that he trained here. What's his name?"

"Conal Ne'Brin."

Frown lines appeared on the magister's forehead. "I don't know that name. When was he last here?"

"About twenty years ago."

Thane seemed even more puzzled. "I should know him in that case."

"You were a Seeker then?" Gidion blurted out. If it was true, Thane was a lot older than he looked.

"It is I who ask the questions," Thane replied, his eyebrow going up again.

"Sorry, Magister."

"Are you sure that was the name he used here?"

And then it struck him. Of course, his father had changed his name, just like he'd changed Gidion's, when they went on the run. "Varn Jameson," he said, the syllables sounding strange on his tongue, not attached to his father at all. "He'd have gone by Varn Jameson. I remember now."

"Varn! You're Varn's son!" Thane tilted his head sideways, eyes narrowing as he looked him over. "You look nothing like him." But then the smile reappeared. "I won't say it's a bad thing."

Thane seemed to be implying something, but he wasn't sure what. Uncertainly, he said, "I-I take after my mother's side. Or so I've been told."

"Aha, and who's your mother?"

"She's ..." Gidion took a deep breath. He hated saying these words. It never got any easier. "She's dead."

Thane's expression softened, and Gidion caught a hint of old pain. "I'm sorry to hear that. It's hard to lose a mother, isn't it?"

"Have you, did you ..." Gidion realized his question was inappropriate and stumbled into silence.

But Thane just smiled again. "She died when I was nine. While it was difficult, it freed me to come here. But tell me, where's Varn now? Why hasn't he come with you?"

"I think he's dead too," Gidion said. Saying the words threatened to bring tears of shame to his eyes, and he furiously worked to calm himself.

"I have a feeling this is going to bring us to the next part of your tale."

Gidion nodded, trying to get a grip on his emotions.

Thane just sat still, waiting for him to speak.

"It's a long story," he said at last. "And you might not believe me."

"I'll be the judge of that," Thane said gently.

"Right." Gidion nodded, considered where to begin, and decided he might as well start with Malai's first appearance.

Thane listened quietly as he spoke, his eyebrows twisting or arching at the more dramatic or puzzling points. He broke his silence only when Gidion had finished. "So this Ilk mage appears—with Ilk—and tries to steal you away but kills your mother. Then you flee to the Federation with your father?"

Gidion wasn't sure if he heard skepticism or not. "Yes, that's about it."

"But why? Surely, your father must have had some idea?"

Gidion shook his head. "He always said he didn't know. And he got angry every time I asked about it." Again, Gidion felt the clouts across his ears.

"And you're sure they were Ilk?"

"My father said that's what they were."

"Describe them for me."

Gidion did as he asked, with Thane listening intently.

When he'd finished, the magister abruptly rose to his feet. "A moment." He left the room, soon returning with a slim but large volume. He set it on the table between them and opened it up to reveal drawings of skeletal monsters. "Did they look like this?"

"Yes, pretty close to that," Gidion said.

"And the Gloom, could you sense it?" Thane seemed eager, excited.

"Both times they came, I had this horrible feeling of despair," Gidion said. "It just made me want to curl up and let them kill me."

Thane rested a finger on his lips, looking thoughtful. "Quite a tale you tell."

"You don't believe me?" Gidion said heavily.

"I believe *you.* But I don't believe that Varn was ignorant of the reason. He was probably trying to protect you from some truth."

Gidion said nothing. Could Thane be right? Had his father known? He remembered what Malai had said to him. *Have you told him yet?* Told him what?

"But where's Varn now? Why isn't he with you?"

Gidion described the Riftlanders' raid in Tine, how Malai had found them again. But he mentioned nothing about his use of the stun power. That was something he wanted to understand better for himself first. And who knew how Thane would react?

"You also mentioned in your note that Jerald Kiltour has died," Thane said. "He was a friend of your father's, wasn't he? His old mentor at the Spire?"

"I think the Ilk mage killed him too," Gidion said. "But I can't be sure."

Again, Thane asked him to describe everything that had happened. "We'll certainly need to investigate that. It was clever of you to weave-lock the door."

"What do I do now?" Gidion asked. He was starting to feel very tired, as if his tale had drawn all the energy out of him in its release.

"I need to think about the best course of action," Thane said. "But you did very well in coming to me first. The other weavers—most of them would have sent you off with a whipping."

Gidion frowned.

"They have no interest in the past," Thane said. "And they think the Ruin was the end of the Ilk. I've always thought that to be an extremely short-sighted attitude."

"But you can make them see, can't you?" Gidion's voice came out weak and strained. He was almost done.

"Let's discuss that another time. I can see you need some rest, and no doubt some food. He frowned at Gidion's leg. "Your injury—have you had it properly tended?"

"Not really."

"You have other wounds?"

"Mostly scratches and bruises," Gidion said.

"Well, let's start with food, and while we're waiting, I'll take a look at the leg. I might not be as skilled a ranger as your father, but I know a few things."

"Thank you, Magister." Gidion found himself loosening further. It was such a relief to have someone who took him seriously, who offered to help and protect him.

Thane rang a bell and a knock soon sounded at the door. Thane opened it with a mere twirl of his forefinger and a whisper of magic, admitting a skinny, dark-haired youth with puppyish brown eyes. "Simion, I'll eat here tonight. And bring some for my guest."

"Yes, Magister. Anything else?" He spoke with no identifiable accent, as if he'd squashed a previous way of speaking.

"We'll also need some fresh bandages and healing salve."

"Yes, Magister." Simion bowed with hands over chest, then disappeared.

Rising, Thane said he was going to wash his hands before looking at Gidion's wound. He went out through another door, soon returning and approaching Gidion. "Let me see."

Feeling awkward, Gidion pulled down his breeches to expose his bandaged thigh.

"No blood, that's a good sign," Thane said as he unwrapped the bandage.

His hands were careful and gentle, reminding him of his father when Gidion was younger. Before the loss of Gidion's mother had made him hard and angry. Gidion hadn't looked at the wound since Conal had bound it. Now, he found it troublingly raised and red.

"We may have some infection creeping in," Thane said. "But it does look like it's healing. Does it pain you a lot?"

"I can manage," Gidion said, trying to project strength.

The left side of Thane's mouth curled up. "No doubt. You strike me as someone who doesn't give in to weakness easily."

Gidion's back straightened at the praise.

A knock at the door. It was Simion, carrying bandages and salve. "I'll go to the kitchens now, Magister," he said as he handed them to Thane.

Thane thanked him. The healing salve was in a pot, and Gidion recognized it from the smell and color. It was the same that Conal had always used and had taught him to prepare. Again, with great gentleness, Thane smeared the salve over the wound, then carefully re-bandaged it. He then put the things aside and left again to wash his hands, while Gidion restored his dignity.

When Thane came back, he went to his drinks cabinet, which was of a similar dark wood to the table and chairs, with ornate leaf motifs in gold and mother of pearl. "I believe it's time for something a little stronger. Wine?"

Gidion wasn't sure he wanted wine. He was so tired and foggy already, but Thane was already pouring himself a glass, so he accepted.

"While we wait for food, let's talk about your weaver training," Thane said as he handed the glass to Gidion. "What have you learned so far in the five disciplines?"

Gidion started by listing all the standard weaves, Thane interjecting from time to time to get clarification.

"And have you shown any talent in artefaction?"

"I can make glowglobes and heatstones," Gidion said. "They were our main source of income, in fact."

"I hope you haven't been selling them here," Thane said sharply.

Gidion was taken aback by the sudden change of tone. "Why?"

"You can't trade in glowglobes and heatstones in Vycenia without a license from the Spire. Didn't your father tell you that?"

"We were selling them in the Federation, not in Vycenia. But—why do you need a license here?"

"Ostensibly to guarantee quality and repairs." Thane's mouth twisted. "In truth, to keep the monopoly on glowglobe trade among the Wyven family. And trading without a license is a quick way to prison. Don't even think of it."

There were layers of emotion in Thane that Gidion couldn't quite grasp, even with his intuitive sense. "How do I get a license?"

"You can't get one until you've officially graduated from the Spire."

"How long will that be?" Gidion asked in dismay.

"It depends on what year we can place you into," Thane said. "If you can already make such advanced artefacts, we might be able to start you into the Apprentice Cycle, which would be consistent with your age. My main concern is your lack of book knowledge. But you have a couple of months to catch up before the Selection Trial."

Gidion's ears pricked. Jerald had mentioned it, although his father never had. "What is it exactly?"

"Anyone who wishes to enter the Apprentice Cycle must pass the Trial. We need to be sure that Seekers are ready for the rigors of more advanced weaving," Thane said. "And especially that they've achieved a good enough level in warcraft to be assigned to the army should they be needed."

It sounded rather daunting. "And what do you need to do to pass?"

"The first part takes place in a maze. Seekers work in teams of three to four, collaborating to overcome various challenges related to the five subject areas."

"What are the challenges?"

"I can't give you any details, I'm afraid. Some require knowledge and quick thinking, while others test your weaving skills."

"But then how will I know what to prepare?"

"I'll make sure you get all the books you need," Thane replied. "But the labyrinth is just the first half of the Trial. Two days after, you must take part in the Selection Tournament. You'll have to fight the other Initiate 4 students in a series of duels. The object is to demonstrate your warcraft skill level."

"And what if you win? Is there a prize?"

Thane's lips pressed into a thin smile. "If you win the Maze Trial, all members of the team get a battlestaff made by Faringale Torenson."

The most renowned maker of blades and battlestaffs in all of Vycenia, if not the entire continent. Gidion would never have been able to afford the man's work himself.

"If you win the Tournament, you get an enormously powerful focus stone—the likes of which are only owned by the greatest of the Great Families."

"And if you win both?"

"You get both prizes, plus the right to request whoever you want as a mentor, and that weaver is obliged to take you on as an apprentice."

"Including Arianna Velden?" Gidion said excitedly. He'd dreamed of training under her for much of his life. She was the Guardian of the Spire, the most powerful warweaver in Vycenia.

"Yes, but don't get ahead of yourself. The overall winner is *always* one of the Greats."

As Thane spoke, Gidion sensed a deep, simmering anger in the man. But it was so buried that none of it showed in Thane's expression or tone. "You mean the Great Families?"

"Varn told you about them?"

Gidion reeled off what he remembered. "There are thirteen historic weaver families who have accumulated a lot of power and wealth over the centuries. They're among the strongest weavers."

"Exactly that. In Vycenia, they're as close as we get to a ruling aristocracy. They're incredibly powerful both inside and outside the Spire."

"But weavers aren't allowed to rule."

"Indeed, we're not."

And now Gidion sensed another emotion in Thane. A powerful, seething emotion, like the whipping winds of a storm. Not anger exactly, but something close to it. And need. An all-consuming need. It made him re-evaluate the magister. On the surface, he might appear warm, almost glib, but there was iron determination beneath. This was not a man to be crossed. The fact reassured him, though. There was strength here that Gidion would need, as long as he stayed on Thane's good side. "If they can't rule, how do they have power?"

"Wealth is power," Thane replied. "They own much of the land, a fact that dates back to long before the Ruin. And they have a monopoly over the trade of many goods, most notably, weaver-made artefacts."

"Why weren't their lands taken from them after the Ruin if they weren't allowed to rule anymore?"

"Even the Lumin heretics knew better than to try," Thane said. "It would have required another war, and no one had the appetite for that."

Gidion took in the evident wealth of Thane's chambers, the fine cloth and cut of his robes. "Are you from one of the Families?" he asked hesitantly.

"Great Spinners, no!" Thane said, laughing, although it sounded forced. "I come from Tarsis." Then, with an elegant wave of his fingers, he said, "But enough history. Tell me, what do you know about the first two cycles of study?"

"The Novice and Initiate Cycles," Gidion said. "Four years in each, and Seekers usually start as a novice around age nine or ten, which is when weaver powers tend to manifest."

"Correct. Some Seekers will do more than four years as an initiate as the graduation to apprentice is a big leap. Some, the weakest, will never become apprentices at all. But somehow, I don't think that's a problem you'll have." Thane bestowed his smile on Gidion again.

He warmed at the praise. "My father told me that in the Apprentice Cycle, you just specialize in one subject that you study under a mentor."

"Yes, unlike the earlier cycles, where you study all subjects equally."

“I want to specialize in warcraft.” He needed to. He needed to make himself strong enough to defeat Malai, avenge his parents. “I’ve always wanted to study under Arianna Velden.”

“I wouldn’t advise that.”

“Why not?”

“Warweavers can only serve the Spire or the Vycenian army—or, of course, go into exile and fight in another country like Tarsis. A place I do not recommend."

Upon mention of Thane's home country, Gidion sensed the storm rising in him again. He clearly didn't have happy memories of the place.

"But while there’s a lot of prestige to warweaving, there’s virtually no money, so you need to be from a wealthy family that will support you. The few commoners who have gone that route studied ranging or artefaction first to earn a living. They did their warcraft studies after.”

“But I need warcraft,” Gidion said.

“Revenge is rarely as satisfying as it seems,” Thane replied.

“It’s not revenge,” Gidion replied. “It’s ...”

Thane raised a skeptical eyebrow.

“It’s just—I need to be able to protect myself.” But Gidion knew he was lying. Revenge was what kept him going, what filled his fantasies at night.

“Don’t worry, you can still train to fight if you specialize in something else. You should really do artefaction, given your abilities,” Thane said. “Then you can become wealthy, as I did. Even the Great Families would have to give you respect.”

Gidion heard the reason in what Thane was saying. But then he thought of Malai. Of his dead mother and missing father. How helpless he’d been when the isaurs and Ilk had struck. No. He needed to turn himself into the best warweaver in the world. He needed Arianna Velden to train him.

A knock at the door. Simion, with their food. He set it on the table, and Thane invited Gidion to sit and eat. It was succulent beef with gravy and potatoes, and Gidion devoured every mouthful.

Thane ate more slowly, cutting his meat delicately and raising it to his mouth with an elegant hand. "You can stay in my apartments until we can enroll you officially in the Spire," he said when they'd finished eating. "I have a spare bedroom here."

"Thank you, Magister."

Thane had Simion show Gidion the room. "We'll talk more in the morning when you're feeling fresher," he said. "But don't worry, you're safe tonight."

The room contained a dresser and a large bed that Gidion soon discovered to be the most comfortable he'd ever lain on. But despite his exhaustion, it was a long time before he fell asleep. So much had happened in a few days that he was barely able to make sense of it all. He found himself thinking back to Tine, to Nessa, wondering what had happened to her. *My one chance with a girl and look what happens.* But that had hardly been the worst of it. His father was gone, the Ilk mage after him again.

Thane, at least, inspired confidence. He seemed willing to help, even if there was a dangerous edge to him. But he needed someone dangerous, someone who could stand up to Malai. Still, he wasn't sure he was going to follow Thane's advice about artefaction. Warcraft was calling to him, had always called to him. He needed power and strength. Power to defeat his enemies and avenge his parents. Power to carve his own path.

Chapter 7

Once Gidion had gone into his room, Thane locked him in with a weave, as much to stop him from coming out as to stop anyone else from going in. Then he went to his library, his mind circling and prodding at all he'd learned. Duty dictated he tell the First Weaver about the boy. But he was reluctant to do that until he'd decided what kind of advantage he might be able to wring from the situation. And anyway, he knew what Elwin was like. The man would take all control, insist the boy be with him while failing entirely to recognize the wider possibilities.

No, he needed to find this Ilk mage and learn what she wanted with Gidion—if Ilk mage she was, of course. The boy was young, perhaps traumatized by the loss of his parents. He might even be lying, an audacious hoaxer. But Thane was usually good at picking out liars, and this boy gave no indication of being one—although Thane strongly suspected that he hadn't told him everything. Which made Thane admire him—wise to know when to keep quiet. Of course, though, he'd have to prize out the boy's secrets, whatever they were.

But if what he said was true, if the woman was an Ilk mage, much bigger questions emerged. Had she survived the Ruin or been born after it? Were there others? There were rumors of the Ilk mages' longevity, of the magic they used to lengthen their life spans far beyond that of ordinary mortals. Now *that* was something he'd dearly love to learn. How much he could accomplish if he had more time! He poured himself a glass of Northlander goldwine, his mind skipping through possibilities.

But as he put the glass to his lips, he thought again of Gidion. The boy's looks—his eyes the same color as the liquid in the glass that was now sliding into his mouth. And the coppery sheen of Gidion's skin, his fine, black hair—coloring Thane had never seen before. He certainly hadn't got it from Varn. And whatever Gidion might claim about his mother, she was no Javan. He'd seen more than one in his time, and while they had dark hair, their eyes were equally dark, their skin even darker. But he suspected what the boy might be. Oh yes, he suspected. He just needed confirmation.

He spun on the spot and began pacing. What was to be his next move? Clearly, he needed to investigate Gidion's claims about Jerald Kiltour and find out exactly what had happened in Tine. Maybe Varn was still there somewhere. Yes, that was someone else Thane had to find, if he was still alive. The man could answer many questions. And he'd need to speak to the mercenary who had accompanied Gidion here. No doubt, the man would have more to tell.

At the same time, he needed to keep Gidion close to him—very close—to ensure the Ilk mage didn't steal him away from under his nose. And to ensure the boy didn't talk to anyone else. The guards at the gate would have to be dealt with in some way. They'd heard Gidion's tale of Ilk, and that absolutely needed to be kept quiet.

But this might be it, the moment at last, the sign I've been waiting for. His fingers curled as desperate yearning surged through him, squeezing his chest, making his head spin. He paused before an oval, gold-framed mirror and regarded himself. His cheeks were flushed, his pupils black and large. "I will rule Vycenia," he said to his reflection.

"One day, I will rule Vycenia." It wasn't enough, so he added a new affirmation. "I will become the most powerful mage in the land." Still not enough. Old Yana's advice floated into his mind, as it had so many times since she first uttered them to his ten-year-old self. *To make something happen, you have only to say the words. Say them with complete conviction, visualize the outcome you desire, and you'll make that outcome a reality.* Advice that had served him well thus far, taking him away from misery and starvation to the Spire—to wealth, status, and power. A small power still, in the grand scheme of things, but a power that was growing. The weavers of the great families were blind. They thought that being Head of Seekers was demeaning. Macio Wyven had no doubt believed it would be enough to stop Thane from seeking further power, the type of power the Greats kept for themselves.

What they didn't realize was that Thane had made himself a close friend of all the young Seekers who'd trained in the past seven years. Some, now graduated, sat on the Conclave. But in a decade, there would be many more, all of them loyal to him.

He clenched his fists. "I will restore weaver rule to Vycenia, and I will rule the weavers and the land. I will become the most powerful mage in the world and discover the lost secrets of artefaction to make Vycenia the foremost power on the continent. I will make it greater than Eleusia ever was." Then he laughed at himself. *My ambition is not small.*

He cast his eyes around the room and the many books it contained. Best he refresh his memory with everything he knew about the Ilk mages and the time before the Ruin. He went to the locked bookcase where he kept his most precious books, removing one extremely old and rare tome that he'd acquired for a small fortune. By rights, he ought to have delivered it to the main Spire library so others could share the knowledge. But Thane didn't want too many people knowing its contents. It was Eleusian, dated from many years before the Ruin, and discussed the wars with the Chelaki people who had once shared the continent of Teleriol with them. He read for two hours, then finally summoned Simion, pressing the bellstone next to his desk.

Moments later, his attendant appeared. "Yes, Magister?"

As always, Simion exuded a combination of impudence and servility, a combination that Thane found endlessly intoxicating. "Go to the room and prepare yourself," he said. His blood was on fire. And yes, there was something about Gidion that had stirred it. But he couldn't indulge in such fantasies with him. Thane needed him for a higher purpose. Simion would always serve, though, and well.

"With pleasure, Master," Simion said, leaving with a bow that wasn't as low as it should have been.

Thane followed him shortly afterward into a room reserved only for their activities. A large bed covered in black silk sheets dominated it, and on one wall hung a collection of crops, gags, and ties. Simion was naked except for a leather collar around his neck. His skin was smooth and shaved all over, as Thane required of all his young men. It glowed with youthful health, the muscles beneath firm but not over-developed. A far cry indeed from the dirty, skeletal creature Thane had plucked off the streets of Glade several years ago.

He crossed the distance between them and kissed Simion deeply, hands exploring his lithe body, enjoying how it reacted with desire for him. Then, when he could wait no longer, he grabbed a fistful of Simion's hair and bent him over the bed. Thane freed himself of his robes, his impatience such that he let them fall to the ground as they were. When he finally mounted Simion, there was a violence in him that caused the youth to cry out.

Chapter 8

Gidion was woken by a knock on the door the following day. He'd expected Thane, but it was Simion.

"Breakfast time," he said with an impish smile. "Would you like it here or out in the living room?"

"Where's Magister Thane?"

"Teaching. He'll be back by lunch," Simion said.

Gidion hesitated. Should he stay in his room, hiding, or try to strike up some kind of relationship with the youth, find out more about Thane and the Spire? "I'll have breakfast out there," he said.

"There's a privy and shower through that door if you'd like to wash first. I'll take some clean robes into you."

"Shower?"

Simion's lip twitched. "Don't have showers in the Federation, do they?"

Gidion shook his head, not much liking Simion's snide tone.

"It's for washing yourself. You'll see." Simion left, closing the door behind him.

Gidion used the privy, then curiously entered the shower room. It was tiled at the back, with glass on the sides and a glass door at the front. Something that looked like the end of a watering can stuck out of the wall above his head. He spotted an activation panel and pressed it. Immediately, warm water streamed out of the watering-can head. He found lemon-scented soap on a tray and began to wash several days' worth of dirt from his hair and body. When he returned to the bedroom, he found a white robe neatly folded over a chair and put it on. It was plain, soft linen in the style of weaver's robes. Gidion couldn't help but smile as he regarded himself in the mirror. He was finally starting to look the part.

Then he went to the living room to find plates of cold meats, cheeses, and fruit on the table. The sight set his stomach rumbling, and he sat down to attack the food. Meanwhile, Simion moved about the room, tidying and dusting. When Gidion had finished eating, he took away the plates. "The magister said you might enjoy reading some of the books in his library while you wait for him."

Gidion wasn't much in the mood for reading but politely inquired where it was.

"Follow me." Simion took him into an adjoining room whose every wall was lined with full bookcases. Some particularly ancient tomes were locked behind glass, perhaps to preserve them from dust. The room was windowless, lit only by glowglobes, and there was a comfortable leather armchair to one side and an elegant desk nestled between two bookcases to the other. Gidion reckoned the contents of the room were probably worth a small fortune.

"Are you his apprentice?" Gidion asked as Simion was about to go.

Simion laughed. "You think apprentices are asked to serve like this?"

"So you're just a servant?"

A flash of something passed over Simion's face, and Gidion perceived a curious mixture of shame and pride. "I'm an attendant," he said. "But my only role is to serve Magister Thane." With that, he left, leaving Gidion to wonder exactly what he'd meant.

But he didn't think on it long. There were a lot of books here, and it occurred to him that maybe he'd find something useful on the Ilk War. He quickly found a tome that recounted the Siege of Arindel, but found himself distracted, his mind constantly playing over the events of the past few days.

Thane came sometime later, dressed again in silken robes of midnight blue. There wasn't a single crease in them, as if he'd just put them on. "My apologies for leaving you this morning without explanation. But you were sleeping soundly, and I didn't want to disturb you," the weaver said. "Come join me for lunch, and I'll share my thoughts on what we should do next."

It was Simion who came again with their lunch, this time a chicken pie served with salad. He also poured red wine for them both at Thane's request.

"I've been thinking about everything you told me yesterday," Thane said when his servant had left. "It's clearly dangerous for you to be out in the city, but I think even in the Spire, it's a risk."

Gidion paused in the act of bringing a bite of pie to his mouth. "You think she can get to me here?"

"The Spire was built to prevent splicing in and out of the grounds, so you're protected from that, at least."

Gidion put his fork down, his appetite entirely gone. "What's splicing?"

"The power you described to me—the Ilk mage's ability to disappear and then reappear instantaneously in another place. It is a known ability of the Ilk mages."

"So if she can't get in, I'm safe here?"

Thane winced and shook his head. "She may have other ways of getting in, or may have spies here already. We'll need to develop your powers so that you're able to protect yourself."

Good, he sees it too. Maybe he can introduce me to Arianna Velden.

But Thane was still speaking, and Gidion realized he'd missed something. "... that you accomplish at least basic training. So here's my proposal. You'll stay here in my rooms until the next academic year starts. I appreciate that sounds confining, but they're heavily warded, and impossible to break into. You can come with me on trips outside the Spire from time to time, and we'll do some of your training in Arindel Woods. I'll train you in warcraft. And you'll study to make sure your lore and statecraft knowledge is up to apprentice level. You'll apply to specialize in artefaction, and once you pass the Selection Trial, you'll join as my apprentice."

"But I want to specialize in warcraft, not artefaction," Gidion objected.

"I know, but believe me, this is for the best. If you're my apprentice, you'll keep the room you currently have, and you'll be officially under my protection. And artefaction has so many possibilities beyond glowglobes and heatstones. I'm sure you've heard of some of the magical weapons the Eleusians used to fabricate?"

"But no one knows how to make those anymore," Gidion said, echoing his father.

"We've discovered a few things," Thane replied with a wink. "And together, we could develop more. This could be what gives us the edge over this Ilk mage. If there are Ilk, we need effective weapons against them. Ordinary steel does little."

"But lightbolts work," Gidion said.

"Yes, but you know the rules," Thane replied. A pause. "Don't you?"

"Of course," Gidion said. "There's only so many you can throw without warping the Tapestry dangerously."

"Which is why the Ilk were such a successful force. And look what happened when we tried to eliminate them completely."

The Ruin. A cataclysm that had destroyed the continent of Teleriol, taking the entire Eleusian population with it. Gidion shuddered. Malai wasn't going to start another Ilk war, was she? "Are you planning to find her?"

"Eventually. We'll need to find out what she wants with you. Even more importantly, we need to know her broader intentions and if she's discovered the means to make Ilk again. But it would be foolish to rush in."

It sounded sensible, and despite Thane's resistance to Gidion specializing in warcraft, he felt a measure of relief to have the magister onside.

"I'm going to investigate what happened to Jerald and your father first of all."

"Can't I come with you?"

"No. As I said, it's not safe," Thane replied. "If the Ilk mage is hunting you, she may try to catch us unawares."

Gidion couldn't deny that, given what had happened in Tine. But it still irked him to be left behind.

He opened his mouth to argue, but Thane continued. "You'll be much safer here. And it gives you plenty of time to catch up on the lore and statecraft reading you'll need to do to pass the Selection Trial. Simion will be here, too. You can talk to him as long as you don't distract him from his duties. He's a good card player, too."

"I don't want to be a prisoner," Gidion said.

"You're not a prisoner," Thane replied smoothly. "But I urge you not to leave these rooms. They're warded. And we don't know who in the Spire we can trust. Your Ilk mage might well have agents here."

Gidion reluctantly accepted, and they finished their meal in silence. But Gidion struggled to eat, the food like ash in his mouth. He had barely eaten half of the meal when Thane rose, saying he had to go and pack. He told Gidion he could return to the library, though, and having nothing better to do, Gidion did as he suggested. Thane finally left a couple of hours later with a further admonishment not to leave his rooms.

Gidion obeyed Thane's instructions for the first night. But he was restless, itching to see more of the Spire and the city. He was used to being constantly on the move, on the road or in a new town. By the second day, he was prowling around Thane's apartment like a caged animal. How long before Thane would come back? He tried to distract himself with books, but his body was full of nervous energy, impelling him to his feet, making him feel like hitting something.

When it came to the third day, he decided he could take no more. If he didn't get out, he was going to scream or break something. He waited until nighttime, when Simion had gone to his room. Then, heart thumping, he tried the door. But it wouldn't open when he pressed his hand on the activation panel. He made the Tapestry visible and examined the weaves in it. It had been weave-locked, but not using the simple weave-lock that he knew, which kept ordinary people out. No, this was vastly more complicated, designed to keep out weavers. He cursed. Locking weaves of this complexity could only be triggered by their maker or using a keystone created by their maker. And skilled weavers created highly personalized signatures in their weaves, using threads that ran through their beings. Gidion reckoned that was what he was seeing now. It meant Thane could feel if someone had unlocked his weave.

Fury rose in him. How dare the magister keep him prisoner like this? He was just as bad as his father! But anger wasn't going to get him out of this. So he trampled down his emotions and pondered the situation. He'd seen Simion go in and out, so the servant must have a keystone. Gidion would have to steal it if he were to leave. But how to do that without the youth noticing? The answer soon came to him. He could use his stun power to knock Simion out, and the boy would be none the wiser. He'd just think he'd had a fall or sudden turn. The downside was that Gidion had killed someone the last time he'd used it, and Simion had done nothing wrong to him. He was just Thane's servant. *But it's that or I stay locked up in here, and I'm not having that. I'm not.*

So Gidion waited until the next evening, then asked him if he wanted to play a game of cards.

Simion agreed eagerly. "Do you know Knaves and Fools?"

Gidion shook his head.

"I'll teach you. It's easy enough, but good with two players."

"Are we allowed to have a drink?" Gidion asked.

"We're allowed most of what he has here. What do you want?"

"Red wine?"

While Simion went to get the wine, Gidion embraced the threads and put himself into the frame of mind he'd been in when the Rift-landers had attacked him. There had been panic, a desire to shield himself, to knock away all his enemies. It was the same the first time. The panic had created the instinct. He fed on his fears of Malai and the Ilk, on his rage at being imprisoned. But he needed to hold back, not push out as strongly as he had that time. He didn't want Simion to die. It wasn't him who had trapped Gidion. And it would be incredibly difficult to explain away.

As the boy was returning with the drinks, Gidion launched his attack. But Simion just paused for a second, his brow creasing. "Bit of a turn there," he muttered.

Clearly, Gidion needed to push harder. He marshaled his power and tried again. This time, Simion's eyes rolled up in his head and he slumped sideways, almost coming off the chair. Gidion first checked the boy was alive, discovering a weak pulse. Relieved, he went to Simion's pocket, finding the keystone as he'd hoped. Triumphantly, he went to the door and opened it. He was about to slip the keystone back into Simion's pocket, but then hesitated. He didn't know when the boy would wake up again, but with any luck, Gidion would be back before he'd realized what had happened.

Chapter 9

By the time Gidion was on his way down the levitator, he'd decided to try to find Ruadh at the Silver Sword. He was the only person other than Thane who might help Gidion. And even if he couldn't, he could at least offer a few hours of companionship.

The inn was a loud place, full of men drinking, cursing, and talking. He saw games taking place too—pinboard, cards, dice. No one paid him any mind as he shoved his way over to the bar to ask for Ruadh.

"He's still 'ere. Who will I say is askin'?" the barkeep said.

"A friend of his—Gidion," he replied. He eyed the casks behind the bar.

"Got a dark ale from Kiligan's brewery that's only a vic a pint," the barkeep said.

"I'll take one." Gidion hadn't yet had a dark ale, and when he sipped on it, he found it bitter but not entirely unpleasant. He took a stool at the bar to wait, but couldn't relax, his eyes constantly scanning for danger. Before long, though, Ruadh was pushing his way toward him.

He clapped a heavy hand on Gidion's shoulder, almost making him fall off the stool. "Good to see you, lad! But what brings you here? Things not work out for you in your weaver's needle?"

"I'll tell you everything, but maybe at a table?" Gidion looked for one that offered some privacy, but the room was rammed. "Or maybe we can go somewhere else?"

"No fear, there's a space we can use." He hollered to the barkeep. "Gared, couple of pales and we'll have them in the small room."

Then Ruadh led Gidion to a door next to the bar, which Gared opened with a key. "You can have it for an hour. It's booked after that."

"That'll do us," Ruadh said, slipping the man a coin.

The room beyond was indeed small, with only a single table with benches on either side. They'd barely seated themselves before the barkeep was back with tankards of beer the color of pale honey.

"To good company and ale!" Ruadh cried, holding his tankard aloft when the man had left.

Gidion raised his ale in turn, echoing Ruadh's words, then took several gulps. It went down more easily than the dark ale, having a light, almost fruity taste.

Ruadh put his tankard down and leaned forward on his elbows. "So, tell me."

Gidion explained how he'd got into the Spire and how Thane had promised to help, only to keep him locked in his rooms.

"Sounds like he's just trying to protect you," Ruadh said slowly, but there was a question at the end of it.

"I won't be a prisoner," Gidion said emphatically.

"No, I hear you. I wouldn't like it either. But did you tell him about the Riftlands and all?"

"About the Riftlands, yes, but not what happened in Tine."

"Aye, sensible. Always best to keep some information back if you can. Know your audience, eh? But what's your plan?"

Gidion sighed. His annoyance at Thane had faded now that he'd managed to escape. But it might be best to have a backup plan, just in case. "If I don't go back to the Spire, I'd need to hide somewhere—and find a way to make money." He gave Ruadh a meaningful look.

To his relief, the warrior took the bait. "Well, we might be able to help each other out," he said, leaning in on his elbows.

Gidion gulped down some ale. "How?"

"Before I went to the Federation, I was working in Arindel. Reason I left was a mix-up with the City Watch and a shipment of silks my boss was getting in. Boss is still mad at me for leaving, but so is the Watch, and between them they have me right screwed."

"How can I help you with that?"

"Well, I need to find something useful for the boss, something that would make him want me back."

"Who's your boss?" Gidion drank again. He was starting to feel the ale's effects, and the anger and fear he'd been carrying around was melting away.

"Known as Moth, runs the city, in a sense."

"He's on the Consulate?" Gidion said, surprised.

"No, no, no. The politicians, they run one side of things. Moth—he's underground, fixing and dealing. He's pretty much the only thing keeps New Arindel standing."

"Are you saying he's a criminal?"

"You might say that," Ruadh said. "Depending on your perspective."

Gidion frowned, unsure how to react. He'd thought Ruadh an honest type, the dodgy coin aside. But his father had said never to trust a sellsword.

Ruadh leaned in, voice low, soothing. "Things aren't black and white, lad. That's the way of the world. The politicians—they use him when it suits them, and he uses them back. Works well both ways and has done for years."

Conal would never have agreed. The man was as straight and narrow as a plank. And now he was probably dead, but Ruadh was here, and he seemed to know his way around the world. There wasn't much choice in it. "So, how can I help?"

"Moth loves artefacts, and he runs his own trade in glowglobes and the like. If I bring you to him, it might be enough to swing things in my favor. And he can get you a hideout if you need it."

"So you want me to make glowglobes for him?"

"That and other things. Moth's always keen to have fireflies in his employ."

"Fireflies?" Gidion echoed in confusion.

"The word we use for weavers."

"I can't sell glowglobes here, though. You need a license, Thane told me."

"Like I said, Moth runs the underground. It would all be very under the table," Ruadh said.

Gidion's hope rose despite his misgivings at the thought of working for a criminal. "I'd need materials."

"He can sort that out, no problem."

Gidion still wasn't sure, but said, "Alright, I'm in."

"Excellent! This definitely calls for another round!"

"I'll get them." Gidion made to get up.

"No, no, no, lad, not here."

He paused. "Where, then?"

"Let's go to Missy's."

"What's Missy's?"

"Only the place with the finest whores in town."

Gidion blushed. "Oh, I don't know—'

"What age are you? Eighteen years?"

Gidion stood straighter. "In four months' time."

"High time, then. You can't count yourself a proper man until you've had a lass."

The words made Gidion feel a different kind of embarrassment, a worse kind than the thought of what might happen in a whorehouse. Not a man? Well, he'd show Ruadh who was a man. "Let's go, then."

"Great." Ruadh swiped up Gidion's remaining ale. He'd already finished his own.

Gidion tried to grab it back. "Hey!"

But Ruadh just knocked back the ale and then slammed the tankard down with a satisfied grin. "I'll cover you when we get to Missy's. Come on."

They left the bar and stepped out into the warm night. "We're going to the Rainbow Quarter. Only a couple of blocks away," Ruadh said. "Just remember this one thing—hold on to your purse like your life depends on it. The only place that's worse for thieving is New Arindel."

Gidion had little in the way of money, but he held onto his purse all the same. The Rainbow Quarter was as colorful as its name implied, probably because of the strings of small glowglobes that crisscrossed the main streets. He was so busy staring at them that he stumbled over something and almost fell. Ruadh grabbed his arm and righted him.

"Remember what I said," Ruadh said. "Don't let yourself get distracted. The fleas here are at the top of their game."

"Fleas?"

"Pickpockets. Watch out for the women, especially. They use the pretty ones to get your attention."

Gidion looked about him, at the sheer, writhing mass of humanity. *This is life*, he thought. *This is how it should be.*

At last, they passed through an archway into a narrower street that was lit by only by glowglobes of a deep golden red color. Women lounged outside the doors to the buildings, breasts pushing through translucent material, showing dark nipples beneath. Gidion yearned to touch them, but when they called out promises of what they would do to him, he shriveled and ducked.

Ruadh stopped outside one of the doors and was greeted by a curly-haired young woman. "'Ello big man, back already? Plum mustn't be working you 'ard enough."

"Plum's a delicious treat, but a big man has big appetites," Ruadh said with a wink. "And I've brought you some fresh meat."

She looked at Gidion. Her eyes large and shining, her red lips curling into a slow smile. "You're an 'andsome cub. Such strong shoulders." She reached a hand out to his face and he flinched. This made her laugh as she ran her long nails down his cheek. Her scent came to him, musky and heavy.

"Is Plum on tonight?"

The woman withdrew her hand. "She is, but you might 'ave to wait."

"I don't mind, as long as there's wine," Ruadh said. "Come on, Gid. Let's go meet the ladies."

The woman gently pushed the door open for them to go inside. They went straight up a narrow stair into a dimly lit room filled with soft furnishings. Groups of men sat around low tables, drinking. Women attended them, wearing half-open robes of thin gauze, pouring wine, letting themselves be stroked, pressing lips to temples or cheeks. Gidion's desire stirred as he looked at their bared flesh, which seemed to have absorbed some of the light from the glowglobes on the tables and radiate it as promise. But this wasn't how he'd imagined his first time. Paying for sex instead of winning a beautiful woman on his own merits, a woman like Nessa. He'd gotten so close with her. Was she even alive?

He almost turned and left, but a tawny-haired woman in a thin, fuschia robe hailed them. Her face was heavily painted, not enough to hide the lines on her forehead and around her eyes and mouth. “Hello, Redhawk.” Then, looking at Gidion appraisingly, “Who’s this young buck?”

“My friend, Gid. He’s all ripe for the plucking.”

Gidion thought he might evaporate from embarrassment, but stood his ground, meeting her gaze with a forced smile.

“Oh, the girls will love you,” she said in a liquid tone, her hand brushing his forearm.

He should leave. He should definitely leave. But before he could speak or move, Ruadh had sat him down firmly on one of the cushioned couches.

“Bring us some sweet wine,” Ruadh said. “And some lasses. Plum for me, if she’s free, and someone who’ll give Gid here the full go round.” He pulled his purse out, opened it up, and stuck it under the madam’s nose.

She glanced inside, then gave him a wide smile. “Relax gentlemen, and all your desires shall be fulfilled.”

The wine was soon brought on a tray by a long-limbed girl whose fair hair tumbled in waves down her back. “Who is Gid?” she asked in a low, husky tone.

“That’s him,” Ruadh said, pointing at Gidion. “You’re new, aren’t you?”

Her smile showed white teeth. “I been here some months.” She set the tray down on the table. “Where you have been, handsome?” Her accent was strong, rolling on the r’s.

“Too far, if this is the first time I’ve seen you,” Ruadh said, running his hand across her rump.

The girl sat next to Gidion, so close that her thigh brushed against his and her perfume filled his nose. Hints of orange blossom and other spices. She leaned over him to pour the wine from a decanter into long-stemmed glasses, resting one hand on his leg. Her barely covered breast brushed against his arm, and he had a sudden urge to grab her and hold her tight against him. She finished pouring the wine, three glasses in total. Then she lifted and uncorked a small green bottle. "Bliss?"

"None of that filth for me," Ruadh said. "I'm a full-blooded man."

Gidion looked at the bottle uncomprehendingly.

"It's a pleasure drug," Ruadh said. "You won't need it. Trust me."

Gidion shook his head, blushing harder, and the girl tipped two drops of clear liquid into one of the glasses. This one she kept for herself, handing the other two to him and Ruadh.

"What's your name?" Gidion asked her uncertainly.

"Meadow," she replied, taking a sip from her glass, her blue eyes holding his, glinting in the light of the glowglobe.

"That's an unusual name." Her thigh was warm, her perfume filling his senses, making him feel dizzy.

"You do not like it?"

"I do, it's lovely, I just hadn't heard it before," he said, feeling stupid. He took a large drink from the wine cup. As he put it back down on the table, he became aware of her hand stroking his leg, moving up from his knee toward his groin, which had begun to stir in response. Some part of him was calling him to get up and leave, but it was quickly buried under the sensations the girl sparked in him.

Another girl arrived and sat on Ruadh's knee, but Gidion barely paid any mind, for Meadow's hand had reached higher, to the bulge between his legs. He let out a small groan and then found himself taking her face with one hand, pressing his mouth against hers. She opened to him, her breath rising with his. He ran his hand down the length of her body, feeling the swell of her breast and the curve of her ribs and hip.

She got up and took his hand to lead him out of the reception room and down into a dimly lit hallway. They entered a small room, its sole feature a large bed covered in red sheets. As she closed the door behind them, he took her in his arms again. As they kissed, she began to unfasten the laces of his shirt, to tug it free of his breeches. She ran her hands up and down the length of his back, then around to the laces of his breeches, inside his breeches. He pushed against her circling palm, groaning, but she stepped away, drew him to the bed. Sat him down, pulled his shirt off and then his trousers. Air soothed his inflamed skin. She shrugged out of her robe, showing small breasts and a flat belly.

He realized he didn't know what to do next and wilted. *Go, before you shame yourself.* But then she was lying him down on his back and taking him into her mouth, her hair tickling his thighs. Thought fled, leaving only need. He groaned again, hips jerking, wanting her to take him deeper. But she held back, caressing gently, sometimes harder, then just as he thought he would reach his peak, she withdrew.

"No," he moaned, trying to pull her down to him again.

"Patience, young buck." Her voice was low, throaty. She slid toward him and then straddled him, taking him with one gentle hand and guiding him inside her, hips circling and thrusting. He closed his eyes, but it was Nessa he saw. The silken warmth of her more than he could stand. He reached and she gave. Reached more, more. *No. Not enough. Can't be enough. But yes, there. That's it. That's it!* He shuddered and quaked like a stone caught in a breaking wave, felt he would crumble under the force of it. But she held him, contained him, until the fury had passed and his tremors subsided. Then she slid off and lay next to him, resting her head on his shoulder and stroking his chest.

He stayed on his back, listening to the hoarseness of his breathing and the half-muffled cries that penetrated through the walls on either side. He half turned to look at the girl. Her eyes were closed, but her hand continued its gentle trailing through the hairs on his chest. Should he say something to her? He should, really, after all this. "Where ... er ... do you come from?"

Her eyes opened, blinked at him. "Tarsis."

"Why?" Why did you become a whore, he wanted to ask, but that seemed rude. "Why come here?"

The hand stopped its movement. "This is greatest city of the world. I want to see it always."

It sounded like a rehearsed reply. But he realized he didn't really want to know the truth. Instead, his gaze rested on her slender form. He hadn't looked at her properly before, so lost in what she was doing to him. Her skin was very pale. So pale that it was almost translucent, blue veins crisscrossing beneath the surface. Like porcelain. Fragile, delicate. Breakable. The thought excited him. He rolled over onto her. Her body beneath his, tiny like that of a bird. He could crush her. He looked into her eyes. The pupils were very large, the black almost swallowing the blue. The sheets were red beneath her porcelain skin, red like blood. His hips moved—against her, into her. Oh, he was strong, and she was so tiny. She loosed little cries, like a wounded animal, bucking beneath him. He fought back.

His mind expanded, turned porous. Her emotion bled into him—a sort of weariness edged with ... No, he didn't want this. He blocked her out. No thoughts. No feelings. Just the rhythm he had set up. He reached under, grabbed fistfuls of flesh, pressed hard. Wilder now, her body tensing and arching against his. She wanted this too. No, she couldn't want it. She was a whore. She was pretending. Paid to pretend. But, oh, feel her breath on his face. Hot, fast little gasps. Her tiny body. His strength. Little bird, like porcelain. He could break her. Grind her to dust. Break her, break her!

When he was done, he slid out but stayed for a moment on all fours, looking down at the thin, white body, slick with sweat, his and hers, noticing for the first time the purpling bruises on her thighs, where his seed gleamed thickly. Revulsion knotted his guts. He pushed away from her. He was empty. He wanted to vomit. He needed another drink. He wanted to fuck her again.

"You are alright?" she said, touching his arm. "You are not unhappy with me?"

"No, no." He lay on his back and closed his eyes. "No." *This is what men do. Ruadh was right. I'm not a boy anymore. I'm not a boy.*

"Looks like you enjoyed your little fucking session."

The voice was familiar but utterly unexpected, and his eyes flew open.

Nessa. Standing by his bedside, black hair tied back, dressed in fighting leathers, but looking even more beautiful despite them. Or maybe because of them. His mouth worked, but no words came out. Was he having some kind of vision? He looked next to him. The whore's eyes were closed, and she hadn't stirred. Unconscious? Not dead—he could hear her breathing. He looked back to Nessa. She certainly seemed real. And he was naked. "Were you watching me?" he choked out as he yanked the bedclothes up over him.

"Would you like it if I had been?" She smirked, eyes going to the unconscious whore, then up and down the length of Gidion's body.

His face burned. "What are you doing here? How did you find me?"

Her expression sobered. "I came to talk to you."

"Talk to me? Why?" Gidion wriggled until he was sitting up. He was feeling distinctly at a disadvantage.

"I was sent by your grandmother."

"My grandmother?" he repeated dumbly. "What grandmother?" Conal's mother and father were long dead. Gidion had never known them. He knew even less about his grandparents on his mother's side.

Nessa cocked her head. "Ah, you really don't know."

"Know what?" He cast his eyes surreptitiously toward his clothes, wondering if it would be more embarrassing to levitate them toward him or pretend he didn't care about being naked in front of her.

"Who Malai is."

"The *Ilk* mage?" he said, even more confused. "You know her?"

"So it's true, your father never told you?" Nessa sat down on the edge of the bed.

Malai's words to his father in Tine floated into his mind. *"Have you told him yet?"* "Told me what?"

"That's she's your grandmother."

This was ridiculous, some kind of con. "Are you playing tricks on me?" he demanded.

Nessa's eyes and voice softened. "No tricks here. Why do you think she's been looking for you?"

"Is she here? Has she put you up to this?" He cast around the room frantically but saw no sign of Malai. Nonetheless, he gathered the threads, then remembered his focus stone was in the pocket of his breeches.

"Don't worry, you're not in any danger from me."

Gidion leaned over the side of the bed, stretching out as far as he could to grab his breeches. But there was no focus stone inside. *Pits!* Had she taken it while he wasn't watching?

"It's under your shirt."

He whipped his head around to face her. "What?"

"Your focus stone."

How did she know what he'd been thinking? He scooped up his shirt, and sure enough, there was the stone. Snatching it, he prepared a lightbolt.

"I'd appreciate it if you didn't try to burn me to a crisp—at least until I've said my piece," Nessa said drily.

Gidion finished his lightbolt but didn't release it. "Who are you, really?" Then, remembering how they'd met, "Why did you lie to me?"

Nessa folded her arms across her chest. "I didn't lie. I just didn't tell you everything."

"That's still lying." He needed to get dressed. Fighting naked was ridiculous. So, keeping an eye on her and his focus stone in his hand, Gidion awkwardly pushed a foot through the right leg of his breeches.

"I had to make sure you were the right person first."

Gidion put the second foot through and risked standing up. He yanked the breeches up to his waist, painfully aware that she was getting a view of his naked behind. Buttoning them up, he turned back to her. "So, what, Malai sent you to find me?" *And was it all pretense? Were you never interested in me at all?*

"She's been trying to find you for years."

"I know," he said bitterly. "What does she want? To finish me off, too? Is that why you're here?"

"She's not who you think she is," Nessa replied.

"What do you mean?"

"She's trying to protect you, not attack you."

"It certainly didn't seem that way," Gidion retorted. "And she killed my parents."

"Your parents aren't dead," Nessa said. "Well, your mother isn't. Not sure about your father."

Gidion froze in the action of picking up his shirt. "What do you mean, she's not dead?"

"She's with Malai."

Gidion stared at her, feeling like he was having a conversation where he didn't understand a word the other side was saying. His mother, not dead? It couldn't be. So many years, and they'd never heard from her again. If she wasn't dead, then why hadn't she come back for him?

Nessa looked sympathetic. "I can see how this is a bit of a surprise."

A surprise? A surprise! "How do I know you're telling the truth? Why didn't Malai come herself?"

"You have a tendency to attack first and ask questions later," Nessa said wryly. "She thought you might at least hear me out."

"She sent Ilk against us." He dragged his shirt on. This was a trap. It had to be. He had to get out of here.

"The Ilk weren't there to harm you. They were there to save you from the Riftlanders."

"Right." His boots. Where were his Ilk-damned boots?

"Don't you want to know about your father?" she said at last.

Gidion turned his eyes to her again. "What about him?"

"He was taken by the Riftlanders, but we're looking for him."

His father still alive? Could it be possible?

"I didn't just come to tell you about Malai and your parents," Nessa said.

"More surprises, just what I wanted," he said, resuming the hunt for his boots.

"Not a surprise—an offer," she said. "I can train you in your Chelaki powers so you don't accidentally knock out your allies next time you get into a fight."

It took him a moment to realize what she was talking about. "You mean Tine? My shout power?"

"It's a Chelaki ability," she said.

This was becoming infuriating, and he still couldn't find his damned boots. "Who the pits are the Chelaki?"

Nessa was about to answer but was interrupted by a loud knock on the door.

"Come on, lad. We old men need to see our beds at some point." Ruadh.

Gidion cursed. He wanted Nessa's explanation. "Just a moment!" he called. But the doorknob twisted. Damn Ruadh.

"I'll find you again," Nessa said. "Think on what I've said."

The door opened, and she vanished, just like Malai had done before. How did she do that?

"Wore her out, did you?" Ruadh said with a grin as he stepped in.

Gidion looked and saw Meadow stirring, her eyes opening woozily.

"Come on, our time's up," Ruadh said.

Gidion wondered whether to say anything about Nessa to Ruadh but decided not to. Who knew how he'd would react if he learned Gidion was supposedly related to Malai. He needed to find out more first, figure out what Malai really wanted. "Just looking for my boots," he said.

"By the end of the bed." Ruadh pointed them out, and Gidion went to put them on before following Ruadh out.

When they were out on the road, Gidion considered what to do next. Nessa had found him so quickly that it seemed it really was dangerous for him to be out of the Spire. He was reluctant to put himself back under Thane's power, but he could steal the keystone again if he needed to. And the weaver had been good to him. There was so much to learn, too. He sighed.

"So, you staying with me, lad?"

"I've been thinking about it more. And I think I should just go back to the Spire." Thane hopefully wouldn't be too mad with him for escaping. Simion might not even have noticed yet. "But I'd like to meet your boss and organize the glowglobes." One thing he definitely needed was money. Without it, he was most certainly a prisoner.

"Alright, if you're sure," Ruadh replied. "Probably is safer for you in there than out on the street. And that Thane fella can't keep you locked up forever either."

"I hope not."

It was late now, and there weren't as many people on the street. Gidion walked as fast as he could, hoping Simion hadn't woken up. And indeed, when he returned to Thane's chambers, he found the boy still unconscious where he'd left him. Breathing a sigh of relief, he put the keystone back into Simion's pocket.

Chapter 10

Thane turned onto Jerald Kiltour's street. What in the name of the Spinners had possessed him to live in such ugly surroundings? And the stench. He'd had to keep a handkerchief over his nose since they'd sailed into port. But this neighborhood reminded him unpleasantly of where he'd come from. There was the same meanness. The same pinched faces. No, Waldar had been worse. *No point in fooling myself.* He shuddered. Were any of them still alive? Not that he cared. He hadn't been back for thirty years. The city was no doubt in an even worse state than before, with the civil war on the verge of breaking out again.

He stopped outside Jerald's house, finding that it had indeed been weave-locked. He examined the weave. A simple one, but neatly done. Gidion was precise in his work. Optimism swelled inside him. This boy could be the future! But no time for such thoughts now. He needed to face what lay beyond the door.

He unraveled the weave with ease. It had never been made to keep out the likes of him. But when he opened the door, he immediately regretted not having put a thicker handkerchief over his nose. The sickly-sweet stench of rotting flesh was so powerful it made him want to vomit before he'd even stepped inside. Insects buzzed around the hallway like angry warnings. Gingerly, he stepped through the door, shutting and weave-locking it behind him.

He made his way down the dark, dank hallway and took a left into the living room. Jerald was lying by a writing desk, black flies crawling all over the bloated corpse, fat maggots wriggling among the entrails. The vile sight made Thane lose control of himself, and he had barely whipped the handkerchief away before he was vomiting noisily into the corner. *Pathetic.* But he hadn't been built for such things. Even the slightest specks of dirt were repugnant to him. And the dirt was everywhere here. It made his skin prickle.

Even so, he needed to make some attempt at an examination, verify if Gidion had been telling the truth about the manner of Jerald's death. Swallowing bile, he approached the body and hunkered down next to it. The flesh was indeed charred. He'd never seen anyone burn themselves with the Tapestry before, but he'd seen lightbolt injuries, and this was similar.

He straightened and did a reconnaissance of the room. There was little of interest. Jerald had some books, but they were histories, along with some novels. In the kitchen, he found a handful of withered carrots and half a loaf of moldy bread but nothing else.

Upstairs, things were just as barren. Jerald's room was simple, just a bed and side table, along with a chest of drawers. It stank almost as bad as his corpse did. He went to the bed, knelt down, and sniffed. Urine. Curious. Had Jerald become incontinent? Or was it that he'd spent time in this bed without being able to leave it. Ill? Perhaps imprisoned?

A search of the chest of drawers revealed that Jerald only had a few items of clothing—three pairs of plain grey weaver robes and some worker's smocks. Thane wrinkled his nose. *Why live like a peasant when you could live like a lord?* Jerald had been a talented weaver, by all accounts. He mightn't have been very strong in artefaction, but his skills as a ranger should have been enough for him to afford a decent house in a much better part of the city. At the least, you'd expect a better wardrobe. But no. Jerald, it seemed, had remained as humble as his origins. Thane carefully refolded the clothing and then wiped his hand on his robe. He felt a strong need to wash, but that would have to wait.

He made the Tapestry visible and examined it in case it provided any additional clues. At first, he saw nothing of interest, but as he was about to leave, he spotted something odd—a slight warp in the threads, as if someone had cut and then rewoven them, leaving a scar like a stitch in a mended garment. Excitement shivered through him. Was this a mark of splicing? Could there have been Ilk mages here? He walked all over the house again, keeping the Tapestry visible, hoping for other clues. But there was nothing.

Reluctantly accepting that he would find no more answers in Jerald's house, he decided to speak to the man's neighbors to find out if they had seen anything or anyone suspicious.

A stocky man with a shiny head answered Thane's knock on the next door to Jerald's. "Good morning. I'm Mikel, a friend of Jerald's. I was wondering if you'd seen him recently?"

"Devlin." The man stretched out a hand.

Realizing he was expected to shake it, Thane reached out his own hand. The man's skin was hard and callused, his grip strong. Afterward, Thane wiped his hand discreetly on his robe.

"Knocked in to him a few times but no reply. Door was stuck fast," Devlin said. He had a thick workman's accent that Thane struggled to understand.

"How well did you know him?" Thane asked.

"I'm hearing a past tense. Is he dead?"

"I'm afraid so."

"Damned shame, that, damned shame. He was a good sort, always there to lend a hand," Devlin replied. "And asked little for it in return when he could have had a lot more."

"Did he start behaving strangely recently?" Thane said.

"We've hardly seen him last couple of months. He said he was ill. My missus brought him some soup. So I guess whatever illness it was, it got to him?"

"Perhaps. We'll need to investigate further. But tell me, did he have any enemies?" Thane asked.

Devlin shook his head. "Everyone liked him, even the gangs. He helped anyone who came to his door, whether they could pay or not. But why you asking this? You think he was murdered?"

"That's what I'm trying to find out," Thane replied.

"I don't know why anyone would murder him," Devlin said. "He's as good a soul as you could get."

Thane bid goodbye to the man and knocked on more doors along the street. But they all echoed what Devlin had said. Jerald had been well liked, not seen much recently. Everyone shocked and dismayed to hear of his death.

Thane returned to the inn he'd booked himself near the port. It was the finest establishment in the quarter, housing mostly wealthy merchants and their retainers. As soon as he arrived, he ordered a bath to his room. It came shortly after in the hands of two young men, both regretfully plain. They filled it with buckets of warm water, to which Thane added a touch of lavender oil before undressing and sinking into the tub with a sigh of relief. But even as his body relaxed, his mind churned over the possibilities. Gidion had been telling the truth about Jerald it seemed, but how would the rest of his story play out? And what was he to do if he found evidence there *was* an Ilk mage?

He wanted to ride for Tine immediately, but he had to restrain himself, not get too excited. It was a weakness of his. He knew this. Excitement could lead to impulsiveness, and he'd made errors before. So he ate, he read, and he went to bed early to rise with the dawn.

When he arrived in Tine two days later, dressed as a trader, he found to his surprise that the wall appeared undamaged. Perhaps the raiders had come via a different entrance? But this gate was the closest to the Riftlands.

Soldiers stopped him as he tried to enter, requesting his identification documents and purpose. They let him through without issue once he slipped them a silver stag each. He made his way straight to the marketplace, now seeing evidence of the Riftlander attack everywhere. People were crawling all over burned buildings to fix the damage or knock down what was beyond repair. It was lucky that most were made of brick and plaster rather than wood. Or perhaps luck had nothing to do with it. The citizens of Tine were probably well used to the depredations of their barbaric neighbors and had constructed their homes to hold strong against fire.

In the marketplace, he was faced with a bleak sight—a dozen golden-skinned men hanging from gallows, dead no more than a day or two, many more cuffed to pillories next to them. Their faces were bruised and swollen, crusted with blood and what looked suspiciously like excrement. Thane didn't go close enough to find out, but he saw a man with a black eye pause in front of one and spit in his face.

The market itself was quiet, the people subdued. Surveying it, he concluded it must be missing at least half its usual stalls. It was surprising it was running at all. But then, life did go on. The other noteworthy thing was the number of soldiers around. He counted at least fourteen on his way to the inn that Gidion had told him of. Quite a few soldiers inside it, too, but only a handful of patrons.

He approached the wiry man standing behind the bar. "I'd like a room overlooking the square."

"Won't be a problem, quiet here at the moment." The man went to fetch a ledger and put it down in front of Thane, along with a quill and ink. "Make your mark there." He pointed at an empty column next to a number.

Thane scratched out his initials. "I see you've had trouble here," he remarked when he'd finished.

"Nothing the soldiers couldn't handle," the barkeep said, eyes flickering behind Thane.

"What happened exactly?"

The barman's face screwed up and he looked like he wanted to spit. "Rift Rats attacked us on the Day of Long Light."

"But you fought them off?"

"Not before they burned half the town," the man said. "Some traitorous bastard let them in."

"I was wondering why the wall didn't seem to have any damage. Have you found out who did it?"

"There's a few theories going round." The barkeep looked left and right, then said in a voice so low it was barely more than a whisper, "Might been one of the Feds."

"Why would they do that?"

"It's them manning the walls." Then suddenly, he stiffened and put on a bright smile. "I'll get you your key, sir. Will you be wanting anything to eat?"

Thane realized that two Federation soldiers were approaching the bar. "Yes, I'll have a meal and a glass of your best red wine."

The innkeeper had a boy show Thane his room. It wasn't terribly large, but the boy assured him it was the largest one overlooking the square. Thane thanked him with a couple of coppers.

When he returned downstairs, he took a table with a clear view of the common room and awaited his food and drink. He noted that the barkeeps were effusive with the soldiers, scurrying to pour their ale.

It wasn't long before his wine was placed in front of him, the food following shortly after. As he ate and sipped his wine, he observed those coming and going, seeing no one of note. When he'd finished, he decided it was time to employ a method that often worked well for him. He rose and went out to the market, scanning the people closely. They were always easy enough to spot, the thieves. But he was looking for the young ones, those he found most amenable. He finally spotted a likely target, a small, skinny boy of perhaps eight years who had nimbly picked the pocket of a passing merchant. Smiling, he approached the thief. "Tell me, did you get his purse?"

"Dunno what you're talking about," the boy said, legs coiling to run.

"Don't worry, I won't turn you in," Thane replied, placing a hand on his shoulder to steady him. "In fact, I'm hoping you can help me."

The boy took him in with a glance. "I ain't no breech puller," he said flatly, shrugging himself free of Thane's hand.

Thane chuckled, impressed by the boy's astuteness as well as his impudence. He would be perfect. "That's not what I'm looking for. I need information."

"'Bout what?"

"Were you in the marketplace on the Night of Long Light?"

The boy stiffened. "Everyone was."

"Can you tell me what happened?"

"I ain't done nothing." The boy's shoulder twitched, first the left, then the right. Skybark addict. Sadly common among his type.

"Like I said, I'm just looking for information about that night, and you look like a sharp boy."

He hesitated.

Thane opened one of his purses and showed the boy the coppers inside it. "Easier to talk for coin, I imagine?"

The boy bit his bottom lip. "Not here."

"Lead the way."

The boy made for the western exit of the marketplace.

"What's your name?" Thane asked him.

"You can call me Nim."

"Very well, Nim. Have you lived in Tine for long?"

"All my life," he said. He turned several corners until they were in a quiet but filthy alley, where he stopped.

Thane repressed the urge to place a handkerchief over his mouth and very carefully did not look at the stinking heap just beyond the boy.

"What you want to know, and how much do I get for it?" Nim asked.

"It depends on how valuable the information is. But let's start with three ravens for telling me everything that happened in the marketplace on the Day of Long Light." *And quickly, so we can get out of here.* The filth was a living thing, and he could feel it crawling toward him.

"Yeah, I was there along with everyone else. The Procession was still on when the Rifters came into town. They torched half of it, killed hundreds in the square before the Feds got 'em out."

"And how did you survive?"

"I hid in a barrel."

"Clever. Now tell me, did you see any weavers? Any magic being used?"

Nim rubbed his cheek, a jerky, twitchy motion. "Another couple of ravens for that," the boy said at last.

"You've barely told me anything yet." Thane admired the boy's boldness, but he wasn't going to be robbed. "But you'll get more if your information is good enough. No lies, mind you. I'll know."

The thief didn't answer straight away, and Thane was about to press him again when he said, "I did see some odd things. Could have been weavers."

Thane held his breath. Was this where he finally learned the truth that Gidion had been hiding from him? "What exactly did you see?"

"There was this lad, seventeen or eighteen. He was fighting off the Riftlanders, and then he musta done something 'cause suddenly everyone around him fell to the ground."

"They just fell to the ground?" Thane repeated.

"Yeah, just like that. I was pretty near when it happened, and it felt like someone hit me on the inside of my head. Had me spinning for a bit."

The Ilk mages had been associated with mind magic. There were hints about it in the books he'd read. Could this be what they'd described? If so, it made Gidion incredibly dangerous to be around. Thane had no idea how to defend himself against that. For the first time, he felt afraid.

"Earlier on, he was with an old man, maybe his pa, selling glow-globes and the like at market. So they might have been weavers."

"And what happened to the old man?"

"He wasn't in the square at first, but after the young one knocked everyone out, he came with a couple of horses, and they left together."

"Did the young weaver talk to anyone else at all?"

"He was fighting with a big foreigner, skin white as milk and hair red as an evening sky. Reckon he was a sellsword. He left with the weaver and the old man."

This was the man, Ruadh, that Gidion had mentioned. "No one else?"

Nim screwed his face up, thinking. "Can't really say. The square was packed. I only saw them after the Rifters had attacked and they was fighting their way out."

"Did you see any more magic being used?"

"Nah. That was the last I saw of them or anything else, 'cause I climbed into the barrel then, and stayed there 'til it all ended."

A shame the boy hadn't seen more. But what he'd said largely corroborated Gidion's story. He would have to get the rest out of the sellsword. "Did you pick up any other information about the young weaver at all?"

The boy shook his head.

"Thank you, you've been very helpful," Thane said. He plucked out five ravens. "I can give you these now. Or—" Here, Thane took out a stag, causing the boy's eyes to widen. "You could ask around, find out more information for me, and I give you this instead."

"What else you want to know?"

"Anything more you can find out about that young weaver and the Riftlander raid."

The boy twitched and scratched, and Thane repressed an impulse to reach out and still his motion. "Can I have the coppers now, and I'll give 'em back to you for a silver tomorrow? In case you scarper, and I get nothing."

Thane smiled. Good, the boy wasn't stupid. "Very well." Thane dropped the ravens into his grubby hand.

Nim turned them this way and that, then pocketed them.

"I'll be staying at the Market Inn tonight. Come to me before breakfast tomorrow if you want that silver."

"They won't let me in there."

"Been caught before, have you?"

The boy just rubbed his arm.

"I'll stop by here in the morning before I leave. At ninth bell."

He nodded and scampered off, fast as a rabbit.

Thane returned to the Market Inn in a state of excitement. His suspicions about Gidion were as good as confirmed. The boy must be of Chelaki descent. But did he know it or not? He'd probably hidden his use of the stun power because he knew it wasn't weaver magic. Thane didn't blame him. But there was so much more to all of this. And he could see the future opening out, filling with possibilities. This was the key he'd been waiting for all his life. It had to be. He spent the rest of the evening in the common room, listening to conversations, but didn't pick up much that was new or of interest.

The next day, he found Nim in the alleyway waiting for him. The boy was wearing the same rags as the day before and carrying nothing else. "Found out couple of things more about the weaver," he said.

"Oh?"

"The old man was a weaver too. Someone saw him shooting blue magefire out of a staff when they was fighting their way out. And there was a woman with the young weaver during the Procession. But she disappeared after the Rifters attacked—at least, no one I spoke to saw her again."

A woman? Gidion had made no mention of her. Interesting. "Did you get a description?"

"Black hair, really pretty, wearing a green dress. That's about it." Nim rubbed his arm, waiting expectantly.

But Thane made no move to pay him. "Would you like to come back with me back to Arindel?" he said. "I can make good use of someone with your observation skills. And you're clearly very bright."

The boy was instantly suspicious. "Told you I ain't no breech puller. You said you was gonna give me the stag."

"It's yours, and you can even keep the ravens I gave you yesterday," Thane said. "I'm merely offering you the chance to make more. And don't worry, it's not your body I'm interested in. You're only a child."

"I'm nearly twelve," he said indignantly.

Small for his age, but it was often the case with these urchins. They never had enough food. *I never had enough food.* "As I said, a child," Thane replied. "But I have a house in Arindel where I keep other boys like you. You'll always be well fed and clothed, you'll have your own room." It was such a little thing to do, and so many he couldn't help.

"What do you want from me?"

Good that he was still suspicious. "Your eyes and ears, that's all."

"So like I'll be a spy?"

"Yes, you could put it that way."

The boy frowned, looked Thane up and down.

Thane plucked out a stag and handed it to him. "This is yours whatever you say."

The boy examined it as carefully as he had the ravens, bit on it just to be sure, then pocketed it. Then he scratched his arm and shoulder, still considering. Thane would have to do something about that if the boy agreed to come. "Alright," he said at last. "Nothin' keepin' me here. But my eyes and ears is all you get."

"Excellent," Thane replied. "Let's go get you some traveling clothes and a pony."

"I can't ride."

"I'll show you how."

They went to a tailor, where Thane bought the boy a cloak and some old clothes that had belonged to the tailor's son. Then they picked up a placid, dappled gelding from the stables at the entrance of the town. The boy mounted it nervously with Thane's help but proved to be a quick study.

They traveled mostly in silence, Thane mulling over what he'd learned about Gidion. His greatest concern was how to protect himself against the boy's powers. He had no defenses against mind magic, and he hadn't come across any books that discussed this. He could wear nicoleum, but that would stop him from using his own powers and would be uncomfortable, to say the least. But the Eleusians must surely have invented some protections. He'd need to research, put some feelers out in case there was an artefact that could be used. A thrill of anticipation ran through him. Still today, the hunt for new knowledge was as addictive to him as the lips of a beautiful young man. To find out what had been lost to the world was as good a conquest as any of the flesh.

He glanced at Nim. The boy claimed not to be inclined toward men, but he was too young to know himself yet. Thane could see it in him. He was never wrong. So he would protect and nourish the boy, ensure he was able to grow strong, hone the intelligence that lurked in his brown eyes.

The boy looked in his direction, and catching his gaze, Thane smiled. The boy uncertainly smiled back.

When they sailed into Arindel several days later, Thane ordered a cab that took them to the Rainbow Quarter. At his request, the driver dropped them a few streets away from their destination. Thane preferred no one to know exactly where he was going, and the cabs always had a difficult time with the crowds and narrow streets.

"Lots of people here," Nim said, rubbing his elbow.

His twitches had subsided, though. Thane had made him give up every bit of skybark he had. He'd passed a difficult night or two, but already his color was better. "Almost a million people live in this city,"

Thane said. That was if you didn't include the wretches in the slums of New Arindel, a place he abhorred and avoided at all costs. Who knew how many existed there. No one had ever bothered to count them. And they died frequently, quickly replaced by new influxes from the provinces or from Tarsis.

They stopped outside a three-story house, one of the few that had survived the destruction of the Great Siege. Painted sky blue, it had two white doors and flowers spilling from boxes in the windows. It was, in fact, two houses joined together, but Nim would live in only one of them until he came of age.

He opened the nearest door with his key and pulled the cord inside the entrance. A bell rang out, and moments later Lucien had appeared, his long fingers stained with chalk.

"Magister," he said with a bow. "Welcome home."

"I'm sorry to distract you from lessons," Thane said, "but I have a new boy for you. His name's Nim."

"Pleased to meet you, Nim," Lucien said with a broad smile.

Nim just shuffled his feet.

"I met Nim here in the Federation. He speaks a dialect of Vycenian as he comes from near Kharas. But you'll want to teach him how we speak and write it here."

"Of course."

"Find him a room and have him join the lessons. He's also going to help you track down a sellsword called Ruadh who arrived in Arindel a few days ago. It's an urgent task, so I'm setting you all to it as soon as morning lessons are over." He had Nim repeat his description of Ruadh before bidding him goodbye and crossing over to the other house via a locked door that could be opened only by him or Lucien. It wouldn't do for the younger boys to know what went on in *this* house.

Chapter 11

Gidion woke the day after his escapade with a pounding head, his mind replaying the scenes in the brothel. But instead of the whore, it was Nessa who lay beneath him, crying out at his thrusts, her legs wrapped around his hips. He tried to tell himself that he couldn't trust her, that she'd been sent by Malai, but his mind stubbornly fixated on the fantasy until he had spent himself on the bed. Only then was he able to consider what had happened with any kind of reason.

Nessa had been sent by Malai, and so quickly that the woman must be spying on him. Which meant there could well be a spy or spies in the Spire, just as Thane had warned. But then why not kill him? Because Nessa was telling the truth? Malai was his grandmother, and he was descended from the Ilk Lord? No, it couldn't be. She was playing tricks on him. Making him out to be a fool. There was some other game being played here, and it made him crazy that he didn't know what it was.

Maybe he should tell Thane about Nessa's visit. He'd be better able to protect Gidion if he knew the true extent of it. But it could backfire. Gidion would have to confess how he'd gotten the key from Simion, which meant also admitting that he hadn't told the whole truth about Tine. And if Thane thought he was an Ilk mage, he might hand him over to the Spire authorities. In the end, that was what decided him.

He would stay quiet but obey Thane's instructions to remain in his rooms, and hope for the best.

Several more days passed before Thane returned. Gidion battled fresh temptation to escape his rooms but managed to restrain himself. When the Magister appeared, utterly without warning, one evening, Gidion sensed a blank around him. He couldn't perceive his emotions as he had before. But his expression was serious as he bid Gidion join him in the library, and Gidion didn't need his other senses to know that trouble was coming. "Your story about Jerald stands up," Thane said.

At first, Gidion felt relieved. Thane believed him.

"And I've good reason to believe there was an Ilk mage in his house at some point, as you suggested. You definitely didn't see anyone?"

Thane was fixing him with an intense look, making him pluck nervously at the cuff of his robe. "No, but it seemed like he was talking to someone in his head."

"You didn't say that before."

A note of warning in Thane's tone that made him want to shuffle his feet. But he held his ground. "I thought I did. I wasn't really sure what I was seeing, to be honest. It did seem like he was talking to someone invisible, not just us."

"Invisible?" Thane repeated sharply.

Gidion nodded. "But that's impossible, right?"

"Not for someone with Eleusian magic," Thane said.

"The Eleusians are all gone," Gidion said automatically.

"Indeed," Thane said, his eyes distant and thoughtful. But suddenly they sharpened and focused once more on Gidion. "I also went to Tine." He paused meaningfully.

Gidion tried to keep his expression blank, but inwardly, he cursed. He should have known Thane would investigate there.

"I heard an interesting description of how a group of Riftlanders were felled by an invisible power on the Night of Long Light."

Gidion chewed the inside of his lip, unsure what to say. Thane didn't seem angry, exactly. But he was watching Gidion closely to see if he would slip up. It was time to tell the truth, or at least a version of it. "I was afraid to tell you," he said at last, doing his best to look contrite. "I don't understand what I did. It just happened."

Thane placed a hand on Gidion's shoulder. "I understand. And luckily for you, the Federation soldiers you killed can easily be passed off as having been murdered by the Riftlanders."

Gidion panicked. He didn't remember any soldiers being affected by his stun strike. But then it had all been very chaotic. Was Thane going to give him up to the Federation for justice? "I didn't kill any soldiers, I swear," Gidion said. "It was the Riftlanders."

"Well, it seems like some soldiers got caught in whatever it was, and they're looking for you."

"If I did, it was an accident. I didn't mean to—"

Thane raised a hand to interrupt him. "Don't worry, even if they did trace it to you, the Federation has no authority over the Spire."

"So you're not going to hand me in?" Gidion said hopefully.

"Of course not. But you need to tell me everything from now on," Thane said. "I can't help you if you aren't open with me."

He paused again, and Gidion debated whether to mention Nessa. But instinctively, he wanted to protect her, even if he didn't trust her. To hide this truth, he told a different one. "I used the same power when the Ilk mage first came to find me," he said. "It was an accident too. I was so mad with Ma. I'd been playing a game, and I didn't want to stop. She was calling me for dinner. I knocked her unconscious, and a few days later the Ilk mage appeared." He paused, because this part was painful for him. "I think it must be related."

Thane's gaze sharpened. "What, she can track you when you use the shout power?"

Gidion shrugged. "It could be coincidence." But was it? He'd used it against the Riftlanders and his mother, and both times Malai had come. After he'd used it against Simion, Nessa had come. He should tell Thane about her visit. He should. But something silenced him.

"You'll clearly need to learn to control this power," Thane said.

Gidion's hope rose. "Can you teach me?"

"I'll try, though I'm not sure how much help I can be. It's a Chelaki power," Thane said.

The same word Nessa had mentioned. "Who are the Chelaki?"

"To us, most commonly known as the Ilk mages," Thane said drily.

The Chelaki were Ilk mages? Did that mean Nessa thought Gidion was an Ilk mage, too? "But, I don't know how to make Ilk. And I don't want to. I'm not—"

Thane rested a soothing hand against his upper arm. "Don't worry, it doesn't automatically make you an Ilk mage," Thane said. "The Chelaki are an ancient race that lived on Southern Teleriol until the Eleusians wiped them out about five hundred years ago."

"But I thought the Eleusians were a peaceful race."

Thane dropped his hand. "Once the Eleusians had established their empire, they were indeed generally peaceful and focused on beauty and art. But they warred a lot with the Chelaki before, or so I believe. There aren't many sources on that period of history. The Eleusians probably had better records, but of course, Teleriol is no more."

Teleriol, sunk under the sea in the Ruin and all the Eleusians gone with it. Gidion shuddered at the thought. "So what do we do now?"

"I'd like you to show me how you use your stun power," Thane said.

"But what if she tracks me again?" Gidion said.

"You'll be with me. And anyway, the Spire is enveloped in a powerful concealing weave. What happens in here doesn't resonate well outside it."

So maybe Nessa had been telling the truth. The shout power wasn't how they tracked him. It was all coincidence? He wished he knew who was telling the truth. Everything seemed upside down.

"I promise, I won't let anything happen to you," Thane said, touching him lightly on the arm again.

The magister's concern finally broke him. "If you're sure, then yes."

"Wonderful, let's go out to the Water Garden." Thane got to his feet.

"But it's almost dark."

"Which is precisely why we'll go now."

They exited the tower, going to the garden that had been visible from Thane's rooms. The sounds of water were everywhere, rumbling, gurgling, splashing, and spraying, the air filled with the scent of green things.

Thane stopped by a small pond scattered with white water lilies. "Here will do."

"You don't want me to use it against you, do you?"

"Of course not," Thane said with a laugh. He pointed to an owl sitting on the branch of a nearby tree. "That bird there. Can you stun it, cause it to fall?"

Gidion opened himself to the Tapestry, his entire being humming and vibrating in response. Then he found the threads to the bird and sent his power out against it. Several birds and insects fell to the ground.

"Impressive," Thane murmured.

Gidion warmed at the praise.

"Can you target just the bird itself?" Thane said.

"That was what I was trying to do," he replied, chagrined.

"No mind, you just need to practice," Thane said. "I suspect you need to be very deliberate about the threads you choose."

So Gidion tried again—and then again and again—until a blinding headache built up, and his left eye screwed up with pain.

"One more time," Thane said.

Gidion tried, but the headache was so bad he couldn't keep the Tapestry in focus. "I'm sorry, Magister, I can't," he said. He was frustrated. His net had been tightening with each attempt, and he was sure he was only a few away from achieving his target.

"That's enough for today," Thane said, seeing Gidion's pain. "Let's go in and have something to eat, and we can discuss the readings you've been doing.

When Thane returned to his apartment the following evening, he called Gidion into the study and said he wanted to assess Gidion's artefaction abilities. He placed a small round marble on the desk. "I'd like to watch you weave a glowglobe."

"Now?" Gidion was tired and in little mood for work. Glowglobes took an immense amount of concentration.

"Don't worry, you don't need to complete it tonight," Thane said. "I just want to see how you get started."

So Gidion began the arduous work of weaving the threads into the complicated pattern that would make the stone give off light.

Thane stopped him after about half an hour. "And you've never had anyone show you how to do this?"

Gidion shook his head.

"You've taken a somewhat unusual approach," Thane replied. "But it's an effective one, perhaps even a little faster than the standard."

Thane sounded genuinely impressed, and Gidion couldn't help feel a measure of pride.

"Tomorrow, I'd like you to come along to my Advanced Artefaction workshop."

"I thought I couldn't attend classes until I've passed the Selection Trial and officially enrolled in the Spire," Gidion said.

"This one's different," Thane said. "It's an extra class I do for those with full artefactor abilities who intend to specialize in artefaction."

Gidion wanted to object that he didn't plan to specialize in artefaction. But he decided against it, thinking there might be more advantage to be gained from going to the class. "How many other students are there?"

"Just one, and it will be good for you to meet him."

"Only one?" he echoed in surprise.

"Full artefaction talent is extremely rare among Vycenians—it was always more of an Eleusian skill—which is why it's so valuable."

Conal had told Gidion his ability wasn't common, but Gidion hadn't realized just how uncommon it was. "Is that why the Wyven family are so strongly associated with the glowglobe trade in Vycenia?"

"I'd go further and say they have a monopoly over it. Nearly everyone with full artefactor abilities is related to them by blood to some degree."

"Does that mean you're ..."

Thane laughed. "No, no. But I work closely with them."

Gidion sensed something else lurking beneath the surface of his words, something dark and bitter. And Thane's laughter had sounded forced. But when he spoke again, it was with such lightness that it made Gidion think he'd imagined it.

"The Seeker you'll meet in the class is called Jasper. He's a younger son of Macio Wyven, the current head of the family. A bright boy and an excellent student."

Gidion felt a pang of jealousy at Thane's description of him. Did he consider Jasper more capable than Gidion?

"Try to get on good terms with him," Thane continued. "The Wyvens can make you wealthy if you accept their patronage. Prove yourself, and they might even let you marry into a minor branch of the family."

Irony had crept into Thane's last words, and Gidion wanted to ask him if he'd ever been offered marriage. But he worried the question would sound rude, and instead asked, "Will I be able to take part in the class?"

"Of course. I'll be preparing you both for the project you'll need to complete as part of the Selection Trial."

"What will it be?"

"You'll find out along with Jasper in class tomorrow."

Chapter 12

Thane pushed open the door to the Silver Sword. It was everything he disliked, full of loud men who stank of sweat and too much alcohol. His instinct, as always in such places, was to curl in on himself. But he reminded himself he could dispatch the lot of them with a blast from his focus stone. So he pulled himself up straight, walking as if they couldn't touch him. And none tried to.

"Good evening to you. I'm here to meet Ruadh Sturmson," he said to the barkeep, a slimy little man with a ferret's face.

"He's waiting for you. Follow me." The man took him into a small back room.

The sellsword was indeed there, but he didn't get to his feet when he saw Thane. This irritated him, but he carefully hid it behind a smile as he sat himself down on the bench opposite. He looked like many of his type—hairy, over-muscled, a patchwork of scars across his face and arms. But he had a surprisingly friendly face despite the lurking suspicion in his green eyes.

"Ruadh Sturmson. How can I help you?" A tankard of golden ale was sitting on the table between his elbows.

"As I said in my note, I wanted to thank you for taking Gidion to me."

"You could have done that in the note," he said. "Why are you really here?" The words were delivered bluntly but without malice.

Even so, the man's directness put him momentarily off kilter. He'd become used to the evasions and misdirections of politicians. "I'm glad we can get straight to the point," he said to cover himself. "In fact, I wanted to hear your account of what had happened at Tine while you were with Gidion."

"I'm afraid the lad's story is his own." He grasped his ale in a huge paw and slugged a good third of it down.

Thane waited until he'd set the tankard back onto the table. "He's put himself under my protection, and I'd be doing him a disservice if I didn't try to get a full picture about this Ilk mage who's been following him."

"Was it him told you I was here, then?" Ruadh didn't seem particularly concerned about it.

"No, he barely mentioned you, in fact. But I've just come back from Tine—and Kharas."

At the mention of Kharas, the sellsword's mouth twisted.

"It was a very strange event, wasn't it?" Thane said. "Gidion told me."

"Not sure what the pits went on in there, but we got away as quickly as we could," Ruadh said, taking another gulp of his beer.

"Well, I learned something when I went there. I'll tell you what if you'll tell me what you saw."

The sellsword still had a stubborn slant to his expression. Thane slid a full purse across the table. "Perhaps this will help."

The man loosened the strings with a show of reluctance. But when he looked inside, his eyebrows rose high. "I'm not sure I have anything valuable enough for what's in there," he said, sitting back and grasping his tankard again.

"Just tell me everything that happened since you first met Gidion," Thane said, "and it's yours."

"Why don't you tell me what you know, and I'll see what else I can add to it?"

Not quite as stupid as he seemed. And not as easily bought as he'd expected. "Very well." He recounted all he'd learned, leaving out only some details that should be known to the mercenary to test him. "So, will you tell me, how did you first meet him?"

Ruadh glanced down at the purse, pressed his lips together, then slapped his paw down on it and scooped it toward him. "I met Gidion at the market in Tine," he said. "Bought a glowglobe off him. As good quality as you'd find anywhere."

"He has a natural genius for artefaction," Thane said. "One of the best I've seen for years." Thane suppressed the niggling feeling that Gidion might be even better than he was. "But tell me, did he speak to anyone apart from you?"

"He probably talked to plenty. He and his pa had a stall at market, after all," Ruadh said with a shrug.

"But no one in particular who stood out?" Thane pressed.

Ruadh shook his head, then narrowed his eyes. "Well, there was a lass we met in the bar before the Procession. Dark-haired, very pretty, not my type."

This might be something. "And did you get her name?"

"Nessa, she called herself. Can't remember the second name. The lad was like a puppy for her." He laughed.

"What happened to her?"

"She disappeared when the Riftlanders attacked. Probably made a run for it, and I don't blame her." Another gulp of beer. The man certainly liked to drink.

"Can you tell me in detail what you saw once the attack started?"

"I managed to get a sword off one of them. Gidion used magic that knocked a bunch of them unconscious, including me. That part was all a bit of a blur."

Thane moved in for the kill. "That power he used. Did you know it was one the Ilk mages had?"

Ruadh's fist tightened around his drink, his thick red eyebrows drawing together. "I don't know much about magic," he said at last.

"But you must agree that the Ilk mage must want him for some related reason," Thane said. "And that reason, whatever it is, can't be good."

"She's trying to kill him," Ruadh said. "She had Ilk with her. Saw them for myself."

Another confirmation of Gidion's story. Either that or the mercenary had been trained to say it and was an exceptionally good liar, which Thane doubted. He knew his type. Would say whatever came to his mind and not an ounce of subtlety to him. He'd already slipped Gidion's secrets with barely any prompting. "Describe to me in detail everything that happened during the Ilk attack."

"Well, we were making a dash for it when we were stopped by Riftlanders. The Ilk came out of nowhere, started killing the bastards. Bunch of them ran away."

Thane's ears pricked. "The Ilk didn't attack you?"

"I wrecked one of the fuckers. Had to chop it right to pieces before it would stop."

A gleam entered the man's eyes, and Thane had no doubt he was replaying the scene in his mind with some relish. "But did it attack you first or did you attack it?"

This brought Ruadh up short. "Now that you mention it, *I* attacked *it*. The foul thing had just finished with one of the Riftlanders and I came up behind it."

"And did you see any attacks directly on Gidion?"

Ruadh shook his head.

"So, you see what I mean?"

The man looked uneasy. "Aye, I see what you mean."

Good, his allegiance was shifting. Sellswords were all the same, their loyalty only as strong as the coin you paid them. "I'm going to do all in my power to protect the boy," Thane said.

"He says you're keeping him captive."

"Oh, I hadn't realized you'd spoken to him since you arrived."

The sellsword swore.

Thane suppressed a smile. He'd revealed something he shouldn't have. "Did he see you here?"

"That's a question for him," Ruadh said, draining his tankard.

"As I said, I'm trying to protect him," Thane said. "I advised him not to leave my rooms for his safety while I was gone, but he's not a captive. Surely, the fact he came to see you proves that." *How did he get past the weave-locks? Did Simion let him out?*

"Aye, well, I've told you all I know," Ruadh said, getting to his feet.

"What if I were able to help you out of your current troubles?" Thane called.

Ruadh froze.

"I hear you aren't very well liked by the City Watch."

"The Watch aren't fond of many people." But the man didn't make another move toward the door.

"It wasn't Gidion who told me," Thane said. "He's been good about keeping your secrets—if he knows them. But I imagine it's quite inconvenient for you. They don't come in here much, do they? The owner has a tidy arrangement with them. But it stops you from being able to get around the city, find work."

"I've got a plan for the Watch," Ruadh growled, turning toward the door.

"I could quite easily sort them out for you," Thane said. "But please, come, sit down. I'd rather not shout." The mercenary turned back toward the table but didn't sit. Ah, the little resistances. They always amused him.

"What's your price?"

"Information, of course. I just want you to discourage Gidion from leaving the Spire to see you, but if he does, I'd like to know what he's up to, if you hear anything else about Ilk or the Ilk mage. Oh, and I'll protect you if she does come after you. I think that's a pretty good deal."

Ruadh said nothing, but it was clear that the cogs were churning in his mind.

Thane watched him, careful to maintain a patient expression. This wasn't a man to press too much—there was an air of barely restrained violence in him despite the friendly demeanor, and who knew how many of those ales he'd had already.

His patience was rewarded. "Come back to me with confirmation of the Watch, and you have yourself a deal."

Thane smiled. "Consider it done." And with that, he took his leave and went to his second appointment of the evening.

He picked up a horse cab on the main road to take him to the Merchant's Quarter. At his request, it dropped him off two streets away from his destination, a bank in a nondescript building.

Inside, he asked to speak to Rafaelo, one of the bank's owners, and was ushered through to a well-appointed room. It was a reflection of Rafaelo and his business, the shelves and walls filled with curious objects from all over the world—a long, white horn from an isaur in the Riftlands, delicate porcelain from Tunis, a jeweled Tarsan dagger.

And a collection of paintings in the style of the Kharasian Awakening—they looked very like Kriadans, the colors sharp and in relief. Those were new. Last time, Rafaelo been showing off a collection of pre-Ruin canvases from Western Vycenia.

"You like the Kriadans?" Rafaelo said, getting to his feet behind his huge redwood desk.

"How did you manage to assemble so many?" In truth, they weren't much to his taste. He found the colors vulgar.

"A collector died without making a will. We bought the lot."

Thane's eye was caught by one piece in particular. The storming of Kharas by the Federation army. A brutal and bloody battle by all accounts.

"I can do you a good deal on them as you're a valued customer," Rafaelo said. Like all Tunians, his black hair and beard gleamed with oil, and he gave off a distinct smell of spices that made Thane's nose wrinkle.

"I'm not here for paintings, you know that."

Rafaelo grinned. "Well, sit and tell me what it is you *do* want."

"I have a challenge," Thane said as he took a chair opposite Rafaelo. "And it will be worth a lot to you."

Rafaelo's little eyes brightened greedily. "Tell me."

Really, the man was repulsive. But he was useful—very, very useful. "I need an artefact that can protect against Chelaki magic."

Rafaelo clasped his hands together. "Something Eleusian, in that case."

"Most likely."

"I'm afraid I know of nothing off hand," Rafaelo said. "However, we've been looking for funding to do some diving in the Straits of Ruin and along the Carian coast." He looked meaningfully at Thane.

"Do you have reason to believe there's something under the water?"

"Undoubtedly, there is," Rafaelo said. "But as you know, it's expensive and difficult to dive. We only have a single Eleusian breathing apparatus for deep waters."

Thane considered. It was likely to lead to nothing, but he knew also that Rafaelo and others like him had already combed North Myrna, and much of South Myrna, for Eleusian artefacts. The sea might well be the only place left to look.

"How much do you need to get started?"

"Five thousand consuls," Rafaelo said immediately.

A small fortune. "I'll give you a thousand and I want a full accounting of how it's being spent," Thane returned.

But Rafaelo shook his head regretfully. "That won't be near enough to get a ship."

"You have ships."

"Not ships that are able to go out in the deep ocean."

"You mean to look near the Maelstrom?" he said with surprise.

"We mean to get as close as we can," Rafaelo replied. "There may be shipwrecks or artefacts that survived the Ruin."

Disappointing. He thought Rafaelo knew better. "People say Teleriol sank under the sea. But it didn't actually sink. It was unmade. You're more likely to be sucked into the storm than find anything."

Rafaelo's expression turned smug, irritating Thane further. "Yes, we're aware of that. But we believe that things may have been thrown aside by the unraveling. Like when there's a fire blast."

Thane considered. Was it worth the risk? It was a lot of money, even for him. But his gut was already providing the answer, even if his head said no. "I'll give you three thousand to help fund a single expedition," he said. "But no more until you actually find some evidence that there are items to be recovered."

Rafaelo grinned. "It's a deal."

Chapter 13

The Advanced Artefaction workshop took place in a small classroom in the Tower of Artefaction. The room contained three parallel pairs of workbenches facing a single one on a dais at the top of the room. Thane was standing by a bench in the first row, talking to a boy with red-gold hair. Jasper no doubt. There was a conspiratorial air about them that made Gidion's stomach clench. It was quite obvious the boy was enraptured by Thane. Thane, for his part, was leaning in close to the young initiate. *But what do I care? It's Arianna Velden I want as mentor.*

As soon as Thane noticed Gidin's arrival, he stepped away from Jasper, beckoning Gidion in with an elegant wave of his fingers. "Gidion, welcome. This is Jasper." He touched Jasper lightly on the arm as he introduced him. "Jasper, say hello to your new classmate."

Gidion saluted Jasper warmly, but the other only nodded coolly in response.

"Take this bench," Thane said, indicating one opposite Jasper's.

Gidion did as he was told, his fingers curling around its edges.

Thane took position behind the teacher's bench and spoke in a lecturing tone. "Today, I'll show you how to refine the amount of heat you produce in your heatstones. In the past, you've adjusted heat by using different types and sizes of stone. But this time we want to set up the weaves to produce a precise level of heat which is only partially dependent on the stone's size and type. Can either of you tell me a use for this?"

Jasper jumped in to answer before Gidion had even opened his mouth. "To produce heat for floors. It's preferable to use larger stone slabs for floors, but obviously you don't want them to be very hot. And some types of stone are more suitable for floors than others as they don't wear quickly."

"Excellent, Jasper," Thane said.

Jasper ducked his head, his mouth curving with pleasure.

"And the ability to produce different levels of heat will then lead us to the most advanced form of heatstone making, which is ...?"

"Heatstones that produce different amounts of heat using a linked activation stone," Jasper said.

"Exactly. But that's apprentice-level work." Thane glanced at Gidion as he said this. "We'll start with medium-sized soaprock today. It's easiest to work with."

"Jasper, come help me." Magister Thane went to a chest at the back of the room and unlocked it.

Jasper went to him like a pleased puppy. Gidion gnawed the inside of his lip, feeling like the outsider and not much liking it.

"Take two of the medium and give one to Gidion," Thane instructed as they both bent over the chest, heads close together. Thane took another stone for himself.

Jasper set a thin slab of grey rock down on Gidion's workbench. It was similar in size to those Gidion had worked with before, although he'd never tried this particular exercise.

"Before we continue, can either of you tell me the particular advantages of using soaprock for heatstones?" Thane said.

Gidion quickly put his hand up and Thane nodded at him. "Soaprock holds heat well and transfers it quickly. The weaves are also more stable than with basalt, for example, so it's less likely to lose its power."

"Good, Gidion. And who can tell me how long on average soaprock keeps its weaves for?"

This time Jasper got in first. "Ten to fifteen years, depending on the skill of the artefactor."

"And if we compare that to basalt?"

Jasper and Gidion both put their hands up, but Thane pointed to Jasper. "Seven to eight years before it needs to be redone," the youth said.

Gidion gripped the workbench harder. He was certain his hand had gone up first. Was Thane favoring Jasper?

"Very good, Jasper. Now, turning to the task at hand—you already know how to manipulate the pattern of threads in the stone so that rubbing the stone's surface creates heat. But over the coming month, we're going to work on finer alterations to the pattern to create three gradations of heat. If you show yourself able to do it, you'll pass the Advanced Artefaction section of the Selection Trial.

"Come close to me and watch what I do. First, see which threads I choose."

Gidion and Jasper crowded around him as he put on a pair of odd-looking spectacles that gave him a bug-eyed look. Gidion let the threads come into view so that he could sense which ones Thane selected.

"So, Jasper, do you notice anything different from the usual?" Thane asked.

The other boy squinted, answering slowly. "Erm, yes, I think so."

Gidion shook his head, knowing Jasper to be categorically wrong and wondering why the pits Thane was directing all his questions at him. But even as this thought popped into his mind, Thane invited him to give his opinion. "They're exactly the same threads," he said. "We'll just need to weave them differently."

"Yes, Gidion, very good. You're absolutely right," Thane replied.

Jasper scowled and Gidion repressed a pleased smile.

Thane continued with his explanations, demonstrating how to reweave the threads and set them vibrating to the right frequency. He repeated the demonstration a handful of times, then had them practice on their own stones.

"Gidion, take these goggles," he said, coming to him with a pair of spectacles like those he'd been wearing.

"What are they for?"

"To protect your eyes in case the stone explodes."

Gidion had never had a stone explode, hadn't even considered the possibility of it. But he took the goggles and put them on. They were made of thick glass that had been altered by a weave to make it stronger. Wearing the goggles made him feel stupid, but Thane and Jasper were wearing them too, so he tried to put it out of his mind.

While they worked, Thane moved between his bench and Jasper's, making corrections and offering advice. It was extremely draining, and a steady burn had built up in Gidion's chest by the end of the lesson. However, he succeeded in approximating the level of heat in the magister's stone, unlike Jasper, who was still struggling with the exact heat levels.

"Right, time for lunch. Good work both of you," Thane said. "Gidion, stay back a moment."

It was clearly an instruction to Jasper to leave, and Gidion caught a burst of unease from him. The other youth walked out stiffly, not even saying goodbye. He smiled to himself.

"You did well today," Thane said. "I'm confident you'll pass the Advanced Artefaction portion of the Trial."

"Thank you, Magister." Gidion paused, nervous about annoying Thane with his next question. But it had been pressing on him with ever-growing urgency. "I was wondering when I'll be able to prepare for the Selection Tournament?"

"Don't worry, we'll get to it," Thane said. "It's just not the priority right now. You've fought Riftlanders—and worse—and survived. The other students have never tested their skills outside an arena."

But while Gidion felt pride at Thane's belief in him, he wasn't satisfied with the answer. "I don't know the rules or anything, though." What he really wanted to say was that he wanted to win the Tournament so he could study under Arianna Velden. But he could guess how Thane would react to that.

"As I said, we'll get to it. Classes end in a few weeks, and then I'll be able to give you my full attention," Thane replied. "But now I do have to prepare for another one."

Gidion gritted his teeth. He was getting the impression that Thane was deliberately avoiding his warcraft preparation. But the magister was already turning away from him, and Gidion decided against pressing him further. So he left, intending to find a quiet place in the Water Garden where he could at least practice the fighting drills he already knew.

To his surprise, he found Jasper standing by the levitator. Deciding he'd rather be on the youth's good side, he smiled and raised his hand in a wave. "Hey, were you waiting for me?"

"You going down?" Jasper didn't return Gidion's smile.

He kept his tone cheerful all the same. "To the ground floor."

But it had no warming effect on Jasper. "I'll come with you." He pressed his palm to summon the levitator, his posture stiff.

Gidion made another attempt to defuse the tension. "Good to meet another artefactor today. I'd never known anyone else who could make heatstones."

"First time I've ever had anyone share my class, too."

Jasper's tone was neutral, but Gidion sensed confusion and worry from him. "I'm honored, then," he said with a grin.

But Jasper didn't relax. "So what's the deal with you and Magister Thane?"

The levitator arrived, giving Gidion a few seconds to consider his answer while they stepped inside and sent it down. "He's helping me prepare for the Selection Trial," he said at last.

Jasper's eyebrows rose. "Thane doesn't normally do that kind of thing. You must have known him before?"

Gidion had already prepared this answer with Thane. "He knew my father, who sent me to him when it was time for me to study."

"Oh? What was your father's name?"

"Varn Jameson."

"Ranger, then?" Jasper said.

"How did you guess?"

"Process of elimination," Jasper replied. And now there was a trace of a smile, or more of a smirk. "Why didn't you come here before to train?"

"We lived in the Federation. My father trained me himself. But now I plan to study warcraft here as an apprentice."

"Not artefaction?" Surprise from Jasper, but also relief.

Gidion shrugged. "Thane wants me to do artefaction, but my dream has always been to study warcraft." The levitator reached the bottom of the shaft, and they stepped out and walked to the tower exit. "Thane still hasn't let me practice for the Selection Tournament, though."

They'd reached the huge doors leading out of the tower, and Jasper was silent until they'd passed through them. "We have a sparring class this afternoon," he said. "You won't be able to join in, but you can watch."

"Really? They'll let me do that?"

"The arena is open to anyone," Jasper replied. "If you can get into other towers, I don't see any reason why you can't get in there too."

"I have a letter that gives me access," Gidion said.

Jasper gave him a tight smile. "See you later, then." He marched toward the Seekers' Tower. Gidion watched him, puzzling over his attitude throughout their conversation. At first, he'd seemed threatened, but toward the end, condescending. What he hadn't been, despite his invitation, was particularly friendly. But maybe that was just how he was. And it did provide an opening for Gidion to get to know some of the other initiates he'd be up against in the Selection Tournament. So he decided that, on the whole, it had been a positive outcome and went with a lighter step toward the Water Garden.

Chapter 14

The arena was just beyond the Seekers' Tower, surrounded by high walls, with only two entrances on the Spire side. One of these was for fighters or students, the other for spectators. Gidion handed his letter to the man standing watch at the latter entrance, then passed through a dark tunnel before climbing a set of steps that took him out into the seating area.

It was an impressive sight, rows of seats ringing the oval-shaped arena, with room for thousands. No one else was watching, and he felt self-conscious as he made his way to the first row, where he had the best view. The initiates filed out for their lesson, dressed in tunic and trousers rather than robes, wearing leather armor that covered their head, torso, and legs. It made them look like regular soldiers. There was one key difference—every one of them had a battlestaff, although none had a focus stone in it.

Jasper caught Gidion's gaze and nodded in acknowledgment. A large-boned, curly-haired girl standing next to him said something, her eyes also on Gidion. Then they both laughed, leaving Gidion to wonder what had caused them such amusement.

Shortly after, the teacher walked out, and the sight of her caused Gidion to straighten with excitement. She was very tall, with auburn hair bound in a tight knot at the back of her head and a long, fine nose.

This was exactly how he'd heard Arianna Velden being described. But if the initiates were being taught by the Guardian herself, why had Thane not mentioned it? He sat on the edge of his seat, watching intently, as she set them to running laps before putting them through loosening exercises. Then she demonstrated a partner drill where one person shot unpowered lightbolts and the other blocked them using a shield powered by a focus stone on their wrist. Gidion had never seen a wrist shield like this and wished he had his own. It gave them a lot more flexibility as the shield didn't have to be powered by the focus stone in the staff, which could be used for fighting instead.

Gidion noted that Jasper was the most competent of them all. The Guardian, if it *was* her, picked him out often to demonstrate a drill and always regarded him admiringly. His movements were efficient and graceful, and he always seemed to be a fraction quicker than the others, whether he was attacking or defending. *He's the one for me to beat.*

He was so intent on watching them spar that, at first, he didn't notice someone was approaching him. It was only when he heard her voice that he realized she was there.

"Trying to pick up some tricks?"

His head swung around, his heart lurching at the sound of the voice. Yes, it was Nessa. Her black hair was done into tiny braids, gathered together at the nape of her neck in a leather thong, and she wore a white shirt and breeches like a man. The top laces of the shirt were loose, displaying smooth, tanned skin. As for the breeches, they did nothing to hide the curves of her hips and legs. He reminded himself that she was working for Malai, but it cooled his desire only a little. "What are you doing here?" he croaked.

"Got myself a job with the Spire guards," she said with a shrug.

Gidion blinked at her. How had she managed that so quickly?

"I'm actually quite good with sword and spear," she said with a wink.

He cleared his throat. "And what – they just let you join?"

"All you need is a letter of reference from a weaver and prove that your skills are up to it," Nessa replied. "I had no trouble with either."

This put Gidion on alert. So Thane and his father had been right. Malai did have someone here. "Who's the weaver?"

Nessa just tapped her nose. "I can't reveal all my secrets."

Gidion decided to switch tack. "Are you spying for her?"

Nessa laughed. "Malai, you mean? I suppose I am. But mostly, I'm here to help you."

"Help me how?"

"Like I said, I can teach you more about your Chelaki powers." She tilted her head. "Although I can also take you to your mother if you want."

Did he want that? No, he still didn't trust Nessa. Malai even less. This could all be a huge con. "I'm not leaving the Spire."

Nessa shrugged. "Fine."

Despite his wariness, Gidion couldn't stop himself from asking about the Chelaki. "I've never heard of them before." No need to tell her what Thane had said. In fact, better not to, so he could decide if she was telling him the truth.

"No one has heard of them before," Nessa replied.

"Why not?"

"Because the Eleusians and Vycenians banded together to wipe them out five centuries ago," she snorted. "And it seems that no one wanted to be reminded of their people's part in the genocide, so there are no histories about the Chelaki, nor about the genocide. That's what I've gathered, anyway. Maybe you'll find more information in the library here. I'm certainly hoping to."

"If they were all wiped out, then how is it possible that Malai is Chelaki?" And that he was by extension, if what Nessa said was true about his relationship with Malai.

"Some elkiri—Chelaki mages—escaped the genocide and traveled to the Riftlands. That's why you and I have certain powers in common."

"You're Chelaki too?"

"Only partly, like you."

Gidion thought of the surprise his features had always caused—so unusual, like no one he'd ever seen. And now that he looked at Nessa, there was a similarity in the shape of their eyes and nose. "Are you related to me?" he asked, dreading the answer.

"No, thank goodness." Nessa looked out at the training initiates. "So, are you doing the Selection Trial?"

"You know about that?" he said in surprise.

"It's the only way you can become an apprentice, right?"

Gidion nodded.

"And there's a tournament?"

He nodded again.

"I can help you train for it too if you like."

"So you can weave?"

But Nessa shook her head. "I can't do lightbolts if that's what you mean. I've tried to learn, but I just seem to be missing something. The type of thread manipulation you can do is linked to your ancestry. You're lucky, you've got Chelaki, Vycenian, and Eleusian blood in you."

"Eleusian?" Gidion said, surprised.

"Ilis'Elkir was half Eleusian. Which makes everything that more ironic."

"Who's Ilis'Elkir?"

Ness's eyebrows rose almost to her hairline. "Oh, you don't even know that."

"What?" Gidion said, becoming annoyed. She seemed to like being obtuse.

"That was the Ilk Lord's name." Nessa paused. "Elkir means skyrider. You know they used to fly on these great birds called drakiri? Before the Slaughter, of course. I would have loved that. Riding on the drakiri, obviously, not the Slaughter."

But Gidion wasn't paying attention. His mind was fumbling with her earlier words, trying to decipher the implications. "Are you saying I'm related to the Ilk Lord?"

"Ah, so you don't know about him and Malai either?"

"Please, just tell me," he said, trying and failing to keep the snappiness out of his tone.

She raised her hands, palms out in surrender, the smile falling from her face. "I'm sorry. I realize it's a lot to take in."

Gidion controlled himself with an effort and waited for her to continue.

"So your grandmother—Malai, I mean—was a kind of wife to Ilis," she said. "The Chelaki don't have the same concept of marriage that we do. In fact, they don't even have the concept of fidelity to one partner, whether you're a man or a woman. Which I think is quite enlightened, given it's usually only men who get that privilege."

"So, you're saying that ..." Gidion was still trying to tussle with the idea, hardly able to credit Nessa's words.

"Yes, the Ilk Lord is your great-grandfather." Nessa regarded him intently.

Gidion said nothing. Was she playing a game with him? He wasn't descended from the Ilk Lord. He couldn't be. *Then why can I do what I can do?*

"I'm telling you the truth," she said, again showing a disconcerting ability to read his thoughts. "Why do you think Malai is so keen to get you on side?"

"I've no idea," he said. Had his father known? His mother? "What *does* she want of me?"

"She wants you to inherit his powers."

"The Ilk Lord's powers?" he said incredulously.

"I mean, you have them already, technically. It's the memories she wants you to have, so you can learn everything that he knew."

"How would that work?" he asked, both curious and repulsed.

"He left his memories in a memory stone. It's a Chelaki ritual, a bit like the Eleusian soulbindings. But while Eleusian Keepers bind the souls of others to theirs to access their memories, the Chelaki put their consciousness into a stone to pass on their knowledge to blood descendants."

"I don't want his memories," Gidion said. "He was evil. He killed millions."

"Well, not exactly," Nessa said. "I mean, fewer people died in the Ilk War than in the Federation's Unification War. He used Ilk, not human soldiers. And most battles were finished before they even began."

"But Teleriol," Gidion said.

"Teleriol was destroyed because of the magic of the Final Hundred," Nessa said. "It wasn't his doing."

Gidion couldn't argue with that. It was well known that the power they'd summoned against the Ilk Lord and his army had torn a hole so great in the Tapestry that it had sunk the continent and all its people, leaving an impassible maelstrom in its place. "The Gloom," he said instead. "It destabilized the Tapestry so much it made the cataclysm more likely."

Nessa shrugged. "That's true. But still, don't you think it's a more effective and less bloody way to conquer?"

Gidion's mouth worked. Nothing good had come out of the Ilk War. To even suggest ...

Nessa's tone hardened as she continued, "Nobody calls the Federation evil even though tens of thousands died in the Unification War—or rather, nobody but those who suffer under its yoke."

She was right. Why *did* no one talk about the price of the Unification War? He'd lived in the Federation half his life, knew many of the stories about the battles fought. Knew how its officials were often resented. But it had brought peace to South Myrna where there had always been war.

Would it be a price worth paying? To have all the Ilk Lord's memories, some of which must be dark, terrible, in exchange for power? Power to impose peace if he willed it? To live his life in the open and free of control at last?

"I don't blame you for being unsure. I'm not sure I'd want the memories either," Nessa said. "But even if you don't want them, I can still teach you to use the powers you inherited from him."

"Like the stun power?"

"And how to splice the Tapestry."

Again, Gidion decided to pretend he didn't know, see if her words matched with Thane's. "What's that?"

In answer, Nessa vanished from sight and reappeared a few paces to his right.

"How *do* you do that?" he said.

"I can show you, like I said."

Gidion had to admit that this would be a great thing to master. But he was still suspicious. "And what do you want in return?"

"From you, just a willingness to learn."

Again she smiled, showing dimples to rival Thane's, and his chest ached. But he reminded himself that she was quite openly working for an Ilk mage. "Thanks for the offer," he said. "But I think I'll just stick to my weaving lessons for now. I have a lot of catching up to do before the Trial." And that was true.

Nessa shrugged. "Up to you."

The initiates seemed to have finished their class, for Arianna Velden was leaving and the others were chatting to one another. Gidion leaped up to follow her, but to his surprise, Jasper came up to them.

Jasper flicked a glance at Nessa before focusing his attention on Gidion. "Fancy a spar?"

"Isn't there another class?" Gidion said.

"Not for an hour."

Gidion hesitated. He wanted to see how he measured up against Jasper, but he didn't want to miss the opportunity to talk to Arianna Velden. And there was Nessa.

"Go for it," Nessa said. "I'll be here."

Thinking it might be a chance to impress her, Gidion decided to accept Jasper's offer.

"Come on, then, and we'll get you a staff and armor."

Gidion looked for a way to get into the arena from the seats.

"Just hop over."

Indeed the barricade separating the seats from the arena was very low, and soon Gidion was crossing the hard-packed dirt next to Jasper. A handful of Jasper's classmates were still there, watching Gidion with undisguised curiosity. Gidion caught the eye of the girl who'd been laughing with Jasper at the beginning of the class. She was attractive, with a button nose and dark hair bound in a ponytail, loose strands kept away from her face with a yellow headband.

"Hello," Gidion said, waving at them.

A few of them started giggling and nudging each other.

His unease growing, Gidion followed Jasper through an arched doorway that led under the seating area and then down a passageway that ran along the perimeter. But they only took a few steps before Jasper was pushing open a door. The room beyond turned out to be an armory. It was filled with racks of blunted weapons—battlestaffs of various types, but also swords and regular spears.

Gidion picked a battlestaff with a curving blade that was similar to his own. Then Jasper took him down to the end of the room, where various pieces of leather armor were stacked. "Take your pick," he said. "They have every size."

"I can do without," Gidion said. He'd never worn armor in his life and hadn't any idea how to put it on.

Jasper eyed him. "I'll help you."

"It's not that ..." Gidion said, although it was.

"They don't let us spar without armor," Jasper said. "Otherwise, I'd be perfectly happy to break your bones. So, come on, let's choose what you need."

Jasper had a keen eye for size, and most of his selections were spot on the first time around. Soon, Gidion was trooping back out, covered head to toe in boiled leather. It was uncomfortable and restrictive, not to mention hot.

When they entered the arena, Gidion discovered that some of Jasper's classmates had stayed behind to watch. Jasper gave them a thumbs up as he marched into one of the fighting circles. They cheered him on while casting amused looks at Gidion.

Disconcerted but determined to prove his ability, Gidion squared off against Jasper. They circled one another, feinting and testing, looking for gaps in the other's defenses. Gidion knew Jasper was good, had seen how well he did against the others, but he felt confident he'd find a way through. He'd always loved sparring with his father and was able to beat him more often than not.

But to his shock, Jasper landed such a fast blow against his mid-section that he barely even saw it coming. He tried to counterattack, but too slowly, and the other boy easily evaded it. His next attempt only gave Jasper another opening as he pirouetted out of the way and struck Gidion from the side. Gidion's confidence drained away. Jasper's style was completely different to Conal's, making it hard for Gidion to guess where he'd strike next. He realized how limited his training had been, how much he'd relied on Conal's predictability to succeed against him.

Finally, he managed to land a glancing blow against Jasper's shoulder. But the other responded by swinging at him with blinding speed, staff whirling in his hands. Gidion ducked as it whistled over his head. He'd barely gulped in a breath before Jasper attacked again, blade streaking down. Gidion parried the blow but had no time to counterattack before Jasper was sweeping at his legs. He jumped, the blade skirting the ground just beneath his feet. Jasper spun the staff so that the end of it crunched into Gidion's hipbone, just below the chest protector.

Gidion bit back a cry of pain, but Jasper gave him no time to recover, thrusting the blade at his mid-section. He leaped backward, the tip of the blade just scraping his armor. Jasper pressed forward, using his superior speed to full advantage—sweep, chop, thrust, side-step, chop, thrust—a relentless barrage that gave Gidion no time to think, never mind formulate an attack. He found himself increasingly backing away, his arms and shoulders aching from parrying so many blows.

Then came a jarring strike with the staff that left Gidion's right arm numb from wrist to shoulder. Jasper was on him in a flash, ripping Gidion's staff out of his grip, then swiping out a leg to send him stumbling off balance. He swung his staff around, the blade coming to rest against Gidion's neck.

"I yield," Gidion said, furious with himself.

Jasper smirked and lifted the blade away, and Gidion went to pick up his staff. But as he crouched down, Jasper's foot connected with his behind, sending him onto his face. Dust filled his eyes, nose, and mouth, making him sneeze.

"You fight like a novice," Jasper hissed.

Tears of rage came to Gidion's eyes, and he blinked them away furiously as his hand closed around the staff.

Jasper was already walking off, laughing with his friends, who loudly talked about how inept Gidion had been. He glared at their backs, breathing heavily. How dare they humiliate him in this way? He'd make them pay. He'd show them.

"I'd advise against doing anything rash."

Gidion jumped, whirled around to find Nessa standing nearby. He hadn't even heard her approach.

"You fell for a pretty obvious trap, I'm afraid."

His humiliation burned hotter. She must think him pathetic.

"I've heard Jasper is one of the best staff fighters to come through the ranks," Nessa continued. "Ever."

"I need to be better than him." He felt tearful and then angry at his weakness, and averted his gaze from hers.

"Why? You only need to pass if you want to become an apprentice, and you're easily good enough for that."

Gidion blinked back his tears and turned to face her again. "Because I want to specialize in warcraft."

Nessa folded her arms. "Do you need to beat him for that? Is there only one spot?"

"I do if I want to be guaranteed a position as a warcraft apprentice. And especially if I want to have Arianna Velden as mentor."

"Well, I can help train you for it if you want," Nessa said.

"I've got Thane," he said sullenly. Apart from the fact he didn't trust Nessa, he didn't want her to show him up.

"I've no doubt he's a good teacher," Nessa said. "But there'll be things I can teach you that he can't. Remember, I've had a weapon in my hands since I could walk. And Thane strikes me as the more scholarly type."

Several contradictory impulses warred inside him. Strong was the instinct not to let her in. But almost as strong was the desire to know her better. Plus, she could be his key to beating Jasper and the other initiates. Not just them, but Malai too. How ironic, though, to accept the help of a possible Ilk mage to beat another. He also had a fear that Nessa's true purpose was to humiliate him further. He didn't think he could bear that.

"You've nothing to lose and everything to gain by accepting my help," Nessa said. "If Malai or I had wanted to kill you, we'd have done so by now."

He'd already considered this. "But what do you really want from me?"

"Like I said, we just want you to come into your full powers, return to your family."

It was all so neat. So helpful. Far too good to be true. But how much did he really have to lose by learning from her? If he mastered the same powers Malai was able to use against him, he might figure out how to beat her. And he could keep his distance from Nessa, learn from her without befriending her. "Fine," he said. "I'll take your help. But can we start with the warcraft training?"

Nessa beamed in delight, and despite his concerns about her, seeing her happy couldn't help but make him feel happy. "We can start right now," she said. "I don't have anywhere to be for a while."

Gidion only had books waiting for him, and he doubted he'd be able to concentrate after the drubbing he'd received. "No time like the present."

"Show me where I can get a weapon?"

Gidion led her into the armory. She picked a battlestaff much like his, regarding it with curiosity. "A bit like a poleax," she said, examining the blade at the top. "We trained with these in the legions, although I much prefer a sword."

Then she went to get some armor, asking Gidion to help her fasten it. Being so close to her made his pulse beat harder. He could see the individual pores on her nose, the silver flecks in her violet eyes. And he could smell her. Vanilla and musk, overlaid by leather.

They returned to the arena, where she took a position opposite him. "To start with, you could be more efficient with your swings," she said. "You're leaving yourself open to a fast thrust under the arm. Attack me, and I'll show you."

Gidion did as she said and found the tip of her blade against his armpit.

"Keep your elbows tucked in closer to your body to protect yourself."

Gidion nodded, and she had him repeat the swing several times until she was satisfied.

After that, she put him through another drill that he'd never done before. By the end, he was panting and sweating, but she barely seemed winded.

"You need to run more," she said, a hand on her hip as she regarded him critically.

"What?"

"Your stamina," she said. "If you want to build it up, you need to run—a lot. Come on, we're going to do fifty laps to finish."

Fifty! He began to unbuckle his breastplate.

"What are you doing?"

"Taking my armor off."

"Don't be ridiculous," she said. "What's the point if you can't run in armor?"

Gidion flushed. But he wasn't going to give her the satisfaction of a retort, so he just started running. By the twentieth lap his lungs were burning. By the thirtieth, his legs were wobbling. By the fortieth he was leaning against the fence, a stitch in his side, his breathing so hoarse he could hear nothing else.

Nessa, infuriatingly, did the full fifty, even picking up the pace after he dropped out.

"You need to run every day," she said when she was done. "You should be comfortably able to do a hundred laps if you want to have any hope of keeping up with the other initiates."

Gidion said nothing, still breathing too heavily, sweat pouring down his face.

Her lips curved into a half smile. "I'll get you some water." She went to the fountain at the side of the arena and returned with a full skin.

He took it from her in relief and guzzled fully half of it. Water had never tasted so delicious.

"Do you have anywhere to be?" Nessa said.

Gidion shook his head, handing the skin back to her.

"Want to get something to eat? I'm starved."

Gidion agreed eagerly, so they returned their equipment to the armory and went out to the food stalls in the main grounds to buy some meat pasties. On Nessa's suggestion, they took them to the Rose

Garden, where they found a bench to sit on, surrounded by the heady fragrance of the flowers.

"You said before that you're not related to Malai. But how did you meet her?" Gidion said, crunching into his pastie. A rich flavor of gravy and venison burst in his mouth, making him suddenly ravenous.

"I told you before that I come from a farmstead on the border with the Riftlands?"

"I remember."

"We've suffered Riftlander raids for decades, but the Federation has always seemed happy enough to take our taxes while doing nothing to protect us against them," Nessa said bitterly. "My brother Kye and I decided to become legionaries at first, thinking we might be able to help that way. We were only sixteen. But we discovered that they preferred to station their soldiers away from home. I think to make sure no one ever got too friendly and took the notion to rebel. But if that was the case, it backfired."

"How so?"

"We quit the army a year later and decided to form a resistance to try to free Kharas from the Federation so we'd have control over our own soldiers again." Nessa cracked out a short laugh. "Yes, I know it sounds crazy. We were very young and stupid and thought somehow we'd be enough. Plus, Kye and I had both come into our powers. We were untrained, of course, and the stun strike was unreliable, but it helped us in a few sticky situations. Malai heard rumors about us and came to offer us help."

"She's *helping* you?" Gidion said, confused.

"She's not the terrible person you think," Nessa said.

"She's an Ilk mage," Gidion said, although with less conviction than before.

"The Ilk are just a weapon," Nessa said with a dismissive wave. "And anyway, she can't actually make Ilk. The only person who could do that was the Ilk Lord, and he's gone."

"But she had Ilk!"

"The only Ilk remaining from the last war," she replied. "Malai keeps them as bodyguards. She has her children studying how to make them. But none can channel the prime force. She's certain you can, though."

"What's the prime force?"

Nessa gave him a surprised look. But for once, she didn't try to taunt him with his ignorance. "Pure chaos. Destruction and creation together. It's where the Tapestry came from in the first place. The llk Lord—he could channel it and give a kind of life to the Ilk."

"How do you know all this?"

"Malai told me."

"Is that what she really wants me for, then?"

"To make Ilk? Yes, I'd say that's part of it. But it's not just that—you're her family, Gidion. And believe it or not, she loves her family fiercely. Even if some of them are—how do I put it—unusual."

The emphasis she placed on the final word pricked his curiosity. But he was more concerned with the first part of her sentence. "I'm not making Ilk," he said. "Those things are ..." He remembered the terror they had provoked in him. The sense that everything he did was futile.

"Let's not think about Ilk now," Nessa said.

But Gidion wasn't finished. "You said Malai is helping you against the Federation. How?"

"I can't tell you very much about it. But she's going to help us get rid of the rats forever." Nessa's fingers closed into a fist.

"I'm sick of not being told everything," Gidion muttered.

"If you come with me, you can ask Malai yourself," Nessa replied. "We're not trying to keep secrets from *you*. But we do need to be sure that no one leaks our plans to the enemy."

"And my mother? Is she part of all this?"

"She's helping too," Nessa said.

"Why doesn't she come for me?" Gidion asked. "Presumably, she knows I'm here."

"That's not her decision to make," Nessa said.

"What do you mean?"

Nessa sighed. "Malai doesn't really let her leave—after what she did, taking you away, hiding you."

Gidion frowned. "That seems harsh."

"If Malai gets you back, I think she'd be open to letting Seila go."

Gidion pondered her words for a few minutes. It sounded like a trap, though. A lie to make him go and try to save his mother. "I'm not going to Malai," he said. Not yet. Not until he could figure out the truth of it all.

"As I've said, your choice. But will you tell me more about you?" Nessa asked.

The softness in her eyes melted him, and he found himself telling her all about his wanderings around the northern states of the Federation with his father. She knew the land well, having traveled to different parts as a legionnaire. Even though she occasionally teased him, he enjoyed talking to her. She was quick-witted and observant, with a sarcastic jibe always on the tip of her tongue. And she made him laugh, something he seemed to do little of these days.

The bell rang the twelfth hour of the day, and Nessa said she had to leave. "I'm on shift soon in the Tower of Succor," she said, referring to the spire that contained the infirmary. It served both weavers and those wealthy outsiders who could afford the high prices charged there for treatment. “But shall we meet again tomorrow? I’m free at midday, but I think the arena is busy all day,” she said.

“Maybe we could meet in the Water Garden? I know a bit that no one ever goes into,” Gidion replied.

She agreed, and he watched her regretfully as she walked off. Their conversation had made him feel more connected with her. And his other senses gave him no hint that she’d lied about anything. Plus, her backstory made sense. Could it be that Malai wasn’t as evil as all that after all? Despite what his father had said? At the thought of his father, he experienced a pang. Captured by Riftlanders, but was he still alive? They didn’t seem like the type to take prisoners.

And then there was the fact of his mother. But he didn’t know what was worse—discovering that Nessa was lying and she was dead, or knowing that he’d mourned her pointlessly all these years.

Chapter 15

Thane returned to his rooms to find Gidion poring over a book in the library. At the sound of the door opening, the boy whirled around to face him. As jumpy as a rabbit—had he broken Thane's commands again or was this his general state? The latter wouldn't be surprising given all he'd been through. But then, neither would the former. "How have you been?" he asked, watching him carefully for clues.

Several expressions flitted over Gidion's face, too quickly for Thane to catch them. "Just reading the books you set, Magister."

Thane noticed a graze on Gidion's cheek. "Did you have an accident?"

Gidion flinched as if Thane had struck him, his fingertips going to the cut. "Jasper and I had a sparring bout."

So, they were meeting outside class. He'd been curious to see if that would happen, and if so, what form the relationship would take. "I hope you took sensible protections."

Gidion nodded, but his golden eyes were clouded. "We sparred in the arena. Jasper got me some armor."

"Jasper's idea, or yours?"

"Jasper's."

Gidion was angry but trying to hide it. Thane could guess what had happened. "And how did you find it?" The red suffusing Gidion's cheeks was all the confirmation he needed.

"I ... learned some things," the boy said in a choked voice.

So, Jasper had trounced him. This was good. Gidion was overly fixated on studying warcraft. Perhaps, he'd be put off by it now.

"But I need to practice more," Gidion said, giving him a pleading look.

Thane wouldn't be easily swayed. "We'll go out together soon," he said. "But it's late now, you should rest. The books can wait for tomorrow."

Gidion frowned, opened his mouth, then closed it again. Thane noticed he often did this, was used to swallowing whatever it was he really wanted to say. But the restraint cost him. Thane could see it in the rigid set of his jaw and shoulders.

Thane went to him and put a hand on his shoulder. "Don't worry, Gidion. I'm with you all the way. We'll find your father and this Ilk mage of yours. I won't let her hurt you."

But if anything, Gidion looked even more at war with himself.

"Is there something you need to tell me?" Thane prodded.

Gidion's mouth worked, but then he shook his head. "It's been a long day. You're right. I should rest."

The boy was hiding something, but what? Frustration welled in him. But he just smiled. "Very well. We'll talk in the morning."

The following day, Thane summoned Jasper to his workroom in the Tower of Artefaction. If Gidion wouldn't tell him what had happened, Jasper surely would. "I believe you and Gidion had a sparring match yesterday?"

A smile crept onto Jasper's face. "We did, after class."

"And how did he do?"

Jasper's mouth twisted into a sneer. It made him ugly, and Thane was reminded of how little he liked the youth. "He's no match for me."

"Indeed, few are."

Jasper looked pleased at Thane's words, but the sneer didn't quite leave his face.

"I'd like you to keep an eye on him for me," Thane said.

Jasper looked even more pleased. So easy to manipulate. "What am I looking for?

"Nothing in particular," Thane said. "I just want to know what he gets up to, who he talks to."

"He was talking to a Spire guard while he was watching the class," Jasper said instantly.

Thane raised an eyebrow. "Which one?"

"She's new. I don't know her name, and I've never seen her before."

Now Thane was all ears. "New, you say? Describe her."

"Clearly from South Myrna, near black hair, attractive if you're into women." Jasper gave him a knowing look, his lashes fluttering.

Thane quirked his lips into a smile—not a real one, just enough to show complicity. "Did you see the color of her eyes, by any chance?"

Jasper frowned. "I didn't get close enough."

"Would you be able to point her out to me if you saw her again?"

"Almost certainly. She stands out."

"Excellent. Be sure you do. Now off you get, I know you have lessons in a few minutes."

Jasper left, and Thane waited a few minutes to ensure their paths wouldn't cross before making his way to the administrative offices. He walked briskly, his blood singing. If this new guard was who he thought she was, things had gotten very interesting indeed.

He entered a room filled with rows of desks—scribes and attendants busy behind each one. Thankfully, he knew the man whose responsibility it was to catalog everyone who officially resided in the Spire—a balding Arindeler with a cheery aspect. "Good afternoon, Carrick," he said. "How have you been?"

Carrick broke into his usual beaming smile. "Hello, Magister. I'm doing alright, doing alright."

"And the baby?"

Carrick's smile widened. "Walking now, would you believe it?"

"It happens quickly, doesn't it?" Thane said. Not that he knew much about children. It was just something he heard other people say.

"She'll have flown the nest before I know it," Carrick said with a shake of his head. But then he sobered. "What can I help you with today?"

"I'm looking for some information."

"Anything you want, Magister." Carrick smiled, showing a broken front tooth.

Not for the first time, Thane wondered why Carrick didn't get it fixed in the Tower of Succor. He had the right as an attendant. Trying to ignore the distracting sight, Thane said, "Have you had any new guards sign up in the past week?"

Surprise flitted across Carrick's face, but he said nothing. Just went to a shelf and removed a huge tome that he set down carefully on his desk. His eyes narrowed as he scanned the lists of names and dates. "Yes, there was one who came only yesterday."

Thane's pulse quickened. "Her name?"

"Nessa Ne'Teele."

The same woman who'd been in Tine! He fought to appear calm. "And who sponsored her?"

"Bailin Cavelish."

Interesting. Bailin was known to be a friend of Arianna Velden despite the fact that Cavelish was one of the minor Families and hers was one of the most prestigious. "Do you know much about the Cavelishes?" Thane said.

"Not really, Magister," Carrick said regretfully. "But I can get the Register of Families?"

"Yes, that would be helpful."

Carrick got up and returned with another large tome.

"Can I take it somewhere to read?" Thane said.

Carrick pointed at an empty desk next to his. "Sara's not here today."

"My thanks." Thane took the book to the desk and turned to the entries under "C." He quickly learned that the Cavelishes had only been established after the Ruin. But when he looked into it in more detail, he discovered that it was because a Cavelish had married the only surviving woman of another minor family, the Ninevals. By all accounts, the Cavelish was a weaver of common birth, but for some reason, the Nineval had accepted to change her surname to his. Unusual among the Families, where the name of the most prominent Family in a pairing was almost always retained. Although, as he recalled, in the immediate aftermath of the Ruin, when people blamed weavers for the catastrophe, it was less common. More than one Family had thought it sensible to become invisible, at least for a time.

He returned the book to Carrick and left in a state of distraction. Should be speak to Bailin directly, ask him why he'd sponsored this Nessa as a guard? But he didn't want the man to know Thane was onto him. What he first needed to do was confirm that this Nessa was indeed the same woman who had appeared in Tine. And that shouldn't be terribly hard to do.

Chapter 16

The next day, Gidion took his books to the arena in the hope he might see Arianna Velden again and have the opportunity to introduce himself to her. He was in luck, because the Initiate 4s were doing a sparring class, and she was in charge again. He watched intently, trying to fix in his memory the strengths and weaknesses of the students. But it was to Jasper his eyes often went. He had to find a way to beat the little prick.

When the class ended, he determinedly hopped over the barriers and jogged over to Arianna, pretending Jasper wasn't there. She was already leaving the arena, so he ran faster, calling her, "Guardian!"

She paused and turned to him with a frown.

He stopped before her, panting. "I'm sorry, I ... just wanted to introduce myself."

She looked bemused. "Indeed?"

Gidion could hear Jasper sniggering with his friends, but determinedly plowed on. "I'm doing the Selection Trial this year, and I'm going to specialize in warcraft."

"Good for you," she said, turning away.

"I plan to request you as a mentor," he blurted out.

At this, Arianna stilled, eyebrows arching into a triangle above her nose. "And who are you, exactly?"

"My name's Gidion. Gidion ... Jameson."

"Jameson," Arianna repeated to herself thoughtfully. Then, her expression cleared. "Varn Jameson's boy?"

"That's right," Gidion said, relieved she'd heard of his father.

"Well, Gidion, I'd advise you stick to ranging like your father. I only take on one apprentice." A tight, dismissive smile.

"I could be that apprentice," he said, heating.

"I'd advise you to turn your efforts elsewhere, perhaps follow in your father's footsteps." She almost sounded sympathetic, but before he could respond, she was striding off toward the exit.

"She got a great impression of you, didn't she?" Jasper said, laughing.

Gidion ignored him and made his way back to the seating area, even more determined to prove himself to Arianna Velden. He'd show her he was the best and make Jasper pay for the humiliation he'd visited on him. Nessa would help, maybe show him a way to use his Chelaki magic to his advantage. This reminded him that he was due to meet her in the Water Garden, and his spirits lifted as he made his way over.

She was already there, dressed in fighting leathers. When he saw her, he realized she wasn't at all like the image he'd had of her in his mind. That image was rigid and stale, but the real her was a vital force that tangled and scrambled him, left him feeling uprooted and exposed. He tried not to stare at her, and especially not at her chest, to which his eyes had now wandered, nor at the narrowness of her waist and curve of her hips. He kept his eyes averted from her bared forearms, slender yet knotted with muscle from sword practice. And most of all, he avoided gazing at her lips, which he longed to feel against his.

"Hello," she said, kissing him on both cheeks in the Kharasian way. She smelt of fresh soap and that other heady scent that was hers alone.

"Yes, er ... you too." He wanted to put his arms around her but instead stepped back. A flashing memory of the girl in the brothel. Pits, if that had been Nessa ...

They began to walk under the shade of the trees toward the waterfall. He'd imagined sitting with her there many times in the night, holding her hand, feeling her head on his shoulder. He'd decided upon the exact weight her head would have and how her dark hair would tickle his chin.

They crossed a wooden bridge over a running stream and found themselves by a shaded pool crowded with white and pink lilies. Further on, they came to the waterfall, which tumbled down from a rockery into a small stream. On the bench in front of it was a pair of kissing initiates. Gidion wished it was him and Nessa.

"Through here," he said, pointing at a stand of sweeping willow trees. He was feeling light-headed. Nessa was more mesmerizing than ever, more beautiful than ever.

They entered a small clearing surrounded by trees and shrubs. It was empty except for a small stone bench beneath an aged statue covered in spots of yellow and white lichen. This was surprising because no other stone he'd seen in the Spire had been affected either by the elements or by nature.

Nessa regarded the statue with open curiosity, then approached it to read the inscription at the base. "'Chareia Venios, builder of the Spire,'" she read out. "I wonder why she's hidden away here, when the others are so visibly honored around the grounds," she mused.

Gidion was surprised by her observation. She was correct, of course. There were statues of the builders everywhere, along with other high-ranking weavers. "She liked this part of the garden?" he ventured.

"Yes, that's what I thought." She seemed delighted that he'd had the same thought as her, and it delighted him in turn. As one, they moved closer to the statue.

It was made of white stone. Gidion touched it with his fingers—rough and grainy, but in a pleasing way. The statue was tall, a head taller than him, and he wondered if that had been her real size. Probably, if what they said was true about Eleusians' superior height. There was a mischievous expression on her face, her mouth curling slightly to the left, the matching eye in a half-wink. She was holding a ruler in her right hand.

"She was different to the rest," Nessa said. "She didn't fit in."

"Yes." He brushed his hand along the length of the extended arm. "I think you're right." He would find out about her so he could tell Nessa more the next time they met.

Nessa sat on the bench, so he joined her, the statue spinning out of his mind. He groped for something to say, but she was ahead of him. "I think we should work on splicing," she said. "It's probably the hardest thing to master, but it has incredible uses."

Her practical, matter-of-fact tone disappointed him. With difficulty, he focused on her proposal. "But you can't splice in the Spire, can you?"

"You can't splice in and out, but you *can* splice within it, as long as you're in a portal location."

Did Thane know that? If so, why hadn't he mentioned it? Gidion sighed inwardly. It was so difficult to know who to trust. "Where's the nearest portal?"

"Here, as it so happens." Nessa grinned, showing her dimples, and he repressed the urge to rearrange a strand of her hair that had fallen against her cheek. "The gardens are one giant portal, probably because they're public."

Gidion clasped his hands together to stop himself from doing anything stupid. “So how do we start?”

“Watch me first,” she said, getting to her feet. “You’ll need to kind of push yourself through the Cloth, force all the threads apart.”

“The Cloth?”

“Sorry, the Tapestry. The Chelaki call it Chel’s Cloth after their creator god. *Our* creator god, I suppose.”

The mention of the god, who he’d never heard of, sparked his curiosity. But he was keen to move on to the practice, so he didn’t quiz her further on it.

“I’ll begin now,” she said, raising her hands.

Gidion looked closely as Nessa made like she was opening a pair of curtains. It was a relatively slow gesture, as if it required great effort. But as she parted the threads, a greyish swirl appeared. Immediately, he felt the call of it, a thrill of power, potent and wild. “Is that the prime force?”

“Yes. At least, that’s what Malai calls it. She tells me the Chelaki usually refer to it as Sīut’s Realm.”

“Who’s Sīut?”

“The Chelaki chaos god, father of Chel the Creator. According to Chelaki myth, Chel spun the fabric of the world out of Sīut’s chaos. So when you splice the Cloth—the Tapestry as you weavers call it—you’re essentially stepping out of this world and into pure chaos.”

“So, what, you can just go through?”

“Not quite. You have to create a tunnel, which is even more exhausting than splicing in the first place. But if you don’t create one, you’ll be unraveled instantly.”

There was something truly intoxicating about the power he sensed beyond the Tapestry. The more he regarded it, the stronger the pull.

"And the prime force doesn't leak through when you splice the Tapestry?"

"No, it needs a channel to enter this world."

But Gidion barely heard what she was saying. He'd become fixated on the siren call of that swirling power. He walked up close to the hole Nessa had made and peered at it. Standing right in front of it, he could almost make out the shape of the trees on the other side.

"Don't try to go through it yet," Nessa warned.

The warning came too late. Transfixed, Gidion had allowed the threads of his being to connect to the alien force. It slammed into him, twisting and contorting his body, forcing his mouth into a silent scream. His blood seared like molten rock, his bones stretched and popped, as if trying to burst through his flesh. No nerve, muscle, or tendon of his body escaped the mind-breaking pain. It was all consuming, all destroying.

Cursing, Nessa closed the splice, cutting him off.

His knees buckled, but he never even felt his head hit the ground. Next he knew, he was slumped on the bench. Nessa was standing before him, peering at him with concern. "Are you alright?" she asked.

He didn't reply. Sweat was pouring down his face and soaking his back and armpits. The world was spinning wildly. He felt like he was going to be sick. "I ..." he began. But his stomach rebelled, and he leaned over to spew out the food he'd just consumed.

Nessa leaped out of the way. "At least it didn't kill you." But she still looked worried.

He raised his head, remaining hunched over, elbows on his knees. "What ... happened?"

"You decided to be a complete idiot." Despite the words, her tone was gentle, still laced with concern.

"I touched it, didn't I?" he said. "Somehow, I touched it."

"You did more than that. You tried to channel it," she said. "You might be Ilis's great-grandson, but you're far from ready for that kind of thing."

Slowly, he straightened and wiped his mouth with the back of his arm. But the world continued to spin alarmingly. "Is that what he used to make the Ilk?" he asked hoarsely.

"Basically."

"I didn't mean to channel it." His stomach heaved again, and out came a fresh portion of his lunch.

Nessa's nose wrinkled as she regarded the pool of partially digested food between them.

She definitely wasn't going to like him now. "Sorry," he mumbled, trying to straighten. But he felt like he might be ill again, so he returned to his hunched position. Waves of hot and cold ran through his body, as if he were struck by fever.

"I'd definitely advise not doing it again anytime soon," she said. "People have died trying. You need a conduit at the very least."

He tilted his face up to look at her. "Like a focus stone, you mean?"

"The prime force would destroy your weaver stones," Nessa replied. "Or so I've been told."

"What, then?" His head seemed to be settling, so he risked sitting up again. He still felt sick, but more in control of his stomach.

"Ilis'Elkir used a sword made of a metal that he claimed came from outside this world."

"And where is that now?" Another wave of heat, and he sucked in a breath to steady himself.

"I believe Malai has it somewhere, but she's never shown it to me." Nessa cocked her head appraisingly. "I think we should get you some water."

But Gidion was determined to continue. He didn't want to end the session having made no progress at all. "Show me again how to splice." He did his best to look hale and well.

But she looked doubtful. "It can wait for another day."

"No, I want to do it now," Gidion said. He stood up, wanting to get away from the stink of his own vomit. His knees were weak, his legs shaky, but he tried not to show it.

Nessa regarded him silently for a few heartbeats, then shrugged. "Alright, if you feel up to it. Just don't touch the prime force this time."

"No chance of that."

She raised her hands and parted the Tapestry for him to see.

This time, he ignored the pull of the prime force, just tried to observe it, understand it. It was so alien and strange. Both destructive and generative, as she'd said. The power of the gods. Gidion shuddered. Surely, no human being should touch it? At the same time, it called to him, intoxicating as a woman's perfume.

"You're not going to try to channel it, are you?"

"No," he said softly. Then again, more emphatically, "No."

"Good, try parting the threads like I did."

But when he tried, nothing happened. He just felt sick again, a headache building behind his right eye.

"It's hard to do it consciously. No one gets it first time."

Gidion tried again, but still had no success. "I'm missing something," he said, frustration tightening his chest. A deeper fear in him, though, was that despite what Nessa said, he didn't have the ability to do this.

"You really need to think about separating all the threads, not just those you can sense."

"How do I do that if I can't sense them?"

"That's why you have to imagine yourself pushing through, like you're forcing your way through very thick mud. The Cloth will resist you, but you can get it to move around you if you push hard enough."

Gidion tried again but had no more luck.

"Don't worry, the ability comes to people at different times," Nessa said. "And touching the prime force probably hasn't helped."

But Gidion was used to picking things up quickly, and he was annoyed at how long it was taking him to do just the first step. He tried one more time, then cursed when he failed again.

"It's also a lot harder to splice in the Spire," Nessa said. "I think it's because of all the protections around it. The Tapestry is so warped here."

She wasn't wrong about that. The patterns and weaves were dense and knotted, beyond the understanding of even the weavers who lived there.

"Maybe we can go out into the city another day, and you can try where it's not so difficult."

"I'm not leaving the grounds," Gidion said.

Nessa eyes narrowed, as if she had guessed what he was thinking. "You won't come to any harm."

Gidion didn't answer. "Let me just try one last time."

But he came no closer to parting the threads than he had before. Instead, he felt ever sicker, the very effort of holding the Tapestry in view causing him to break out in a sweat. It was Nessa who finally called time on it.

"Let's try again tomorrow," she said. "You're not in good shape for it right now."

Gidion gritted his teeth in frustration. "Fine."

They walked together to the garden's exit, where she took her leave from him. It felt like she took some of the light of the day with her. But at least he had the promise of seeing her again the next day.

Chapter 17

It took Gidion a few days to fully recover from his attempt at channeling the prime force. He would have sudden dizzy spells accompanied by blinding headaches. But it didn't stop him from persisting, and he finally managed to part the threads three days after the first attempt. Initially, he could only make tiny splices, but day by day, he built up the strength that enabled him to push the threads open ever wider.

At the end of the second week, he was finally able to throw objects through a tunnel he'd formed in Sīut's Realm so that they landed exactly where the Tapestry reopened. But Nessa counseled him against trying to move himself through the tunnel. "It's very difficult," she said. "And dangerous if you don't know what you're doing."

"But I have to try some time," Gidion protested.

"Malai said most people don't do it for at least six months after they first learn how to splice," Nessa said. "It takes time to build up resistance to the prime force."

After what had happened to him when he'd touched it, Gidion was willing to believe her. But he was equally determined to prove that it would take him less than six months. Nessa had shown him how effective splicing could be in a fight, enabling you to attack from behind or escape if you'd been disarmed or downed. Skills he needed to beat Malai and her Ilk.

"One way to build up the strength is to pass through Sīut's Realm with someone else," Nessa said. She spliced the Tapestry and took his elbow. "Come with me."

The pressure of her fingers on his bare skin made him tingle. But he forgot it as soon as they stepped into the tunnel and was subjected to a bone-breaking pressure that made him feel like an insect being crushed beneath a boot. The sensation only lasted an instant, but when he emerged, he looked down at himself, fully convinced he'd see blood coming out of his pores. To his surprise, though, both he and Nessa were unharmed. "That's ... not pleasant," he said.

"So you see what I mean," she replied. "If you were to lose control of the tunnel while you're out there." She ground her palms against one another.

"Does passing through it get any easier?"

"A little, but honestly, it's always painful," she said. "I don't think we're made to go there."

"I think I can do it myself," he said. "It's not that different from sending something else through a tunnel, is it?"

But Nessa refused to allow him to try. "It's far too soon."

After that, Gidion practiced splicing every spare moment he had. He pestered Nessa relentlessly to show him how to send himself through, but she remained adamant. Eventually, he decided to try it by himself. He was feeling confident in his ability to keep a tunnel open, had started sending objects across one end of the Water Garden to the other. But when he tried to create a short tunnel for himself, it collapsed as soon as he tried to enter it, expelling him so hard he landed on his backside. That, of course, didn't stop him from trying again, usually in the quiet part of the Water Garden where he and Nessa met.

And finally, of course, she caught him at it while he was waiting for her.

"Are you ignoring everything I've told you?" she demanded, startling him as he was trying to step through his tunnel for the seventh time that day.

"I want to know how to do it," he said. "Please, show me, or I'll just keep trying myself anyway."

Nessa shook her head in exasperation. "Malai would *not* be happy with me."

"She'll be less happy if I kill myself trying to do it without instruction." He tried his most charming smile on her. Not hard when she was so captivating to look at.

She snorted softly. "You're incorrigible."

"You said you'd teach me."

She rolled her eyes. "Fine, fine, I'll show you. Splice the Tapestry."

Grinning, he did as she said.

"You've gotten very fast at that," she said grudgingly.

"See, I *am* ready." His grin broadened.

"No, I don't see. But I soon will." She made a splice near his. "You need to stabilize the tunnel before you enter it yourself."

"But how?"

"You hook the tunnel opening to the threads around it." She demonstrated the technique as she spoke.

Gidion squinted at what she'd done, then tried it for himself. The threads resisted his efforts, though, snapping away and closing the tunnel.

"Use more threads."

Gidion tried again a few more times before finally managing to copy what she'd done.

"That's actually quite good," Nessa said in surprise. "Normally, it takes people a lot longer to figure out this part."

Gidion smiled broadly. "So can I go through now?"

"Make the tunnel shorter, just a couple of paces," she said. "That way, there isn't much time for things to go wrong."

He did as she said, then stepped through. The pressure lasted less than a heartbeat before he was out the other end. He cast Nessa a triumphant look.

"Fine, I'll admit you're good at this," she said, raising her eyes heavenwards, this time in a fond manner. "But please, keep the tunnels short for the moment."

"As you say, mistress." He made a short, teasing bow, and she walloped him on the shoulder.

At his insistence, they kept at the same task for the rest of their session. And later, when he was away from her, he mostly stuck to his promise about the length of the tunnels, focusing on stabilizing them more quickly. Very soon, another week had passed, and Thane finally fulfilled his promise to train Gidion in warcraft.

Gidion had said nothing of Jasper's humiliation of him to the magister, not wanting Thane to think less of him. And he found that despite what Nessa had said about Thane being more inclined to scholarship than war, he was a very able fighter with lightning-fast reflexes. He also gave Gidion a wrist shield similar to the one Gidion had seen the initiates wearing in their sparring class. As Gidion wasn't used to fighting with one, their training mostly consisted of this.

"I'm surprised Conal had a staff for you but not a shield," Thane said. "Not everyone uses them, but they're common."

Gidion shrugged. "He didn't use one himself, so I suppose that's why." It was yet another indication to Gidion of how lacking his training had been, another reminder that he was behind where he should be. And yet Gidion found himself aching for his father. The man could be stubborn and bad-tempered, but he was the only person Gidion had truly known.

As for Jasper, Gidion avoided him where he could. When they were in Advanced Artefaction, though, he made a point of acting friendly toward him. Let Thane think that it was Jasper who was being the churl. And in fact, he did once overhear Thane tell Jasper he should be more welcoming to Gidion. "He's not your enemy, you know. I still hold you in the highest regard," Thane had said, his expression largely paternal, but with a flirtatious undertone.

Jasper bit his lip, looking away as if he didn't trust himself to speak.

Gidion, for his part, discovered he didn't like hearing that Jasper was Thane's apparent favorite.

"And I know you'll pass artefaction with flying colors," Thane said. "You have nothing to concern yourself over."

"If you think so, Magister," Jasper said, his stance relaxing somewhat.

"I know so." Thane put a hand on his shoulder.

Gidion sensed Jasper's excitement at feeling Thane's hand on him. He wanted Thane. But did Thane want him? If so, he kept his desires in check, for Gidion couldn't sense them despite the flirtatiousness in his tone and eyes.

He heard no more of the conversation, deciding to slip away before they saw him. But it left him with much to consider. So Jasper thought him an enemy? Well, that made two of them. And the most perfect revenge might be to show Jasper that it was Gidion who Thane regarded higher. To do that, Gidion needed to excel in the thing that Thane wanted him to excel in—namely, artefaction. But he also needed to win both the Selection Trial and the Tournament if he was to be guaranteed his choice of mentor, so every subject needed dedicated attention. Driven by these needs, he threw himself even more diligently into his studies, forgoing sleep to squeeze extra hours into the day.

Before he knew it, the Selection Trial was upon him, and he still felt barely prepared. The Advanced Artefaction test came first. As Thane had said, their task was to create a heatstone with set levels of heat, and they had an entire day to complete it. Gidion knew he could do it in half that time. His speed had won him frequent praise from Thane, so he got to work confidently on the stone that Jasper had handed to him.

His first inkling that something was wrong was a little jolt, a reaction of the existing weaves to the new one he was forming. He stopped what he was doing to see what the problem was, carefully revising each of his weaves. But they all seemed correct. Maybe he'd imagined it? He got to work again, but a little more slowly, double-checking each piece of work.

But the next time it wasn't a jolt. It was a loud explosion and a flash of blinding white light. A thousand darts of pain shot into his exposed skin. His hands flew to cover his face, where he felt fragments of stone and sticky wetness. An acrid burning smell filled his nostrils, mingling with the tang of blood.

"Gidion! Are you alright?" Thane said, rushing over. He removed Gidion's hands from his face to regard him.

Gidion blinked dazedly, his vision still spinning with spots of light. His hands were dotted with tiny cuts, all bubbling blood. Where not bloodied, the flesh was raw and blistered. Shards of stone were strewn all over his workbench and glittering motes stuck to his robes like tiny stars.

"Jasper, fill a bowl with cold water," Thane said, seeing Gidion's hands, now burning with pain.

"I'm doing my test," Jasper objected.

"That's not a request," Thane snapped.

Jasper went to a tap in the corner of the room to do as Thane said. When he returned with the bowl, Gidion plunged his hands into the water with a groan of relief. Thane began to dab at his face with a wet cloth.

"I was doing everything right," Gidion said, his voice muffled by the cloth. "It was the stone. Something was wr—"

"The stones are all carefully checked upon purchase," Thane interrupted. "And again before they're distributed." He dunked the cloth into the water and wrung it out, creating a swirling current of red.

But Gidion knew it wasn't his fault. He'd never exploded a stone. He was too careful, too precise. He glanced over at Jasper. The boy was studiously working on his heatstone. "It must have been tampered with," he said loudly, keeping his gaze on Jasper.

The boy continued to ignore him. That alone would have told Gidion the truth—Jasper wasn't looking over because he was too cowardly to face Gidion. And Gidion's other senses confirmed the suspicion. Jasper was full of smug delight, even if a measure of guilt ran through it.

"I hope you're not throwing around unfounded accusations," Thane said sternly. "You most likely made a mistake with a weave. It's not so uncommon." Thane began to dab at his face again.

"It was him," Gidion said, jerking his head back furiously.

"I won't say it again," Thane said, a warning note sounding. He dipped the cloth back into the bowl and wrung it out. "Hold this here, you have quite a deep cut." He pressed the cloth against the middle of Gidion's forehead.

Gidion put his hand over the cloth, his rage undimmed. *Ilk take Jasper, I know it was him. Prick. He's trying to make me look bad.*

What's he got against me anyway? Wasn't it enough that time in the arena?

"You'd best get to the hospital to get that cut sewn up," Thane was saying. "I can see the bone."

"I want to finish the heatstone. I still have time," Gidion said. "Can't I just start again? I'll be fine."

Thane pressed his lips together, contemplating.

"I can do it, Magister," Gidion said again, pleading.

Thane sighed. "Go and get your wounds tended, then come back."

Gidion ran all the way to the Tower of Succor, praying the whole time that an attendant would be free. To his relief, they saw to him straight away when he explained his predicament. He rejected any kind of pain-numbing potion, not wanting to risk clouding his head. It was hard not to cry out each time the needle sank into his skin, but he gritted his teeth to fight the urge, sweat trickling down his face and back.

"You're a brave lad," the attendant said, a matronly woman with soft cheeks, as she dabbed the lesser cuts with antiseptic. "Off with you now, and good luck with your test."

Gidion thanked her profusely and sprinted back to the Tower of Artefaction.

Thane gave him another stone and Gidion worked feverishly to accomplish his task. He was determined to not only do the stone to perfection but finish before Jasper, despite the amount of time he'd lost. In the end, though, he finished as Jasper was tying off his last weaves.

"Excellent work, both of you," Thane said as he examined the stones. "You may consider yourselves as having passed the Advanced Artefaction portion of your Selection Trial." He beamed at them both. "Congratulations."

"Thanks, Magister," Gidion said, unable to stop a note of triumph from entering his voice. *Up yours, Jasper.*

"Gidion, stay a moment, would you?" Thane said as they prepared to leave.

He waited until Jasper was gone, then closed the door after him.

"You did well to catch up, and I never doubted you would," Thane said. "Stones explode from time to time, which is why we wear the goggles. So don't be too hard on yourself. I won't be."

"It wasn't my fault," he said. "It was—"

Thane raised a finger. "Now, now, what did I say about unfounded accusations?"

But Gidion wasn't going to give up so easily. "Jasper is the one who handed out my stone."

Thane's voice hardened. "And you don't think I would have noticed if he'd tampered with it in front of me?"

"It's not that, Magister, it's just..." Gidion trailed into silence, realizing that Thane was only likely to take offense if he pushed harder.

"I know you're an excellent artefactor, Gidion. What happened today hasn't changed my opinion. I've seen you work many times now. This was just the formal part," Thane said.

"Thank you, Magister." He wasn't entirely successful at keeping the sullenness out of his tone.

Thane evidently noticed and laid a comforting hand on his upper arm. "Yes, Jasper is arrogant, like any member of the Great Families. But that will also be why he won't resort to cheating. Someone like him believes they're naturally superior."

"If you say so, Magister."

"I see I haven't convinced you, but the matter's done. Get yourself off to my chambers and ask Simion for anything you need—food, a pain remedy, a hot bath. You want to be in good form for the team selection tomorrow."

This was when Gidion would learn which of the initiates would be on his team for the maze run in the Selection Trial. The reminder of how close it was set his heart to racing. Had his preparations been enough? Would he be matched with initiates good enough to help him win the Trial? He had to have Arianna as mentor—he *had* to.

But as he returned to the magister's rooms, he fixated on how he might get his revenge on Jasper. Because whatever Thane had said, Gidion was convinced that the youth had tampered with his stone. And he wasn't going to let the little prick win. He just needed to find his moment.

The team selection was held in a classroom in the Seekers' Tower. Gidion arrived with Thane to find the other inmates there already. He had some pleasure in seeing Jasper's unhappy expression when he saw that they'd come together.

Thane ascended the dais at the end of the room to address them collectively. "Finally, a day has arrived that I know you've long been waiting for," he said. "You're all on the cusp of finishing the Initiate Cycle, and you will become men and women of the Spire. Your training hasn't finished, of course. A weaver's training is never truly done. But this is a highly important juncture for you all, when you start to specialize in your chosen area of mastery. Of course, we also need to know you're fit to enter the Apprentice Cycle, so you must show you have the strength of character, knowledge, and fighting skill to be worthy of your new positions." Thane stopped, his eyes roving the assembled initiates.

A tremor of excitement ran through them.

"The first stage of the Selection Trial, as you all know, is a team event. It will test not only your knowledge and weaving skills, but also your ability to cooperate under pressure. Please listen carefully now, while I call out the names of each team." Thane again paused for dramatic effect, and the initiates shuffled nervously.

"Sapphire Team: Jasper Wyven, Emilie Morgan, Gidion Jameson. Please come to the front," Thane said.

What? Thane had put him with *Jasper*? Jasper seemed equally incredulous but quickly switched his expression to one of disdain as Gidion joined him. Emily, it turned out, was the button-nosed girl who'd witnessed Gidion's humiliation at Jasper's hands in the arena. She exchanged a smile with Jasper but paid less attention to Gidion than she might have to a bug. Gidion gritted his teeth. Why had Thane done this? Was it a punishment? Something to do with Jasper's tampering of the heatstone? Or because Thane wanted Gidion to fail?

He was so full of these thoughts that he didn't hear the names listed for the Ruby or Emerald teams, only saw that Ruby had three people like his team while Emerald, rather unfairly, had four.

"Remember that from now on in, you rise and fall together," Thane said. "Whatever friendships or grudges you've had with each other until now, you must set aside to win." Thane shot a look in Gidion and Jasper's direction. "Weavers don't always get to choose who they work with, and a mark of adulthood is being able to collaborate under pressure. I advise you to spend the rest of the afternoon with your team to discuss your collective strengths and weaknesses. Tomorrow at eighth bell of the morning, we'll start the Trial."

Gidion decided he would just have to get through it. He'd had enough experience pandering to guards in his peddling days. What was another day or two? He girded himself to face Jasper and Emily. "Where shall we talk?"

Despite her shorter stature, Emilie managed to look down her nose at him. "I think we all know your weaknesses, scrubber."

"Wit is one of yours, I see," he returned, his determination to keep them onside wiped in an instant.

Emilie flushed, opened her mouth to speak again.

But Jasper pulled her away. "Come on, let's find better company. See you tomorrow, scrubber." He made the words sound like a curse.

Gidion glared at them as they left the room with the other initiates, who were all talking excitedly among themselves. His throat and belly clenched. Would they ever think him one of them? But then he remembered that Thane was behind this and rounded on the magister, who was stepping off the dais. "Was that deliberate?" he demanded.

"Could you be more specific?" Thane asked coolly.

Thane's tone infuriated him further. He surely knew what Gidion meant. "Did you deliberately put me with them?"

Thane seemed unfazed. "They are the best two students in their entire year," he said. "You can't do better."

"But Jasper ..."

Thane raised an eyebrow as if daring Gidion to repeat his accusation.

Knowing a warning when he saw it, Gidion bit down on his words. "Jasper doesn't like me," he said. "I don't know how we're going to work together. And his friend—girlfriend, whatever—hates me just as much."

"So it will be a good test for all three of you to see if you can overcome your differences to work together. My speech wasn't just for show," Thane said. "There will be times when you have to collaborate with people you despise. And nothing brings out tension and stress more than war. We can't have any weak links."

Thane talked about war as if he knew it firsthand. "You've been at war?"

"Tarsis has been in an almost perpetual state of civil war for decades," Thane said.

"So you ..."

"No one escapes the consequences."

Gidion sensed a complex web of emotions in Thane as he spoke of Tarsis. Regret, loss, pain, relief, anger. And the yearning that so often came through. Thane's background, whatever it was, had left scars. It made Gidion reconsider the man. He seemed so strong, so capable and well liked. But there was a wounded core to him, just like there was to Gidion. "Why did they call me a scrubber?"

Thane's mouth twisted. "Because Seekers who can't afford their tuition fees are given attendants' work to help pay them off. That includes quite a lot of pot scrubbing."

"But I'm not even enrolled yet."

"It doesn't matter. Usually, the only ones who can afford the tuition fees come from the Great Families. So they just apply the term 'scrubber' to any commoner."

"Does that mean I'll have to do menial work when I become an apprentice?" Gidion said in dismay. He'd thought that once he came to the Spire, he'd be freed of such tasks. He was a weaver, for pits' sake, not a servant.

"Not if you apprentice with me to study artefaction," Thane said. "I'll cover your bond, and you can repay me by helping me on artefaction projects."

What would it mean, then, if Gidion chose warcraft instead? Would Arianna Velden make him her servant, akin to Simion?

But he couldn't let that put him off. He might still be able to make glowglobes for Ruadh's boss, even if Ruadh had ignored every message he'd sent since they'd last met. And if not Ruadh's boss, there would be someone else. Glowglobes, as Thane himself had pointed out, were a route to wealth.

What was most important was his mission to defeat Malai and her Ilk. And, if what Nessa had said about his father was true, to rescue him from the Riftlanders, too. Winning would also impress Nessa, although he tried to tell himself that this didn't matter. She was working with the enemy—ultimately, no matter how much Gidion wanted her, no matter how much she occupied his fantasies, she was off limits, dangerous.

But still, it was a matter of pride. He'd show her and everyone else how good he actually was. He'd just need to try harder with Jasper and Emilyy tomorrow, ensure they were working together at their best despite their enmity.

Chapter 18

Once the teams had been organized for the Selection Trial, Thane went out to meet his artefact dealer Rafaelo again. He'd sent word that he'd found something Thane might be interested in, and Thane was filled with hope. When he entered Rafaelo's study, his attention immediately went to a small bronze chest on his desk.

"Naturally, you're the first person we've spoken to about this," Rafaelo said. "We had quite the time trying to open it, I'll tell you."

"You've got me most curious," Thane said lightly as he approached.

Rafaelo lifted the lid of the chest. "Go on, take a look."

Inside it were some scrolls and an assortment of jewelry. But Thane could tell immediately that it was no ordinary jewelry.

"We uncovered it underwater."

"You got a ship out to the Maelstrom already?" Thane said. Impossible, surely—it would have taken weeks to go and come back.

"No, no, not that far. This was on the West Carian coast under quite a lot of debris."

"It's from the time of the Ruin?" But he didn't need to ask. The chest was clearly of Eleusian make, and it would only have survived this long because of the weaves impregnated in it.

"We've assessed all the contents, of course," Rafaelo said. "There's some ordinary jewelry, but also a lot that's been woven.

Rafaelo first removed a small silver box, inside which nestled a pair of silver rings. "These, when activated, will enable you to sense the other wearer within a range of about five miles."

Thane's heart pumped faster. "Does that go two ways?"

Rafaelo smiled. "Yes. To make it work, one person must activate the weave. You just have to rub the gemstone briskly five times. This sends a pulse to the other ring, whose wearer must also rub the stone on his ring. Then, both wearers will be able to find each other. Would you like to try?"

"Do you need to ask?" Thane held out his hand, and Rafaelo dropped the ring into it. He slipped it onto his finger, while Rafaelo put on its twin.

"Activate yours first," Rafaelo said.

Thane rubbed his thumb on the stone and felt something shift in the Tapestry in response, although he couldn't see what threads were affected—Eleusian magic that was beyond him and anyone else living today.

"Got it," Rafaelo said, rubbing his own ring.

A moment later, Thane felt a distinctive pull from his ring toward Rafaelo. The broker stood up and walked around the room. Thane could feel the pull moving with him. This was incredible. Thane had read about such tracking ring pairs, but it was the first time he'd ever seen any. If only he could replicate this!

"I don't believe the like of these has been found yet," Rafaelo said meaningfully.

"They could be useful," Thane replied, keeping his expression and tone bland. "But let me see what else is in here." He returned the ring to Rafaelo.

The broker removed several pieces of amethyst jewelry. "These appear to be purely decorative." He shook a necklace, and it began to sparkle as if light were striking it. The effect, though, was produced by the weaves in the stones, and was one Thane had produced many times himself. "What about that collar?" Thane said, peering at a slender band of bronze.

"We haven't found any use for it yet. But it's been woven." Rafaelo plucked it out and held it before him.

Thane brought the Tapestry before his eyes and examined the piece. It didn't have the kinds of patterns he associated with Eleusian or Vycenian weaving or artefaction. He couldn't make sense of them. The old frustration bubbled in him. They'd lost so much knowledge in the Ruin. "May I touch it?" he asked.

Rafaelo handed it to him.

It felt cool, but there was a resonance through the threads. He felt an impulse to fasten it around his own neck, and uneasily, he returned it to Rafaelo. The desire drained away.

Rafaelo looked at him knowingly. "It's an odd artefact, isn't it?"

"You've really no idea what it does?"

"I was hoping you might."

"And the scrolls, do they shed any light?"

Rafaelo spread his hands. "Most of them are related to business transactions, records of where the rings and collar and other pieces were acquired."

"But nothing that describes how the collar works?"

"Doubtless, the owner already knew that when they acquired it."

Frustrating, but he had to investigate for himself. "How much for the ring and collar, and the scrolls pertaining to them?"

"Four thousand consuls." Rafaelo smiled, showing golden teeth.

Thane laughed. "A wonderful joke, Rafaelo. Tell me the real price."

"A lot of effort went into finding this hoard. Each piece alone is worth a fortune. We have men and women to pay. Do you know how difficult it is to hunt underwater?"

"I've already helped fund an expedition," Thane pointed out. "And you don't even know what the collar does."

"But it and the rings are the only thing of their like that have ever been found," Rafaelo said. "They're probably worth even more than that."

"I'm not a fool," Thane replied. "Unless you can tell me exactly what it all does, I'm not taking the collar for less than a thousand consuls."

It was Rafaelo's turn to laugh. "That doesn't even cover the cost of acquiring them. But I'll be generous, as we've had such a long and fruitful relationship, and reduce the price to three thousand."

"A relationship that gives you access to Wyven-quality glowglobes at a vastly reduced rate."

"Where *are* my glowglobes, by the way?"

Thane hefted a satchel onto Rafaelo's table. The broker didn't bother to look inside it. "Two thousand five hundred is my best offer."

"One thousand five hundred," Thane insisted.

"Others will pay what I'm asking. And I know exactly who to go to."

Thane didn't doubt the truth of this. The only reason he got first look at everything was their arrangement with the glowglobes. But wealthy buyers of Eleusian artefacts weren't rare. The Greats liked to collect too. "Very well, I'll have the funds transferred from my account." It wasn't a terrible bargain.

"A pleasure doing business as always," Rafaelo said.

He reeked of smugness, and Thane wondered if he hadn't paid over the odds. Never mind, the artefacts weren't of use to him just for their abilities. They also presented opportunities for research, a chance to expand his knowledge of artefaction. And he could afford it, just about. "Until next time."

Rafaelo opened the door for him, and he returned to the street. But he wouldn't go to the Spire yet. His blood was up, a fire burning in him that demanded quenching. Cabs waited hopefully on the street, but he couldn't endure the thought of being trapped in one when his legs demanded so urgently to walk. At the same time, instinct stopped him from striding so quickly that he would appear indecorous. He mustn't draw attention to himself. So he forced himself to maintain a steady, unhurried pace, all of his senses alert for any sign of a footpad or thief. Arindel was a relatively safe city, especially in these parts, where the Watch patrolled constantly, but one could never be too careful, and he had no desire to lose his prize.

Soon, he was facing the wild bustle of the Rainbow Quarter, squeezing his way through the throngs of drunkards and revelers to reach his house. As always, it triggered a sense of relief in him. Here, he could be entirely himself, free of the mask he wore before all those at the Spire. But he didn't enter by the door through which he'd taken Nim. He wasn't looking to spend time with the young ones tonight. Instead, he knocked out a set pattern on the other door. He had a key, but it pleased him to have someone open it for him.

Almost instantly, the head of the house, Makir was ushering him in with a bow and a smile. "Magister, you're most welcome."

Thane stepped through and greeted him with a lingering kiss on the mouth, a reminder of how their relationship had started, even if they no longer shared a bed. At twenty-seven, Makir had become too old for his tastes, but he'd pleased Thane so much that he'd kept him on purely practical purposes.

"What will you want tonight, Magister?" Makir asked.

"Let's all have a drink together, I'm in a mood to celebrate," Thane replied. He went to the drawing room, a large, open space on the ground floor decorated in ancient Eleusian style. Acquiring the pieces hadn't been easy. Some were genuine antiques, others mere copies. His greatest pride was the four chaises longs upholstered in deep blue velvet around a low marble table. Those had allegedly come from the house of the Eleusian ambassador to Arindel before the Ruin.

Sitting at the gaming table at the opposite end of the room were Loki and Wyntir. They were playing cards, their handsome faces sharp and intent. Thane's blood stirred. They were his youngest, just sixteen years old, and he'd only had them a handful of times. Loki spotted him and leaped to his feet, cards still in hand. Wyntir took his cue but was slower in rising, a smirk twisting his lips. Thane knew it was deliberate, designed to provoke, and it made him want to take the youth there and then.

"Makir, a Rastian red for us all," he said, taking himself to the nearest of the chaise longues. "Loki, set out the glasses. Wyntir with me."

Wyntir strutted toward him, hips swaying like a girl's. He had very large blue eyes and a fine nose over a full, pouting mouth, and was clad in tight breeches of fine cotton that showed him off to best advantage. He curled up at Thane's feet, and Thane ran his fingers through the youth's soft hair.

Loki placed wine glasses for them all on the table before reclining on one of the other chaise longues. He was evidently disappointed not to have been chosen, shooting envious glances at Wyntir when he thought Thane wasn't looking. But Thane had favored him on his last few visits, and it was best to remind him he wasn't indispensable.

As Makir poured, Thane quizzed all three about the gossip they'd heard on the street. He did it for form rather than out of genuine curiosity, and by the time he'd finished his glass, his blood had been stirred to a peak. Plus, there was the collar to try out. "Wyntir, upstairs with me. The rest of you may do as you please."

Wyntir made a show of taking his time to get up. As he strutted out, Thane followed close behind him, admiring the roundness of his rump. They went upstairs to his bedroom, and as soon as they were inside, Thane commanded him to kneel.

"If I must," Wyntir said.

"You must," Thane said firmly.

Wyntir did as he asked, his mouth twisting impudently.

It aroused him even more, but he had business to take care of first. Taking the collar out of the satchel, he placed it around Wyntir's neck. He kept the Tapestry in sight as he did so, hoping to see some change in the threads, but there was nothing. Either he couldn't see the relevant threads, or the collar was activated via some other kind of trigger.

"What do you feel?" Thane asked him.

"I don't like it," Wyntir said, tugging at the thing. He liked to play at defying Thane, but this time, his disgust seemed genuine.

"That's not what I asked. Do you feel anything from it? Any change in yourself?"

"Something about it makes me feel ill," he said, and there was no playfulness in his tone.

Thane delved into the collar, pulling and tweaking weaves with little discernible effect other than to occasionally cause Wyntir to yelp in pain. Finally, frustrated, he abandoned the attempt and took the collar off the youth. "You've pleased me. Now let me make it up to you." He gripped Wyntir's hair and pulled him to his feet before levering him toward the bed.

Chapter 19

Gidion woke early on the morning of the trial, filled with anxiety about the day ahead. He disciplined himself to do some reading, telling himself that every piece of information he could absorb might be useful.

Thane wasn't long in joining him, but then, the magister always woke early. They breakfasted together, then Thane accompanied him to the basement of the Seekers' Tower, where the entrance to the Trial maze was located. The levitator opened into a medium-sized room with walls of slick black stone, glowglobes in silver, claw-shaped sconces casting a soft, golden light.

Many of the initiates were there already, including Jasper and Emily. "Go to them," Thane said. "I have to prepare."

Reluctantly, he joined his team members, who were talking quietly. They returned his greetings coolly, then resumed their conversation, shutting him out with their shoulders. Gidion's anger began to simmer, but he stayed quiet, reminding himself that his mission to win mattered above all.

The last stragglers arrived, and Thane announced that they were to begin. "Remember, the tunnels will take you through challenges that your team must work together to pass. In the final challenge, you'll have to steal the standard of at least one other team while holding onto your own. Each standard is located in a base that matches the color of your team name, and the bases will be easy to see."

Gidion had heard this all before several times but paid close attention nonetheless. He couldn't afford to put a single foot out of place if he wanted to achieve his aim.

Thane waved at an iron door at the opposite end of the room. "Pass through here and at the first junction, Team Sapphire, you take the left passage. Team Ruby, you take the one straight ahead, and Team Emerald you take the right passage. You'll have eight hours to complete all the trials."

The door opened, and they filed through silently. It clanged shut after them, sealing them in darkness. Gidion triggered the focus stone in his staff to create light. The others did the same, revealing a corridor made of the same slick, black stone as the room outside. A few paces along, they came to the junction Thane had mentioned.

"I guess this is where we split up," Jasper said. "Let's get going." He started jogging down the lefthand passage.

Gidion and Emilie ran after him, but very soon, they came to a dead end.

"What now?" Emilie said, looking around.

"Only those who know the past can know the way ahead," boomed a deep male voice.

Gidion jumped, looking around for the source of the sound, finding none. Magic?

The voice boomed again. "When was Eleusia united into a single realm and by whom?"

"The Lore questions," Emilie whispered excitedly. "I'll answer."

Jasper nodded.

But as Emilie was opening her mouth to speak, a loud roaring and crackling started up from behind. Gidion whipped his head around to find a wall of fire moving rapidly down the corridor toward them.

"Shit, answer quickly," Jasper hissed.

"Eleusia was turned into a single realm in BR 410 by Queen Anthea I," Emilie cried out.

A brick about the size of a hand vanished in the wall to their left. Did that mean Emilie had got the question right? He *thought* she had.

"Why don't weavers sit on the Council of Eleven in Vycenia?" said the voice.

"The Council was created after the Ruin. People blamed the weavers for causing the cataclysm, so they were banned from holding power in the country again," Emilie said.

Another brick vanished in the wall to the left. Surely, the correct answer, too.

Gidion could feel the heat of the fire on his back. He glanced back to see it had already come most of the way toward them. How many more questions did they have to answer? Quite a few if they were supposed to go through the gap in the wall.

"What caused the Ruin?" asked the voice, barely audible over the advancing flames.

"The Final Hundred summoned an immense amount of power to destroy the Ilk Lord and his army of Ilk. But it was too much, and the rebound effect tore a huge hole in the Tapestry," Emilie said.

Another gap in the wall to the left. But the heat of the fire was intense, moving so quickly it was surely going to overcome them before she'd finished answering. Gidion tried to see what was causing the fire. It wasn't burning anything, so it had to be woven. But the weaves were so dense and knotted that he couldn't make out how they worked, let alone unravel them. He noticed that Jasper's focus stone was glowing. "What are you doing?"

"Saving us from getting fried, since you don't seem too eager," Jasper snapped.

"But how?"

Jasper ignored him and completed his weave—a blast of cold that just dissipated in the face of the flames. Jasper cursed.

Maybe water would work, only Gidion couldn't weave water himself yet. It was difficult at the best of times, and you needed high moisture content in the air. This tunnel was dry as a bone. "Can you make water?" he asked Jasper, hating to admit his weakness but more concerned about burning alive.

"The steam would scald us, scrubber." Jasper pursed his lips, then his expression cleared. "A shield barrier," he said. "With two of us, we should be able to block the whole passageway."

Gidion suspected a trap. "It's a *fire*. Shields are for keeping out weaves."

"Exactly," Jasper said. "This fire isn't real. It's woven." His focus stone glowed again as he got to work.

The fire was almost on them, so hot Gidion was surprised his clothing hadn't combusted yet. Lacking a better idea, he joined Jasper in creating the shield. They finished it just as the wall of flame hit. It felt like a physical assault, the weaves that generated the flames constantly eating at the weaves of their shield, draining his strength at an alarming rate. But it did keep the fire at bay. Meanwhile, Emilie continued to answer questions behind them until finally, she shouted that there was a gap large enough for them to pass through.

"You go first," Jasper called to her. "Then, I'll go, scrubber, and you hold the shield."

"Worried you're not strong enough to hold it alone?" Gidion taunted. But he was panicking. He didn't think he could hold the shield alone either, not when the fire was eating at it so ferociously.

Jasper released the shield and squirmed through the gap in the wall after Emilie. Without Jasper's power, the shield began to dissolve. Terrified, Gidion wrapped protective weaves around himself as the flames engulfed him. They kept the heat fire off him but wouldn't last long. He dashed blindly for the gap, feeling for it with his hands before pushing himself through headfirst. He landed heavily against Jasper who cursed and stepped away. The flames died as Gidion scrambled to his feet, the skin of his arms and legs prickling where he'd grazed it. Amazingly, though, he hadn't been burnt.

"Nice work, Emilie," Jasper said. "We made good time there."

"Thanks for keeping that fire off my back." She didn't look at Gidion when she said the words.

He ground his teeth together. *My moment will come.*

"Come on, let's go," Jasper said, again starting before the words were out of his mouth.

They ran down a twisting corridor and into the next room. It was small, and along one wall sat a table covered with various phials, jars, and packets, as well as a pestle and mortar and some empty bottles.

"Each bottle you must drink, each poison must you counter," said the voice, male, again.

A low table stood in front of them with three red bottles on it. Each bottle was no taller than his thumb and had a label saying, "Drink me."

"Poisons," Jasper said, taking in the table and its contents. "They want us to figure out which one it is and make the antidote."

"They're not seriously trying to kill us, are they?" Emilie said, frowning at the bottles.

"Scrubber, you can drink the first one," Jasper said. "Seeing as you're a ranger's get."

"No problem, I'm not a coward," Gidion said, going for the first bottle. He unstopped it and sniffed. A bitter smell. Eyebright? It was severely poisonous. Was he supposed to drink the whole lot?

"Go on, then," Jasper said. "Or are you afraid?"

Here goes nothing. Gidion tasted the poison. Yes, it was eyebright, and he told them as much. Thankfully, he also knew the antidote and went to the table containing the phials of liquid and powder. But then he discovered that none of them were labeled. Even worse, the bottles and phials were made of green or brown glass so he couldn't determine the contents immediately by sight.

"Could they have made it any harder?" Emilie complained as she opened a bottle and smelled it. Her nose wrinkled. "Great Spinners, that's vile." She set it aside and opened another.

Gidion's mouth was drying, his heart speeding into a rapid patter, making it hard to stay calm. And he trusted neither Emilie nor Jasper to hand over the antidote if they found it, especially after the way Jasper had abandoned him to the flames. So he picked up every bottle they'd dismissed to confirm it wasn't what he was looking for—beak bean extract.

"You're slowing us down, scrubber," Jasper said when he realized what Gidion was doing.

"Like you said, I'm ranger's get," Gidion said. "I probably know these better than you do." He was starting to feel dizzy. How long before the hallucinations began?

"I think I've found it," Emily said, handing a small jar to Gidion.

He peered into the jar. The paste in it was the right color—a brownish red. He picked up a spoon from the table and scooped out some of the paste. Yes, that might be it. He ate up the lot. It didn't make him feel better straight away, but that was to be expected. He'd just have to hope for the best.

"Next one," Emilie said, picking up a red bottle.

"Go on, scrubber," Jasper said to him.

"No, we should take it in turns," Gidion said. He wasn't going to let Jasper bully him. "Too many toxins for one person could mess up the antidotes."

Jasper scowled at him, and Gidion crossed his arms over his chest defiantly. "You know it's best if we all make it through this trial."

"Fine, I'll drink it," Emilie said, rolling her eyes. She popped the cork out of the bottle and downed the liquid inside.

"What is it?" Jasper asked her anxiously.

Her eyebrows drew together. "I ... *think* ... it's sleepfast."

"I know the antidote," Gidion said. He began searching for lanial oil. There, a thick, golden liquid. He unstopped it and sniffed. A faint, almost fishy smell. Yes, that was it. He poured some into an empty bottle. He needed an emulsifier to make it mix with the water—but even as he thought this, Jasper was bringing him an egg. He cracked it into a bowl that Emilie provided and beat it, before adding some of it to the bottle along with water. This done, he gave the bottle a good shake and passed it to Emilie. They watched her intently as she drank it down.

"Stop staring at me," she said. "You're creeping me out. Let's start on the next one."

"Do you think you'll be alright?" Jasper asked.

"We'll find out," Emilie said. "Now, which of you is going to drink the last bottle?"

In answer, Jasper picked it up, unstopped it, and had a sniff.

"What is it?" Emilie demanded.

"I'm not sure." He took an experimental sip, his mouth twisting. "Still not sure."

"What kind of taste does it have?" Gidion asked.

"Bitter, although there's a hint of sweetness." Jasper sipped again, but still seemed uncertain.

Gidion went through the potions he knew according to their taste and started to throw names out. But Jasper shook his head at each one.

"Give it to me," Gidion said at last in exasperation. He was still feeling woozy from the eyebright, but if they didn't get the antidote soon, something bad was going to happen to Jasper. And that wasn't going to be good for their prospects of winning, even if he thought Jasper deserved it.

"I ... need to sit down," Jasper said breathlessly, sinking to the ground where he was.

Gidion took the poison off him, discovering there was only the tiniest drop left. He tipped it into his mouth, but there wasn't enough left for him to be certain of what it was.

Jasper's limbs started spasming, the color draining out of his face.

"Jasp, Jasp, can you talk?" Emilie cried. She crouched next to him, peering down at his face with panic.

He didn't answer. His teeth were clenched tight, his eyes bulging as they fixed on the ceiling. The rictus led Gidion to the answer. Heartsbane poisoning! He hurried back to the table and snatched the bottles and seeds he needed. By the time he'd finished preparing the antidote, Jasper's body was as stiff as a plank.

"Get his jaw open," he said to Emilie.

With difficulty, she prized his teeth apart, and they forced the remedy down his throat using a funnel Gidion had found on the table. A few minutes later, the stiffness began to reduce. They waited more agonizing minutes for Jasper to become conscious again.

"Pits, that was ... awful," Jasper wheezed. "What was it?"

"Heartsbane," Gidion said.

"I thought you were going to die," Emilie said, tears in her eyes.

"It looks worse than it is," Gidion said. "I don't think he had enough to kill him, but certainly enough to knock him out for the rest of the Trial." He looked at the door and found to his relief that it had opened. They'd passed.

"Can you walk?" Emilie asked Jasper.

"Help me up."

They took an arm each and got him to his feet. He took a few unsteady steps. "I'll be fine," he said. "Just a minute." He stumbled to the door while they watched in concern, but then straightened. "Come on, I'll be fine."

Gidion again noted the lack of thanks, of any acknowledgment that he'd just saved Jasper's ass. *Next time, he can go rot in a pit.*

The next room was split in half by a huge chasm, a door on the far side. It was much too wide to jump across, but three bridges spanned it. The furthest was solid, reassuring stone, while the middle was a span of metal so slender it would only be crossed by putting one foot directly in front of the other. It had no railings to hang onto. The nearest was just wooden slats attached to two lengths of rope, many of them broken or missing. It had no rails either. "Let's go," Emilie said, making for the stone bridge.

"Wait!" Gidion cried. "I think this is a test."

"Of course it's a test," Jasper snorted.

Gidion's first instinct had also been to go for the stone bridge, but Pa had always taught him to look beneath the surface of things. Maybe the stone bridge wasn't what it seemed. He opened his mind to the Tapestry, focusing on the bridges, hoping the threads would teach him something. There was something distinctly off about the threads around the stone bridge. "I think that bridge is broken," he said.

"How can you tell?" Emilie said skeptically.

"Can't you see how strange the threads are?"

"They're strange everywhere," Jasper said.

"This is different." But different how? Why was he so convinced there was something wrong? It was true that the Tapestry was very knotted in the maze. But there was a pattern in that bridge that he didn't recognize, and the other two bridges didn't have it.

"It's probably just one of those double bluffs where they make you suspect the good bridge," Emilie said. "They love doing that kind of thing to us. Come on."

"Or maybe we're each supposed to take one bridge," Jasper said. "There's three of them and three of us. It was that way with the poisons."

"Well, I'm taking the stone bridge," Emilie said, stepping onto it.

Jasper considered the metal bridge and then the wooden one. "Do you see anything strange about these two?" he asked Gidion grudgingly.

"Only that we can fall if we make the slightest misstep," Gidion said.

"Fine. I'll take the metal one," Jasper said, making for it.

Which left Gidion with the most dangerous bridge. It didn't even have any handrails. He slung his staff across his back and placed his foot on the first of the wooden slats, trying to ignore the yawning abyss on either side. The bridge creaked and swayed in response to his weight, making the blood rush through his veins. He gingerly moved forward with the next foot. The bridge swayed even more, and he nearly lost his balance. His heart lurched off rhythm, making him feel so faint he almost slipped off. By the fourth step, he was sweating freely, cursing himself for not having followed Jasper on the other bridge.

A shriek pierced the air.

Gidion froze and looked around. Emilie had disappeared from the stone bridge. It still looked intact and had high sides, so she couldn't have just fallen off. "What happened?"

"She fell through it," Jasper said with a frown. "Must have been an illusion." He was well ahead of Gidion but had paused just shy of the half-way mark, as if considering whether to continue.

Nessa had told Gidion he had Eleusian blood in him through the Ilk Lord. Was that why he'd sensed something was wrong with the bridge? Illusions were Eleusian magic, and of course, Eleusians had helped construct this maze.

"Check my bridge again," Jasper commanded.

"If you ask nicely," Gidion said.

"We're down to two. You don't want to end up having to steal a standard and guard our base on your own, do you?"

Knowing Jasper was right, Gidion carefully analyzed the threads around the bridge. "It seems fine to me, but just take it easy, alright?"

He took his own advice and lowered himself onto his belly, clutching the sides of the narrow bridge in a white-knuckled grip as he propelled himself forward. The bridge continued to creak and sway alarmingly, but he made faster progress than when he'd been walking.

Jasper made it safely to the other side, waiting with obvious impatience while Gidion slithered the rest of the way across. "Come on, scrubber. We're down one. We've got no time to lose," Jasper said when he finally made it to solid ground. He stretched out a hand to help Gidion get to his feet.

"What do you think happened to Emily?" Gidion said, ignoring the hand. "She's hardly dead, is she?"

"No point thinking about her now," Jasper replied. "Come on. We need to move even faster and get to the base before the other teams."

Surprised at Jasper's coldness, Gidion followed him down the corridor at a jog. But he was angry, too. If they'd just listened to him, Emily would still be with them. Now, they were a team member down, and their chances of winning had plummeted.

They soon came up to a door shut by seven bolts, each one with a heavy padlock. Hanging from hooks high on the wall to the right were seven golden keys. The voice boomed out. "Order the keys from base to precious and most pure, and you will pass."

"They want us to test alloys," Gidion said, peering up at the keys.

"Evidently. Help me up and I'll toss them down."

"Why don't you help *me* up," Gidion said.

"Are we really going to waste time on this?" Jasper said. "I thought you wanted to win."

Gidion did, of course, want to win. And that desire was even stronger than the desire he had at that moment to punch Jasper in the face. Arguing was going to get them nowhere. "Fine, get up." He bent his knees so that Jasper could get onto his shoulders.

The youth quickly tossed the keys to the ground, and then they crouched over them. Jasper pointed out one. "This is the most impure, I think."

Gidion analyzed the threads running through it, then started on the other keys to compare.

But Jasper didn't wait for him to answer and took the key to the door. It didn't work. Cursing, he tried it in other locks until he finally found the right one.

Meanwhile, Gidion continued analyzing the remaining keys and then shifted them into order. It was a task his peddling days had left him eminently suited to. "This is the most impure," Gidion said, plucking the correct key.

"What makes you so sure?"

"I've got a lot of experience in testing alloys."

"Why's that?" Jasper said.

"I tested coins all the time when trading."

Immediately, Jasper's features twisted into a sneer. "Right. And how long have you spent studying artefaction at the Spire?" he said. He picked up another key, but it didn't work either.

Exasperated, Gidion elbowed him out of the way and inserted the one he knew to be correct. It turned in the lock. After that, Jasper silently stood aside while Gidion swiftly opened the remaining locks. Again, he received not even the slightest acknowledgment from Jasper for his success.

The next room they entered was extremely odd. It was made up of bricks, like the walls of the tunnel with the Lore questions. But in this case, the bricks were square, and those on the left-hand side displayed glowing mathematical symbols. Meanwhile, each of those on the right-hand wall bore a number between 1 and 150. Straight ahead of them was a closed door.

A female voice boomed out, making them jump. "Thirty problems you shall solve before the portal opens. Fail one more than that and you will fall."

Instinctively, Gidion looked down, seeking a trapdoor. But the floor didn't look any different.

"Do they mean we'll fall if we get more than thirty wrong?" Jasper said.

But before Gidion could answer, the voice spoke again. "Beware the sands of time." An image of a giant hourglass appeared on the wall near the exit door. Then the voice asked a question, the hourglass turning so that sand seemed to pour into the empty part: "A woman takes some baskets to market and comes home with a total of thirty vics. If she sold three baskets at four vics each, three baskets at three vics each and the rest of the baskets at one vic each, how many baskets did she sell in total?"

Gidion's father had often teased him with puzzles of this nature as a child. He did a quick calculation in his head. "Fifteen!" he shouted.

Nothing happened.

"Wrong answer, scrubber," Jasper said. But he sounded puzzled, as if he'd come to the same one.

Gidion went through his calculations again. "I'm sure it's right." They both stared at the wall, then Jasper raced to the number 15 and pressed his hand against it.

The brick pulsed once with a blue light, and the voice asked another question. "Two men on horses set off from the same point to travel the same journey. The first man sets off thirty minutes before the second man. If the first horse travels at three miles per hour and the second travels at four miles per hour, how many miles after the starting point will the two men draw level?"

Gidion calculated in his head. "It's six miles."

"I've come up with four," Jasper replied. And before Gidion could move, he'd pressed his hand against that number.

A lightbolt shot out, striking Jasper squarely in the chest. He crumpled to the ground.

Shit! But Gidion didn't have time to check whether Jasper was alive or dead. The sand was continuing to trickle through, and he'd be damned if he let Jasper's idiocy ruin it all. He ran to the number six, pressed his hand against it, and was rewarded with the blue glow.

The voice asked him to solve another puzzle of the same type, but more difficult. Again, his time as a peddler served him well, and he was quickly able to make the calculations in his head. But then the questions took a different turn. "What number should appear next in the sequence? 3, 8, 35, 48, 99."

Gidion tried multiplying and dividing the numbers in various ways but could see no logic to it. Something was scratching at the edge of his mind. If he could just place it. Then it came to him in a burst of insight. The numbers were 1x3, then 2x4, then 5x7, then 6x8, then 9x11. Which meant the missing number was 10x12, or 120. He ran to press his palm on the number. To his relief, it answered with an affirmative glow. There were three more like that, and each time, he was able to answer correctly.

But then the nature of the questions changed again. "What is the square root of 25?"

What was a square root? He looked at Jasper. The boy was still unmoving. Gidion went over to him, pressed his fingers against his neck. Not dead. Gidion tried shaking him, but still no response. Then, using a trick he'd learned from his father, he injected a tiny bit of his own energy into Jasper. The boy began to rouse.

"What happened?" he mumbled, eyes half open.

"You were hit by a lightbolt."

The voice was speaking again, repeating its question with a warning that their time was running out.

"Do you know the answer?" Gidion asked Jasper.

"Not learned any calculus?" Jasper said, slowly pushing himself to his knees. Gidion offered a hand to help, and Jasper took it, then staggered over to the number five and pushed his hand against it. It glowed blue.

"What is the ratio of a circle's circumference to its diameter?"

Ratio, Gidion understood. But circumference, diameter? He'd never heard the words before.

Jasper knew this answer, too, but told Gidion to go and answer it.

Gidion couldn't resist a taunt. "Afraid you have it wrong?"

Jasper's mouth twisted. "We'll take it in turns to press the answers," he said. "We don't want us both knocked out because we got hit too many times."

Gidion used his other sense to try and tell if Jasper was playing a trick on him. But the boy seemed confident of his answer. So Gidion pressed the numbers and ratio symbol. He raised a shield and braced himself to be struck by a lightbolt, but the answer was correct.

The questions continued, each of them more bewildering than the last. Circles, triangles, probabilities, x's and y's. He'd never studied any of it. *Pa only ever wanted me to be a peddler,* he thought bitterly. They each suffered further lightbolt attacks, the sand running ever lower. But finally, on the fortieth question, the door opened, and they passed through.

The next corridor took them into a kind of sitting room. Gidion took the scene in quickly. An unlit standing lamp in the corner, an inactivated heatstone beneath a mantlepiece, a green velvet couch, and a low wooden table on which rested a teapot broken into five pieces. On the wall above the couch, a clock with both hands on the 10. Opposite, a large, rectangular mirror with a gilt, leafwork frame. But when he looked into the mirror, he discovered it wasn't showing the room behind him. Or rather, it was, but it looked very different. The teapot was mended, and the clock was ticking, showing the hour of twelve.

"They want us to fix everything!" he exclaimed. It was the typical work of a ranger. Many of the jobs didn't require full artefaction talent to complete, which was why most rangers could do them. Creating the artefacts in the first place was the greater difficulty. "I can fix that glowglobe and heatstone," he said. And for once, Jasper didn't ignore him or disagree with him, instead going to the clock.

But as they moved around the room, a loud explosion cracked the air. They threw themselves to the ground, covering their ears.

"What was that?" Gidion said.

"No idea," Jasper replied, craning his neck to look around.

Gidion gingerly got to his feet. But he'd no sooner done that than another deafening explosion sounded, sending him back to the ground. A series of rapid cracks followed. But again, they could see no source or effect.

"I think they're just trying to distract us," Jasper said, already back on his knees. "Let's just get on with it."

Easier said than done. The explosions came frequently but unpredictably, each one deafening. Soon, Gidion's ears were ringing, his heart racing in a constant state of alarm.

But finally, they finished, and the door swung open for them. Exultant, Gidion ran through after Jasper. It opened into yet another tunnel, but as soon as they rounded the first corner, they saw it—their base, floating in the air above them.

Chapter 20

They walked around the left side of the base, looking for an entrance, but saw none. And they couldn't get around to the front of it because they were blocked by a wall that stretched from floor to ceiling. They tried the right side, but there was no entrance there either.

"How do we get in?" Gidion said, frowning at the wall.

"Levitation," Jasper replied. "Can you do it?"

"Of course." Annoyed he hadn't thought of it himself, Gidion began to pluck the threads he needed, weaving them to create a solid cushion of air that would propel him upwards. It was slow, so much slower than splicing.

Once inside, he spotted their standard, a blue flag stuck into a hole in the ground in the middle of the base. There were two other holes, presumably for other standards they captured. The base itself was about six paces wide by four paces long, but the front wall had an opening wide enough for one and a ramp that led down into the darkness. From the top of the ramp, they could see another maze. But unlike the wall on either side of the base that had blocked their route forward, the walls of the maze itself didn't reach the ceiling. Above the maze, to the left and right, were and red and green glow respectively. The Ruby and Emerald bases. Gidion stretched out his lifesense to see if the other initiates had reached them yet, but the dense patterns confused him.

"We should go after Ruby," Jasper said. "They've got the weakest fighters."

"Shouldn't one of us stay here to guard the flag?" Gidion said.

"I think we got here first. I don't see anyone, do you?"

"No, but they could be hiding. And it's pretty dark down there."

But Jasper wasn't swayed. "If we move fast enough, we can get to their base and back here again."

It was a risk, but it appealed to Gidion. "Let's go, then."

They sprinted down the ramp, plunging into almost total darkness. The walls were so high that only the faintest glow was visible. Gidion lit his focus stone, but Jasper told him to put it out. "Better they not see us coming."

Grudgingly, Gidion agreed Jasper was right, so he let the glow die. They picked a path that led roughly in the direction of the Ruby base. But the maze twisted and turned frequently, full of alcoves and dead ends that forced them constantly to backtrack. Gidion was on high alert, expecting at any moment to be jumped by the other teams, but they reached the other base without mishap. There didn't seem to be anyone inside it, but Gidion was suspicious.

"Let's go," Jasper whispered excitedly.

Gidion stretched out his lifesense and encountered the resonance that told him people were present. "No, they're in there."

"How can you tell?"

"I just can," he said. He knew his sensitivity wasn't something many weavers shared and didn't want to go into any awkward explanations.

Jasper frowned at him but hesitated.

Gidion could use his stun power if he was able to get out of sight somehow. But he risked knocking out Jasper too—he didn't have enough control of it. And if he killed someone here, he'd be in big trouble. But he had another idea. "Can you draw their fire and I'll levitate up to get the standard?"

Jasper's eyes narrowed. "You won't be able to take them on alone."

"That's why I need you to take the bridge. You're better at head-on combat than me. I'll run around the back while they're distracted by you."

As Gidion had hoped, this appealed to Jasper's vanity. "I can make it seem like there's more than one person attacking."

"Even better."

So Jasper ran out into the open, toward the ramp that led up to the entrance of the base. Fire shot out from three places, but he raised a shield in a blink, and the attacks bounced off. They would have been no more harmful than the bolts during the math challenge even if they *had* hit, but Jasper would still only be able to maintain the shield for a short time. And he'd have a hard time making any counterattacks.

A moon-faced youth took position at the entrance to the base, also in a full-body shield. His teammates were on either side of him, protected by the sides of the base, but shooting fire at Jasper over the top. To Gidion's amazement, Jasper split his shield in two, protecting his flanks while he fired back at Moon-face. Gidion had never seen or heard of such a technique.

Then, Jasper cast his explosion of light. Gidion sprinted to the back of the base, but he had no intention of levitating. No one was watching—they were all intent on Jasper, which meant he could splice unseen.

So he opened a hole in the Tapestry, a murderously difficult task with the patterns being so dense. But he reckoned they'd never designed the Trial to counteract splicing, whether by accident or design, and he persevered. At last, he had a tunnel just large enough to step through. A fraction of a second later he was in the base, snatching the standard, then back on the ground again.

"Done!" he yelled at Jasper, running back around the front.

"Cover me!" Jasper cried.

Gidion blasted lightbolts to hold the other team back while Jasper retreated. As soon as the latter was off the ramp, they turned and sprinted back to their base. But when they got there, breathing heavily, they found a pair of Emeralds charging in to grab their standard. They ran up the ramp after them, taking one each.

Gidion found himself against a powerful youth who was extremely fast with his staff. But Gidion managed to hold his own, had, in fact, just managed to beat him into a corner, when the entire Ruby team appeared, levitating up on every side.

"Get my back!" Jasper yelled.

Out of the corner of his eye, Gidion saw that Jasper had stuck the Ruby standard next to their own standard in the center of the base and was pressed against both. Gidion retreated until he was back-to-back with Jasper, the standards between them.

"We just need to hold on," Jasper gasped. "Shields only."

Gidion was already raising a full body shield to protect against magical and physical attacks. If they could keep it going long enough, they had a good chance of winning. But both he and Jasper were already depleted, and the others were throwing everything they had at them. Soon, Gidion was starting to feel ill, his shield flickering unsteadily.

How long until the bell sounded the end of the Trial? A blow landed on his arm, numbing it completely and almost causing him to drop his staff. If another blow landed, he was done for. He made a snap decision. He wouldn't lose when he was so close to the win. He wouldn't.

To hide what he was doing, he blinded everyone using the same trick that Jasper had. Then he unleashed his stun power. With so many people to target, he didn't even try to isolate the threads. He didn't have that level of skill. So he just blasted everyone in a radius around him, trying to ensure it wasn't strong enough to kill.

They all slumped to the ground, and Gidion anxiously stretched out his lifesense to check if they were still alive. Their resonance was at a different pitch to normal, but there was a resonance, which meant they were alive. Giddy relief burst inside him.

But what now? Did he try to drag them out of the base? Did he go after the Emerald standard? Even as these thoughts came to him, the bell rang to signal the end of the Trial. Gidion's relief turned to exultation. They'd won!

A grinding sound from the bottom of the ramp that led to the maze—the floor had opened, revealing steps going down. He grabbed the standards and ran down. Thane was standing at the bottom of the ramp, radiating fury, and Gidion stopped in his tracks. "You fool!" Thane hissed, arms out as if he wanted to shake Gidion. "What were you thinking?"

Gidion knew he was talking about the stun power but was defiant. "I made sure no one could see what I was doing."

"They could feel the effects!" Thane exclaimed. "And it's not even the initiates you need to be concerned about. It's the people who were watching you in the maze."

"You were watching us?"

"Of course, we were. It's a test!"

"You didn't tell me," Gidion said, still defiant. But he was worried. He'd thought he'd got away with it, that he'd be able to explain it away. Winning had been everything for him in the moment. But now ... he didn't want them locking him up as an Ilk mage.

"Luckily for you, I was the only one watching your base. The others were assigned to Ruby and Emerald. But tell me, did you use the stun strike anywhere else?"

"No," Gidion said, relieved. He'd spliced, though. Had someone seen him do that? Should he tell Thane? But Thane didn't know he'd learned how to do that, so he kept quiet. Hopefully, it could be explained away if there were questions. A glitch. Someone seeing things.

Thane's eyes narrowed as if he wasn't sure whether to believe Gidion. He peered around behind him. "Are they alive, at least?"

"Yes, I checked."

It was Thane's turn to look relieved. "Well, that's something, at least. Take the standards and follow me," he said. "We'll let the rest of them join us when they wake. And whatever you do, don't admit to using the stun blast. Tell them you don't know how you did what you did. It will keep them guessing for a while."

"But will I have to tell them eventually?"

Thane hesitated. "Probably, but I want to find your Ilk mage first. The other weavers won't be as understanding as I am. They know little about the time before the Ruin and even less about the Chelaki."

"I'll do as you say," Gidion said, chastened.

"And don't even think about using that trick tomorrow. The Tournament is a very formal affair. You're expected to fight with staff and lightbolts only."

This seemed utterly ridiculous to Gidion. It hardly counted as a win if your opponent wasn't able to use everything at their disposal.

"It's for the pride of the Greats," Thane said, as if reading his thoughts. "Honor and grace count above all."

They'd reached the bottom of the short steps, turning a sharp corner into a dimly lit corridor. At the end of it was a levitator which took them back up again. It opened into another tunnel, which in turn brought them back to the starting point of the first maze. The entrance door was wide open, and they stepped through to the mirror room. Already there were Emily and two members of the Emerald team.

"What happened to you?" Gidion asked Emilie.

"I fell into a levitation weave and then got sent through a tunnel back to here," she replied sullenly.

Gidion bit down on a smile. *Maybe, you'll think twice next time before ignoring my advice.*

The others were beginning to trickle in behind them, and Thane waited until everyone had arrived before announcing that the Sapphire team were the winners of the Selection Trial. "Congratulations to you all. Your names will go on the Honors Register, and, of course, you each win a battlestaff crafted by Torigan Faringale."

Gidion grinned proudly, but everyone was congratulating Jasper and Emilie, giving Gidion only the most cursory nods. Again, his anger stirred.

"Off you go now and eat. You must all be hungry," Thane said, waving a hand in dismissal.

They trooped toward the levitator, but Jasper pulled Gidion back. "I want to talk to you."

The inevitable question over the stun blast, coming already. Could he just shake Jasper off? But the youth seemed anxious. "Why?"

"I'll tell you when we're away from the others," Jasper said. "Let them go ahead of us."

His curiosity piqued, Gidion halted and let the rest flow around them.

"Jasper, you coming?" Emilie called from the levitator.

Jasper waved her away. "Go on, I'll follow."

She frowned, but then shrugged, allowing the levitator door to close.

"What's this about?" Gidion said once they were alone.

Jasper rounded on him. "You won't beat me in the Tournament."

"If that's all you have to say, then don't waste your breath," Gidion said angrily, stepping toward the levitator.

But Jasper stopped him with a hand on his shoulder. "Whatever it was you did to knock us all out in the base, you won't be able to do it tomorrow. The rules for the Tournament are very strict."

"I don't know what I did," Gidion said, then cursed silently. He sounded too defensive.

Jasper didn't seem to pick up on it, though. "Over the years, people have tried other tricks, and it never works for them. It's a strict staff and bolts affair."

"I don't need you to tell me the rules," Gidion said, shrugging free of Jasper's hand to call the levitator.

"If you promise not to put Thane down anywhere on your list of preferred mentors, I'll let you beat me."

Gidion froze. "Why?"

"I want to apprentice with Thane. All Wyvens are expected to," Jasper said. "My father has long had an alliance with him. But if I'm not the best, Thane won't take me. And it will be me who gets in trouble, not him. The only way to ensure he takes me is for you not to be in the running."

Gidion's sense told him that Jasper was being genuine. He was afraid of his father. But it wasn't just that. He'd seen how Jasper looked at Thane. "Is that why you tampered with my heatstone in the artefaction test?"

"I didn't do anything to your stone," Jasper said, shifting his feet. "You think I'm that stupid? Thane would have noticed. You messed it up all on your own."

But Gidion's other senses told him clearly that Jasper was lying. "You're full of shit. I'm not helping you." Gidion tried to sidestep him, but Jasper blocked his way.

"You want to win the Tournament, right? So you can train with the Guardian?"

Gidion hesitated. Was Jasper trying to trap him? "Don't *you* want to win the Tournament?" he said instead of answering. "It would mean you could choose Thane and he'd have to take you. You won the Selection Trial."

Jasper snorted. "No—*you* won it."

"But Thane said we all did ..."

"Yes, it's a team thing. But they still need to rank us," Jasper said. "Emilie fell into the chasm, and you knocked me out, which meant you were the only one left standing at the end. So you placed first, and I placed second. The only way I can guarantee to apprentice with Thane is if you take his name off your list and I let you win."

Gidion still hesitated. His instincts told him that Jasper was being truthful. And he remembered how infatuated Jasper seemed to be with Thane. Plus, it made sense why Jasper had tampered with Gidion's stone. So, much as it stuck in his craw to accept Jasper's help, he agreed. "Fine, I'll leave Thane's name off my list. But if I don't win, I'll say I made a mistake."

"I'll play my part." And with that, Jasper stepped into the levitator. Gidion waited until he was gone before calling the levitator for himself.

They were all due to hand in their list of mentors the following day, ranked from one to ten in order of preference. Gidion filled his top four slots with the names of warcraft mentors, with Arianna Velden's name in first position. It cost him little to leave out Thane, but Jasper, mistrustful, asked to see his list before he handed it in.

And then it was done, with only the Tournament left so that he could prove himself.

Chapter 21

They were supposed to rest the day before the Selection Tournament. But Gidion was too anxious and cajoled Nessa into training with him.

"Let's skip the physical training and talk about the mental game," Nessa said when she came to him in the Water Garden the evening before.

"I'm not allowed to use my Chelaki magic," Gidion said, thinking this was what she referred to.

"That's not what I meant."

"What, then?"

"Winning is as much about psychology as skill," Nessa replied. "Surprise and misdirection—they'll give you the edge, even with someone who's technically better than you," she continued. "And don't be afraid to cheat. Fighting honorably is a sure way to a quick death. Blind them with dust. Kick them in the nuts. Stab them in the back. Whatever works in the moment."

"Thane said they don't approve of things like that," Gidion replied.

"Do you want to impress them, or do you want to win?"

"Win, of course." And he had his pact with Jasper, so really, it was too late to be concerned about cheating.

"Remember, at the start of the fight, stay predictable. Keep using the same feints and attacks. Let them have an easy score. They'll let their guard down, think you an easy victory. Then you land your killer blow, something they haven't seen you do yet." She proved her point by suddenly diving into a roll, coming up to the side of him with a knife against the back of his knee.

Her words were still ringing in Gidion's ear when he made his way over to the arena the following morning. He went alone, Thane having told him he had to go earlier to meet with other mentors. That had him thinking about Arianna Velden. Today, at last, he'd have a chance to show his worth to her, convince her he was the apprentice she needed.

He found the initiates standing in front of a noticeboard outside the entrance of the arena, pointing excitedly. Gidion peered over their shoulders to see that it was a list of matchups. As Thane had told him, the initiates were divided into two groups for the first round and would have to fight each person in their group first. The top two from each group would then go against the top two from the other group to determine the overall winners. To Gidion's relief, Jasper wasn't in his group. Best he came up against him in the final—that was, of course, if Jasper held up his side of the bargain.

"In you go and get ready!" called a man in pale brown attendant's livery.

The initiates filed inside the entrance and went to the armory to select weapons and armor. They had to fight with blunted blades, but they could use their preferred staff type, and Gidion opted for one similar to his own. To keep things fair and prevent accidental death, they all had to use regulation focus stones, tiny emeralds that wouldn't generate much power. These were handed out to them once they'd selected their staff.

The initiates ignored Gidion as they got ready, chattering nervously among themselves. It hurt him, but he made no attempt to engage. He wanted to focus on what was ahead, and it was better if he regarded them as enemies to be defeated.

The first pair trooped out for their bout, which would last fifteen minutes or until someone was knocked out, whichever happened first. The remaining initiates weren't allowed to watch the fights. Instead, they had to stay in the changing area, but they could hear the roars of the crowd whenever someone scored a hit. Mostly, they waited in silence, the tension thick and heavy between them.

Finally, it was Gidion's turn, and he walked out to the applause of the crowd along with his first opponent, a girl called Annina. Gidion couldn't help but gawp as he entered the arena. People were jammed into every seat, several thousand of them, at least. The best seats, in the shade, were clearly for the most high-ranking families. They wore rich clothing, some of them weaver's robes, and weren't so closely packed.

Spire weavers also had their own section, and among them, near the front, was Thane. But Gidion was more eager for the sight of another weaver—Arianna Velden, Guardian of the Spire. She was sitting next to Thane, clapping politely, the barest hint of a smile on her face. Their eyes met. Gidion thought silently at her, *You will choose me.* She cocked her head, her gaze sharpening, holding his, as if she'd heard him.

"Take your positions!" cried the referee, a hook-nosed man whose shock of thick, dark hair was peppered with grey.

A circle ten paces in diameter had been marked out in white paint, with a spot in each half of it. They would have to stay within the circle throughout the bout or lose a point. And if they were pushed out three times, it was an automatic loss. Gidion stepped onto his spot and dropped into a fighting stance.

Opposite him, Annina did the same. She was tall and willowy, her face set in determination. Gidion repeated to himself, *I will beat her. I will beat her.*

The referee cried, "Fight!"

Gidion wove the beginnings of a shield but didn't complete it, hoping to lure Annina into a hasty attack. At the same time, he closed the distance between them with three fast hops. She sidestepped and threw a lightbolt, but he strengthened his shield just in time to break it before jabbing the spear at her neck. She jerked back and skipped to the side, the blade missing her by a whisper.

The rest of the fight was similar. He allowed her to lure him in, and she would try to strike him with a lightbolt from a side angle. But when the bell rang to announce the final minute, Gidion unleashed his plan—a feinted spear thrust from the front, just as he'd been doing, followed by a lightbolt that caught her squarely in the chest when she sidestepped. Had the lightbolt been real, she'd be dead, so the bout was over, his arm raised in victory. The applause was muted and hesitant. Searching the faces around him, Gidion saw confusion. *You'll know who I am after today.*

As he walked back into the waiting area, his eyes went to Thane and the Guardian. Thane smiled at him, but the Guardian merely cast him an appraising look before turning to say something to the woman beside her. The woman looked remarkably similar in features, and Gidion guessed she might be a sister.

"Congratulations," Jasper said drily when he returned to the changing area.

"I'll look forward to our bout later."

Jasper smirked. "If you get that far."

His taunt sparked doubt in Gidion. Was this all an elaborate ruse on his part? A trick to humiliate Gidion? A questing of Jasper's emotions told him only that he was in a state of anxiety, which surprised him. But he decided not to reply, instead going to the water fountain to cool his face and wet his parched mouth.

His next opponent was the freckled youth he'd seen with Emilie at the end of the Trial. He presented no great difficulty, and Gidion soon lured him into overextending before taking him down with a sweep to the legs. The fall sent his staff flying loose from his grip. Gidion kicked it away and pressed the tip of the spearhead against the youth's throat until he yielded.

His third opponent, though, was one he knew to watch out for—Harald. He'd won each of his fights in the first minute and was still looking worryingly fresh. Gidion didn't need to beat him to go through to the next round. But if he didn't win, he'd likely face Jasper in the semi-final and then Harald again for the final—which wouldn't be good for his overall chances. This was probably the most important—and dangerous—fight of the tournament for him.

Harald's staff closely resembled a halberd, reaching a good arm's length above his head. Gidion knew from watching him sparring that he'd use it to try to keep Gidion out of reach, running a shield off it that went all the way to the ground to keep out any lightbolts Gidion might throw. Then he'd try to score a kill with the blade. Lightbolts weren't Harald's forte, which was probably why he adopted this tactic, but he was incredibly effective with it.

As they squared off, Gidion considered his options. He could try to move around to Harald's side fast enough to throw a lightbolt before Harald could swing around to block it on his shield. Or he could abandon lightbolts entirely and make it a straight-up blade-against-blade battle. Only thing was that Gidion's staff was a lot shorter than Harald's. And if he didn't have a shield ready, Harald might still send a lightbolt against him.

The referee called a start, and they began to circle one another. Gidion decided to test the speed of Harald's defense, dodging around the side to try to catch him with a lightbolt. But Harald swung around just fast enough to catch it on the shield, before stepping in with a counter.

Gidion parried it with his staff, observing that Harald did as he so often did in sparring—he stepped to his right after he attacked. They exchanged more feints and attacks, neither scoring a hit on the other. But each time, Harald showed the same tendency to step to his right. Gidion just needed to figure out his timing.

When the moment came, it was pure instinct that moved him. He parried Harald's staff, then stepped to his left and pirouetted, landing his blade at the side of Harald's throat. A clean kill. Harald yielded, eyes hot with fury.

He'd won! He glanced at Arianna Velden and then Thane. The Guardian's expression was one of undisguised surprise. Thane initially looked contemplative, but when he caught Gidion's eye, he beamed a congratulatory smile. The spectator response, though, was distinctly muted. Harald had no doubt been expected to defeat him easily. But Gidion didn't care too much, or at least told himself he didn't care, as he marched back into the changing area, keeping his head high. *They'll know me now. They'll know me, and they'll mark me.*

He passed Jasper on the way in. The youth gave him a questioning look, and he responded with a slight nod. Jasper's lips pressed together, but Gidion's other sense told him that he was trying to conceal surprise. He hadn't expected Gidion to beat Harald, had no doubt expected to both win the tournament and have Thane as mentor. Gidion smiled. He was starting to learn about Gidion. They all were.

When the initial rounds were over, they were given a break of an hour to refresh. The initiates who hadn't made it to the final went to join the spectators in the arena, leaving only the four finalists. They were offered light food, but Gidion could barely swallow a mouthful. He was too nervous, too close to his prize. And winning mattered more than anything else.

"I've got some tips for you." Gidion started at the unexpected sound of Nessa's voice in his mind. How was she doing that?

"I'll teach you how to do this when you're ready. But listen to me, I've been watching the bouts."

"You have?" How had he failed to see her?

"The girl, Laurelle, who you'll be up against next. She's canny. She's using attacks we haven't seen during her sparring sessions. But I have an idea of what might work."

"Okay, tell me." He didn't know if Nessa could hear him, but she laid out the plan for him, and he agreed it was sound.

At last, it was time to start again. Gidion's bout was first. Like him, Laurelle had chosen the standard setup of staff and shield. The blade on her staff was shaped like a spearhead, designed for stabbing.

Following Nessa's instructions, Gidion activated the shield on his arm and pointed his staff at Laurelle, shooting lightbolts so quickly that she was forced to do nothing but defend. After a few minutes, he slowed, pretending he was exhausted and allowing his shield to flicker. Gidion had been certain that she'd see through the ruse, but Nessa had been adamant it would work.

"Even though you've made it this far, she can't imagine you'll beat her. She won't think anything of your abilities, she thinks it's all a fluke," Nessa had said. Bruising words that had caused his anger to rise, but he saw the truth of them when Laurelle's mouth curved into a smug smile.

She dropped her shield and sent out a horizontal sheet of blue light. The only defense against such an attack was a shield that covered the entire front of the body. Laurelle didn't think Gidion had the power left for that. So she'd put everything into this one mighty attack, one that would knock him unconscious if it landed, giving her the win. But Gidion held his staff directly in front of his body, summoning a full-length shield through his focus stone that sliced the sheet in half. It passed on either side of him and crashed harmlessly against the magical barricades that protected the spectators.

But even before he heard it strike the barriers, Gidion was in motion, crossing the ground to thrust the spear blade at Laurelle's throat. And with that, he'd won.

It was Jasper against Harald next. Gidion had to go back into the waiting area, so he didn't see the bout, but Nessa gave him a blow-by-blow account. Jasper won with relative ease, soon returning triumphantly.

"He's going to be tough to beat," Nessa said.

"I have a plan for him," Gidion said.

"What is it?"

"You'll see."

"You'll need to use every trick you have. But his overconfidence could be your friend. Wait for him to think he's got you."

"I told you, I've got this one," Gidion returned.

He sensed confusion from her, but she didn't press further.

Jasper's name was called out, and he headed back into the arena. A roar rose up from the spectators. When it came to his turn, Gidion tried to inject swagger into his walk, but he just felt stiff and uncomfortable, a feeling that was magnified by the decidedly less enthusiastic welcome he received. He glanced up at Arianna Velden, found her watching him closely. Thane was also watching, but when Gidion's eyes caught his, he made no sign of recognition, as if his mind was elsewhere.

"On guard!" the referee called.

Gidion faced Jasper and settled into his fighting stance. The other stared at him with a disdainful curl to his lip. A front, or did he intend to break their bargain? Gidion couldn't figure it out from his emotions. He was tense, focused on the fight.

"Ready!" called the referee.

Gidion pointed his staff at a forty-five-degree angle from his body, preparing to attack or defend.

"Fight!"

Jasper blasted a lightbolt at him. Surprised at the speed of the attack, Gidion only just deflected it with his shield. He was still recovering his wits when Jasper darted in and scored a hit against his chest with the blade of his staff.

"One point, Wyven!" cried the referee.

Pits! He threw a pair of lightbolts in quick succession, one at Jasper's head, the other at his chest, but he caught them both on his shield before returning one of his own that hit him in the foot.

"One point, Wyven!"

Jasper came at him with his staff, a whirling barrage that had Gidion seriously wondering if he'd broken their pact. He blocked the first few, then tried a counterattack that was cut short when Jasper hooked his blade around the back of his leg and pulled him off balance. He just about managed to stay on his feet and hop free, but Jasper had already thrown another lightbolt at him. Whether through luck or intention, it crashed harmlessly against Gidion's shield. But Jasper had received a point for the successful hooking maneuver, leaving Gidion three down.

Moving so quickly he was a blur, Jasper attacked again with his staff, scoring a strike against Gidion's helmeted head that left his ears ringing. Desperate, convinced that Jasper had no intention of letting him win, Gidion tried to gain an advantage, tossing bolt after bolt as fast as he could. But Jasper evaded or deflected them all.

The half-way bell pealed. They'd planned the next part, but Gidion was sure Jasper had set a trap for him and hesitated to make his move. Instead, he circled round, jabbing and feinting, but staying out of reach, agonizing over what to do.

"What are you waiting for?" Jasper taunted. "You made it this far and now you're too chicken to fight?"

It seemed like genuine puzzlement. And he was holding off, giving Gidion a moment to breathe. Maybe it wasn't a trap? But then, Jasper hardly needed a trap to beat him. He was the far superior fighter. *Pits with it, here goes.* He cast a full-body shield, using the stones in his staff and wrist to power it. But he was already drained from the earlier bouts, and immediately felt dizzy.

Jasper stopped tossing lightbolts at him. None would land, and the standard tactic was to wait for the opponent to run out of energy, at which point you could take them rather easily. But he still had to keep Gidion out of reach.

With a yell, Gidion ran straight at Jasper, throwing his staff like a spear at Jasper's head and forcing him to duck. Gidion's shield collapsed at the same time—he didn't have enough in him to maintain it. But it didn't matter. He dived into a forward roll, coming up into a low crouch before Jasper. Then he wrapped his arms around Jasper's legs, just below the knee, and yanked up to smash him down onto his back. Jasper fell heavily with an unfeigned cry. Gidion threw himself on top of him to keep him down, reaching for his staff, now lying in the dirt. Jasper writhed beneath him, trying to push him off and almost succeeding. But Gidion prevailed, and his fingers closed around Jasper's staff. Then he whipped out his knife and held the blade to Jasper's throat.

Gasps all around, then a shocked silence. Then a cheer from the rangers section of the weavers. Nearly all were commoners, and it seemed Gidion had just become their unexpected hero.

"I yield!" Jasper shouted. Then he added in a low voice that only Gidion could hear. "Now get off me. I can feel your dick swelling."

"I'm wearing a codpiece," he said flushing.

Jasper just laughed while Gidion scrambled to his feet.

Then Jasper stretched out a hand. "You can help me up. Or do you want to seem unsportsmanlike?"

Gidion silently took his hand and pulled him to his feet.

The referee had them stand on each side of him. Then he raised Gidion's arm and pronounced him the winner of the Tournament. But again the cheers were muted, mostly coming from the rangers and other scattered pockets. He even thought he heard a few jeers.

Jasper had prepared him for that. "It won't be considered an honorable way to win," he'd said of the tactic they'd formulated. "But it's legal, and winning is winning. Plus, they'll find it more believable."

Easier a defeat for Jasper to swallow, too, no doubt. But Gidion felt no satisfaction in it. He'd rather have won fair and square, and cheating made him feel dirty. But again, he reminded himself of his higher purpose and pushed the guilt away.

"Well done!" Nessa said. *"We'll have to celebrate."*

"When?"

But she didn't reply. She was gone or hadn't heard him.

The prize-giving ceremony took place after they'd showered and dressed. Gidion waited to be called up with a mixture of shame and anticipation. He knew he didn't deserve the prize, even if his skills had improved greatly through Thane and Nessa's tutelage. At the same time, he felt vindicated. They'd all have to reassess their opinion of him. And no one would go against him if he had Arianna Velden as mentor.

At last, the announcer was calling them, and he and Jasper made their way to the center of the arena to receive congratulations from Thane and the First Weaver. Thane pinned a badge to each of their robes, a simple staff with a tiny white diamond. They'd wear it for all of their time as apprentices so everyone would know they'd been finalists.

"And the winner of this year's Selection Tournament is Gidion Jameson!" the announcer cried.

It was the First Weaver who handed him his award, a wiry, grey-haired man with a slight stoop. Gidion had expected a focus stone, but what he hadn't expected was the sheer size of the thing. It was a sapphire the size of his fist—worth thousands of consuls and at least three times as powerful as his current stone. With this, he surely had a chance against Malai.

Thane stepped forward to congratulate him. "Well done, Gidion. Your promise is showing," he said in a loud voice. Then, too low for anyone else to hear, he added, "I'll speak to you in my rooms later."

He was angry. He probably knew that Gidion had put Arianna Velden's name down as his top choice. But Gidion was prepared to face him down. No one controlled him. No one.

Chapter 22

Dinner was served after the prize-giving ceremony in the Seekers' mess hall. Family members were allowed to attend, so it was a busy affair. Of course, Gidion had no family or friends, and Jasper and Emilie had both made it plain they wanted nothing more to do with him. But Thane invited him to the top table as the winner of both the Tournament and the Trial. He was unusually cold with Gidion, who reckoned Thane must know about the list of mentors. Gidion didn't give it much thought, though, because Arianna Velden was sitting opposite him, and he was determined to speak to her. Her robes were shimmering silver – a color that told everyone she was the Guardian of the Spire. Embroidered along the cuffs were intertwining threads that marked her three specialisms – warcraft, statecraft, and lore. The triumvirate of ruling weavers. Her deep auburn hair was wrapped into a knot at the back of her head, but slender strands fell around her face, making her look surprisingly youthful.

Their hands touched as they both tried to take a bread roll from the basket sitting between them. Gidion blushed and snatched his hand back. A trace of a smile hovered on her lips as she took the bread and set it on a white porcelain side plate. Gidion took a roll of his own, trying to think of a way to open the conversation, but she beat him to it.

"Congratulations on your win," she said, deftly slicing the roll open with her knife.

Gidion had been about to tear his roll open with his hands, but seeing how Arianna did it, he opted for the knife instead. "Thank you, Guardian. I've trained very hard for this. I'm very eager to learn." He stopped short of saying he'd selected her as a mentor, not with Thane sitting right next to him, giving off a distinct aura of anger.

"Where did you train before you came here?" Velden started spreading butter on her roll.

Butter was something else he'd had to get used to since arriving in Arindel. People preferred oil in Federation lands. He still wasn't sure if he liked it but dipped his knife into the butter dish. "I didn't go to a school," he replied.

"But you must have learned somewhere?"

Gidion put down his knife, still covered in butter, to fix his attention fully on her. "My father trained me himself."

"Varn?" She sounded surprised.

Gidion nodded, bracing himself for the inevitable next question.

"Why didn't he send you here?"

"Varn had him traveling the length and breadth of the Federation," Thane interjected. "And saw no reason to send him for training among us."

"Rangers can be like that," Velden said. "Although they'll usually obey the law."

Was she implying he'd cheated? Or was it something else? "I always wanted to come here," he said. "But he didn't give me a choice."

"I've no doubt you'll be a valuable asset," she replied. Her tone implied she was just being polite, that she didn't think much of him one way or another.

"Guardian, a word?" A young female attendant who then whispered into Velden's ear.

Velden's expression changed to irritation. "If I must," she said, pushing her chair back. "Of course they call me away just as the meal comes, but you'll have to excuse me." Her words took in the whole table generally, and she didn't look directly at Gidion. He was disappointed. He'd hoped to establish rapport with her now that he'd finally got her talking.

When they'd finished eating, Thane said it was time for them to leave. His tone was short, barely masked with a veneer of warmth. Gidion followed him with increasing unease. He caught a glance from Jasper as they went out. The youth looked away quickly, but Gidion could sense his envy, sharp as a knife. It was Thane who worried him more, though, and he said nothing as they went up the levitator.

As soon as they were inside Thane's rooms, the magister turned on Gidion. "It was quite practical of you both to help each other get what you want. I commend that—it's good to use allies when you can." His tone was flippant, but his emotions said much more, and his smile seemed carved in ice.

Gidion decided to feign innocence. "What do you mean?"

"Let's not pretend either of us is an idiot."

Gidion fought to keep his expression neutral. "I really don't know what you're speaking of."

Thane allowed his exasperation to show. "Jasper is by far the better fighter than you are," he snapped. "Everyone could see that. And yet he fell for a very obvious trick."

Gidion swallowed, trying to think of a way out.

"It was just about believable," Thane continued. "Believable enough to fool the other magisters, I'll admit. But you won't specialize in warcraft." Thane stepped closer to him, lifting Gidion's chin with his fingers so that their eyes met.

"I've won the right to," Gidion replied, taking an involuntary step back. "That's what I want to focus on so I can defeat the Ilk mage."

"I've already told you I'd help train you in that too."

"With all respect, Magister, Arianna Velden is known to be the best warcraft practitioner in the Spire."

"The only reason she holds that rank is because of her family," he said with a dismissive wave. "They don't let commoners rise to the top levels, and if you think that having her as a mentor will help you rise, you're sadly mistaken. She'll do the bare minimum with you, try to bully you out. And she certainly won't pay your bond for you, so you'll find yourself slaving in the kitchens at the same time."

"I don't care about rank," Gidion said, although he did. "I care about staying alive and avenging my parents."

But Thane was shaking his head. "You have to change your selection preferences and put my name as your first choice."

"But I'm free to choose as I want, aren't I?"

"I won't be able to protect you if you're apprenticed to Arianna," Thane said. "You'll be assigned to her rooms, you'll shadow her everywhere."

Good. He didn't like feeling he was entirely dependent on one man. But Gidion did still need Thane. "I really appreciate everything you've done for me so far, Magister," he said. "And I won't share with her anything about the Ilk. But I'd rather study artefaction on the side with you."

"It wouldn't be in your interests to refuse me," Thane said. "You want to finish your studies here, don't you?"

The threatening note in Thane's words made him pause. "What do you mean?"

"I could explain how you've cheated," Thane said. "How you both admitted it to me."

Would Thane do that? And would Gidion be able to deny it? Would Jasper deny it? Surely, the Spire authorities would listen if they both did. "I've admitted nothing."

Thane snorted. "And whose word do you think they'll take?"

It was a risk, so Gidion opted for another angle. "Isn't it too late to change my preferences?"

"Not with my authority," Thane replied.

But Gidion wasn't ready to give up yet. There had to be *something* he could do to salvage the situation.

"I *will* tell them," Thane said. "And you've passed the Selection Trial, which means the Spire is no longer legally obliged to train you. You'll be expelled with no specialization—and no protection."

He hadn't thought of that. Weaver training was only obligatory until the end of the Initiate Cycle. At that point, Seekers were considered able to control their magic and at least minimally useful to society, so they could safely be released. Of course, most people continued through the Apprentice Cycle to graduate as full weavers—unless they failed the Trial or were expelled. If that happened, maybe he could go back to his earlier plan, hide out with Ruadh? But Ruadh had ignored every note Gidion had sent him, and Gidion hadn't dared venture out of the Spire to find him either. He still didn't know whether to believe Nessa about Malai's intentions. It made him sick to bend to Thane's wishes, though. Gidion had thought him better than his father—kinder, more giving with praise—but he was equally controlling.

"This is all in your best interests," Thane said more gently.

They always said that. When would *he* get to decide his own interests? Complaining wasn't going to help, though, and he needed

Thane. So with great reluctance, he said, "Fine, I'll change my preferences."

Thane smiled. "I thought you'd see sense. You're a practical boy, aren't you? Just like your father." He pulled a paper from inside his robes and set it on the table. It was Gidion's list of mentors. "My name at the top."

He watched while Gidion scratched out Arianna Velden's name and replaced it with Thane's.

"I know this feels like a defeat, Gidion," Thane said as he took the paper from him. "But your talent for artefaction is truly outstanding. You'll discover it gives you far more power than warcraft does. And I can arrange for you to have a personal tutor for warcraft in your spare time. You won't lose out too much. I'll pay off your bond, and we'll hunt your Ilk mage together."

But Gidion's anger was undiminished. "Can I go to my room now? I'd like to rest," he said stiffly.

"Of course. It's been a trying few days, hasn't it?"

Gidion went and lay on his bed. At first, he thought he wouldn't sleep, he was so consumed with rage at what Thane had done. *I trusted him too much,* he thought. *Should have listened to my instincts when he locked me up at the start. Is there no one in this world I can trust?* Tears pricked his eyes. Everything had gone wrong that first time he'd used the stun power. He'd called Malai upon them and that had led to his mother's death, which his father had rightly blamed him for. And now his father was probably dead, too, as a result of his actions. It seemed that no matter what he did, things just got worse. Tears leaked down his face, but he made no effort to wipe them away. Soon, they turned to great sobs that wracked and contorted his body, forcing him into a fetal position, arms wrapped tightly around his knees. The sobs died only when exhaustion overcame him, whereupon he fell into a broken sleep full of half-remembered dreams.

The next morning, he woke aching all over, his mouth gummy and eyes swollen. He lay staring at the ceiling. The despair of the evening before had left him, although he was still angry at Thane. But he determined that he wouldn't give in to self-pity and weakness again. Fine, he was stuck with Thane for the moment. He'd just have to learn all he could from the bastard, and when the time came, he'd make his break for freedom and have his revenge. At least he had the new staff and focus stone he'd won in the Selection Trial and Tournament. And now that he was officially an apprentice, he would have much greater freedoms in the library and the Spire. He could make renewed efforts to contact Ruadh, start making those glowglobes for Ruadh's boss so he could earn his own money. He'd need it if he was ever to strike out on his own.

He washed and dressed, then called for Simion to bring him breakfast. Shortly after, a knock sounded on his bedroom door, but he discovered not Simion but Thane on the other side. Gidion put on his best smile. From now on, he played a game with the man. "Good morning, Magister."

If Thane was surprised by Gidion's warmth, he didn't show it. "I'm pleased to see you well rested," he said, returning Gidion's smile. "If you're up for it, I have a rather interesting artefaction project I've been working on, and I'd love your input."

"Will Jasper be joining us?"

"On this one, no. Anyway, he'll be spending the break at his family estate in the countryside."

Thane was referring to the four-week holiday that traditionally took place between the Selection Trial and the commencement of the Apprentice Cycle. Most apprentices were out of the Spire during this period, although the lower cycles would return to their studies sooner, having started their break before the Trial. "I've just asked Simion for breakfast."

"Of course. When you're ready, join me in the study."

Simion appeared with his breakfast, and Gidion took his time with it, pondering his strategy, before going to find Thane.

"I want you to help me with this." Thane picked up a slender bronze band that was resting on a workbench.

"What are you trying to do?"

"I'm trying to work out how to use it. It's an old Eleusian artefact. I think it might help us capture your Ilk mage."

Despite everything, Gidion's curiosity was piqued. "Do you know what it's for?"

"I'm not entirely sure, which is why I need your help. You've already shown you can manipulate weaves that I can't."

Gidion liked this reminder that however powerful the magister might be, Gidion was even more so. *And doesn't even know half of it.* "Can I delve it, then?"

"Go ahead."

Gidion opened himself to the Tapestry and looked at the collar. It was very different from any other artefacts he'd delved so far, using a mixture of thread types. Some he associated with weaving, threads that were visible to his eye. Others he was aware of only as a vibration or a hum. And was that a trigger weave to activate the collar? It seemed so, but he couldn't quite figure out how the trigger worked. He told Thane what he'd been able to perceive. "It might tell me more if we put the collar on someone," he added.

So Thane summoned Simion, who came not long after, his face flushed as if he'd been running. Gidion fastened the collar around Simion's neck, immediately noting a difference. The resonating threads that he associated with being able to read emotion had latched onto the threads comprising Simion's being. Perhaps even those associated with his mind? All of Simion's emotions were amplified for Gidion. He could feel the youth's trepidation at wearing the collar, a mixture of anxiety and love for Thane, repressed resentment toward Gidion. The last surprised him, but he pushed it aside and examined the trigger weave to see if anything had changed with it. It hadn't. Something was still missing.

"What do you see?" Thane asked with barely restrained impatience.

"It seems to provide some kind of mental connection with the wearer," Gidion said. "Like an amplification."

Thane simmered with excitement. "And can you activate it?"

"No, it still needs a trigger," Gidion said. "Maybe something similar to a keystone."

"So an external trigger, another artefact?"

Gidion nodded.

"Do you think you could make the trigger?"

"I'm not sure. I could try." He pondered. "Maybe a bracelet or something?"

"Well, let's make it your first project as my apprentice," Thane said. "I'll teach you all I know about keystones, and perhaps something will come to you."

As Thane had no classes due to the break, he spent all day with Gidion, showing him how to make different types of keystones. And while Gidion didn't have any particular inspiration for the collar, he learned a lot, pleasing Thane with his rate of improvement. And this couldn't help but please Gidion in turn.

Three days later, the initiates all gathered in the Great Hall of the Conclave to discover who they'd be apprenticed to. It was on the ground floor of the First Tower, occupying the entire north-west quadrant of the building. There were five rows of tiered seating against the outer wall, facing into a broad dais with a lectern. As it was a notable rite of passage, all weavers who lived in the Spire were required to attend, and the hall was bustling and loud when Gidion arrived.

He scanned the room, noting that the weavers who'd attained magister status sat together according to their specialism. Instead of white, their robes were in various shades associated with their primary specialism. Rangers wore green, the warweavers red, the loremasters yellow or brown, the artefactors blue, and the envoys in grey. Looking more closely, Gidion saw that many had slashes of other colors in their robes to indicate secondary or even tertiary specialisms.

Weavers who hadn't taken magister exams wore white hemmed with a single color, again to show their area of specialization. There were far more of these than there were magisters. Gidion recalled what Thane had told him—that only the most gifted weavers attained magister status.

Thane was already on the central dais, in his usual midnight blue, hemmed with yellow and grey thread to indicate his secondary specialisms of lore and statecraft. Of course, because he was a ranking weaver, and a wealthy one at that, the yellow and grey were, in fact, gold and silver. As the initiates gathered in front of the dais, the other mentors filed in to stand on either side of Thane. As Head of Seekers, it was Thane's role to read out who was apprenticed to whom.

When Thane announced that Gidion would be apprenticed to him, Gidion glanced at Jasper. The youth looked stricken, then turned to Gidion with murderous fury. Gidion mouthed that it wasn't his fault, trying to project contrition, but Jasper seemed only to get angrier.

"Also apprenticed to Danial Thane, Jasper Wyven."

Jasper's expression turned to shock, then relief as he turned his eyes back toward Thane. Gidion didn't know how to feel. Part of him was relieved, as it eased his guilt about breaking their pact. But he knew it could only bring further complications because now they were both Thane's apprentices and would presumably be expected to spend more time together. Gidion would have to try to smooth things over with him. His desire for revenge had largely dissipated after Jasper had let him win the tournament. It now seemed more useful to have Jasper as an ally against Thane, the one who exerted the real power.

There was a feast afterward to celebrate the new apprentices. It took place in the Feasting Hall, which occupied another quadrant of the central tower, next to the Hall of the Conclave. The most high-ranking weavers were seated at a curving table along the inner side, while the new apprentices were along the outside, by the glass wall. In between them were the masses of magisters and ordinary weavers.

Gidion was quick to sit next to Jasper, taking the opportunity to explain in a low voice. "He made me do it. He knew what we did."

"Did I hear a mouse squeak?" Jasper said loudly, looking at his friends, who were sitting all around.

They laughed, but the laughter was hesitant. Gidion sensed a mixture of condescension and envy from some of them. Because they'd realized he was a full artefactor? Because Thane had taken him on as an apprentice? Because he'd won the tournament? He should have felt vindicated, but instead all he could think was that he didn't belong among them and would never belong. His good intentions to get Jasper onside evaporated. "It must be so disappointing for the cat when he's beaten by a mouse."

A stiff silence as Jasper's friends looked at him, unsure how to react.

"Winning through trickery isn't as noble as losing with honor," Jasper returned. "And mice have no option but to use deceit, don't they?"

This prompted some confused looks. But a few laughed awkwardly. Did they know about the bargain Jasper had made with him?

"No one ever awarded a prize to a loser," Gidion replied. *They'll soon realize what I am.*

The first course arrived, a creamy seafood soup served with hunks of dark brown bread. For a while, everyone turned their attention to it, but the atmosphere remained tense. Jasper said little, his laughter in response to his friends' comments sounding forced. Gidion found himself increasingly angry, hurt at their rejection of him despite how he'd proven himself. It soured his appetite, and he left as soon as he'd finished the main course.

But once he was outside, he discovered he didn't want to go back to Thane's rooms, his hurt and anger fizzing violently in his veins. Perhaps he could go find Nessa? It would be good to see her, to hear her laughter, even to be the butt of her jokes. She seemed the only one who could banish the emptiness he felt. So he made for the barracks, hoping to find her in there.

"Didn't realize she had a sweetheart," the woman at the barracks door said. She looked a little older than Nessa and had a long scar across one cheek.

Gidion blushed. "I'm not ... We're not ..."

The woman just laughed.

"Well, is she in?" Gidion pressed.

But the woman shook her head. "Try the Crooked Staff."

That was a tavern in the Spire grounds that was mostly frequented by attendants and guards. Gidion had only ever seen it from the outside.

The guard took a closer look at him. "You one of the new apprentices?"

"That's right."

"Shouldn't you be celebrating?"

"I'm not much one for crowds," Gidion replied, turning on his heel to leave.

"Have a drink for me!" she shouted after him.

The Crooked Staff was on the other side of the Spire grounds, and he strode toward it quickly.

At last, he was in front of the tavern, a squat building not far from the main forge. His breath caught in anticipation as he pushed the door open and looked around the busy common room.

There she was, amidst a group of men and women who were talking loudly, their gestures animated. Gidion watched her from a distance. Her violet eyes were bright and alive, her dimples showing as she laughed at something someone said. Her hair was free of its braids, spreading across her shoulders in silky waves. But she was still dressed in men's clothes—breeches and shirt—the front of the shirt open enough to reveal smooth skin and the first hint of her breasts. He went toward her, wishing he could call her to come outside, away from all the people.

She caught sight of him as he approached the table, a grin spreading over her face. "Gidion! Come on!" she exclaimed. She sounded drunk, her words not as clipped as usual.

Several faces turned quizzically toward him. None were weavers. Most were guards, scarred and knotted with muscle.

"This is Gidion, new apprentice of the Spire," Nessa proclaimed to her companions.

Her companions made a great noise of congratulating him, all of them too drunk and too loud. He repressed the urge to fidget under the scrutiny, smiling and nodding at words he barely heard.

“What do you want to drink?” Nessa asked. “I owe you one.” She slung an arm across his shoulders.

Normally, he would have delighted at this gesture of intimacy. But it just made him feel tenser. “Can we leave here?” he said in a low voice.

She frowned, peering closely at him. “Are you alright?”

“I’ve just had enough of people.”

She shrugged, her arm sliding away from him. “I’ve had enough to drink, to be honest. Let’s go.”

They bid goodbye to the group and wandered outside. Free from the noise of the tavern, Gidion began to relax, to wish she would put an arm around him again.

"Water Garden?" Nessa said.

Gidion agreed, and they wandered in its direction.

“So, how did it go earlier?” she asked.

Gidion found himself spilling it all out. Thane forcing him to choose him as mentor. The rejection of the other apprentices. “I feel like there’s no place for me here.” Sudden tears threatened to come to his eyes, and he blinked them away rapidly, hoping she didn't notice. She'd think him such a child.

Nessa touched his arm, and he shivered despite himself. “You do have a place with your family, you know," she said.

“I’d like to believe that.” And he did. He longed for a family so much that it hurt.

“Do you want me to take you, then?”

He wanted to go anywhere with her. Wanted to kiss her and touch her. Wanted to feel the silk of her hair between his fingers. Too late, he tried to repress these feelings.

But if Nessa sensed them, she didn't show it. "All you have to do is say the word."

He was tempted, more tempted than he had been yet. But his mistrust was still too strong. "No, I'm not ready for that." He groped for something else to say. "Tell me more about your brother." They were nearing the entrance to the Water Garden, the sounds of its gurgling streams and fountains reaching his ears.

Nessa's voice raised in surprise. "What do you want to know?"

Gidion shrugged. "You've mentioned him a few times, but you haven't said much about what kind of person he is."

"He's my best friend," Nessa said.

Her lover for her brother filled each word she'd uttered, pricking Gidion with jealousy. What he'd give to have Nessa speak of him that way. "Are you very alike?"

"In looks, yes. He's basically a male version of me." She laughed. "But our personalities are different. Kye is more easygoing, despite everything that happened to him."

"Oh, what happened?"

"He was captured by Riftlanders as a boy and made a slave."

Gidion missed a step. "You never mentioned that before."

"I don't like to talk about it."

He could sense the hurt in her, causing him to weigh his next words carefully. "Can you share how he was captured?"

"A raid on our farm. Kye was so brave, he stood up for me against one of the raiders who wanted to ..."

She didn't finish, but Gidion could guess what she meant to say, and felt sick. "It was the first time I used the stun strike," she said. "But I knocked out Kye as well. And before I could drag him away, another raider came and took him. He didn't see me, maybe because it was too dark, so I wasn't taken."

"What age were you?"

"Ten years old."

"It wasn't your fault," Gidion said immediately.

"Of course it was my fault," Nessa shot back. "I used the stun strike, didn't I?"

And then Gidion realized that he and Nessa were the same. That he felt the same guilt and shame radiating from her now. Their powers had a cost. "How did you get him back?"

"He ran away from them a year later," Nessa replied. "He'd come into his own powers. But he wears the slave brand still."

"No wonder you hate them," Gidion replied.

"Kye still won't talk about what happened," Nessa said. "Whatever it was, it was awful, because I can feel the darkness coming from him. He buries it deep, but I know him better than anyone." She fell into silence.

"Is that why you joined the legions?"

"Yes. We both signed up as soon as we were old enough. But we fought many more raids before that time came."

They'd reached their spot in the Water Garden, by the statue of the builder. Gidion stood awkwardly, unsure of what to do. Nessa was being more vulnerable and open with him than usual. Maybe because of the alcohol. But did it mean more than that? "I'm sorry you've suffered all that," he said at last, daring to put an arm around her, as if in comfort.

She sagged against him, and for a moment, he thought she'd return the embrace. But then she stiffened and pulled away. "We have to say focused."

Was that an indirect way of telling him she didn't want him? He returned his arm to his side.

Nessa laughed.

"What?"

"You look like a sad puppy."

He blinked. "I'm not a ..."

She traced the line of his jaw, making him shiver. "You're still so young," she murmured. "No need to rush into things."

That seemed like a very definite rejection. But Gidion felt neither hurt nor angry. Instead, he found himself nodding along, agreeing with her. "Yes, we need to focus," he said. "I've got a lot to learn still."

"Let's practice your splicing again," she said. "You're getting better at it, but you need to learn how to take someone through Sīut's Realm with you."

Gidion sighed but gave his agreement. It seemed he wouldn't get what he really wanted that evening. But he could at least grow in strength.

Chapter 23

Gidion had few opportunities to see Nessa over the following weeks because Thane, who was no longer teaching, demanded almost all of his time. And that time was spent almost entirely on designing the trigger bracelet for the collar. He always worked in Thane's study because the magister insisted both bracelet and collar remain there. But Thane had also been true to his word and had assigned a young weaver to train Gidion daily in warcraft. It reduced some of his anger toward the magister for forcing Gidion to choose him as mentor, but not all of it.

Not seeing Nessa frustrated Gidion, although he told himself it was for the best. He'd been rash that night after the feast, ignoring his own strictures not to let her get too close. But after what Thane had pulled, it was hard not to think she was the only person left whom he *could* trust. Ruadh might have been another, but he still hadn't responded to Gidion's notes. For all Gidion knew, the mercenary was no longer at the Silver Sword.

He finally solved the problem with the trigger bracelet after a flash of insight one evening. Thane immediately summoned Simion and placed the collar around his neck, while Gidion wore the bracelet. As before, the youth's emotions were sharply projected to him. But when he set off the trigger, Simion cried out, his shoulders hunching, his mouth and eyes screwing up in pain. It looked like some of the weaves had embedded themselves in his mind. And now Gidion could do more than sense his emotions—he could read the youth's thoughts. They were panicked, and Gidion recoiled.

"What does it do? Thane asked eagerly.

Gidion hesitated. He wasn't sure he wanted Thane to have that much power. What if he made Gidion put on the collar?

"Tell me," Thane said, an edge to his tone.

He decided to say nothing about being able to read Simion's thoughts. Maybe Thane wouldn't have the same effect from the collar that Gidion did. After all, Gidion was the one who'd made the trigger, the one who had mind magic. "I can sense his emotions."

Simion's alarm increased, his hand touching the collar but stopping short of trying to tug it off. He was afraid of displeasing Thane, and that was strong enough to counteract his disgust with the collar.

Thane's eyes lit up. "Give me the bracelet."

Gidion reluctantly slipped it off his wrist and handed it over. Thane snapped it around his wrist and triggered the weave, which Gidion had designed to be usable by him. "I see what you mean," Thane said delightedly. Then, his gaze unfocused.

Suddenly, Simion ran to the other end of the room with his tongue sticking out. Gidion frowned while Thane laughed. Next, Simion started hopping about like a rabbit, two hands flopping in front of him like paws. What was going on?

"Alright, that's enough," Thane said, grinning broadly. "Thank you, Simion." He took the collar off his servant and sent him away.

Gidion found himself expelling air from his chest, as if he'd been holding Simion's panic inside. But he still didn't understand what Thane had done.

"Did you know what else it could do?" Thane said, now more serious.

Gidion realized Thane suspected him of lying and put all his effort into appearing innocent. "No, what do you mean?"

To his relief, Thane's delight at his discovery bubbled over once more. "The collar has the power to read emotions, yes. But even more, it can compel the wearer to do what you want them to."

"So it was you controlling Simion's actions just now?"

"Simion is generally obedient, but he hates more than anything to look like a fool. When I ordered him to behave in that idiotic fashion, he showed no resistance at all." Thane's eyes gleamed feverishly.

Gidion shuddered. The collar was dangerous, and Thane's expression made him wonder if he shouldn't have made the bracelet. "You were able to speak to him mind to mind?"

"Yes. And even read his thoughts."

Thane was positively shaking with excitement now. Gidion had never seen him so out of control, and it frightened him. But then another thing occurred to him. "So, you could make someone tell you the truth?"

Thane grinned conspiratorially. "You're thinking what I'm thinking?"

"If we can get it on Malai ..."

"Yes! This is how we can learn everything from her," Thane said. "Not just why she's looking for you, but where her Ilk came from, how she made them, what her plans are, if she has allies."

Gidion couldn't help but be swept along by the possibilities Thane was setting out. Wasn't this what he wanted most of all? To know the truth at last about everything? "But how do we capture her in the first place?"

"That's what we need to work out next." Thane started pacing, hands clasped before him.

"Can we get help from the other weavers?" This had been much on his mind of late. Surely, they needed to know there were Ilk in the world once more?

Thane came to a halt. "I'm still cautious about telling them anything. I don't know what they'll do with you if they know about your past."

Gidion reluctantly agreed that Thane was right. He didn't know whom he could trust. Nessa had made it clear there was at least one weaver in the Spire on Malai's side. It could be anyone. But maybe he could find out who it was? Was it time he told Thane about Nessa? He quickly discounted it. The idea of Nessa being controlled by Thane and the collar revolted him. And Thane might be angry that Gidion had been keeping her a secret all this time.

"I need some time to think alone," Thane said. "But you've done excellently." He laid a hand on his shoulder. "I'm very proud of you."

Gidion smiled at the praise despite his worry over the bracelet. *Take that, Jasper.* "Thank you, Magister."

"A moment." Thane disappeared into another room and returned with a small purse. "A reward for your work," he said. "Try not to spend it all in a single tavern." He winked.

The purse was full of silver, enough for many trips to a tavern. Gidion thanked Thane with surprise. The purse seemed to him a sign of trust as much as anything else. Money was freedom, after all.

"Off you go, then," Thane said. "We'll speak again tomorrow."

Gidion escaped gratefully. It was already late afternoon, and he decided to find Nessa to see if she'd come to a tavern with him. But he discovered she was on duty in a part of the Spire he couldn't access, so instead he wandered around the Water Garden, trying to think of ways to win her over. Perhaps a gift. Did she wear jewelry? He'd never noticed any on her, but that was because she nearly always dressed like a man. The first time they'd met, though, she'd been in a dress. He wasn't sure how he preferred her. Something about her strength, her toughness and ability to fight, attracted him strongly. But he also wanted her like a woman, wanted her soft and powerless in his arms.

He tried again to find her after her duty was finished, but they told her she hadn't returned. That wasn't entirely unusual. She had a habit of disappearing without telling him where she was going and what she was doing. But her absence left a hole in him.

Not knowing what else to do, he went back to Thane's apartment. The magister, apparently, was out, and he took to his own room, the sense of emptiness growing inside him. He wanted desperately to fill it, but he didn't know how, so he lay on his bed and stared at the ceiling, thinking about his absent parents, about Jasper and his friends' rejection. Even Nessa didn't seem to want him—but he shouldn't want her either, should he?

Eventually, he could bear it no longer. He couldn't just lie here, friendless and alone. The yawning chasm inside him would swallow him entirely, or else madness would come to fill it. He sat up abruptly, eyes lighting on the purse Thane had given him. He could go into the city, try to find Ruadh. The man hadn't responded to any of Gidion's notes, but there could be a good reason for that—maybe he'd never got them.

Feeling revived, Gidion dressed in plain breeches and shirt and headed out into the city. It was the first time he'd left the Spire since he'd last seen Ruadh. But he told himself it mattered little. If Malai wanted to get to him, she could probably do so whether he was in the Spire or out of it.

He headed straight for the Silver Sword, hoping to find the mercenary there. It was even louder and more raucous than the last time, with men shouting and swearing drunkenly over various games of skill and chance. But when Gidion went to the bar to ask for Ruadh, the innkeeper told him he wasn't staying there anymore.

The hole in his chest expanded. "Any idea where he went?"

"He didn't say," the man replied, wiping down the counter as if he considered the conversation closed.

But Gidion wasn't giving up so easily. "Are you able to get a message to him at all?"

He stopped his cleaning. "Who's asking?"

"A friend of his." Gidion remembered something that Ruadh had said about weavers. "A firefly."

The innkeeper clearly knew the term, as his expression cleared. "Name?"

"Pep Ne'Brin."

"It will cost you a silver."

"What?" It was an extortionate amount of money for passing on a message.

The man shrugged. "You said you was a firefly."

"That doesn't mean I'm rich," Gidion replied. "I'll give you a couple of vics."

"Can't help you." The man started wiping his bar again.

Gidion clenched his fists. Was the man asking for so much money because he wanted to put Gidion off? Was it some kind of test? Or was Ruadh deliberately keeping Gidion away? Why hadn't he mentioned he'd left the Silver Sword? The hole in Gidion grew even larger. Ruadh had been his last hope as a friend. But friends didn't disappear without a trace. "You know what, it doesn't matter," he said heavily and turned away.

He pushed his way back out onto the street. But once there, he didn't know what to do. He looked left and right, taking in the lively crowds. It seemed everyone had friends other than him. Black despair rose in him. He was alone in the world. Ruadh had abandoned him. His mother was probably dead, his father too. All because of him, because of this cursed magic he was able to wield. Thane helped, but he was controlling, and despite his warmth and praise, Gidion couldn't escape the feeling that the magister was just using him for his own ends. That left only Nessa. But she was connected to Malai. She probably thought him the greatest of fools, pining after her when she too was using him for her own ends, whatever those might be.

But what was he to do? He couldn't bear the thought of going home. He would die if he was alone one moment longer. Then it came to him. Missy's. He'd go to Missy's. Maybe Ruadh would even be there. The hole in his chest shrunk.

It took him a good deal of searching to find the place. The Rainbow Quarter was a confusing warren, and he only had the vaguest of memories of how they'd got there the first time. Eventually, he had to fight down his embarrassment and ask a passerby. The man winked at him knowingly. "You're not too far, brother. Down that road, then left and left again and you'll find it."

The directions were good, and Gidion arrived to find the brothel much as before. Nervously, he approached the madam and asked for a girl.

"What's it you'll be wanting her for?"

Gidion's face heated. "What are the options?"

"Hand, hole, or mouth," a grey-haired man said lewdly next to him. "Or all three." He pinched the bottom of the woman who was hanging off him.

Gidion blushed harder, and the madam shrieked an ugly laugh. "Peter, can't you see he's just a young buck?"

Gidion almost ran out in mortification.

The madam leaned over to him. "How good is your coin?"

Gidion cleared his throat before answering with as much confidence as he could muster, "I've got plenty."

"That could mean many things," she replied, "depending on who you're talking to."

Gidion removed two silver pieces from his pouch and held them up.

"An 'andsome buck like you can have his pick for that amount," she said with a wink. "Stay the whole night if you like."

Gidion set his silver down on the counter, wondering if he was being ripped off.

"What looks do you prefer?"

Gidion thought to ask for Meadow again. But then Nessa came to his mind. "A girl with dark hair," he said. "As dark as you have."

"I've just the one. Will you have a drink, too?"

"A bottle of wine," he said. "Will the silver cover that?"

"It will, and some bliss?"

A drug to heighten the senses Ruadh had told him. Gidion decided to accept. He didn't want to inhabit the real world anymore.

"Have yourself a seat. Plum will be with you shortly."

Plum was the name of the girl Ruadh was so fond of. Already, Gidion felt misgivings. He didn't want Ruadh's cast-offs, even if she was a whore. But he said nothing, wanting to be away from the leering madam.

When Plum came to him, his disappointment deepened. She was nothing like Nessa, her skin pale, her belly rounded and her breasts falling heavily. But it seemed rude to reject her, and he wasn't sure they'd let him do that. So he allowed her to pour him his wine and told her to pour one for herself, too. She showed him a small blue bottle and tipped several drops of transparent liquid into his wine and hers.

He'd only taken a couple of sips of the drink before the feeling began to spread through him—a warmth that thawed the cold in his heart and caused his nerves to tingle. The light of the glowglobes took on a mystical aura, the sounds of laughter around him making him want to laugh too. Every touch of the girl's hand was magnified. Her body, which had repelled him, now called to him.

"Time for a room, my love," she said, pressing a soft kiss on his mouth.

He wanted to take her there and then but let her pull him away down the corridor. The room she took him to was much the same as the last time. But he paid little attention to it. As soon as the door closed behind them, he was on her.

She laughed and slapped him aside. "Come here."

She had him lie on the bed while she took off all his clothes and then her own. Then she stroked him from head to foot, turning him into a cat, purring from the delight of her touch. But soon he became a dog, rising to overpower her, turning her over to rut her from behind. She gasped and cried, and he doubled his efforts, wanting her to scream her submission to him. Again and again, he spent himself until, at last, the bliss and the wine combined with his own exhaustion to send him into sleep.

Next he knew, he was being jolted awake by Nessa's voice in his mind. *"Come! Thane's got me!"* And then all sense of her abruptly went.

At first, he thought it might have been part of a dream. But the more he pondered it, the more worried he became. She'd sounded afraid, her emotions pressing themselves sharply into him.

"Please, Gidion, come!" There was no mistaking it, this time. She was terrified.

He hurriedly dressed, his head pounding, and ran out into the street. It was very late, and the crowds had diminished to a trickle.

"Where are you?" He wasn't sure it would work. She hadn't trained him in this, but whatever link she'd opened to him remained open, for he immediately got a response.

"Here." She transmitted a street address to him. It was in the Rainbow Quarter.

He pulled on his clothes and ran out of the brothel, finding the house with the help of a couple of drunks. The ground-floor rooms were dark, but there was a glow in the top window. How would he get into there? He couldn't splice because you could only splice to somewhere you already knew or could see. That gave him his idea. He snuck up to the door and pushed open the letterbox, peering into the corridor beyond. It was dark, but maybe he could form a tunnel into there.

It worked, and soon he was creeping up the narrow stairs. He could hear voices and followed them. Pressing his ear against the door, he heard Thane speaking. He tried it. Locked, but with a mundane rather than magical one. Gidion wove and tripped the mechanism to open it.

Nessa was standing before Thane with the collar around her neck. The magister was in the middle of saying something but stopped speaking upon Gidion's entrance. He looked surprised but not upset. "Gidion, I'm glad you've joined us."

The magister's reaction confused him, but his fear for Nessa was stronger. It made him sick to see her so helpless before the magister. "Let her go," he demanded.

"She's an Ilk mage," Thane replied.

"She's not an Ilk mage," Gidion said. It was his fault that she was trapped. He'd made the damn bracelet.

"He's right. I can't make Ilk," Nessa said. "Why don't you let me go and we'll explain everything to you?"

Her tone was matter of fact, but Gidion sensed layers of anger and fear beneath it. Her pupils were large and black, her posture rigid. It was unbearable, seeing her like this. He started to marshal his power against Thane. He'd knock the man out with his stun power and free her.

"Don't be hasty," Thane said to him. "It's perfectly reasonable for me to question her, don't you think? Wouldn't you like to know if she's been telling you the truth?"

Gidion paused. Thane was right. Attracted as he was to Nessa, he still didn't trust her. And Thane didn't appear to have harmed her. "What has she told you?"

"We were just getting to that." Thane smiled, but it didn't reach his eyes.

Gidion didn't know how to feel. He hated that Thane had trapped her, forced her to call him. It reminded him of how Thane had forced Gidion to accept him as a mentor. But he also felt a desperate yearning to know the truth once and for all.

"You can ask the first question," Thane said.

"You'll let me wear the bracelet?" It wasn't that he wanted to control Nessa, exactly. He just didn't want Thane to be the one to have power over her.

"I don't think that would be wise of me, do you?" Thane said, the side of his mouth curling up.

Damn you. Gidion considered what to do next. The stun power was still an option. Thane had no protection against it. Gidion could wear the bracelet himself and get the truth out of Nessa. But the idea of that repelled him, too. She would never forgive him if he did that to her. And rightly. He ground his teeth, trying to resist a sense of overwhelming helplessness.

"I'll relay any question you like to her," Thane said. "Anything at all."

The offer decided Gidion. It was a way out of his dilemma, a way to get the truth without being the one to compel it from her. He looked at Nessa squarely. "What does Malai want with me?"

Thane repeated the question to Nessa, and she rolled her eyes. "As I've told you, Malai is your great-grandmother, and she wants to take you home to your family."

"Is that the only reason?" Gidion asked.

"She wants you to fulfill your destiny."

"What destiny?"

"You're the Ilk Lord's descendant. She wants you to inherit his powers and finish what he started."

A cold lump settled in Gidion's stomach. He hadn't quite believed it before.

Thane, for his part, looked as if he was going to jump out of his very skin from excitement. "Why did she send you here?" he asked.

"So that I could ..." Nessa stopped, winced as if she had wanted to say something else but couldn't. "She sent me to gain Gidion's trust and convince him to go see her."

There was another question Gidion wanted to ask, but he didn't dare. Had it all been a front? Did she care for him at all? Or had this always been about manipulation? His anger surged forth. Everyone was using him, even Nessa. But she was still the one person who had told him the truth. "Is my mother alive?"

Nessa regarded with a strangely sad expression. "Yes, as I told you, she's with Malai."

Thane looked like the cat who'd got the cream. "And the Ilk. Are they real?"

Nessa hardened as she faced him. "I'm not sure what you mean by that."

"The Ilk who attacked Gidion. Were they truly Ilk?" Thane said.

"They didn't attack Gidion," she said. "But yes, those were Ilk."

"My father?" Gidion said hopefully.

Nessa's eyes softened again. "Captured by Riftlanders."

"I would very much like to meet with Malai," Thane said.

Was the man insane? Why would he want to *meet* Malai?

Nessa started laughing. "You must have a death wish."

"Tell me, does she like to strike a deal?" Thane returned.

"What could you possibly offer her?" Scorn was thick in her tone.

"That's between me and her," Thane replied.

What was Thane playing at? Did he think he could take Malai and her Ilk on?

"Fine, free me, and I'll summon her as you wish."

"I'm afraid I can't take that risk. I have no protections against you," Thane said.

"Worth a shot," Nessa said, showing her teeth in an impression of a smile. "But if you want me to summon her, I'll need to splice and send through a note."

"Very well." Thane went to his writing desk and removed paper and pen, then bade her use them.

Gidion watched as Nessa scratched out an angular symbol that he didn't recognize.

"What does that mean?" Thane asked.

"It means I need her to immediately come to the place I send it from."

Gidion trembled. Was he ready for this? Did Thane know what he was doing?

Nessa spliced the Tapestry and sent the note through it.

"What happens next?" Thane asked her.

"We wait."

"You're Chelak too, aren't you?" he said, cocking his head at her. "The features aren't as obvious in you as they are in Gidion, but I can see it."

"How observant of you," she said drily.

"Where have you all been hiding? Are there more of you?" Thane pressed.

Nessa was about to answer, but before she'd said anything, the Tapestry reopened where Nessa had sent the note through. Out Malai stepped, seemingly alone.

The sight of her made Gidion feel nauseous, and he grabbed the threads, ready to defend himself. Thane had done the same, but he smiled at her. "Welcome. My name is Danial Thane. I've had much desire to meet you."

Malai ignored him. "Has he harmed you?" she demanded of Gidion.

Gidion shook his head, unable to speak. Too many thoughts were racing around his head, his emotions a jumble he could make no sense of.

Malai turned to Nessa. "And you?" She caught sight of the collar, stepping closer to peer at it. "I haven't seen one of those in a long time," she said. Then to Thane, "Remove that immediately if you value your life."

"I only wanted to speak to you," Thane said smoothly. "Perhaps we can help each other."

"We have no use for you, weaver," Malai said contemptuously.

"With respect, I disagree," Thane said. "Tell me your purpose, and perhaps there is something I can offer you in return."

"I won't share my plans with a giki," Malai said. "Now, remove the collar."

"As you wish," Thane said, removing the collar from Nessa's neck. But he had barely done this when he screamed, clutching his head. Malai had sent something through the threads, attacking his mind. Thane fell to his knees, moaning and weeping.

Gidion watched numbly. It was strange to see Thane so reduced, when Gidion had always seen him as so powerful. Some part of him liked it, appreciated the irony of Thane kneeling before him, helpless and undone. Abruptly, the crying stopped, and Thane slumped to the ground, eyes closed.

Was he dead?

"He'll wake and remember nothing of this," Malai said. "Are you ready to come with me? I won't force you. But this ... *man*—he doesn't have your interests at heart. He thinks only of himself."

Gidion looked at Nessa, who nodded. He looked back down at Thane, thought of how he'd forced Gidion to take him as a mentor, how he'd trapped Nessa with the collar. Thought of Jasper and Emilie and everything he'd learned about his chances to rise among the weavers as a commoner. In truth, the Spire was no place for him. Ruadh had seemed a friend, but he'd disappeared without a word. The only person who'd shown him nothing but kindness was Nessa. And everything she'd said had been true so far. But still, he doubted. Malai had come twice with Ilk, and a parent had disappeared each time. He only had Nessa's word that they were both still alive.

But he also knew that if Malai wanted him dead, she'd have killed him by now. She'd undone Thane with laughable ease. He stalled. "I'm officially enrolled in the Spire. People will ask questions if I disappear."

Malai waved a dismissive hand. "There are ways to handle that. So what do you say, will you come with me and meet your mother?"

His mother. Could it be true? A wave of longing hit him. Family. He still had a family. There seemed nothing more important now than to claim it, to find a place where he was loved just for being himself. "Take me to her."

Malai smiled. "Come here, then."

Gidion glanced at Nessa, who nodded encouragingly. Cautiously, he approached Malai.

"Be sure not to let go of me." She looped an arm around his and then reopened the portal. Together, they stepped through, emerging in some kind of underground room. The walls were bare black rock, lit with glowglobes in golden sconces. He and Malaier were standing on a raised platform in the center of the room, two slender pillars of the same black rock rising on either side of him.

Standing across from him was a woman he instantly knew, even though it had been over a decade since he'd last seen her.

His mother.

Chapter 24

Gidion's mother, Seila, was largely as he remembered her—long, straight black hair, eyes golden like his, slanting up, much narrower than those of Vycenians. But she was shorter than him now. He'd probably only been up to her waist when he'd lost her. It was disconcerting. The woman who'd been his world, his goddess, now reduced to ordinary proportions. And she'd lied to him.

Malai pulled him forward, away from the portal, and he was vaguely aware of Nessa coming through behind them.

"My boy," his mother whispered, tears in her eyes as she moved toward him.

Gidion took a step back. It was hard to believe that she was really there. And with all the years that had passed, he didn't know what to say to her, how to be with her.

She advanced on him, put her arms around him, held him close. But he stood stiffly, hands clenched by his side. Her scent filled his nose, and he was unexpectedly taken back to the cottage that had been their home.

"Look at you," she whispered, stepping back, her eyes taking in every inch of him. "All grown up. I've missed so much." She wiped a tear from her eye. "Are you well?"

Was he well? Was he *well*? Fury seized him, hot and bitter. "How can I be well? I've had nothing but lies for years!"

Seila flinched.

He swept his gaze around the room. "Where are we?" His voice sounded harsh to his ears, but he was beyond caring.

"This is our home," Seila said in a quiet voice.

"It doesn't look like a home," he said, frowning at the smooth rock walls. They weren't terribly unlike those in the maze of the Selection Trial.

"We're inside a mountain," Malai said. "It keeps us safe from the outside world. No one knows we're here. You'll find other parts of it more comfortable."

But he barely listened to the answer. A more pressing question had come to him. "Why did you run away?" he demanded of his mother. "Why did you leave us?" Something raw and wild was opening up in him, a kind of hysteria that had his legs shaking.

"Because she doesn't want you to come into your birthright," Malai said.

Gidion ignored her, keeping all his attention on his mother, straining for any sense of a lie. Her face was a picture of warring emotions—pain, fear, anger, resignation. But he got nothing through his second sense. No doubt, she was shielding them from him. It made him angrier, and he inhaled deeply, his fingers curling in on themselves.

"Tell him," Malai commanded Seila.

"You can inherit Ilis'Elkir's power," Seila whispered. It sounded like the words had been forced out of her.

Gidion glanced at Nessa, who nodded. Another truth.

"I wanted a different life for you, Gid," Seila said, pleading. "The chance of an ordinary one, as I never had."

"I never had an ordinary life either," Gidion said bitterly. "I spent it running." Running, running, running. Always running, trying to find his place. He turned to Malai. "Is it true that I can inherit his power?"

"You already have," Malai said. "You're the strongest male descendant born yet. You appear to be as talented an artefactor as he was. You have his genius."

"So I can make Ilk?" Laughter threatened to bubble up inside him, but he pushed it down. He had to focus, had to know whether they were lying or not.

"That and other things," Malai said. "The magic they teach at the Spire is ... very limited. But here you can come into the full range of your powers."

"What if I don't want to make Ilk? They're wrong. They destroyed the Tapestry."

Malai's answer surprised him. "Yes, the Ilk were a danger to the Cloth. But Ilis always believed we could find another way to make them, one less damaging and less draining on the elkiri who controlled them."

"I have no interest in that," he said with a shake of his head. "I just want ..." He stumbled into silence. He no longer had any idea what he wanted. He'd wanted to avenge his mother, but here she was, alive. He'd wanted to become a great weaver, but the Spire had rejected him. And he'd wanted to rely on Thane. But Thane had just wanted to control him. There was still one person missing from the picture, though. "What happened to my father?"

"Captured by Riftlanders," Malai said, "and we're still trying to find him."

Gidion glanced at his mother, who dipped her head in affirmation. Another truth.

“Don’t you want justice for the wrongs done to you? To our family? Our people?” Malai pressed.

That infuriated him. “The ones who’ve wronged me *are* my family!” he cried. “Lies, all lies!” He wanted to weep suddenly, and tears pricked his eyes. Furiously, he wiped them away on the back of his arm. His next desire was to curl up into a little ball, hide from all these impossible truths. He clenched his fists, trying to master himself. “Why do you want me to inherit his power?”

“So you can rule.” Malai's voice was calm, implacable, as if it was the most normal thing in the world.

Again, Gidion was filled with the desire to laugh. “Rule what?”

“The world.”

And now he did laugh. Or rather, he shrieked, a mad sound that made him clamp his jaws together.

Malai’s expression was serious but also surprisingly compassionate. “That is your destiny, Gidion,” she said. “And we’ve been preparing for it for hundreds of years.”

“But ...” He didn’t know what to say. Didn’t know what to feel. The mad, screaming laughter threatened to bubble out again.

“I’ll open my mind to you,” Malai said. “And you’ll see everything. I’m not trying to hide anything from you.”

“You can do that?”

“More importantly, you can do it,” she said. “It’s an extension of the ability to sense the emotions of others. But even among the best of the elkiri, the ability to read others’ thoughts was limited. You need to be in physical contact, and the other person must open themselves to you.”

“You’ll show me how?”

“If you want.”

"Now?" He was certain she'd refuse. But to his surprise, she nodded. So he let her take his hands.

"Open yourself to the Cloth. Follow the threads to my mind," she said.

He traced the threads that usually revealed another person's emotions to him. Usually, when he did this, he'd come up against a kind of wall that blocked him from traveling further into the mind of the person. But this time, it was like a door had opened, and he slipped through easily. A scene played before him.

"I've discovered a way to win this war," Ilis said to Malai. "The Eleusians and their allies will accomplish their own destruction. It will be a perfect revenge."

She gazed into his golden eyes, so fierce and determined, and loved him even more. "Aren't we winning already?"

"It would take years to clear Teleriol of them all," Ilis said. "This way, we can eliminate them in a single stroke, and the continent will be ours—our people will have all the land and resources we could need, with no enemies to fear."

"Tell me, then," Malai said, taking his hand. It was callused and rough. While he didn't often fight directly, he practiced regularly with bow and spear. He'd been one of the greatest of the elkiri. A flush of pride swept through her.

"The best part of it is that they'll be fooled into thinking it is they who have won the war," Ilis said with a feral grin.

"Now you have me very *curious."*

"We'll show them how to bring enough power against me and the Ilk to destroy us. But it will rebound and kill them too—every single Eleusian on Teleriol."

"So, mutual destruction?" she said, confused.

"Exactly."

"But—how does that mean we win? The Ilk will be gone. But so will you."

"The Ilk are putting a lot of strain on the Cloth. The Gloom is getting worse. They've fulfilled their use. We no longer need them."

"But what about you?" she pressed.

"I intend to splice at the last minute. But just in case, I'll perform the Passing Ceremony, and you'll store my memories in the crystal until our son is born. He'll take them when he comes of age."

Malai put a hand on her swollen belly. Entiki was kicking lustily. Her first and only child with Ilis, and he was to grow up without his father? "But you'll be gone," she insisted.

"As I said, I intend to splice away. But if I don't get away in time, it will be more than worth the sacrifice," Ilis said. "We'll have achieved justice against the Eleusians. And eventually, our son will rule all of Teleriol, with you at his side. Our people will thrive again."

"I don't want to lose you," she said, tightening her fingers around his.

"I'll live on through our son." Ilis pressed his hand against her belly. "I can feel him, growing strong inside you."

"How are you going to get the enemy to summon this power against you?"

"Jiki has penetrated the ranks of the Vycenians, and he'll propose the solution. They're desperate. They'll accept it."

"And what if they don't?"

"They will."

Ilis stood on the hill, the Ilk all around him, Malai next to him. The Eleusian army was marching toward them, tens of thousands spreading around to encircle the hilltop. Would it play out as Ilis had predicted? He'd always claimed to have the power of a Foreseer. But everyone knew this power was uncertain, that it didn't always show what you thought it showed. Still, Jiki had reported that the so-called Final Hundred were in the vanguard and would summon the force to destroy Ilis and the Ilk as planned.

"Now, we do it," Ilis said to her as the army stopped close to the hill. He'd made himself visible high on top of it so that they could easily find their target.

Malai felt the Tapestry hum as the enemy mages began to call on the explosive energy that would sever the link of the Ilk with the prime force. She trembled. "Why not just come with me now? I don't want to lose you. You don't need to sacrifice yourself."

But Ilis shook his head. "It must be this way. I've achieved my objective in this life. I'll have cleared Teleriol so our people can return here. But that will be your job, yours and Entitki's and the other few who are left. Return Chel's people to our homeland."

Fighting back tears, she held out the crystal and Ilis put his hands on it, closing his eyes. It glowed brightly as he poured his consciousness into it. When he was done, his body sagged but didn't fall—they'd slid a pole beneath his robes and tied him to it so he would appear alive to the enemy.

The crystal now impregnated, she spliced the Cloth, ready to flee. It was difficult, the Cloth so stretched by the masses of Ilk. If they hadn't already created a waygate, she doubted she'd have succeeded.

A tremendous noise shattered the air behind her as she stepped through the hole she'd made. She felt scorching heat, and then she was in Sīut's Realm and safely away.

Gidion emerged from Malai's mind. The Ruin had been orchestrated by the Ilk Lord! So many souls unraveled, unable to join the gods in the afterlife. And the Tapestry there broken beyond repair, the Great Maelstrom where once a continent had been. It had all been deliberate.

"Not deliberate," Malai said, speaking directly in his mind. *"We didn't foresee the Ruin as it played out. We didn't intend to lose Teleriol."*

Gidion could feel her grief and rage, and believed her. Still, they'd intended to commit genocide against the Eleusians. Instinctively, he was revolted.

"It was justice," Malai said fiercely. *"Do you know what they did to us?"*

He had to admit that he didn't.

"Then learn."

Gidion's mind was flooded with horrors. Settlements pillaged and torched, forests burned to the ground to kill those who fled among the trees. Women violated in front of their children and murdered, the children too. Old people, the sick, slain in their beds. Famine and disease spreading everywhere, taking those who were spared the fire and steel.

The Chelak armies, led by their mages, the elkiri, tried to stop the slaughter, but they weren't enough. Because the Eleusians didn't work alone. They had help from Vycenian weavers, whose powerful, destructive magic the Chelaki had no defense against. And not just Vycenian weavers. Regular soldiers too, sent across the sea on weave-powered ships. Despite himself, Gidion felt his anger rise. The Chelaki had suffered genocide first, and in the most brutal way. *"How is it possible that you were alive then?"* he asked Malai.

"I wasn't. These are Ilis's memories, which he shared with me," she replied. *"He was barely a man when the Slaughter happened and he escaped to Myrna on the backs of the drakiri along with a handful of others."*

"Drakiri?"

She sent an image of a huge flying creature with a bird-like beak containing rows of teeth. It stood on powerful legs and had a long, lashing tale. But it was covered in iridescent feathers in blue and gold. Gidion marveled at its beauty, feeling an immediate kinship with it. *"Do they still exist?"*

"This land wasn't suitable for them," Malai said. *"They went in search of somewhere better and never returned."* Her voice was heavy with regret.

Gidion shared that regret. How magnificent the creature was! Malai returned to his own mind, and he blinked around the cavern. Seila and Nessa were both looking at him. Seila in concern, Nessa with curiosity.

"So you see," Malai said.

Gidion didn't know what to think. With the Ruin, Ilis had repaid the wrong done to his own people. He'd evened the scales. But didn't that make him just as bad as the Eleusians and Vycenians who'd slaughtered the Chelaki? A feeling of helplessness overwhelmed him. He didn't know what to think. What way was right and which was wrong? It was beyond him, beyond anything he'd been taught. "But you've already won," he said at last. "What do you want now?"

“No, we haven’t, not yet,” Malai said fiercely. “Our people still aren’t free. We have no land to call our own. But we’ll take it, and you’ll rule as you were meant to.”

“I won’t commit murder,” he said.

“And you don’t need to dirty your hands if you don’t want to,” Malai replied. “But every ruler must take what is theirs by force. That has always been the way.”

Gidion opened his mouth to object but then thought of the many histories he’d read in the Spire these past months. It was true—no nation had been born without force. And wasn’t it the threat of force that kept people peaceable? “What happened to your son, Entiki? Why isn’t he here?”

“See for yourself.”

Again, he entered her mind. She and Ilis had thought that the child in her womb would be Ilis’s heir, but Entiki died when he tried to channel the prime force, and Ilis’s memories continued, untouched, in the memory crystal. All was not lost, though, because Entiki had planted his seed in several women, and had three children. But while two were mage-gifted, neither had the ability to access the prime force. Another generation of children, none with the right abilities. More generations, eight in total. Malai had despaired, thinking they’d failed. Until Seila's grandmother Reina had come, able to touch the prime force but of the wrong sex. Gidion was the first male to be born with it, making him Ilis's true heir.

"I thought you were my grandmother," he said.

"In Chelak, any female one generation or more higher than your direct parent is called a grandmother."

"How is it possible you're still alive?" She had to be over two hundred years old.

"We have a ritual we can perform to lengthen our lifespans."

There was something she wasn't telling him, but he had a more pressing question. *"How do you know I won't die trying to channel the prime force? I felt like I was going to, last time."*

"The fact that you touched it and it didn't kill you is a sign. But Seila saw you do it first as a baby."

He drew out of Malai's mind. "I need some time," he said. "I need to think."

"Of course," Malai said. "Seila, why don't you show Gidion to his room. It's very late, and we're all tired. We'll meet for breakfast in the Woodlands?"

Seila nodded and held a beckoning hand out to Gidion.

He regarded her coldly for a moment, then walked directly to the door, forcing her to hurry after him. "Have you been here all along?" he asked stiffly as they exited into the passageway beyond. It was surprisingly warm and paved in black stone, reminding him of the maze beneath the Seekers' Tower. But it was brightly lit with glowglobes, and a rich, dark green carpet ran the length of it.

"Ever since that day," Seila said. "I wanted to find you, so, so badly."

"Pa never recovered," he said, intending to hurt.

His strike landed. "What do you mean?"

"He changed after that day," Gidion said, thinking of the sudden rages, the clouts across the ears when Gidion did something he didn't like.

Seila pressed his hand. "I'm so sorry, Gid. It wasn't what I planned. I wanted you to live free."

"A life of hiding isn't freedom." But he couldn't summon the same bitterness as before.

"No, I suppose not. But please, believe me. I had only your interests at heart."

They all said that. But did they mean it? "Why did you leave me that day?"

"What day?"

"That day in the glen, when Malai first came with the Ilk."

"I didn't leave you. Conal did as I asked and took you into hiding, but Malai forced me to come back here. I haven't been allowed to go anywhere since."

She was making herself open to him, and he sensed nothing but sorrow. It made him relent further, and he decided to change the subject. "Where are we exactly?"

"I can't tell you."

He hardened. "Why not? Surely, I deserve at least that by now."

"It's not that I won't tell you. It's that I truly can't. Grandmother has always been very secretive. I don't know where we are either."

"But surely, when you left, you must have seen, traveled somewhere …"

"We only ever go in and out through Sīut's Realm."

"So there's no other way in and out?"

"Not one that I've ever found. And if the others know of one, they haven't told me."

"But why doesn't Malai tell you where you are?"

"So there's no danger of anyone else ever finding out either," she replied.

He couldn't deny the logic. "You must have some idea, though."

"The land around us is all desert," Seila said. "That much I know. We can't cultivate anything, so we portal in all our food."

"From where?"

"Various market towns near Kharas."

So they were likely somewhere in South Myrna. That would make sense given that Malai had found them in the Riftlands. They might even be in the Riftlands somewhere. It was a vast, canyon-filled plateau that took up a huge chunk of the continent.

They came to a T-junction, and Seila led him down the righthand passageway, which had many doors along it. All were carved directly out of the rock, visible as doors only because of their outline and an activation panel to open them. Each had a different symbol on it, too.

"What do the symbols mean?"

"We each have a symbol of our own that we use to identify ourselves to each other."

"How many of us are there?"

"Hundreds," Seila replied.

To go from having no family to hundreds was as shocking as learning the origins of the Ruin.

"And they all live here?"

"No, only a few of us are here at any one time. They have normal lives out in the world, waiting for our time to come. Waiting for you."

"What if I don't want to do all this?" he said. "What if I *do* just want an ordinary life?" But as soon as he said those words, he knew he didn't want ordinariness.

"Malai can't force you to do anything," she said. "And I don't think she'll try to. But be careful when you speak to her. She has a way with words ..."

"She said she wiped Danial Thane's memories."

"Who's he?"

"My mentor at the Spire. And before we came here, she said she'd make him forget everything he knew about me."

"Yes, she has the ability to do that. It's dangerous. You can cause a lot of harm to a person's mind. But Grandmother has never been overly concerned with such things."

Seila was clearly unhappy about it, but Thane deserved it as far as Gidion was concerned. It brought him to another question. "Are the Ilk pits here? Is this where he made them?"

Seila nodded.

"Can I see them?"

"I suppose you can. But you'll need to ask Malai."

"And the Ilk?"

"The remaining ones are here too." They'd stopped outside a door with the symbol of a drakir in side profile, wings folded against its body. "This is yours." She pressed her palm against the rock, and it slid sideways, revealing a large room. She activated the glowglobes set into the ceiling with a press of her hand against the inside wall.

A bed large enough for three, made of dark wood, the legs and ends carved with twining leaves. A desk and chair, an armchair, and a bookcase filled with books. It all looked very normal.

"If you'd like to wash, there's a bathing room through there." She pointed to another door at the back of the room. "You'll find clothes in the wardrobe, all to your size."

"And how do I find you in the morning?"

"I'll come back for you."

She left him, and Gidion stood in the room, dazedly taking it in. But soon he became aware of something calling him, an insistent tug from a single direction. He hadn't been aware of it at first, but now, in the silence of the room, it was all he could think of. What was it? He paced every inch of the room but didn't find the source of the call. It was coming from somewhere in the depths of the mountain. Should he go out, follow it?

He went to the door, fully expecting it to be locked. But it wasn't, and he stepped out into the dimly lit corridor. The call was coming from the right. He started walking, following the call through warm, twisting black tunnels to a door. But when Gidion tried to open it, he found it locked with a complex weave. What was beyond the door? He ached to find out, wondered if he could ask Malai. Then he realized he had little idea to get back to his room, never mind how to find Malai. He'd been so focused on the call that he hadn't taken the time to note which way he was going. Cursing, he turned back the way he'd come, trying to ignore the maddening pull of the locked room. It took many wrong turns and a painfully long time before he finally found his room again.

At this point, exhaustion threatened to crush him. But he decided to wash himself first. He felt sweaty and disgusting, the smell of the whore still on him and making him feel queasy. It embarrassed him that Nessa had seen him like this, had probably known that was where he was. Would she think less of him for it?

The bathing room turned out to be a generous size, with a large copper bath against the wall and water that came out from a tap. It was cold, but it was a simple matter for him to heat it to the temperature he wanted. He eased himself into the water with a sigh and contemplated everything he'd been told. Part of him felt like he was in a dream—a nightmare, more like. He'd imagined meeting his mother again many times, discovering that she hadn't been killed after all. But he'd never imagined anything like this. And he still wasn't sure who he could trust. Did Malai just want to use him, as Thane had? Or was this a real chance at power? He mulled over the conversations he'd had with Nessa, with Malai and his mother, trying to see what truths might be lying behind their words. But he had no answers by the time the water had begun to cool. And all the while, the locked room called to him.

Chapter 25

When his mother knocked on the door the following morning, he was already awake, staring at the rocky ceiling, brooding. At the sound of his name, he reluctantly dragged himself out of the bed and opened it. Seeing her face again, so like his own, heightened his sense of unreality. He blinked at her silently, while she ventured a smile.

"You look tired," she said.

Gidion's anger and bitterness spiked. "Who'd be able to sleep after what I learned yesterday?"

Seila flinched. "I know it's been a lot to take in."

"I need to dress," he said.

"I'll wait for you here."

He closed the door on her and went to the wardrobe to see what clothes had been left for him. There were some loose cotton shirts in the Kharasian style, along with several pairs of breeches. Both shirt and breeches fit perfectly.

He returned to his mother, and they started walking down the corridor, away from the thing that was calling him. They didn't speak. Gidion felt very uncomfortable in her presence, the boy he'd been warring with the man he now felt himself to be. She seemed equally uncertain. He kept sensing that she wanted to say something to him but was too afraid to, and it irritated him.

As they walked, he noted again how warm the tunnels were, and decided to mention it. "There are hot flows of rock beneath us," Seila told him. "It's an old fire mountain."

"You mean a volcano? Aren't you worried it will explode?"

"We monitor it carefully," Seila replied. "It hasn't exploded since Ilis came here."

"And when was that?"

"After the Slaughter," Seila said.

An unsettling reminder of how long his family's past stretched.

They finally entered a room covered in tapestries showing woodland scenes. It contained a couple of round redwood tables with matching chairs, as well as clusters of more comfortable-looking armchairs in the corners. Malai was sitting at one table already, but there was no sign of Nessa.

"Sit," Malai said, indicating a chair to her right.

Gidion did as she bade, while Seila slipped out, saying she'd get their meal.

"Were you able to sleep?" Malai asked.

From the way she asked it, she already knew the answer. She was just inviting him to open up, and he wasn't sure he wanted to. After all, he'd spent his whole life in fear of her. And the guilt—he'd carried it around for years, believing himself the cause of his mother's death, then his father's. "I keep feeling something pulling at me," he said. "Like an itch I can't scratch."

Malai seemed unsurprised. "It's probably Ilis's memory stone. They always call to the people destined to use them."

"Can I go see it?"

"It's too soon," she said. "You're not ready."

Despite the call of the crystal, Gidion wasn't sure he was ready to see it yet either. He certainly didn't want to touch it. But something else was on his mind. "Can I see the Ilk?"

Malai blinked at his sudden change of subject, but then smiled as if at some joke only she had heard. "I can take you to them after we've eaten."

He was surprised, having expected her to deny his request. And now he wasn't entirely sure he wanted to face the creatures again.

His thoughts were interrupted by the arrival of their breakfast—floury cakes filled with currants and nuts, and a red juice he didn't recognize. Seila brought the meals on a trolley as if she were mother to them all. Or a servant. Yes, it seemed more like servitude, the way she held herself, with shoulders hunched, hardly daring to meet Malai's gaze, or Gidion's for that matter. And a mean part of him despised her for it.

"Where's Nessa?" he asked Malai as Seila put out the pastries.

She gave him a knowing look. "She was called away but will be back later."

To mask his disappointment, he bit into one of the floury cakes. It was sweet and lightly spiced, similar to the cakes he'd often had on the road with his father, making him surprisingly nostalgic.

"Now tell me, how did you find the Spire?" Malai asked, biting into a cake of her own.

Reluctantly, he began to talk about his impressions of it, his relationship with Thane. "What will happen to him now?" he asked.

"As I said, we'll ensure he remembers nothing of what happened," Malai said.

"But other people knew I was there. How will you manage that?"

"To them all, you'll simply have disappeared," Malai replied. "Thane will believe the same."

And Jasper would continue as Thane's sole apprentice. He'd be happy about that.

Once the meal was done, Malai fulfilled her promise to take him to the Ilk. The journey took them closer to the source of pull he'd been experiencing since he'd arrived.

But when they stopped, it wasn't at the door he remembered from the night before. Malai opened it with a palm press. The Gloom hit Gidion, potent and sharp, whispering fear into his ears. There were only two Ilk, the tall, wolf-like ones whose jaws looked like they could bite his head off in a single snap. They stood by the wall with red, unblinking eyes, entirely unmoving. Gidion opened himself to the Tapestry, curious to learn how they functioned. As before, the threads around them were warped, but he spotted something else, a thin stream of the prime force coming from outside the Tapestry. He was about to reach out to it, but then remembered what had happened last time and stopped.

"Don't try to channel it yet," Malai said warningly.

He wouldn't, although it called to him. "Nessa said the Ilk L—Ilis—had a sword he used as a conduit."

"It's taken different forms over the years," Malai said. "But yes, he had metal that came from outside this world, and only it is strong enough to contain the prime force without shattering."

"Can I see it?"

"Now isn't the time," Malai replied.

"Why not? I thought you said I was his heir."

"Well, you certainly have his stubbornness," Malai said with a wry twist of her mouth.

But Gidion was impatient. He was here now. He might as well know the truth of everything. "When will it be time?"

"You need more training first. I don't want to risk you like Entiki."

"There's no rush, love," Seila added.

Gidion didn't like this answer very much, didn't like to feel he was being controlled again. His instinct was to push, but he needed to bide his time, figure out a plan.

"We'll start training you this afternoon," Malai continued. "Nessa has told me you're a quick pupil and have already made progress with her. But we've still only scratched the surface of your powers."

So Nessa had spoken well of him? Pride replaced Gidion's annoyance. "I want to learn all that I can."

"And you will. You'll learn, and you'll be even greater than he was before." Suddenly, she tilted her head as if hearing a voice, her eyebrows drawing together. But Gidion's other sense told him nothing. They were all very good at masking themselves from him. Malai's face cleared, and she smiled. "Let's return to the Woodlands. Nessa has news for us."

"About my father?"

"It seems so." Malai walked quickly, and Gidion and Seila hurried to keep up.

Nessa was sitting at the table, munching on a cake. She smiled at him when he entered, showing her dimples, and his heart cracked.

"You've got word about my father?" Gidion asked.

Nessa's smile broadened. "We may have a lead, at last."

Seila's eyes widened and she leaned in on the balls of her feet. It was the most animated Gidion had seen her. "He's alive?"

"We think so. It's hard to tell for sure because the Riftlanders are so secretive, even with each other," Nessa replied.

"So, what next?" Gidion asked.

"Kye and I will follow up on the lead," Nessa said. "I'm just waiting for him to come back."

"When?" Seila asked.

"Later today, I hope."

"Can I come?" Gidion asked.

Nessa hesitated, looking to Malai, who shook her head. "No, the fewer who go, the better, and you have much to learn here."

Gidion sighed heavily. He wanted action, not another bloody prison.

"Nessa, why don't you take Gidion for a lesson," Malai said. "You might as well continue where you left off. I'll let you know when Kye returns."

"Be delighted to," Nessa said, flashing her dimples at Gidion. She swallowed the last of her cake, washed it down with some juice, and got to her feet. "Come on, I'll show you our very well-equipped training room."

Cheered by the prospect of some time alone with her, he followed her into the corridor. But as they walked, his doubts about her kept crawling back into his mind. Did she care for him? Had it all been for show? He had to find out. He had to know. But he couldn't bring himself to ask.

When they reached the training room, Gidion discovered she hadn't been exaggerating. It was piled with weapons and armor. There were weaver's battlestaffs, but also swords, spears, shields, and other, stranger items. Gidion's mouth fell open in surprise as he took it all in.

"One of Malai's sayings is 'Always be ready'," Nessa said. "We train constantly here."

"Who's 'we'?"

"Kye and me, your mother, Malai, but also any of your family when they come to visit."

It still sounded strange to him. Family. Hundreds of family he'd never met, whose existence he'd never known of until yesterday. "Are any of them here now?"

Nessa shook her head. "Not that I'm aware of. There are gatherings from time to time, when everyone comes. Maybe there'll be one soon now that you've finally come home."

"Home" sounded even stranger. The place didn't feel like a home. But then, home had been a peddler's wagon. It was hardly better.

Nessa cocked her head. "Tell me truthfully," she said. "How have you been? It must be a lot."

This was his chance to ask what he really wanted to. His heart speeding up, he said, "I was more worried about you."

She frowned. "Why?"

"Well, Thane kidnapped you."

Nessa waved a dismissive hand. "I've been through worse."

"You seemed … frightened … when you called me." Gidion had hoped that she'd admit vulnerability, that she'd needed him.

"He made me call you."

Gidion was taken aback. "He *made* you call me? But why?"

"I suppose he guessed there was something between us he could use as leverage."

His breath caught. "So there *is* something between us?" He stepped closer to her. At the same time, he quested with his other senses. But Nessa was a blank to him as always.

She smiled, touched a hand against his cheek. His body flushed with heat, and he leaned in to kiss her, but she stepped back and dropped her hand. "It wouldn't be a good idea to get involved."

"Is this what she's told you?" he said bitterly.

An expression of sorrow and tenderness crossed her face. "I never pretended I hadn't been sent to you by Malai," she said. "But I do genuinely care for you, and I want to see you succeed."

"Then why …" he said in frustration.

"So much has happened, you've got so much to take in, to learn."

"I don't care about that. I just want ..."

"Can you even say that you trust me?" she replied.

Gidion bit his lip. "I could learn to."

"Trust is earned, and it takes time," she said. "Sex complicates things."

Her mention of the word made him heat more. "Can't we just ... see how it goes?"

But she shook her head firmly. "We can't let ourselves get distracted," she said. "You need to focus on your training, and I have my missions to accomplish."

"What are your missions?" His voice was roughened by the lump that had hardened in his throat.

"First, I need to get your father back."

"Then what?"

"Then it will be time for Malai to help fulfill her bargain. She'll help me defeat the Riftlanders once and for all."

"Can I help?"

"That's up to Malai," Nessa said. "You still have so much training to do."

Again, that! He was so fed up with being told he wasn't enough. "But you've said yourself I learn quickly. I can already splice."

Nessa smiled. "Not with the speed and precision of someone fully trained. Watch." She vanished and instantly reappeared at the other end of the room, sword drawn. But she'd no sooner done that than she was hovering in mid-air above him, sword slicing down. Before she fell to the ground, she vanished again. Next he knew, the tip of her sword was pressing into his back. The whole thing had taken barely three heartbeats.

"Pits," was all he could manage. He could nowhere near match that speed. But he wanted to learn. He wanted to learn it all, so badly. "What if I touch the stone and take his memories?"

"Ilis's?"

"Yes."

Nessa hesitated. "Honestly, I'm not sure. I don't know what impact that would have on you."

"But I'd have the power to help you with the Riftlanders?"

"Probably, but I don't want that to be the reason for your decision. Take your time, learn what you can from Malai and me. There's no rush."

But there was a rush. She didn't get it. She didn't understand his frustration, his need to prove himself. He stared at her silently, trying to work out what to say next. In the end, he opted to side-step. "Fine, can we practice what you just showed me?" he said. "I want to get that fast."

Nessa smiled. "Grab a weapon."

Gidion forgot his frustration for a while, the training absorbing him. It was only when she called a halt, saying she had to meet Kye, that everything crashed back upon him again. If he could only get good enough, prove to her that he was ready, a man, he might win her over. So he kept practicing after she left, but found himself growing every more tired, the pain in his head ever more distracting.

Again, he thought of the Ilk Lord's crystal. Surely, it was the quickest way to achieve his goals? He dismissed the thought, but it returned almost instantly, even more insistent. Before he knew what he was doing, he was marching out of the room, seeking Malai.

As he was looking for her, he heard a bell ringing. They'd told him he'd hear one when it was time for lunch, so he made his way to the

Woodlands Room. No sign of Nessa, but his mother was there with Malai.

"I want to see the memory stone," he said to Malai as soon as he sat down.

Malai's eyes narrowed. "Not yet."

"Why not? I thought you wanted me to take his memories."

"And you will, but there's time," Malai said. "You're still very young, there's been a lot of change."

Gidion wanted to yell and shout. He was so thoroughly sick of being patronized. But he just said, "Can't I at least see it?"

Malai shook her head. "It's too soon. Now, tell me what you worked on with Nessa. This afternoon, you'll train with me instead."

Gidion gritted his teeth in frustration, forced himself to take a breath, then reluctantly described the morning to her.

Things continued much the same for the following weeks. Gidion trained daily with Malai, his mother, and sometimes Nessa. But Nessa was always coming and going, attending to this or that task. And all the while, he could feel the Ilk Lord's stone calling to him, like an ever-present itch he couldn't scratch. Malai refused every request he made to see it, until at last, out of pure frustration, he returned to the locked room to see if he could find any way to get in.

He waited until the middle of the night before slipping out. But try as he might, he couldn't figure out how to unlock the weave. He thumped his fist on the door in frustration. To the pits with Malai! Was this her work? Probably. And he was willing to bet she hadn't risked creating a keystone either. She was so calculating, so careful, so *controlling*.

He returned to his room angry. The books in it infuriated him. He stalked over to them, pulled them out one by one, and tossed them to the ground. What was the point of it all if he was still a prisoner?

When would they just let him *be*? He kicked at the books, then his bed. It wasn't enough. He smashed his fist against the wall, letting out a long scream while tears of rage flooded his eyes.

Then he slumped to the ground, drawing his knees up and burying his face in them. A heavy weight pressed on him, and he felt like he couldn't breathe. He gulped in more air, but it wasn't enough. His chest heaved, in and out, in and out, faster and faster, but there still wasn't enough air. Panic spread through him, his muscles seizing and spasming, but he couldn't make them stop. It was exhaustion that finally put an end to it. But then the tears came out in great choking sobs, shaming him with his weakness.

When he finally calmed down, he felt guilty about the books. Some were old and fragile, the pages now torn or bindings broken. He picked them up and patched them up as best he could before restoring them to the shelves. Then he sat on his bed and plotted how to gain control of his situation. Things couldn't continue as they were. He wouldn't stand for it. His mother seemed the weakest link. She'd tried a few times to come to him, but he'd rejected her coldly. He couldn't quite forgive her for not telling him the truth before, for the years of absence, even if that was Malai's doing. But he could tell how desperate she was to win him over, and that could be his leverage.

He got to his feet, determined to seek her out. But he ran into Nessa in the hallway. Her face was flushed with excitement. "We've found him!"

He blinked. "My father?

"He's being held by Riftlanders in one of their permanent settlements. Come, I'm on my way to meet Malai and your mother."

Feeling oddly numb about the news, Gidion went with Nessa to the Woodlands Room. Malai and Seila were already there, apparently locked in some kind of argument. The looks they gave Gidion made him think it had been about him.

"Good news, I hope?" Malai said.

"As good as could be. Conal is in the settlement they call Shadow Creek," Nessa said. "Quite a distance from Tine, so he was either traded to another band or the one that attacked Tine had ventured far from their clanland."

"Do you know how he is?" Seila asked, eyes lighting with hope.

"Apparently, he's been teaching their magic users how to use weaver magic," Nessa said. "So they're treating him well enough."

"Where's your brother?" Malai said.

"Here." The man who had entered was very obviously Nessa's twin, Kye, having the same violet eyes and near-black hair. He was also tall, lean, and sharp as a blade. He turned his gaze to Gidion. "So this is Ilis's heir," he said. His voice was deep, melodious. It could have belonged to a bard. But while he scrutinized Gidion carefully, he didn't seem particularly impressed.

Gidion realized that Kye just saw him as a boy and bristled. *He hasn't seen what I can do yet.*

"You haven't seen what I *can do,"* Kye said in his mind, lips curling in amusement.

Gidion slammed down the defenses around his mind. He'd obviously been broadcasting again.

"Have you got any thoughts on how to get him out?" Malai said.

"Pretty straightforward. Seila makes us invisible, and we sneak in and free him," Nessa replied.

"How do you do that?" Gidion blurted out, having never heard that his mother could wield such magic.

"I can spin illusions," Seila replied.

"Like the Eleusians?"

“Eleusian blood runs through our veins,” Seila said.

Of course, Nessa had told him that. He hadn’t thought much about it, having so many other things to worry over. But now he wondered, could he spin illusions too? “Show me how to do it, and I can help.”

“No, we can’t risk you,” Malai said firmly. “You’ll have your chance to fight, Gidion, but I haven’t spent all this time looking for you only to lose you.”

“You keep treating me like a child.”

“Because you are one,” Malai returned. “No Chelak was ever considered a full adult until they reached their twentieth year.”

He swallowed the temptation to argue back. He’d find another way to get what he wanted, one more likely to succeed. *They can’t keep me away. Pa sacrificed himself for me that time. It’s my turn to repay him.*

The following day, Seila, Kye, and Nessa set off to execute their plan. Gidion went to the portal room and watched closely as Nessa spliced the Tapestry, trying to see which path she’d picked. It was difficult, but he felt he got a sense of it. He’d follow as soon as the coast was clear. But there was one more thing he wanted to do first.

“Please, can I see the memory stone?” he said to Malai when they’d gone. “Just a look.”

“It’s too soon,” she said yet again.

“It calls to me,” Gidion said. “I can’t sleep because of it. It’s driving me mad. I just want to see it.”

“Even more reason for you to stay away until you’re ready.”

“But I don’t understand!” he exploded. “I thought you wanted me to touch it?”

“*Ilis* wants you to do that,” Malai replied. “But Ilis was always like a charging bull. He saw only his target, and once he’d fixed on it, he didn’t think very much about anything or anyone else.”

"What do you mean?"

She hesitated. "I'm not sure he considered what impact the memories might have on you."

"Are they so bad?"

"Ilis lived through the Slaughter," she replied. "He saw everyone he loved murdered or violated by the Eleusians. And he never fully recovered from that."

Gidion thought of the scenes of the Chelaki genocide that Malai had shared with him. If Ilis had lived through that... "I don't want to touch the crystal, I just want to see it," he said. This time he employed a technique he'd started learning from her, a pressure on the threads to influence her.

"You're still clumsy at that," Malai said. "But well done for trying." Her tone was ironic rather than angry, and a small smile played on her lips.

So Gidion hid his annoyance at his failure, and just smiled and shrugged. "You did tell me to practice."

"It was strong," she said. "And against the untrained, you would have succeeded. But you have no subtlety yet. That takes a long time to master."

Gidion tried another tactic. He made his mind open, holding a single thought foremost in it. "I just want to see the crystal. I promise I won't touch it. Surely, I've earned at least this much. And you can bind my hands if you're worried."

Malai gazed at him for a few seconds, then gave a tiny shrug. "I suppose there's no harm in a quick look." To his relief, she didn't take up the suggestion she restrain him. That would have complicated his plan. Instead, she just took him to the room he'd discovered, and he watched closely as she dismantled the weave-lock she'd created. It took her a few minutes as it was so intricate, even more intricate than those used by Thane.

As soon as they were inside the room, he made his move—a quick blast of power through the threads of her mind. She was so taken by surprise that she didn't raise a defense. He caught her as she fell, lowering her to the ground.

Only then did he pay attention to the crystal. It was a large chunk of red quartz and pulsed with faint life. His fingers itched with the desire to touch it. This was his destiny. This was why he'd been born. But Malai's warnings returned to him. Did he really want these memories? Malai herself had said he didn't need Ilis's memories to become as powerful as Ilis. He could learn it all for himself. And it wasn't as if he wanted to make Ilk.

It might be safest to destroy it. No, he'd take it with him, ensure that it was in his possession, under his control. So he pulled his tunic off and wrapped it around the stone, then left with it tucked under his arm. He went to his room, where he'd already prepared a pack containing food and water. Shoving the memory stone inside it, he made for the portal room, where he opened the gateway to the Riftlands.

Chapter 26

He found himself inside a shallow cave, Seila, Nessa, and Kye conversing quietly on the ground in front of him. They leaped to their feet, weapons drawn, then relaxed when they saw it was him.

"What are you doing here?" Seila asked, frowning.

"I'm going to help rescue Pa." He stared at them defiantly.

"Did Malai let you come?" Nessa said, narrowing her eyes.

"She couldn't stop me," he replied. And that was the truth, so it wasn't too hard to make them believe it, even if they delved him with their lifesense.

But Nessa remained suspicious, while Seila looked afraid.

"Oh, let him stay if he wants to," Kye said. "It's his father, after all. You can't tell me you'd stay behind if the situation were reversed."

Gidion felt a sudden rush of affection for the man. He got it.

Nessa pursed her lips. "Fine, point taken."

Seila opened her mouth as if to speak, then closed it again with a slight shake of her head.

"Where are we exactly?" he asked.

"Come on, you might as well take a look." Nessa led him outside the cave.

They were high on a rocky plateau broken everywhere by deep chasms. The sky was an intense blue, and fiery heat radiated from the red rock, causing him to break out in a sweat. "Where's my father?"

"The settlement is down in that canyon." Nessa pointed to a narrow crack perhaps a quarter of a mile away.

"So when do we sneak in?"

"*Kye, Seila* and *I* will sneak in," she said firmly. "You'll stay out here."

It was hard for him to be angry with Nessa. But again, he felt he was being treated like a child, being told what he could and couldn't do. "I said I wanted to help."

"You can help by staying out here and keeping watch when we go in," Nessa said. "We'll need someone to alert Malai if things go wrong."

"Why don't one of you stay here if that's the case?"

"We're experienced at this. Seila has hidden us on more than one occasion," Kye said, touching his mother familiarly on the arm.

The gesture annoyed him. "Well, can't you just hide me too?" he said to his mother.

But Seila shook her head. "My ability is small. Hiding three people while we pass through a camp will stretch me to my limits. And it's even harder when there's a lot of nicoleum about. The Riftlanders have a lot of it."

Gidion wanted to argue further, but there was nothing he could think of that wouldn't make him sound petulant. And he didn't want to be that in front of Nessa. "When are you going?"

"Nightfall," Nessa said. "There's no moon tonight, so it's our best chance. You can come near the camp with us and keep watch."

They began to move as soon as night had fallen, using their lifesense to help them navigate the treacherous path in the darkness. Nessa,

Seila, and Kye did indeed seem to be well practiced, moving with grace and silence. But Gidion stumbled more than once, to his chagrin.

"This is as far as you go," Kye said at last with impatience. "You're not trained for this."

Gidion was about to object, but he had to admit that Kye was right. He wasn't able to move with their surety. And he could make out the shape of sentries against the starry night. They were almost upon them. "Will you stun them?"

"Their sentries and elite warriors wear nicoleum, so it won't work," Nessa said. "We'll have to trust in Seila's illusions."

"If anything goes wrong, you'll tell me?" Gidion said. The idea of losing Nessa, along with his mother for a second time, frightened him.

"Yes, I can link with you from that distance," Nessa replied.

It was something, and he lay down on his belly while the three snuck off into the dark. They were so good that he soon lost sight of them. Shortly after, he saw one sentry fall to the ground. Murdered? He kept his lifesense extended, and at first, everything was quiet. Most people were asleep, while Seila, Nessa, and Kye prowled through the canyon, seeking Conal's prison.

But suddenly, he felt an explosion of magical energy. Chaos washed through the threads as the entire camp woke up. Confusion, alarm—and from Nessa, pain.

"What's happened?" he cried through their link, not sure if he'd reached her.

"They've caught us! Get Malai!" Nessa cried.

More pain radiated through the threads before all sense of Nessa was abruptly cut off. Gidion stood frozen, caught in an impossible choice. Malai would probably know what to do, could perhaps come with the Ilk as reinforcements. But if he went back for her, what would happen to Nessa? To his mother? What if the Riftlanders killed them? No, he had to go in himself and help.

He scuttled toward the canyon, keeping as low as possible, hoping that the alarm within the settlement would keep its occupants from paying attention to what was going on outside. There was no visible sign of the sentries, but when he extended his lifesense, he encountered the blank he was starting to perceive as nicoleum. The blankness told him roughly where the sentries might be, but he wouldn't be able to take them down alone, and they were sure to see him.

He'd have to make a bold move, do something to attract their attention. An earthquake? No, it could collapse the cliffside and kill everyone, including Nessa and the others. He remembered the light trick he and Jasper had used in the Selection Trial. That would work. The sentries would be night blind after, and he could use the opportunity to sneak past them. So he summoned the threads, plucking on this and that one to weave the pattern he needed. Then, squeezing his eyes tightly shut, he released the light, before running to the edge of the crack.

A rope ladder dangled from hooks hammered into the lip of the canyon. Below, men and women swarming about with torches, the men armed with knives or swords. No sign of magic users. They hadn't noticed him yet, but he probably had only a few seconds before they did. Could he risk the rope ladder? No, he'd make an easy target. He could see the bottom well enough to splice down into it, but that would take him right among them, not a great outcome either. Another risky idea came to him. Risky, because he wasn't confident of the speed of his splicing. But safer than landing in the midst of them.

He spliced out into mid-air, allowing himself to fall a little while he looked for an alcove in the cliff face. Shouts from below. He'd been seen. He spliced again, emerging once more in mid-air, but lower down. This time he spotted a landing place, a very narrow crack in the canyon wall. He spliced but couldn't quite get the tunnel to open inside it. Instead, he emerged right in front and scrabbled for purchase. But his fingers scraped off the edge of the crack, and he tumbled down into the bottom of the canyon.

The impact left him senseless for precious seconds. By the time he'd come to, armed men had grabbed him and were hauling him to his feet. He blasted out a stun strike. Those holding him let go and fell to the ground. But others were unharmed and closed in, swords drawn. Nicoleum wearers, no doubt, and seasoned warriors, with black slashes on their biceps to show how many men they'd killed.

Gidion surrounded himself with a shield that would repel physical attacks. But there was only so long he could maintain it, and their nicoleum armor might stop it from working properly. *Pits!* He cast about frantically for inspiration, then spotted a young woman, a girl really, staggering about woozily. Dodging a slashing sword, he dropped his shield, grabbed her, and pulled her tightly against him, holding a knife to her throat. "Touch me and she dies!" he cried at the three men approaching him. She screeched and struggled, showing surprising strength. "Stop or I'll hurt you," he said furiously, yanking her harder against him. The men had halted their advance and were regarding him warily. "Where are they?" he asked in the Zenian tongue. "Where are my friends?"

One of the men pointed to his left.

"Lead me to them," Gidion demanded.

The man nodded and beckoned sharply. Gidion followed, keeping the girl close to him as he stepped around sprawled shapes. He was vaguely aware of weeping and wailing behind him. But all of his focus was on Nessa and Seila. He wouldn't lose them. He wouldn't let anyone harm them. He'd kill them all if he had to.

They reached the very end of the canyon, where there was a deep pit. One of the men pointed down into it. Gidion cautiously approached the edge and looked down. They were all down there, including his father, wearing nicoleum handcuffs. Nessa was bleeding from a cut on her face. He moved around the pit so that his back was directly to the canyon wall. “Get them out of there,” he demanded.

One of the men got a rope and sent it down into the pit, shouting at the prisoners to grab the end of it. Kye went first, holding the rope awkwardly with his handcuffed hands and wrapping his legs around the end as the men hauled him up slowly. He was just over the edge when a scaled head loomed over Gidion from above. An isaur. He'd forgotten they could scale the canyon walls.

Opening huge jaws, the isaur sank its teeth into Gidion’s shoulder. Pain lanced through him, forcing him to let go of the girl. She scrambled away while he tried to weave a shield, but before he could complete it, a fine wire net fell over him, and the Tapestry vanished from view. The enormous jaws clamped around his torso and lifted him off the ground, fetid breath heating the air around him. He struggled wildly, thinking he’d be crushed, but instead, he was held in a careful grip while a warrior approached with a pair of nicoleum handcuffs.

“Wear, and not kill you,” he said in heavily accented Zenian.

Seeing he had little choice, Gidion didn’t try to resist as they worked the net away from his hands and fastened the cuffs around his wrists. Only then did the creature drop him, lowering its head so that he didn’t fall from too far. Gidion gazed up at it from the ground. Intelligence glimmered in its swirling green-gold eyes. He cursed himself for not having taken the possibility of isaurs into account.

The warrior who’d cuffed him yanked him to his feet. Then he patted Gidion down, taking his knives and focus stone. Worse, he took the Ilk Lord’s memory crystal. Then, another warrior maneuvered

Gidion to the edge of the pit. Gidion struggled, thinking the Riftlander intended to push him into the pit. It was at least ten feet deep, and handcuffed as he was, he wouldn't land cleanly.

But no one pushed him. Instead, a warrior put rope between his hands. "Go," he said.

Gidion gripped the end of the rope, then sat on the edge of the pit, holding on tightly. A foot in the back sent him out into the air, and he swung wildly before crunching painfully against the side of the pit. They lowered him the rest of the way down, then yanked the rope up and out.

Gidion swept his gaze around the pit. Nessa was bleeding from several cuts on her face and arms, and bruises were swelling all over her. Kye looked little better but was doing what he could to wipe blood out of Nessa's eyes with a rag torn from his shirt. Seila and Conal were sitting close together, Seila with her hands on Conal's cheeks, tears trickling from her eyes. The sight of his parents struck him silent. Such a familiar gesture, yet one that seemed terribly out of place.

"I hope you told Malai," Nessa said around Kye.

"There wasn't time," he began.

"There was all the time, you fool!" Nessa cried, batting her brother away and angling her head so she could look at Gidion directly.

"You were hurt," he protested. "I was worried they'd kill you."

She rolled her eyes. "It's just a few knocks. I've had much worse. Can't you do anything you're told?"

"I'm not your servant!" he said.

"Save me from children!" Nessa cried in exasperation.

He burned with shame. "I'm not a child." Even as he said it, he realized he sounded like one, and the shame burned hotter. So he turned to his parents. His father looked worn and tired and much thinner than when Gidion had seen him last.

"It's good to see you again, son," Conal said.

Fury overtook Gidion, so intense he almost choked as he spoke. "You have questions to answer."

Nessa murmured something to Kye, and the twins rose and went to the far end of the pit. It was only a few paces away, but Gidion appreciated the gesture. He moved until he was standing above his father. "You lied to me."

"Sit down, at least," Conal said.

"Answer me. Why did you lie?"

Some of Conal's iron returned. "If you want a conversation, then sit and stop being a churl."

This only enraged him further. "Did you know she was still alive?" He flicked a look at his mother, who looked anguished.

But Conal said nothing.

Gidion repressed an urge to kick him, instead whirling on the spot and clenching his fists. He spotted Nessa looking at him with concern. It was enough to make him get a grip on himself. He turned back to his father and hunkered down so they were almost at eye level. "Did you know Ma was still alive?"

"I thought the Ilk killed her that day," Conal said steadily.

"I don't believe you." Damn the nicoleum, which stopped him from using his lifesense to sense Conal's emotions.

Conal's eyes remained locked on his. "I swear it, Gid."

"But you knew who she was, didn't you? You knew what Malai was to her—to me?"

Conal nodded wearily. "She told me and made me promise I'd give you a normal life. So we didn't tell you about it."

"How could you have called that normal? I grew up without friends, with no idea of who I was. It was all fear and hiding." His bitterness was so consuming it threatened to bring tears to his eyes.

Conal leaned forward. "She's an *Ilk* mage, Gidion."

But the words didn't strike the same terror in him as before. Malai was also his family, and she'd been more truthful than his parents.

Conal gripped his arm. "Please, don't become him." He looked at Seila. "You've warned him, haven't you?"

Gidion was taken aback by the strength of feeling in his father's words—naked, desperate, pleading. His father never pleaded. Only demanded and commanded. It reminded him that the Riftlanders had taken the Ilk Lord's crystal from him, and he cursed himself for a fool. So he just repeated what he'd said to his mother. "I can take his power, but I don't have to be him."

It was his mother who spoke again now. "Please, Gidion, don't trust her. I know you have no good reason to believe me. But everything I've done, everything *we* did, was to keep her from using you."

Gidion looked at the floor, then at the wall. The tears came despite his attempts to repress them. But he wasn't sure if they were tears of anger or sorrow. He blinked them away. "You should have told me the truth," he whispered.

"I see that now," Conal said, and Gidion was struck by the pain and remorse in his expression.

It softened him a little. "Why haven't they killed you?"

"They want me to teach them. They aren't quite as brutal as we've been led to believe. I think they might even have let me go free eventually. But now ..."

"You don't know that," Gidion said brusquely. "Is it weaving they want you to teach?"

"They have some ability with it, but it isn't as developed as ours," Conal replied.

"So they have magic users here?"

"I know of only one in this band, a woman. I believe all bands have at least one. Their role is a semi-sacred one. Quite interesting, really."

How typical of his father to say something like that. But what would the Riftlanders do with them? Malai would come and rescue them, wouldn't she? Or was there something Gidion himself could do? Some way to bargain with them? If he could figure a way out of this, then maybe everyone would finally stop treating him like a child.

"I need to think." He got to his feet.

"Gidion ..." his father started.

But Gidion ignored him, striding to another part of the pit, as far away from Nessa and Kye as from his parents. He sat down and looked up. The pit had been covered with a heavy wooden grate. The walls were slick stone, with no grips for climbing. *I won't be a prisoner again.* His fingers curled into fists. It felt like there was always someone trying to take him, make him bend to their will. But there had to be something he could do to escape this latest snare.

Experimentally, he tried to bring the Tapestry into view, see if there were any weaknesses at all in the dampening power of the nicoleum. The threads weren't entirely absent, but they were fuzzy, winking in and out of sight. The vibrations and sounds he was used to sensing were absent or erratic. He focused even harder, trying to keep the threads steady, but was rewarded only with a headache. Then he tried some basic weaving, but the threads fell apart as soon as he touched them.

Disheartened, he drew his knees to his chin and rested his head on them, wrapping his arms around his legs. Then he realized, *the threads aren't everything.* There was the prime force. Could he access that with nicoleum on his wrists? He first needed to splice the Tapestry. Would nicoleum block that? Probably, given the others hadn't already spliced their way to freedom. But Nessa had told him you didn't even need to be able to see all the threads to splice.

Girding himself, he tried to cut through the Tapestry and bring Sīut's Realm into view. At first, he failed entirely. The nicoleum seemed to dull whatever sense it was he needed to part the threads. But he continued to focus on pushing through, trying not to let himself be distracted by the fizzling threads. Sweat broke out all over his body, and his heart pounded so hard it was all he could hear, but he sensed he was getting close, and persevered. Finally, he managed the tiniest hole, little bigger than his fingernail. It snapped shut almost immediately. But he'd proved that it wasn't impossible. Just very, very hard.

He tried again, succeeding more quickly this time, the prime force calling to him through the tear. It would be easy enough to touch it, he sensed. The nicoleum would have no effect, perhaps because nicoleum was of this world, and the prime force came from outside it. But he hesitated. The last time he'd touched it, it had made him so ill he thought he'd die. And his grandfather had died trying to channel it. He had no idea what it could do either, other than make Ilk, of course.

So he closed the tiny splice he'd made, leaving the prime force alone. Best to leave it as a last resort. The fact that the Riftlanders hadn't killed Conal was heartening. Maybe they could be negotiated with. And once Malai woke up from the stun strike, she was sure to come looking for them. So he'd wait and see.

Chapter 27

The night stretched on, and despite it all, Gidion dozed off, coming to when a stone struck him on the cheek. He jerked to full wakefulness and looked up. A sheen on the rock told him daylight had come, and the warrior who had cuffed him the day before was hunkering down at the edge of the pit. He raised a hand as if to launch another stone. But when he saw Gidion had woken, lowered it. "You come now," he barked.

The rope came tumbling down, and Gidion pushed himself heavily to his feet. The others all still seemed to be asleep. Nessa was resting her head on Kye's thighs, stirring Gidion's envy. His parents were curled up together, Seila with her head on Conal's chest, and some other emotion struck him at the sight. At the same time, he felt more lonely than ever. They had each other, and he had nothing and no one.

"Come!" said the warrior.

The rope hit the top of his head, and he reached up to grab the end of it with both hands.

"Be careful what you say." Conal's voice. His eyes were open, but he hadn't moved.

Gidion said nothing as the warrior hauled him back up. Once he was over the edge, two others lifted him roughly to his feet. They dragged him along the bottom of the canyon, which seemed quite different in daylight. Now he could see that homes had been built on natural shelves in the rocky sides of the canyon. Where possible, they had used the rock itself for walls, but reddish bricks made up the rest of the structures. The windows and doorways were mostly open, but some had cloth coverings in shades of brown.

Water trickled down the center of the canyon. The riverbed was much wider than the stream itself, indicating that the water sometimes flowed more heavily. Small green plants, some of them flowering, sprouted near the water. He didn't see any homes in the canyon bottom. Instead, there were patches of cultivated land and scrubby trees, along with cloth awnings that served as shelters from the sunshine. Beneath them, men and women were engaged in various tasks. He saw isaurs, too, curled up in the shade or being groomed by their keepers. Many children ran around, screaming and naked.

About halfway along the canyon bed, his captors had him climb up a ladder to a large, round building set deep in the cliffside. The door was a heavy red tapestry sewn with swirling black symbols, and two warriors stood guard outside it.

One of the warriors holding him called out and received a sharp answer from inside. He pushed the tapestry aside while the other shoved Gidion into the room beyond. It was a curious space. The ground was covered in hair mats, but objects of silver and gold, some encrusted with gems, sat in alcoves in the walls or along the sides of the room. Mostly, they were pots or ornate weapons, and their only function seemed to be to impress.

A man in his prime sat on a small stool at one end of the room, wearing a sleeveless leather tunic that stretched across his powerful chest. Black lines striped his biceps and forearms, and his silky brown hair reached down to his shoulders. Sitting on the ground next to him was a strange woman whose face was mottled with swirling black lines.

She looked to be in her late middle years, with fine lines around her eyes and mouth and a wild mane of dark hair streaked with grey. A necklace of feathers, bones, and teeth hung just above her sagging, wrinkled breasts, which were uncovered, discomfiting him.

The warrior on Gidion's right kicked him in the back of the legs, making him fall to his knees. He almost tumbled over, but the other warrior yanked him upright by the hair before his face met the ground. Gidion burned with humiliation.

Then the woman picked up the Ilk Lord's crystal from a table behind her. It flared brightly, but she seemed unperturbed by it. "What is this?" Her voice rasped like there was sand in her throat.

Gidion's mind raced to see what advantage he could wring from the situation. "A magical artifact."

"We can see this," she said. "What does it do?"

Gidion hesitated. "It can only be used by me."

A hardening in her tone. "For what?"

Gidion raced to think how he could take advantage of the situation. "I can use it to help you defeat your enemies," he said. "If you'll set me free."

His reward was a vicious kick in the ribs from the warrior on the right, making him cry out.

"What does it do?" the woman asked again.

"There's knowledge stored in it," he said. "Of very powerful magic."

"How can we access this knowledge?"

"As I said, I'm the only one who can use it," Gidion replied.

Another kick, as sharp as the last, the question repeated.

"I swear it. Look, my father has been teaching you, hasn't he? I can teach you, too. We all can."

"Why would we believe you?" This time it was the chief who spoke. His voice was strong, resonant, and he spoke Zenian with a clearer accent than the others.

"We're not Federation soldiers," Gidion said. "We like the Feds no more than you do."

"The woman and her brother—they have the mark of the Zenian devils on them."

Shit. He'd forgotten that Nessa and Kye had served in the Federation army before they turned rebel. And all legionnaires had a tattoo on the right side of their ribs to show it. "They're not anymore," he said. "They've turned against the Federation, just like you. Bring them here and ask them."

The chief considered his words, then nodded at someone at the back of the tent. Shortly after, Nessa was hauled in. She looked even worse than she had the night before, one of her eyes swelling and blackened. Gidion's instinct was to tear free of his captors and try to release her. But he forced himself to stay still, hoping Nessa would find a way to talk them out of this.

"Why did you come here?" the chief demanded of Nessa.

"To free the weaver you have captured. His father." Nessa nodded at Gidion.

"What is this thing?" The chief pointed to the Ilk lord's crystal.

Nessa's eyes widened when she saw it. She transferred her gaze to Gidion, and the look in her eyes made him feel ashamed of his idiocy in taking it with him. At the same time, he could feel its call, even more powerful than before. It made his whole body itch.

"It's an artifact of great power," Nessa said. "But you won't be able to do anything with it."

At least she'd said the same as him. And it made an impression on both the chief and the woman holding it, because they looked less hostile.

Gidion leaped on the opportunity. "Look, why don't you just free us and we'll leave you in peace?" he said. "Our quarrel isn't with you. We just wanted to get my father back."

But the chief scowled. "Show us how to use this artifact."

"We've told you, you won't be able to do anything with it," Gidion said.

A ringing blow to the cheek that knocked his head sideways. Stars danced across his vision. He gritted his teeth against a growing rage.

The warrior who'd struck him raised his fist again, but the chief raised a hand, indicating no more. "You will show us, or she will suffer." He pointed at Nessa.

"I'm telling the truth," Gidion said, growing more desperate. How could he convince them? What could he give them to make them let Nessa go?

The chief nodded to his warriors. One punched Nessa in the gut, and she doubled over, gasping for breath.

"No!" He tried to get to his feet but was shoved back down.

"Show us," the chief said implacably.

"I told you it has ancient knowledge, but you won't be able to use it." Tears of rage and helplessness threatened to overcome him.

Nessa was still wheezing, but they were forcing her upright. Tears leaked from her eyes.

"She is very pretty," the chief commented. "I think my warriors will appreciate her."

"If they touch me, I'll bite their skinny cocks off," Nessa spat.

The chief laughed. "Some fire. This will make things more amusing."

Gidion fell into a panic. "I swear, I don't have anything more to share with you. But I can show you other magic if you want."

The chief ignored him. "Janabala, you may have her first as your reward for capturing her."

A warrior stepped out from the depths of the house, a savage grin on his face. The two who'd been holding Nessa kicked the legs out from under her and then pulled her hands forward so that she was on her knees, low to the ground, haunches high in the air.

Gidion's panic became fury. "Leave her alone!" He struggled against the guards, but they were as immobile as boulders.

"She's your woman?" the chief said. "All of my warriors will have her until you speak."

The one called Janabala hunkered behind her. She was struggling, succeeding in landing a kick in the man's face as he yanked at her breeches. Other warriors swarmed in to hold her down. Janabala snarled something at her in his language as he shrugged his loin cloth aside.

Gidion snapped. "Fine, I'll show you!" On their heads be it. He made his tiny splice in the Tapestry. The prime force swirled beyond, beckoning. The memory crystal resonated in its presence, causing the chief to frown at it, then at Gidion.

"Tell him to stop what he's doing," urged the strange woman, a frightened look on her face.

"Don't, Gidion!" Nessa pleaded.

But he couldn't bear to see her like that. He couldn't let them have her. And he was tired of being bullied. Tired of being told what to do. This was his time.

So he braced himself and reached out to touch the prime force. Pure agony tore through him, making him feel like his bones were splintering, his lungs imploding, his head exploding. He shrieked, every muscle in his body rigid. The clothes on his body disintegrated, the nicoleum binding his hands melting into his wrists. But the pain of that was nothing compared to holding the prime force.

Yet somehow, he contained it. Perhaps because the splice had been so tiny, the amount of power he was channeling so minute. And with the pain had come an incredible euphoria. This was the stuff of creation itself. The ultimate power over life and death. It made weaving seem puny. If he could control it, he could control the world.

But it was becoming too much. The bricks around them were crumbling, the warriors next to him screaming as their bodies dissolved, the threads that held them to the world unraveling.

"Let it go, Gidion! You'll kill us all!" Nessa cried.

Her terror and pain were enough to bring him back. He let go of the power, falling to his knees as it drained out of him. The warriors who'd been holding him were nothing but a collection of bone fragments and teeth, swimming in pools of blood, dark red and light mingled together.

Those still alive were fleeing. Gidion stopped the feathered woman with a stun strike, his powers returned now that the nicoleum had melted off him. The Ilk Lord's crystal fell out of her grasp as she crumpled to the ground.

Gidion leaped toward his prize. The stone was calling to him, promising power, control, freedom. All of that, plus the knowledge of how to use the prime force. He wanted more than anything to feel it coursing through him again—feel it and channel it as he'd been born to do.

He put his hands to the crystal. It sparked, and a connection tore through his mind, rippling through his consciousness. A deluge of memories rushed through him, too quickly to grasp even one. He felt a rage to match his own, but also a terrifying hunger and a deep, yawning hate. Too late, Gidion realized what he was dealing with. This was more than just memories. There was a spirit in that stone, and it was latching onto the levers of his mind, seeking to supplant him in his own body. He struggled and pushed, tried to shred the spirit, return it to the artifact from which he had released it. *"No, you have no right!"*

But he might as well have tried to stop an avalanche. The being he faced was immensely powerful, knew far more than he did. Had lived for centuries and planned long for this. Gidion was squashed, pushed aside, became little more than a voice in the corner of his own mind.

The boy who had been Gidion was now Ilis'Elkir. And he looked around with satisfaction at the ruin he had wreaked on his enemies. Then he smiled at Nessa. "You have pleased me greatly."

THE END

Fellow adventurers,

I hope you enjoyed reading this book! If you did, please consider leaving a review. It helps readers like you find it, especially on Amazon. To get "Deathstalker," a free short story set in the world of The Unraveling, sign up for my newsletter on www.elmcinerney.com. Signing up also gives you discount codes for direct purchases from my website. Plus, you'll be first to hear when new stories are published and to learn about any prizes and giveaways!

If you haven't read Soulstealer yet, the first book of The Unraveling series, you can find ebooks and paperbacks on Amazon and paperbacks and hardbacks on my website.

Scan the code for my website:

Scan the code for my Amazon author page:

Yours, El

Acknowledgements

This book has been particularly difficult to birth, not least because my beloved father passed away during the writing of it.

But, as always, it would not be the book it is today without the invaluable contributions of several people.

Chief among these is my friend and editor Adam Jackson. He labored through an early version of the manuscript that wasn't working well and was causing me no end of despair. It's thanks to his insightful comments and suggestions that I was able to rewrite the story in the form you see it today. But the work wasn't yet done, and I owe further thanks to Adam and my partner Mim, for applying their creative genius to the second draft and pushing me to dig even deeper.

Also crucial was the input of my beta readers, Kayleen, Michael, Bridget, Katie Norton, and Leyla Parlak. Thank you so much—you read an imperfect version of the book so that others could enjoy a stronger one.

Many thanks also to my second editor, Jonathan Oliver, who combed over the manuscript to ensure people's names didn't change halfway through, among other things!

And, of course, I must say a huge thank you to the Kickstarter backers who took a chance on this novel before it had a single review. You guys have helped bring the book into the world, and your support means so much to me. I'd specifically like to mention the

Archmages—Mark, Louise, Brendan Scarvell, Dave W, Chris M, and Seb—and the Overlords, Miriam and Barry.

Finally, thank you to everyone who has read and supported the series so far. Without readers, this story stays locked in my head, and you are the ones who make it live and breathe.

El

About the author

I live in London, but I'm half Irish and half Belgian, a fact I blame for my wine-drinking penchant and compulsive need to tell stories.

My love of fantasy began at age nine when my father bought me *The Hobbit* as a Christmas present. At first, I thought a story about a man who lived in a hole was supremely ridiculous, but he insisted on reading it to me and my sister every night—soon winning over two eager young fans. He followed this feat with *The Lord of the Rings*, and thus my doom was written.

I graduated to books from the Dragonlance and Forgotten Realms worlds, and then on to David Eddings, Robert Jordan, and Raymond E. Feist, along with many other great fantasy writers of the 1980s and 1990s. Later, I found my way to the darker worlds and deep character work of Robin Hobb and George R.R. Martin.

My whole life, I dreamed of writing an epic fantasy series that combined my favorite elements of all these stories The Unraveling series is the product of a lifetime spent dreaming, writing, and developing my craft.

I've got a PhD in Spanish Literature and Cultural Studies from Trinity College Dublin, and a background as a martial artist, political activist, and musician. Now, my attention is fully devoted to words – those of others, which I edit, and of course, my own.

Also by El McInerney

Book 1 of The Unraveling

An endless feud between nations. Sorcerers who steal souls to feed their eternal life. A world so broken by magic that those who wield it are shunned and despised.

Skilled young hunter Ina hides a deadly secret—she has the dark god's powerful magic, blamed for the genocide of her people five centuries ago. If anyone finds out, they'll execute her. When she learns that her lover's daughter has the same magic, she must decide whether to reveal her secret to save the child.

But her decision will determine not only the child's fate but that of the whole world. Because the cycle of violence has begun again, and prophecy decrees she must be the one to end it. The alternative is the unraveling of all creation.

You can purchase Soulstealer on Amazon or on my website elmcinerney.com.

Printed in Dunstable, United Kingdom

64973157R00188